SHADOW MASTERS

AN ANTHOLOGY FROM THE HORROR ZINE

EDITED BY JEANI RECTOR

SHADOW MASTERS
An Anthology from The Horror Zine

http://www.thehorrorzine.com

FIRST EDITION Trade Paperback

Imajin Books - http://www.imajinbooks.com

May 27, 2013

ISBN: 978-1-927792-04-9

Cover designed by Ryan Doan, www.ryandoan.com

Praise for SHADOW MASTERS

"This anthology is chock-full of wonderfully horrific stories from noted authors as well as talented unknowns. I especially liked *Reanimated* by editor Jeani Rector. It deals with a young widow whose loving husband has come back to life, and it explores not just the wrenching emotional issues surrounding such an experience, but also the enormous cultural, legal and societal issues that would be involved. And it has a powerfully flippant surprise ending!" —John Russo, co-writer of the original film *Night of the Living Dead*

"Veteran editor Jeani Rector delivers the scares again! I have no idea how she manages to pack so much talent between her covers, but she does it over and over, and *Shadow Masters* is her best anthology yet. If you had doubts about the health of the modern horror story, doubt no more. Jeani Rector and her amazing stable of writers have got all the proof you'll ever need that the genre remains vital and compelling. I loved this book!" —Joe McKinney, author of *The Savage Dead*

"Read the first half of *Shadow Masters* straight through; it was like eating potato chips, I couldn't stop! Didn't bother pacing myself through the second half, either. Some old favorites in here, like Bentley Little, Christian Larsen, and Elizabeth Massie. I was also blown away by some new discoveries for me, like Yvonne Navarro and Melanie Tem. A great collection that hits all the big notes: demons, cannibalism, the dead and unquiet, and some subtle surprises. These people are twisted!" —Susie Moloney, author of *The Thirteen*

"When you're stuck in a crypt with only a flashlight and one thing to read, make damn sure it's your copy of *Shadow Masters*. Presenting stories from veterans of their craft, *Shadow Masters* is another winner for Jeani Rector and *The Horror Zine*." —Charles P. Zaglanis, Editor in Chief of White Cat Publications LLC

Acknowledgements

As the editor of *The Horror Zine*, I would like to take this opportunity to thank Dean H. Wild, Assistant Editor; Christian A. Larsen, Media Director; and Bruce Memblatt, Kindle Coordinator. Without these three talented and dedicated individuals, there would be no *The Horror Zine*.

—Jeani Rector

Table of Contents

Editor's Corner

THE HORROR ZINE RIDES AGAIN AND AGAIN
A FOREWORD BY JOE R. LANSDALE

I love horror. I always have. I always will. I love a lot of other story types as well, all the genres: literature, movies, comics, you name it, and I love it all. But I must admit there is, deep in my heart, a special dark and damp place for tales of horror in all its incarnations.

If you are like me in that way, there's a place I need to tell you about.

It's a place called *The Horror Zine*.

You can go there with the click of a mouse.

I love this on-line magazine. It gives me the same feeling I once got when I picked up an issue of *The Horror Show* that Dave Silva used to edit, or *The Twilight Zone* Magazine when it first hit the stands. *The Horror Show* covered all the small press bases, and *The Twilight Zone* covered the mainstream bases. The Horror Zine does both. I'm going to talk about the on-line magazine before I talk about the anthology, because the two are obviously entwined.

It's a damn good magazine, and what makes it good is it's so varied. Stories and poetry, interviews, you name it, it has it. The best thing about it is that it is open to new writers. The editor, Jeani Rector, is willing to work with them, willing to drag out of them what she believes to be their best. She may even blush a little that I have gone to the trouble to mention her. She asked me not to, but to dismiss the editor is to dismiss the magazine, so she certainly deserves an important mention. Without her, no on-line magazine. Without her, no place for great stories and poetry, etc. to appear. Her personality and *The Horror Zine* entwine like some kind of alien plant life and you cannot speak honestly of one without mentioning the other.

I don't remember exactly how I first learned about *The Horror Zine*, but I think it had to do with poetry I was writing. I write very little poetry, and what poetry I had written was lying about inside the bowels of my word processor. I market novels and screenplays through my agents, market some things like short stories, comics, and non-fiction articles on my own, but at that point I had written very little poetry and was not marketing it at all. And then, one day, either Jeani contacted me, or I saw something about the online magazine and wrote her. I don't remember. But she wanted to see some of my poetry and I sent it and she published it. From that point on I've published a lot of poetry there and some short stories.

A lot of fine writers have been published there too, some of them well known, some of them not so well known. It is great to see such writers as Graham Masterton there, the great Ramsey Campbell, Bentley Little, Elizabeth Massie, Melanie Tem, and so many others of that esteemed ilk. It has been great to discover in its contents new writers and poets, like Juan Perez, whose poetry I enjoy and have begun to follow, as well as others. If that isn't enough, there is also art by very talented artists in *The Horror Zine*, and commentary and interviews. The on-line magazine is a potpourri of art forms.

The Horror Zine is not as well known as it should be. Perhaps because it is unable to pay big bucks to writers. My guess is some of that will change with the greater awareness of actual hold-in-your-hands anthologies being put together from the contents of the magazine. Surely e-books will follow and enthusiasm will grow, because each volume is more interesting than the last.

Excuse me while I pause for an aside.

Horror is as much an emotion as it is a genre. Recently I was asked to introduce a special showing of *In Cold Blood* at an Austin Film Festival. It's a favorite film of mine, as well as a favorite book, the brain child of Truman Capote. They are riveting pieces of art. They are about reality, not the supernatural, but what they have in common with any good story of horror is atmosphere. I would argue that *In Cold Blood*, dealing with a real event, the murder of the Clutter family for money that did not even exist, the slow unraveling of events in the book and on film, are just as much a horror story as *The Shining* by Stephen King.

What has this to do with *The Horror Zine*? I mention this to state that horror is a much broader field than many readers might think, and that all the avenues of horror are covered in the "magazine" Jeani edits, including those that might not normally be thought of as horror. From the "real" to the "unreal" to the "surreal," *The Horror Zine* covers the bases. Jeani knows that horror is not so much a subject, as it is an emotion. And there's even comic horror included from time to time; I know a few of my poems fill that bill. I also mention this for all those readers who turn their noses up at horror and think of it as a lesser form. There are no lesser forms of writing, only lesser writers. What you will find in *The*

Horror Zine is the cream of the crop. You will find, no matter in what form it takes, that sense of dread and mystery and riveting entertainment that any good piece of literature or film can provide; you need not be a fan purely of horror to enjoy its contents.

Let me make a proposal. I may not have too many wise suggestions, but I think this is one of them. Find all of *The Horror Zine* anthologies, if you can, because before long they will be collector's items. Not too many years from now there will be testimonials from writers who first appeared in *The Horror Zine* explaining how it started, or boosted their career. Mark my words, the nostalgia will flow. I'm betting on it, and I'm also betting that before long there will be a *Best of The Horror Zine*, because anything this good is bound to actualize just such a book. I know such a volume will contain some of the best of the best when it comes to horror, as well as some of its cousins, and I will be eager to get my mitts on it.

But until then, you have this fine anthology to keep you company. This one is different from the previous *The Horror Zine* anthologies in many ways including original, previously unpublished material, but all the volumes, including this one, have one important thing in common.

They are all good.

Enjoy. I say this secure in the knowledge that I know you will.

The Thing That Was Not There
by James Marlow

*D*amn *Lovecraft. Damn Bentley Little. And Stephen King. Damn all of them*, Chris thought.

Too much heavy reading. Too many nights filled with spooks, specters, and things that eat you in the night. Too many stories of questioned sanity and reality. That's what it was. What it *had* to be. Because if it wasn't just some mental burp brought on by consuming too much spicy literature, then what was it?

"Well, it is," Chris told the room. "So I'm not going to think about it."

He let the curtain fall, once again hiding his view of the thing that wasn't there, and grabbed the book he'd been reading. This time it was a collection of short stories called *Dark Thoughts* by Rudy Jarvis. He returned the book to its proper place in his bookcase and scanned the shelves that most small town libraries would envy. The entire upper floor and the majority of the main floor of his house were dominated by bookcases.

A stroke of good luck when he was twelve—his dad won the lottery—insured Chris he'd never have to work a day in his life. His parents had sat him down and asked him what he wanted to do with his life, which was a question most twelve year olds are in no way prepared to answer.

Chris told them he wanted to be a writer and his parents approved. After a string of rejection letters when he was in college, reality set in and crushed that dream and so he settled on being a reader instead.

He wasn't disappointed in the least.

Now he scanned his westerns, three bookcases full, and almost pulled a Louis L'Amour, but his eyes kept drifting back to where he kept the horror.

He hated not finishing a book once he'd started. Even quite terrible novels were finished. Chris felt that it was the least he could do, as a reader. The author had spent large amounts of time on the book and Chris owed it to the author to finish.

Jarvis was an excellent storyteller, Lovecraftian without being pretentious about it, and Chris wanted to go back and visit the lands the man had created.

That brought him back to the thing that wasn't there.

He looked out a window, thinking. He was tired, he knew, and if he was being honest, his mind was a bit overtaxed. His imagination had always been his best friend and his worst enemy.

He remembered how, as a small child, he refused to sleep in his room for almost a month because there was a clown hiding under his bed. When his father asked him what the clown was doing there, Chris had calmly explained that the clown was recruiting for the circus and that he did not want to live at the circus.

One day Chris walked up to his parents and announced that the clown had moved on. He slept back in his bed. But two days later, he told his parents that the clown had abducted another young boy from the next town over. And it had been true; the TV news confirmed that a boy was missing. So, had the clown been his imagination or a reality?

With an imagination as good as his, reading horror made him live in a myriad of twisted worlds and words. But... "I'll try a different window," he said to himself, grinning. "One with no trees to cast strange shadows."

He walked to the other side of the house. The side where his property abutted the Hurst's. Three years ago Dan Hurst surprised his family with a new pool, and in an effort to keep it clean, removed all the trees in his yard. Chris had played the good neighbor and removed his own trees along their shared border.

He pulled back the curtain and his grin deflated. Down on the lawn, the thing that wasn't there, was there.

Chris dropped the curtain and let out the breath he'd been holding. "This is not good. No, I don't think so at all."

He went downstairs and poured a cup of coffee as he stood at the kitchen counter, his hand only slightly shaking. He frowned at the hand and it calmed. "It's not there. Just relax. It *can't* be there. It's just that it's dark outside, and that makes my imagination go overboard."

He looked out the kitchen window, expecting nothing. But standing just to the left of his little tool shed was the thing that wasn't there. Chris clicked on the porch light, thinking that he would stop seeing the thing that wasn't there if he could show his mind the thing *wasn't* there. That it was nothing but a trick of moonlight and nerves.

Chris turned on the light and quickly turned it off again. He couldn't bring himself to look with the light on.

"It's *not* there," he told himself. "I don't need the light to verify that it's not there." His mind tried to argue but Chris was having none of it. To prove he was right, he dumped his coffee and went to bed.

That night he dreamed of death.

He floated through vast, empty spaces. A heavy darkness pressed in on him and his breath came in short uneven rasps. Sounds he had never heard echoed off the darkness. Trumpets blown by demons long forgotten. Drums beat by the damned.

His head exploded under the pressure of the din, only to have the cacophony multiplied, rattling off the fragments of his skull. Shapes came from the darkness, tearing and biting. Time meant nothing and every wound lasted forever. He tried to tell himself it was only a dream, but as he thought it, he knew it to be a lie.

It was a dream, yes, but it was also something more. A vision? A memory? The answer wouldn't come but he knew this was both real and unreal.

He felt his soul leave his dreaming body and float toward a hideous light. Simultaneously repellant and welcoming, it filled his vision and felt like maggots boring into his skin. As he drew closer, the light transformed into the eyes of an insane god. Something to be worshiped with blood and sex. Something whose very name would cause nations to crumble.

The eyes saw him and the darkness grinned.

He woke with sweat staining his pillowcase, and cursed his imagination.

In the morning, his house was surrounded by things that were not there. Chris screamed, feeling like when he was two and the boogeyman had come creeping out of his closet. He would have thought the emotion of terror was long behind him, left behind with his G.I. Joes and Hot Wheels. Seeing the unreal basking in the morning sun showed him just how wrong he was. About a great many things.

As one, the things that were not there took a step forward. *I've acknowledged them,* Chris thought. *I don't think I should have done that.*

He ran upstairs to one of his bookcases and began ripping through his occult section. Many of the great (and many of the bad) horror authors tackled the subject of other realms, or different dimensions, or alternate universes. In other words, Things That Are Not There.

Lovecraft in particular was fond of the subject, and Chris had bought some "non-fiction" books on the subject as a result. Most were absolute lies, but a few seemed to touch a primal part of his brain with whispers of possibilities.

He remembered that all the authors, fiction and non-fiction alike, seemed to think you needed some kind of portal. A ring of stones, a complex ritual, an ancient burial mound, hell, sometimes just a pentagram some fool drew in his basement.

"There's nothing like that in my house. Is there?"

He ran down to the basement, making sure to keep his eyes off the windows. Whatever was going on out there wasn't really happening and he couldn't deal with that unreality if he was going to stop it from killing him.

The basement was unfinished and a quick glance told him he hadn't been doing any sleep-drawing. A strange hum filled the air. His furnace turned on and began belching spouts of fire at him. *Go*, it seemed to say. *Go see what you have done. Go see what you* are.

A thought struck him and he shivered. What if *he* was the portal? What if somehow he had opened himself and allowed these things that are not there to cross? What if he was the conduit that would birth abominations? Or maybe he was crazy. A happy thought but one he was thinking may be a possibility.

He ran back up the stairs, the sound of hundreds of *things* marching slowly toward his home and drowning out his cries. Someone would come save him. They had to. By now his neighbor, Dan Hurst, had to have seen what was in his yard and called to police. He had cut down his trees for their pool, so they would return the favor.

As Chris ran to his study, he smiled. Sure, the police would be here any second. Yeah, they'd have to call for back up, maybe even the National Guard, but this problem would be dealt with.

He looked out the window and saw the things that were not there were pressed against the house. It would happen soon. Whatever *it* was. The sounds of glass cracking floated to him. The smell of decay filled the house. Chris looked to the sky and saw the clouds had taken on a strange reddish tint, like a thunderstorm sent from hell.

He heard a voice. "They'll come from the sky."

Chris spun and let out a startled yell. The room was filling with things that were not there.

"What will?" he said and choked back vomit.

They were humanoid, but their forms had a liquid quality. *Undulated* was the word his mind supplied, like it was difficult for them to hold this form. Their faces looked like a hastily drawn child's sketch. But they also moved and every so often he'd see the truth. That they weren't faces at all, but empty maws stretching back past eternity. Not the god from his dream but the very darkness itself.

"You have no word to describe us," the thing said. "You think of us as the things that are not there, but we are really the things that should not be."

Their advance was slow but constant. In less than a minute, he knew they'd be touching him and when they touched him, he'd start to scream. He knew if he started to scream, he wouldn't be able to stop.

Outside, the clouds continued to darken and when Chris risked a look at them, he saw shapes moving in the darkness. Shapes he had no concept of...things made of both flesh and fantasy.

"We must close the portal," the thing said right in front of him.

Portal was not the word it used but Chris understood what it meant. He also understood that these things were guardians; watchers who kept the nameless monstrosities locked away in their nothingness.

"Will it hurt?" he asked, knowing the answer.

The things just grinned horrible grins, revealing rows of tiny, nubby teeth.

About James Marlow

James Marlow has been writing fiction in one form or another all his life. He lives with his wife and children in Indiana and is currently working on his first novel.

Red Velvet
by Shaun Meeks

The single fluorescent bulb reflected in the pool of blood on the floor of the small room. David did everything he could to not get on all fours like a dog to lap up the coppery treasure.

The only reason he hesitated was that the others were watching him, and he knew they would think he was some sort of strange, sick monster. How would he explain his compulsion, his near obsession with tasting blood without sounding like he was a crazy person with fantasies about being a vampire?

If only it were that romantic.

He would have loved it if he thought he was an immortal, legendary creature that people wrote books about or featured in movies. That would be better than just being a guy who found something close to a sexual satisfaction with drinking blood. He was happy when he was called to work a scene like this.

A question interrupted his thoughts. "How long will it take you to clean this up?"

David looked away from the pool of blood to the man who spoke. The man was the owner of the building, and he stood with his wife and son in the small bachelor apartment as other tenants looked on from the doorway. The police had already come and gone, and the coroner was now taking the owner of the lost blood to the morgue where they would slice, dice and be done with him.

"Well, that depends. Did the person have any diseases? Did he die of natural causes or was it a suicide?"

"The asshole slit his wrists. Not sure if he had any diseases, but I'm pretty sure he wasn't some AIDS victim. He was too fat for that, and I doubt he had much luck with anyone."

"I doubt even hookers would have touched that human blob." The manager's son laughed and David heard a murmur of disapproval from the crowd in the hall. Some people just didn't have any tact.

"How long?" the manager repeated.

"Three hours tops. But I will need everyone to leave. The chemicals I use aren't good for you."

The manager nodded, ushered his family out and gave David the key. He told him to return it to his mailbox, along with the bill, when he was done. David agreed, and then went to work.

After going down to his van and bringing a large bag full of brushes, chemical and rags, he walked back into the room, locked the door and got ready to go to work. His eyes fell back to the glistening maroon pool of blood as he slid on his rubber gloves, feeling his mouth tingling with excitement. He knew it was going to be coagulated a fair bit since the man had died about six hours prior, but he was desperate.

Before kneeling down, David looked around the sparse room and wondered how anyone could live in such a place. The entire apartment was about the size of the average bedroom in a small apartment, and in there was the kitchen, a dilapidated sofa bed, a table, a chair and a television from about the late 1960s. David knew that the man who had lived and died in the room was a big person, well over three hundred and fifty pounds, and the thought of someone that size living in such a cramped space made him feel slightly claustrophobic.

Don't think too much on it. You have better things to keep you busy.

David smiled, looked back at the blood and went to his knees, slow and easy. He lowered his face toward it, smelling the familiar odor that reminded him of wet pennies, and then finally let the tip of his tongue touch the slick surface.

It was a moment of pure ecstasy, pulsing though his entire body the way the best orgasm never could. It brought him back to the first time he had ever tasted blood, when he was a kid.

*****

He was ten years old and was using a lock blade to cut an apple. When he washed the blade off and tried to dry it, he accidently slid the cutting edge across his thumb, opening an angry red smile there. He dropped the knife and jammed the bleeding digit in his mouth on pure instinct, sucking at it as though he was nursing.

The taste was like nothing he had ever had before, salty and hot. Not sweet, but not bitter either. He sucked at the gash until his mother came in and saw what he was doing, then slammed him across the back of the head and told him that was he was doing was disgusting and rude.

It was that reaction, that scolding, that made the enjoyment of tasting blood even more potent, and started him on his strange path. It is always the things we are told we shouldn't have that we want the most.

After the thrill of his own blood wore off, he found different ways to taste blood; the easiest being websites that specialized in people obsessed with vampire culture and myth. Though David didn't believe in any of it, nor did he enjoy tricking people into thinking he was involved in the culture, it was an easy way to get numerous partners to spill some red for him.

His job was an even easier way to find blood, though not always as pleasant.

Having to clean up blood that had been sitting around for weeks, rotting and becoming inedible was the worst part of the job. It was such a shame to let something so delicious go to waste, but it happened all the time. Too many people died alone and forgotten in the city.

*****

David pursed his lips and began to slurp up the thick blood, taking in a mouthful and then sitting up to let it slowly slide down his throat, tasting it for as long as he could. On his fifth dip down to the shrinking pool, he heard something shift in the corner, and he froze, feeling fear tugging at him.

For a second, he thought that there was someone else in the room with him, though it seemed impossible not to have noticed them. The place was too small, and there was nowhere to hide, so he quickly let the fear go and was ready to go back to the blood when someone spoke.

"What do you think you are doing?"

David jumped to his feet, wiping the blood away from his lips and looked around the room, thinking maybe the manager had returned, or worse yet, the ghost of the man who had killed himself. That was a stupid thought, especially since David didn't believe in ghosts any more than he thought he was a vampire.

Yet something had spoken to him, and even though he looked around the tiny apartment, he could not find the source.

"Didn't your mother ever teach you that it is impolite to take that which does not belong to you? Now get away from the blood."

The voice seemed to be coming from the wall itself, the one on the west side of the room, and he quickly did take a step away. He stared at the water-stained plaster as though it was alive and at any moment, a face was going to appear, like the Great and Powerful Oz. He backed up as far as he could and pressed against the cold surface of the east wall.

The west wall began to pulse and ripple, as though it was not a solid object but made of something intangible like liquid or even smoke. David looked on as the shape of a small man appeared, as if he had always been there, but had been camouflaged somehow and was only now allowing himself to be seen.

The short man stepped out of the wall, his skin at first holding the same color and texture as the plaster, but the further he revealed himself, the more the skin appeared to change. When the flesh finally settled, David felt no better about what was standing before him.

"I have seen some twisted bastards in my time, David, but you are by far the worst."

The man in front of him was only four feet tall. His skin looked as though it was made out of gnarled tree bark; deep gouges and twists ran up and down his small frame and seemed to glow a deep crimson in the grooves. The man's head was squat and he appeared to have a mouth that didn't actually move as he talked; instead it remained open, and a soft blue light flickered wildly when the words came out.

The stranger walked toward David, his feet dragging across the floor, and held out a hand that was made of flexible branches and moss. "I want what you have taken. That was mine."

"I didn't take anything."

"Yes you did. I watched you down on your knees, lapping it up like a dog. I have spent five long years in this room driving Harold mad, and I want what I am owed. Now give it back."

"You mean the blood?"

The man let out a cruel laugh that sounded like someone talking in reverse. "Of course I mean the blood. It holds the essence of what I want. Now return it to me and get out before things get messy here."

"How?" he spluttered. "Should I vomit it up?"

"Are you serious? If you vomit, you will spoil it. I don't need your bile, David. I just want the blood."

David had no idea how he was going to comply. Didn't the little man get how anatomy and digestion worked? There was no way that he would be able to give back the blood without puking it up, pissing it out or worse, shitting it out, and the latter two weren't going to get it all out.

"Who are you?" David asked. "What are you?"

The demonic tree-man didn't answer, but stood, holding out a hand as though David was simply going to pull the blood from himself and give it over. He had no idea what kind of powers were inside the little creature, nor did he want to see what was going to happen when he said he couldn't get the blood out, so he did the only thing he could.

He ran.

He took off for the door and threw it open faster than he thought he would be able to, worried that he would be like some character in a bad horror movie that fumbles with the knob as though they had never touched one before. He ran down the hall, tearing his rubber gloves off as he went and heard a roar behind him that shook the floor. He felt his bladder weaken at the sound, but refused to lose control or stop. He just let his feet take him far from the building where a man had killed himself and a tree-looking demon raged.

He made it to the subway just as the train pulled up to the platform, and he was glad to get inside and finally sit down. It had been a long time since he had used the trains, but now he was relieved he had an escape vehicle, no matter which direction it was headed.

David looked around the subway car as if he expected the tree-demon to appear among the other travelers. Had it been real? Now that he was safely away from the bloody room, he started questioning himself.

Perhaps it was the intensity of the simultaneous lust and shame he felt about drinking blood that made him imagine the tree-demon. How he could feel so free to behave in such a disgusting manner was beyond him, yet he was powerless to stop his cravings.

Judge not least ye be judged, he thought defensively.

"You will be more than judged, David."

He turned his head, and sitting two seats away from him was an elderly man, glaring at him with dark eyes and a scowl on his face. This was too much. Embarrassed, he looked away, but peripherally he could see that suddenly the old man was no longer a man at all. He was the demon creature from the room.

David jumped from his seat, keeping his eyes on the old man, who looked human again. He couldn't think of a rational way he could have been followed here, but reality seemed to bend. "Are you okay, young man?" the old guy asked him, no longer scowling meanly, but full of concern.

"I'm..."

"Go ahead, David. Tell him that everything is just fine."

This time the demon voice came from a woman who was asleep in a two-seater, her head bouncing off the edge of the window. Once again, when he looked out of the corner of his eyes, he saw that the sleeping woman was not a woman at all. The demon turned its misshapen head towards him, a smile creaking across its lips.

"You have something that belongs to me. I worked long and hard to make that man bleed his soul for me, and I want it all. Give it to me or I will take it and so much more, from you."

David moved to the door, pushing his back hard against it as the woman rose from her seat. Her face was slackened, eyes half cast as though she was somewhere between the real world and a dream state.

David turned his head slightly and realized the demon was controlling the woman and laughing as it shuffled towards him.

The demon's voice came from the old woman's mouth. "Normally, when I am sent to your realm, I am not allowed to have any human contact. It's one of the stupid rules that makes my job so hard. Yet, if one of your kind breaks the rules, like stealing what is mine, I am allowed to do whatever I must to retrieve it. For that, I thank you. It has been so long since I was allowed to possess one of you flesh puppets."

As the train sped along, the lights flickered on and off, creating a strange strobe effect inside the car, giving David a view of Hell. The demon was infecting everything in the tunnel, the darkness allowing him to see what was not visible in the light. When the lighting dimmed, David could see the faces of the other passengers alternating between their true selves and states of decay, bones and muscle exposed though graying flesh. Yet when the light came back on inside the car, the passengers returned to normal, as though nothing was wrong. He felt as though madness were engulfing him.

As it moved closer to David, the thing shifted back and forth between the woman and the demon. "You have no idea what madness is. For years I was with that fat bastard in his little hole of a room, driving him to madness and beyond. Then you came along and took what was mine. Now, give it to me."

"How am I supposed to do that?" David shouted.

The demon ignored the question, as though the answer was obvious, and continued to advance, once again in the form of the old woman.

The train came to a stop, and David fell backward as the doors opened, his ass hitting the ground hard. The demon-woman stood in the doorway, looking down on him and David saw a thin darkness bleeding off of her, melting down from her head and pooling at her feet before she stumbled back against the opposing door, a look of confusion on her face. He didn't bother to look at her; instead he turned his attention to the dim shadow moving toward him. Scuttling away from it, David struggled to get to his feet, then turned and ran from the train.

The shadow moved faster, sliding across the ground like a faded patch of ink, liquid. It touched random people and David ducked out of the way of strangers' hands trying to grab him. Fear pulsed though his veins as his feet pounded against the tiled floor, rattling his brain.

He knew he must look deranged; running through the subway station, moving like a football player through the crowd, crying out each time someone possessed by the demon reached out for him. He knew he had to go somewhere the demon couldn't get to him, but where? What place would be safe?

In front of him, David saw the stairs that led up to the street level, but knew that wouldn't be good for him. The outside world meant more people, something the demon would no doubt take advantage of.

Directly ahead were three doors, bathrooms for men, women and a private one for people with kids. He ran straight for the private one, hoping that it was empty so that he could lock himself in, alone. He was lucky; it was open and empty.

He slammed the door, locked it and plastered himself to the far wall, afraid that a possessed body might still try to burst in after him. He waited, expecting the worst, but when nothing happened, he let out a long, sorrow-filled sigh and slid to the floor.

He squinted into the harsh fluorescent light with confusion, wondering once again if he was really running from a demon or from a mental breakdown. Pulling his cell phone out of his pocket, he was surprised to see that it was nearly two in the morning.

As he was about to stand up and risk going to the door to see if it was safe to leave, the lights in the bathroom shut off, except for a small, dull emergency light over the sink. He guessed that since it was almost two, the place was being shut down, with him inside.

"Damn it."

David attempted to stand, but as his hands touched the floor, something shifted in the room, a low crackling noise coming from the direction of the door. Through the dim lighting he could see the wall and the door throbbing, moving in and out like a slow heartbeat. He knew that it wasn't good, that without the light in the room, the demon was coming for him, but found he was unable to move at all, fear holding him down. Crimson light began to glow from small fissures in the wall until a shape formed that could only be the demon.

"Did you really think you could hide, thief?"

The cracks in the wall and the door grew wider as the demon began to push its way out of the drywall. "So glad the damn lights finally went out; I was worried I was going to have to fully possess someone to open the door. It's easy to move and speak through them, but other than that, well, possessions are just not my forte. Now, I think I am just going to take what is mine. I have had enough of this game."

The demon moved across the room, its feet dragging, its movements stiff and heavy. David rose quickly, trying to find any means he could to get around it, to get to the door and run up the stairs just outside the washroom. The room was too narrow to make an escape possible, and there was no other way out. There wasn't even a weapon he could pick up to fight off the approaching monster.

He was screwed and he knew it.

The creature raised one of its twisted hands, holding it out like a panhandler asking for change, and as it did, David felt something pulling from within him, as though the hand had entered his own body and was trying to rip something out.

"It'll hurt more if you struggle."

It didn't seem to matter if he moved or not, fought back or stood still, the pain was more excruciating than anything he had ever felt. The pulling began a fire in him, his veins and skin burning from the inside out.

He screamed out as he looked down and saw thin rivulets of blood coming out of every pore of his exposed skin, through his fingernails, and he could feel more coming out of his face. The trails of blood moved through the air and gathered into a ball of dark liquid in front of the demon, its face as motionless as ever. David dropped to his knees as the pain intensified. He opened his mouth, wanting to beg for it to stop, to leave him alone, but there were no words to be found. Instead, blood poured from his open lips making speech impossible.

When the blood finally slowed to a thin trickle, David was no longer able to hold himself up. His face slammed against the floor, making white light flash behind his eyes, but he fought the unconsciousness closing in on him.

In the dim light, David could barely make out the ball of blood that spun slowly like a crimson planet, obscuring the demon. He was sure that was almost all of the blood he had in his body. There was just enough left in him to keep him alive, though he wasn't sure how much longer he could last.

"So much here, but I am not greedy. I only want what is mine."

The demon's mouth grew wider, the sound of it moving was like twigs snapping under foot. A geyser of blood exploded from the ball, into the creature's mouth. The monster sucked the liquid in, and once the rush of blood stopped flowing, its mouth returned to its normal state.

"Now, was that so hard?" the creature asked. "Don't worry, I told you that I wouldn't kill you, but I'm not just going to let you walk away either."

The demon lowered its hands and when it did, the rotating blood ball fell to the ground and splashed the walls and David's own face. Hot, salty blood touched his tongue and he felt that old feeling again, the lust for blood that had brought him to the end he was facing.

"Since you love tasting blood so much, you filthy dog, the only way you might live is to crawl around this room and lap it up. Or you can just lay your head down and die. The choice is yours to make."

The demon laughed as it moved backwards into the shadows and disappeared as though he had never been there.

David licked the blood from his lips. Even in the state he was in, he felt the ecstasy flowing through him. He looked at the deliciousness pooled in front of him, struggling toward it on his knees and elbows, ready to drink his own essence until consciousness failed him.

He couldn't even be sure if drinking the blood would actually do anything to save him, but he lapped at it with relish.

If not, at least I will die happy.

About Shaun Meeks

Shaun Meeks lives in Toronto, Ontario with his partner, burlesque performer and corsetiere, Mina LaFleur, and their dog, Lily. His work has recently appeared in his own collection, *At the Gates of Madness*, and in *Haunted Path, Dark Eclipse, A Feast of Frights from the Horror Zine* anthology, *Zombies Gone Wild* and *Fresh Grounds Volume 3*.

He will also be releasing his latest novel, *Shutdown*, and a second collection with his brother later this year. For more information go to www.shaunmeeks.com.

THE END OF THE TRAIL
BY BENTLEY LITTLE

"Don't go past the bridge," my mother told me.

I never did.

The bridle trail was just down the street from our house, a relic of the time when Orange County had been much more rural and horses had actually been used for transportation. From its starting point in our middle-class neighborhood, it ran through the greenbelt that wound about the city behind some of the nicer, richer homes, and while there were still a few equestrians using it periodically, the trail was frequented primarily by weekend joggers and bicyclists.

Which meant that on weekdays it was free for us kids.

We played there often. Hide-and-Go-Seek, Red Rover, all the usual games. We caught bugs, hunted for rocks, collected algae water for microscopes, pretended we were hiking along secret paths through hidden jungles like Indiana Jones.

The greenbelt was wide, a low canyon between rows of expensive hilltop homes on either side, and the bridle trail was bifurcated, with a fairly deep drainage ditch running between two parallel paths that started together at the trailhead but separated almost instantly. The paths weaved between trees and brush, growing closer and father apart at various points, sometimes less than a stone's throw away from each other, at other times so distant that a person walking on one side could not see a person on the other. A mile or so in, another path forked off from the north track, leading to another neighborhood. It was from here that most of the hikers and cyclists came, but we kids would always stay on the main trail, which continued on through a piney section before edging closer to the ditch once again.

This is where the footbridge was located.

Presumably, somewhere past the bridge, the two halves of the trail reconnected, but for us, this was the means to get from one side to the other, and we would invariably hike up one path, cross over the bridge, then hike back on the other.

The bridge was oddly elaborate. Instead of a couple of planks placed over the ditch, it was an arched fairy-tale structure with waist-high railings painted white. It was cool looking, and we *wanted* to go over it, probably would have taken it anyway. Even if our parents hadn't warned us not to go past it.

Why couldn't we go past the bridge?

No one knew. But the most popular theory was that it was because of what had happened to Johnny Franklin. A teenager who lived half a block down from us, Johnny Franklin was retarded and the rumor was that he'd been of normal intelligence until he was ten years old and disobeyed his parents, following the bridle trail to its end. He'd gone by himself, continued on past the bridge, and when it was almost dinnertime and he still hadn't come home, his dad went out looking for him.

He didn't find him, though, and neither did any of the search parties. Or the police.

Johnny was gone for three days, and when he finally returned, wandering back down the path from behind the bridge, he was different.

Something had happened to him.

He was retarded.

It was probably just an urban legend, but we all believed it, our parents didn't bother to set us straight, and it kept an entire generation of kids from going past the bridge.

*****

I took June home to meet my parents during spring break. I was teaching at a community college up near Auburn, she was teaching at the local high school, and our times off happened to coincide, something I was assured had not happened for the past six years and might not happen for another twelve. I'd met June a year-and-a-half before, we'd been living together since January, and though I'd told my parents about her and vice versa, they had yet to meet.

The introduction went well. My parents liked June, as I knew they would, and she liked them, as I knew she would. We were staying at a hotel to avoid any awkwardness, but my mom insisted that we take meals at their house, and on the second day after lunch, June said she'd eaten too much and suggested we take a walk around the neighborhood.

"Or we could go back to the hotel and swim," I said.

She smiled tolerantly. "Or we could walk around the neighborhood."

So we told my parents we'd be back and started off down the sidewalk. I pointed out the homes where my friends had lived and even told her a funny story about the time old Mrs. Wakefield squirted us with the hose because she said the sound of our skateboards woke up her dachshund during his nap time.

Ahead, there was an open space between two houses, and I saw the brown wooden sign that said "Greenbelt Trail."

"What's that?" June asked as we approached.

"It's a hiking trail," I told her. "We used to play on it a lot when we were kids."

"That's great! Let's take it!" Holding my hand, she led the way down the dirt path, taking the right fork. We stepped aside for a trio of cyclists speeding toward us, then walked down the gentle slope out of the sun and into the shade. Someone had tied a rope swing to the branch of a tree off to the left, and two boys were taking turns swinging from it.

"I want to live in a neighborhood like this," June said.

"Well," I joked, "when my parents croak, I'll inherit the house."

She punched my shoulder. "How can you say such a thing?"

The hills around us grew taller and the homes farther away as we walked. We saw fewer people, and more trees and brush.

"What's that?" June asked, pointing to the left. "A stream?" She rushed across a carpet of dead leaves over to it, enchanted.

"More of a ditch," I said. "I think it's to catch the runoff from those streets up there."

But she would have none of that. "A stream," she said. "This is so cool!"

We continued walking. I hadn't been here in years, since before junior high, probably. Once my friends and I started hanging out, listening to music and playing video games, we sort of forgot about the trail or decided that hiking was more trouble than it was worth. But I saw it now through June's eyes, and it *was* kind of cool. These days, such prime property would not have been allowed to remain wild; either additional houses would have been shoved into the space, or the yards of homes flanking the greenbelt would have been expanded to include the trail so developers could charge for extra-large lots.

We walked, hand-in-hand, not speaking, listening to the cawing of birds in the trees and the sounds of lizards scuttling through the underbrush at our approach. Ahead, off to the left, as white and elaborate as I remembered it, the bridge arched over the ditch and connected the two halves of the trail.

"Okay," I said. "Time to go back."

She looked at me. "What?"

"We have to turn around here."

"Why?"

I had no answer for that. *Because my mom won't let me? Because no one is supposed to go past the bridge? Because I'm afraid?*

But I thought of Johnny Franklin, and knew I'd better think of something. Because I was *not* continuing on.

"It's getting late," I said. "You wanted to go to Balboa this afternoon, didn't you? At this rate, we won't get there until nightfall."

She was peering past the bridge.

"June?"

Reluctantly, she gave in, and we went back.

Overall, it was a short vacation, and we didn't have time to go on the trail again, although she wanted to. I definitely did *not* want to, and I purposely kept us busy with side trips and visits to family and friends until our holiday ended and we had to return to Auburn.

*****

We made another trip down to southern California in the summer.

June was teaching summer school, but it ended the first week of July, and we went back for a few days to see my parents before continuing on to Phoenix to see her relatives. I'd proposed to her on a weekend spent in San Francisco, and though we'd emailed photos, neither family had seen the ring or been able to congratulate us in person.

We'd splurged for a hotel by the beach, and after a first night dinner with my parents, I'd hoped to spend the rest of our time by the shore, swimming and soaking up the sun. I'd invited my parents to spend the second day with us, intending to take them out to the Crab Cooker, but my mom insisted that we come to their house for lunch instead.

"Why should we drive all the way back there just for a meal," I told my mother, "when you can come out to the beach and enjoy the entire day?"

"Because," she said, in a tone that brooked no argument.

"I think she wants to show us off to all her friends and neighbors," June offered when I expressed my bafflement.

She was right. There was a party waiting for us when we arrived, and the next two hours were taken with showings of the ring and retellings of our story to various people that I hadn't seen in years. It was kind of a potluck thing, and nearly everyone had brought something. I sampled too much of it and wanted to sit down and do nothing, but June was just the opposite and suggested that we "walk it off." I was all in favor of getting out and away from everyone, so I agreed to take a walk, letting her make the excuses.

And that's how we ended up on the trail again.

I didn't want to go there, and I tried to suggest that we just wander up and down the nearby streets, looking at the houses, but June was insistent, and I wasn't quick enough to think of a reason not to take the trail.

As before, we took the path on the right and walked through the widening greenbelt between the trees and bushes, nodding and waving to the other hikers and joggers who occasionally passed by. I was trying to come up with a reason to turn around at the bridge again—*We've been gone too long and we need to say goodbye to people...It's getting late and I want to get back to the beach*—but it was as if June could tell what I was thinking.

"Let's go all the way to the end of the trail," she said.

Panic welled within me. "That's miles away," I told her, though I had no idea if that was true or not. "We won't get back until nighttime."

She nodded. "Okay. But we'll go a little farther than last time. I want to see what's past that bridge."

Heart pounding, I glanced over, looking at her face. Was she doing this deliberately? Did she know that last time I'd purposely kept her from going past that point?

I couldn't tell. But the bridge was coming up, and before I could articulate a coherent argument against continuing on, she was walking past it, pulling on my hand to follow her, and we were hiking into uncharted territory.

"Don't go past the bridge."

I needn't have worried. We crossed the bridge and nothing happened. The path wound around a curve, following the lay of the land, then straightened out, looking just as it had for the past mile or so.

Only...

Only the vegetation seemed slightly different, the trees taller and less leafy, the bushes fuller and wider, the empty spaces between them filled with spiky-looking weeds. It was also somehow darker, though that made no sense. The sparser tree cover should have let in more light, but it didn't, and I put it down to steeper encroaching hillsides, knowing full well that that wasn't the reason.

On a flat open section where neither trees nor brush grew and the ground was covered with dried dead leaves, the two halves of the tail reconnected.

"Okay," I said, stopping. "Let's head back."

"Wait a minute. What's that?"

June was pointing, and I followed her finger. Ahead, past this little barren section was what looked like a row of short, round, very deliberately planted bushes. Beyond that, the trail passed through a small meadow ringed with pines. In the center of the meadow was some type of tall, white gingerbready structure that reminded me of the bridge.

"I don't know what it is," I told her. I didn't like it. "Let's head back."

"Let's check it out."

Ignoring me, she started forward, and I was forced to follow. As we got closer, we could see what the structure was.

A gazebo.

June ran toward it, bounding up the low steps, spreading out her arms and twirling as though she were Julie Andrews. "We should get married here!" she exclaimed. "Next to a bridal trail? How perfect is that?"

"It's not *bridal* as in wedding," I pointed out. "It's *bridle*, as in horse and bridle."

She waved me off. "Doesn't matter. It sounds the same." Placing her hands on the gazebo's railing, she glanced about.

The day was warm, but it was cooler in the shade of the trees and, somehow, there was fog down here. She was looking about the small grassy area, but I was looking beyond to where the trail continued on and disappeared into the fog. *There shouldn't be fog on a summer's day,* I thought, and the fact that there was scared the hell out of me.

"Don't go past the bridge."

"Isn't this just the most perfect spot?" June sighed.

No! I wanted to tell her, but I just said, "Yeah, it's nice," and made a show of looking down at my watch. "You know, it's getting late."

"All right, all right."

We stepped down the gazebo steps, and a woman jogged past us from out of the fog. She was the first person we'd seen in quite some time, and she smiled, waving. She was thin and attractive, wearing jogging shorts and a sports bra, and yet…

There was something not feminine about her.

I watched her as she passed, and June hit my shoulder. "Hey, bud. I'm over here."

"Sorry," I said. "That woman looked familiar."

It was a lie…but it wasn't a lie. That wasn't the reason I'd been looking at her, but something about the woman did seem familiar, though I could not for the life of me figure out what it was, and I was still puzzling over the matter as we walked back up the trail toward my parents' neighborhood.

*****

I hoped that June would forget about the gazebo and the *bridal* trail. The school year started, we went back to work and fell into our old routines, and when the subject of marriage came up, I made every effort to extol the virtues of northern California.

"Wouldn't it be romantic to get married in a glen surrounded by redwoods?"

Or, "What about that cute little church in Yosemite?'

But she was really taken with that gazebo and wouldn't budge. I began to wonder if the site had some kind of *hold* on her, and though I knew that was a stupid idea, I couldn't entirely dismiss it.

When I'd asked her to marry me, I kept the timeframe open-ended. I wasn't in any hurry to rush things, but she had her heart set on a June wedding—her name *was* June, after all—and it kind of became official when she started talking to people about it, especially our parents. That increased the pressure on me, because if I didn't convince her to have the wedding in an alternate location pretty soon, the pre-planning wheels would be set in motion.

I couldn't seem to budge her, however, and I started having a recurring dream, a stress dream. In it, we were getting married, standing in the gazebo. The preacher before us said, "Do you take this woman to be your lawfully wedded wife?" and I looked over at June, and she was retarded.

*****

Eventually, I caved. I had to. There was no logical reason to resist her choice of wedding locations, and the thought of a grown man afraid of a childhood rumor began to embarrass even me. Of course, it was easy to be brave when I was half a state away, but the deeper we got into the planning stages—picking out a dress, picking out a cake, deciding who to invite—the less worried I became. Maybe Johnny Franklin *had* returned from the end of the trail retarded, but we were going to have a wedding party of some thirty people, including a minister. Nothing could happen to a group that large. If it did, it would be the largest incident of paranormal phenomena on record.

I let June handle the logistics, along with my mom and hers.

I stayed out of it.

There was a rehearsal the night before, but it was decided that it was too inconvenient to make everyone traipse down the trail and back, so we practiced in the minister's church, a length of string in a circle marking the dimensions of the gazebo so that the members of the party could be sure they were in their proper places.

Truth be told, I was getting more nervous as the time approached, and that night I did not sleep at all. I was tired in the morning, but I put on a brave face and took pictures with June and my parents and my best man, Patrick, at my parents' house before we all walked down the street in our finery to meet the rest of the guests at the entrance to the bridle trail.

June and I started down the path, following the white rose petals that had been strewn before us.

"This is perfect," June breathed, holding onto my arm.

"Yes," I lied.

I was fine until we passed the bridge.

I looked at my parents at that moment to see their reaction, but there was no indication that they felt any trepidation about continuing further. Apparently crossing the bridge was bad for children but fine for adults. The same lack of concern appeared true for Patrick and the other people who had grown up in the neighborhood. I was the only one affected and the only one who seemed to remember Johnny Franklin. I tried to be brave, but my anxiety grew with each footstep I took.

On the other side of the bridge, the trees had faces. Knotholes looked like eyes, with protuberances for noses, and lines in the bark formed mouths of various expressions. I didn't like those faces. They seemed sneaky and sly, as though they were keeping secrets. They also appeared to be watching me, and as much as I tried to tell myself that thinking that way was stupid, I couldn't make myself believe anything else.

The air cooled but grew more humid, and I saw white tendrils of fog beyond the trees and bushes on either side of the path.

Why had I agreed to have the wedding here? Aside from any irrational fears I might have, it was a stupid and inconvenient location for such an event. If I had pointed out the practical drawbacks to my parents and June's, we could have ganged up on her and convinced her to have it in a church or a park or by the beach or anywhere else but here.

"I don't think I can do this," I told June.

She smiled blithely. "Everyone gets cold feet. Don't worry. You'll get over it."

Ahead, the folding chairs in the meadow and the beautifully decorated gazebo were shrouded in white.

"I don't like this," I said. "It's too foggy."

Her voice became low and irritated. "We can't change anything now."

In the fog behind the gazebo were figures…shapes…things I almost recognized but didn't.

June and I separated, she stepping off to the left with her dad, and me moving next to Patrick.

We reached the meadow, and—

I ran.

I knew how it looked to June, my family, my friends...but I couldn't stay there another second, and I ran like a child back down the trail, in fear for my life, my heart pounding crazily.

Joggers passed me, going in the opposite direction. I heard snatches of conversation as they passed.

"My father was..."

"I told my mother..."

They all seemed to be talking about family. A man in a burgundy track suit approached and nodded at me as I ran past. He looked familiar, but I couldn't quite place him. He reminded me of Mrs. Burkholder, a lady in the neighborhood who'd abandoned her family when I was little. Her son Ritchie had been in my third grade class.

I was out of breath, but I kept running, pushing myself. June probably thought that I had gotten cold feet. I knew she'd be angry. A take-charge person, she was no doubt telling everyone to stay where they were while she hurried off to find me and talk some sense into me.

But I kept going. I passed the bridge and finally allowed myself to slow down, though I continued on a few more yards before bending forward, hands on knees, to catch my breath. I stared at the ground for several moments at the white petals scattered on the dirt. Looking up, I expected to see a furious June storming after me. I was going to suggest that we leave everyone back there and elope, find a justice of the peace and get married. It would be romantic, I would tell her.

But she wasn't there, and as the minutes ticked past and I realized she wasn't coming, my stomach dropped.

I knew what would happen, and the thought chilled me to the bone.

When June finally emerged from the trail beyond the bridge, she would be retarded.

She and all the wedding guests.

*****

Only they didn't come out retarded. They didn't come out at all, and I went back to my parents' house and waited and waited.

When I went to the police the next morning and reported the entire wedding party missing, my claim was met with what could politely be called skepticism but what would more accurately be described as hostility. I took two policemen across the bridge and out to the gazebo, nervous; afraid that even men in uniforms, carrying all the trappings and authority of law enforcement, would be nothing but bait here. But of course nothing happened.

As I expected there was no physical proof to back up my story. The decorations that had been put up were gone, the chairs had disappeared, and there was only the empty gazebo in an empty meadow.

I told the police to check with the minister's church. He had to have a calendar or a record of some sort to indicate that he would be officiating at our wedding. He did, but the location was not listed, and after that the police's involvement basically stopped. I think they thought I was crazy, and though I was given a case number and told to check in after a few days, it was clear to me that no effort would be made to investigate what had happened.

I didn't know June's friends, but I called the families of my friends. I couldn't tell them what had really occurred—none of them would have believed me—but I let them know that their loved ones had disappeared, and I made up a story about how they had not shown up for the wedding. I asked them to have my friends call when they returned home, hoping to get the families to put some pressure on the police, but, bizarrely, not one of them contacted me. I called Patrick's parents a second time a week or so later, and again a week after that, but the reception I received was cold and confusing. Didn't they notice that their son was missing? Or didn't they care?

Or *was* Patrick missing? Had he gone home and told them the story of me running off? Maybe everyone was mad and simply hiding from me.

Either way, it made no sense, because June did not come back, and neither did my mom or dad. I stayed in my parents' house, paid the bills that came in, and waited. But as June turned into July, there continued to be no sign of them.

A month later, on the anniversary of the event, the anniversary of what would have been my anniversary, I walked down the trail again for the first time since I'd gone there with the police. I stopped at the bridge, unwilling to go past it again.

Although the day was not just warm but hot, there was fog beyond the bridge, a thick wall of white that engulfed trail and tree, hill and brush. I saw movement within the white, a silhouetted figure that grew clearer as it approached. Someone jogging. A young woman in a grey track suit who, for some reason, reminded me of my dad.

"Hey!" I called out, but the figure turned and headed into the fog, back the way it had come.

I stood there, waiting, watching, and another jogger emerged from the mist, an older gentleman who ran in place for a moment, staring at me.

June.

It was her.

I don't know how I knew, but I did. The old man looked nothing like the young woman I had left at the altar, had seemingly no physical traits or characteristics in common, but it was her, I was sure of it, and the jogger lifted a hand, beckoning me forward.

I took a single step forward but stopped instantly, afraid to go on.

"Don't go past the bridge."

I couldn't. It was wrong. The jogger motioned for me to join him, and although part of me wanted to do just that, I stood my ground and shook my head. Still running in place, the old man smiled sadly, waved, then slowly turned around, disappearing into the fog until even his outline faded into white.

I watched him go.

"June," I said softly, and my eyes blurred with tears. "June…"

About Bentley Little

Bentley Little is an American horror writer. Somewhat of an enigma, he is the author of numerous novels, short stories, articles and essays. He originally came up through small presses like us.

Bentley has won a Bram Stoker Award for *The Revelation* and a nomination for *The Summoning*.

Same Sex Vampire Wedding
by Garrett Rowlan

WE TOOK BACK THE NIGHT, the sign said, mounted above the southbound San Diego freeway. The message of triumph was clear: The defeat of the vampires.

It was good for me. The ending of the vampire spring, as one wag called it, was now guaranteed work for people in the therapeutic field. The vampires were almost gone, but the impact they had on society brought repercussions that would last for years—or so I hoped, because I'm one of those who has benefitted from the trauma they caused. It was why I was making a business call. The client, a Dr. Primer, had checked my website and phoned a couple of hours ago. He wanted a private consultation. I left the car, crossed the street to his office and rang the bell.

The door opened. Dr. Primer ushered me inside. His features were vulpine, sharp nose and pointed ears, and gentle corrugations around the eyes. His mouth was a scrawl that widened to a crescent as he introduced himself. I noticed the slight serration of his fingernails when we shook.

We entered a small consultation room. He stood behind a high-backed swivel chair and a cluttered desk that seemed like an attempt to intimidate. I was sure he was the type of dentist whose problems weren't as important as proving to me that he could pay to discuss them.

"How can I help you?" I asked.

He gathered a coat from a rack behind him. "You can go to a wedding with me."

"You didn't say that on the phone, and anyway, it's ten at night. What sort of wedding starts so late?"

"These are night people. You'll like them."

"I hope you're not talking about vampires."

"Don't worry," he said, smiling that odd smile, slight and curved as a new moon. "It's a billable excursion. You can keep the meter running."

We walked outside where his black Mercedes S500 was parked. He started the car and let it idle. It did not vibrate; only a faint purr from the engine indicated the engine was running. Pretentious dentist's car, I thought.

"Vampire Dental Therapist," he said. "Just how does one become that?"

"This is the age of the ad hoc profession," I said. His display of wealth seemed to call for a response of pomposity. "We have vampire doctors who administer the serum and guide the patient through recovery; we have vampire lawyers who seek reduced damages or not-guilty verdicts on the grounds of temporary insanity; we have vampire shrinks for those who can't handle being 'human' again; and even ex-vampire reality shows. I fit right in."

"And how did you get started?" he asked. He backed out of his driveway and into the street. It was empty. Though people had begun to believe they could step out at night without the fear of some fanged malefactor pouncing on them, the cities still remained quiet after sundown, and the only people out usually drove with the doors locked.

"I stumbled into my profession," I said. "I had a degree in psychology and was teaching part-time at night. I had personal problems that kept me from sleeping. I started walking at night and I met a fellow insomniac, a dentist named Doctor Wu."

"I expect this was a few years ago, when no one went out at night, not even in a car. Weren't you afraid of the vamps?"

"It was four years ago. The vamps were starting to be contained, and anyway I was depressed. Doctor Wu had his own issues. He had nightmares, he told me, most of them having to do with fanged teeth. He said he wasn't alone. Some vamps were in recovery then, and the dentists who treated them developed fears, you know, phobias. I've heard many stories over the past couple of years, and I think I'm in a position to help."

Dr. Primer drove. His headlights fanned out in a prismatic radiance. "I'm so glad you could come," he said.

"I'm glad you found my website," I said.

"It was a very catchy homepage."

"My wife designed it."

"Give her my compliments."

I nodded. She was dead, but I didn't want to discuss that.

"Well, it was my wife who made the suggestion to contact you," he said.

"Let me ask you something, maybe something you weren't willing to discuss over the phone. Is she a vampire?"

"I'm not sure. She might be becoming one."

"Has she shown an abnormal fixation with flossing? That's often one of the symptoms. The teeth are often painful when they adjust to fangs, and flossing for some reason seems to relieve the discomfort."

"I haven't seen that."

"Is she going to the bathroom as much as she used to? Vampires tend to limit their intake of food. Their stomachs can't tolerate the diet that they used to have. Some can eat a little, but there will definitely be dietary changes."

"She wasn't much of an eater before. 'You eat like a bird,' I used to say."

"You're not being very helpful. Has her bust size improved? It's a side effect of the vampirism, and that's why some women are reluctant to take the serum."

"No," he said. "She…is this confidential?"

"Of course," I said. "You read the conditions."

He took a breath. "Look, she is not becoming a vampire. She *is* a vampire."

"Then she'll have to get registered and take the serum."

"She doesn't want to. She likes being one. She says she's never felt more alive."

"Well, if she's not registered and they find out, she won't be alive for long. Where is she right now?"

Dr. Primer made a hard left and ascended into a neighborhood where the addresses dropped numerals as the properties grew larger. "We're going to meet her. She's at the wedding." He punched a button and the foot-level speakers pumped out music that sounded like a vacuum cleaner slowed down and distorted. "I'm not one of those middle-aged men addicted to the music of their youth," he said. "I like the new, ambient, edgy music. It was in one of those venues where I met Julie."

That was my daughter's name, and I thought ruefully of how I'd grown irrelevant to her, and how love had turned sour. The early years were the best, the times when dependency engendered a bond between Julie and me. That bond—my family—sustained me. Nothing else seemed to be working. My jobs and potential careers were a Sisyphean succession of frustration. The only career I succeeded in was one I invented. I've sat beside a hundred men like Dr. Primer and listened to their problems, but I've been unable to fix my own.

As for Julie, I'd received a message from her last month saying that she got married in a private ceremony. I was not invited. The impersonal touch, however painful, was consistent with our relationship. We had been at odds for years. The first problem was my involvement with drugs. I fell victim to curiosity, to the allure of the illicit, and finally to the craving. The business didn't suffer, but everything else did. As I have told a few dentists who have sought solace in their own pharmaceuticals, when you really want to stop, you will. I did. My wife, however, had fallen ill to the disease from which she tried to rescue me. She never wanted to stop. I stopped her.

Julie's problems began to manifest after her mother's funeral. I made numerous nighttime trips to the police station, and to various clinics. I hate to say this, but I eventually gave up on her. Bail, rehab bills, and lawyers: I was an enabler. Only she could save herself. The last time I saw her, she looked strung-out, and when I tried to dispense some fatherly advice, she cursed me and left. I hadn't seen her in six months when the terse wedding announcement showed up on my email.

"We talked music," Dr. Primer continued. "Julie and I liked some of the same sounds."

"Julie?" I realized I had been distracted.

"You know, my wife. Julie offered to trade blood for sex."

"That should have been a red flag right there, pardon the pun."

"She said she hung out with vamps, and that she had given them blood in exchange for partying with them, but that she wasn't one herself. I invited her to my house. While we listened to music, she drained off a little of my blood, put it in a Starbucks cup. She carried a tube and needle with her."

"Vampire paraphernalia," I said. "Illegal."

"I didn't know that. She took only a half pint. After that, she gave me grape juice to up my body's blood sugar. When I felt ready, we had sex. Having that body in my bed made me young again."

I studied his mouth as he spoke. They say that the eyes are the window of the soul, but you can't brush, floss, or polish the eyes.

The mouth is a better barometer of a person's character. It shows personal concern. Dr. Primer's trap lacked consistency. On one side, the gums seemed to overwhelm the teeth except where overgrown incisors looked like hinges for a door never hung. They made his mouth look incomplete, under construction. It should have had yellow tape and a hardhat warning around its exterior. His lips flexed slightly as if recalling love.

"She left before sunrise, as she always did in the weeks that followed. Over time, however, I wanted a real relationship, not something conducted at night with her leaving before dawn. I confronted her. I demanded to know what she did, and where she lived. When she told me what she was, I encouraged her to take the serum, but she liked being a vampire, the feeling—she called it a natural high. Well, my natural high was love. I pled my case, and she finally agreed to be married."

Having said this, he retreated into silence. The music changed to the sound of indigestion, amplified. We reached the suburbs on the outside of town. He slowed and turned into a driveway. A uniformed guard holding a clipboard stopped us and asked for identification. We both flashed wallets and the guard, satisfied, waved us through. We drove past high walls and thick foliage. In some fifty yards we passed another open gate. I saw chairs and tables and a bower, the trappings of a wedding ceremony.

I was tieless and there was a small stain on my sports jacket. "I'm not dressed for a wedding," I said.

"Don't worry," he assured me. "These people are nonconformists."

He parked at the end of a string of cars. We walked past another open gate. I saw a brick-and-mortar mansion that sloped down to a grove of high, thick foliage. Where the lawn leveled, a long table was set with goblets and white linen. There were about two dozen people in suits and evening dresses.

"These are your friends?" I asked.

"More like my wife's friends, but they're becoming my friends too."

He nodded to people as he moved forward. "Hello John," said one man whose mouth had the long incisors and serrated molars of the fledgling vamp. I noticed the same odd dentition in others, and the pallor of exposed skin. Even a black man looked almost albino. And while their features were young, they spoke with a grain of age.

I recognized the signs. I was mingling amid one of the last remaining covens of vampires.

I didn't quite know what to do. Technically, my being here was illegal. I remembered the 1-800 number on the billboard I saw driving down here. You're supposed to call that number and let the task force do the rest. Dr. Primer made a couple of introductions, and I responded on automatic pilot, hardly remembering whose fanged smile I saw, whose serrated fingernails scratched my palm as we shook hands. Like a wild animal trapped in a cage, I looked for an exit.

It was then I saw my daughter. Julie stood in the doorway of the house, talking to a young man in a tuxedo. I looked at her and then back at Dr. Primer. He nodded. Julie turned and saw me. She made a slight smile and then, as if our entire history had flooded her features, she frowned and jutted her chin, that defiant look I remembered from when she was a child. I walked over to her. Her friend, perhaps sensing her change of mood, moved away.

"Do you love him?" I asked.

By the faint souring in her eyes I suspected this marriage might not turn out well. "I know he won't turn on me," she said. "He won't invite me to go camping and throw me off a cliff."

Just like her mother again, unable to separate her emotions from her reason.

"Your mother loved the changes," I told my daughter. "She loved them too much. She never went for something halfway, you know that. She would have pulled us all down with her."

"We're the superior beings." Julie made a fist. "We should be ruling the world."

"That's exactly the attitude I'm talking about." She took my rebuke with an aggressive shake of her head. I decided to be conciliatory. "As for your mother, I blame myself, my own problems are what introduced her to drugs, and to the vamp underworld."

I took a step closer to her. She was like a skittish animal that retreated from sudden motion. "I had to do it. I've never told you this before. There was a traveling salesman who disappeared, last seen in our neighborhood. She came home with blood on her chin and her blouse. We burned the evidence. I pled with her to stop, to get the cure. She refused. I had to save us, because the officials come after the family. You know the law, no tolerance. We all would have ended up dead."

"So you took her camping and threw her off a cliff."

"The hardest thing I have ever done," I said, though it was relatively easy: a blow to the back of her head, pitching her over the cliff's side, then climbing down and, while she was groggy, driving the stake through her heart. "I did it for you," I added.

Her features were a dialectic in blue eyes, narrow nose, and her mother's mouth, long and bowed. She was still a child yearning to trust a parent, yet enough of an adult to realize the cold, hard truth of what I said.

Or so I assumed. At least, she did not recoil as I took a step closer and held her. A thankless child may be sharper than a serpent's tooth, but the welcoming embrace of a wayward child is the sweetest balm. I felt her face snuggle into the hollow of my shoulder. It was a slight embrace, but one I cherished, even after it was broken as someone announced that the ceremony would begin.

"I'm a bridesmaid," she said, almost as if regretting the small way she had yielded to my embrace.

She hurried away to join three other female vamps, two on each side of the couple, as the presiding minister began by invoking the prohibited vampire creed, "Oh, powers of darkness, who give us our life, let us join these two converts to the Undead in unholy matrimony..."

The invocation wasn't the only break with tradition. I realized it was two women who were getting hitched. They wore black, and their pledges omitted the till-death-do-us-part, and instead of exchanging rings they drank vials of each other's blood, which was at least consistent with typical vampire nuptials.

Still, the odd nature of the ceremony made me think I was the only outsider here, until I noticed someone more underdressed than I, a shabby-looking, bearded man with the sort of complexion you get from being in the sun too much. He wore a torn horsehair coat and mismatched tennis shoes whose loosened soles slapped the earth as he wandered over to the wet bar—as I did—where a woman in a white shirt, tie, and cummerbund poured him wine. He swallowed it like punch as the two female vamps drank to their same-sex commitment and then kissed. The crowd cheered.

"Coupla lezzies," the bum said, winking at me. "I wouldn't mind watchin' what they do later. Maybe that's why they invited me to this thing, an impartial observer."

He drank and laughed again, one nostril expelling a jet of winey snot. "Yeah, I was hangin' in the alley when this fellow come along and ask me if I want to go to a weddin'…well, why not? It's not like I gotta work in the mornin' or any mornin'."

He wiggled his wine glass to explain his joblessness as a huzzah went up around the same-sex couple and the invited vamps rushed forward with hugs and kisses. The tramp looked on with the expression of someone watching a foreign film without the subtitles.

His look of incomprehension deepened as the minister said, "And I'd like to personally thank Mister Clumes for his attendance this evening."

"It's Mister *Coombs*," the homeless man bellowed with alcoholic bravado. "Rhymes with tombs."

The minister corrected himself. "Mister Tombs, I meant, for providing something that makes this wedding even more special."

Sensing something was up, I began to move away from the guest of honor, the hobo Mr. Coombs. I saw his eyes widen and I could see the jolt of fear that moved up his spine. Without looking over my shoulder, I knew what he saw in the crowd, eyes that turned red, nails that turned into claws, teeth that became fangs.

As the group neared, he dropped his glass and ran. He didn't get far. The entire crowd of vampires pounced on him as one. He barely had time to scream. They tore off his clothes, exposing his skin to a dozen fanged mouths slavering with the prospect of warm human blood.

I realized my daughter was among them. I cringed when she smiled at me, her chin smeared liquid-red. That look of ghoulish triumph was a rebuke to the way I had raised her.

That did it for me. I went back to the road and turned in the direction that Dr. Primer and I had driven earlier. As I hurried along, I reflected on what I had seen. Ugly as it was, I recognized a utilitarian process at work. Thanks to the vampires, you didn't find homeless people sleeping on your front porch overnight or defecating on city streets any more, and frankly I felt a little cheered when I read the stories that still popped up occasionally about a vagrant found bitten and bled on a given raw morning.

I was less cheered by my new son-in-law, who was old enough to have a couple of divorces under his belt and hadn't had the courtesy to let my daughter drink first from the exposed body of the fresh-blood victim. Dentists, I can tell you, make some of the strangest people.

These thoughts in tow, I had traveled a mile or so before Primer's black Mercedes pulled over beside me. Beginning to get weary of feet, I got in. I could smell the blood on his breath as clearly as the car's new leather.

"Where's Julie?" I asked.

"She's…cleaning up."

We rolled down the dark road.

"When did you figure out I was a vampire?" he asked.

"Your mouth," I said. "It had that look, and the heavy-black film over your office windows. It's a sure giveaway, and I bet I could have got it for half of what you paid. And could you change the music, that stuff is giving me a headache."

He switched the station to Mozart.

"She wouldn't marry me unless I converted," he said. "I'm not as fond of the vampire state as she is. There are restrictions."

"I'm sure there are," I said.

"But if I can make her happy, it's worth it."

I looked over at my son-in-law, who was a few years older than I. I couldn't say I liked him much, but I had empathy for his state, to be helplessly in love, the way I had once been with my wife, long before I killed her.

"I want your blessing," he said.

I made the sign of the cross in front of him.

"I'm serious," he said.

"You can start by prompt payment of my bill when it arrives."

"Of course," he said, a touch irritated.

I didn't care that he was annoyed. I had been brought here under false pretenses. Even so, I did some pitching as he drove: the Ace Cuspidor that separates a patient's spit from their blood; the private contract, sub rosa, I had with certain blood donation and testing clinics and Biohazard sites; and the sun block that doubled as cologne. I held the patent on all three. The point was to have a steady supply of blood in order to avoid the kind of scene I had just witnessed.

"Are your numbers negotiable?" he asked. Vampires are real skinflints, I've noticed.

"I would have preferred a more traditional introduction to my son-in-law," I said. "But I will give you a piece of priceless advice: caution. Only caution keeps us alive, caution and fitting in, finding a place. Being useful, that's the key."

"Useful," he said. He looked sincere.

My next phrase was nothing but truth. "We're in this together now, the way I see it."

"So a discount is not out of the question?"

We reached the office. I gave him a nod and walked to my car.

"I can bring her back to you," he called after me.

I turned to him. "I'll think about that discount," I said.

I drove up the coast. Past Oceanside, I pulled off the road. I had seen movement.

Sometimes, I thought, the hell with caution: You have to be what you are, or what you have become.

I ran across the highway and slipped through some bushes. On the sand, I saw that my perception was accurate. California, due to its clement weather, attracts a large percentage of the homeless and displaced. In front of me a singular example of that subculture stumbled while holding a bottle. He walked bare-assed, having done his business in the bushes, past a small pile of clothes and toward the dark shore, drinking and singing, "Jesus' blood never failed me," in a rusty voice I found plaintive. He stopped on the shoreline. As he turned, I jumped and tore into his neck.

When it was over, I carried his body out to the water and bore him out beyond the waves and let him sink. Turning, I looked at the highway lights and thought how beautiful they looked from this perspective. I wished then I could have floated endlessly on my back, satiated by blood and looking up at the stars, but I knew daylight would come and I had promises to keep.

I swam back to shore. The adrenaline was beginning to fade, and the sluggish feeling was picking up. I found his bottle. We're not supposed to drink, but a few sips finished the cheap wine and provided a sort of bouquet to my mood. I lumbered across the road and back to the car. I drove a few miles and then pulled over and slept in my wet clothes.

When I woke it was three in the morning, and I still had some time to reach home before the poisonous sun rose. WE TOOK BACK THE NIGHT said the sign some forty miles up the road. They were right, though the night has its own resources, and the night wins once in a while.

About Garrett Rowlan

Garrett Rowlan is a substitute teacher in Los Angeles. His most recent publications are in the *Cafe Irreal* and *Map Literary*.

He is using some aspects of this story in a novel about a post-vampire America.

THE CHURCH
BY MATTHEW WILSON

The church was close to the graves. The earthy bed it sat upon contained bodies dead from the plague, and more recently, the Spanish flu during the First World War. No one had been buried at the church since.

No one spoke of the church. No one worshipped there, no one came to tear it down when the larger part of the roof collapsed in upon itself. No animals wandered in the diseased fields and birds made no nests in the trees. The surface was just as devoid of life as it was underneath.

The Second World War erupted in Europe and mothers talked their children into enlisting, to be anywhere but here, in the town next to the church.

Only Liam and Sam didn't go to war.

Liam knew that as a boy, Sam had snuck into his father's drinks cabinet and broke his leg dancing on the roof, sozzled. The bone had never set properly and he walked funny ever since.

Liam knew that he himself was no soldier and his father had been a manic depressant. His father put his throat into his belt and looped it round a light cord back in thirty-eight. So he had left Liam when the voices got too bad.

Liam found himself wishing he had Sam's limp; some genuine disability from which he could gain sympathy rather than it be thought that he inherited his father's mental illness. He was told that bad blood passed on in any family and the bosses believed they had enough enemies to fight on their fronts without him going ape shit with his rifle in barracks.

The church had always beckoned to Liam; it was a forbidden place. Left alone in the town with all the young men overseas, he had too much time on his hands and that was a recipe for trouble for any eighteen-year-old. Or maybe he decided that since everyone believed he was a basket case, perhaps he should act like one.

Liam was standing on the cracked road that was littered with potholes, studying the church. He had never been this close to it before. He saw the neglect, and the church was so overgrown by a vine that wound up its eastern wall that it appeared haunted, even in the daylight.

A voice at his back made him jump and he cried out.

"Sorry, didn't mean to scare you," Sam said.

Liam turned around. "Why didn't you tell me you were here instead of sneaking up on me?"

Sam laughed and juggled a fist-sized rock. "This place is haunted. I heard back in twenty-nine, all the dead kids from this graveyard flew into Craig Collins' house one night and carried him off through the window inside there."

"That's bullshit," Liam said.

Sam cocked his arm back and threw the stone with all his might. He missed the window by an inch and made a low sucking sound through his teeth. "Damn, the sun was in my eyes. What're you doing here, anyway?"

"No place else to be; might as well be here."

"You're not scared?"

Liam felt a silly need not to piss the church off. He didn't like that Sam was throwing rocks. "I'm not scared," he said, ducking as Sam threw another stone, "but you ought to stop that."

"Who's going to mind, the dead kids who kidnapped Craig Collins?"

"Those stories are hokum that our parents told us to make us behave when we were little kids," Liam said. "Eat your celery, Liam, or else the church will get you. Clean behind your ears, Liam, or else you'll disappear like all the other boys. It's a fucking church! If there are any missing kids, they ran away because this town's a drag. I wish I'd gone to war like the others, to get away from this ghost town and make something of myself."

Did he have to mention ghosts?

Never go to the church, Liam's father always told him. *There's something wrong with the place.*

Never go to the church.

No one except his dad ever spoke of the place. If cancers were ignored then maybe they would go away.

Liam took a rock out of Sam's hand. He was careful to make sure the church's windows had a clear view of him laying the confiscated stone down on the ground. He'd have no part in attacking the church. But then a window suddenly exploded and black glass erupted over the neglected graves.

"Yes! Direct hit!" Sam giggled like a tickled girl. "Take one rock from me and I'll just throw another. Who else in this town of cowards would be brave enough to stand up to the haunted church?"

Liam realized that Sam had been frowned upon so long for his disability, and probably felt impotent because of it. He understood Sam's need to take back some power. He watched as Sam laughed, dancing as much as his bad leg allowed.

But Liam was not joining in.

Just in case.

*****

Later that night, Liam lay in bed and tried to control his breathing as he thought about Sam. He had to let it go. Neither of them had invaded the church's sacred ground. No trespassing.

No, they just beat the shit out of its windows...*Sam did, not me. Not me.*

No good. He couldn't sleep.

Angry at his childish superstitions, he kicked off the sweaty, sodden sheets and headed to the kitchen for a cup of milk. As a boy, it had helped him sleep when an imaginary monster lurked in his toy cupboard, illuminated by a blast of lightning from outside his window. Back then, his father had calmed him with a glass of milk and a theory there were no monsters.

On this side of the road at least.

"Ow." Liam clapped a hand over his mouth when he knocked his foot against the edge of the kitchen table. He didn't want to make noise because his mom was a worker and needed her rest. He would be embarrassed if she knew what he was doing.

Milk? Monster problems again, huh? Oh, honey, you're too old for this.

He'd be all right in a minute. He just needed a sip. He put the glass to his lips, feeling his mouth slowly slacken and relax. The splash of the icy liquid from the glass was an instant balm like the squeak of an old teddy bear. He felt better.

But when he looked out the window and saw the man in the street, he spat his drink on the window.

"What the hell?" he cried, forgetting that he didn't want to wake his mother.

In the illumination from the streetlight, Liam could see that the man had a shovel over his shoulder like a fire fighter carrying a woman from a burning house. When he recognized the limp, realization hit him like a rock wrapped in a snow ball. There was only one person in the whole of town who walked like that.

Sam.

Sam was heading toward the church. In the middle of the night.

*****

The gate was open when Liam got there, but there was no other sign of Sam. He strained his eyes in the pinpricks of star light and noticed foot prints in the dirt just ahead.

"Sam!" he called, not wanting to leave the security of the sidewalk. He knew the church was a presence, a being as living as he. It defended its territory. Was it asleep or only pretending?

Sam was his only friend in a town of ghosts.

Liam could not go to war. He couldn't defend his country in the face of gunfire and be a hero. But here he could make a difference. Here he could save his friend, if he could only find the courage to step off the sidewalk.

He cursed himself, wondering if it was enough protection to simply cross his fingers as he stepped through the mangled gate. He felt like he was crossing from one world to another, a lost explorer in the desert, low on water, hoping this first step in the dark was toward the right direction.

He ducked, expecting some kind of attack when an owl hooted in the air. It did not land on the dead tree, but instead chose to keep flying. Nothing good stopped here.

Walking cautiously on the church grounds, he felt the slight breeze as it rustled the leaves on the overgrown shrubs. The path was dangerous to maneuver in the dark, with uneven concrete pavers that alternatively sank and protruded. To the right and left of the path, wild trees grew at odd angles that had limbs untamed from lack of pruning.

By the time he reached the first granite slab that gleamed in the silver moonlight, the sound of digging assaulted his senses. Liam followed the sound, until he saw that Sam was bringing a spade up and down like a pick axe, breaking open the ground.

Liam paused, fearing what Sam might bring up from the bowels of the earth. A dead hand might reach up from the grave at any minute and drag him down. Liam silently asked mercy from whatever force looked after young men.

He had been stepping only on the pavers. He did not trust the poisoned earth. If the dead souls beneath it minded being trod upon, they had not grabbed his ankles yet.

Coming closer, Liam called, "Sam? It's me, what the hell are you doing? Come on, let's get out of here."

Sam stopped digging and Liam could see him smiling in the moonlight. His eyes were closed, but he was talking. "It's quite all right, Liam. I know what I'm doing. I haven't gone mad. Remember, you're the crazy one and I'm just the one with the bum leg."

"Come on, Sam, let's get out of here," Liam repeated.

"I can't leave. I'm buried here and now I have to dig myself up again. The church told me it would help me."

Liam nervously glanced over his shoulder at the church. It still seemed to sleep. He advanced, one step, two—"Sam. You're not buried in this churchyard. We have to leave this place. It doesn't like us."

"What are you talking about? It invited me here; it wants me here. It wants me to dig."

Liam stopped walking. The spade was barred at him like a knight's lance warding off a dragon.

"Sam! What are you doing?"

"I should never have thrown those rocks. You were right. I see that now."

"You don't see shit. Let's go."

"You want my body to rot down there? You don't want me to breathe, to feel the sun? You're just like your crazy father. He's down there too."

"My father is buried across town, not here. Listen, Sam, that's someone's grave. They're gonna be pissed, you digging it up—whoa!"

Liam threw his head back like a boxer avoiding a KO blow. The head of the spade missed him by inches, cutting the tips off his hair which fluttered to the ground like autumn leaves. The hair frazzled and smoked like spent match heads, sinking into the earth like worms fleeing crows.

Laughing, Sam swung the shovel like a maniac samurai. Liam was afraid of the earth flinging off it, sizzling like acid as it hit the stones he stood upon.

The church tasted and woke. A blue candle came on in the window.

Stay away from the church, his father had said. Suddenly Liam remembered the rest of what his father used to say: *Only the dead are welcome there, and you have so much life in you.*

There would be no heroics now. Liam ran for the gate, skipping over the stones, sure he would disappear into the soft earth.

Sam's laugh chased him and he called, "You can't escape. This place already has us. Both of us!"

But Liam continued to run, his heart in his mouth with fear. He nearly fainted as the gate closed before him, swung shut like a bouncer who did not like his patrons. He was a prisoner in the churchyard.

"You won't be leaving," the church whispered, awake and alert now.

He changed direction, spat on his hands for traction like a goal keeper about to make a save, and leaped onto the fence. His fingers bled as he broke a nail on the ugly wrought iron. It didn't matter if he was impaled; better that then to fall into the church's abyss.

He thought he was going to make it. He thought he was going to climb the fence and land on the other side. But Sam grabbed his ankles hard enough to bruise the skin. "Where do you think you're going? Always running away. No wonder the church chose us, it's because we're both defective. Get down here!"

Sam tugged at his ankles, and all the air left Liam as he hit the hard earth, his lungs shrinking like broken bagpipes.

Despite his bad leg, Sam dragged Liam toward the church. Sam pushed the door open and said to the church, "Your ghost-boys kidnapped Craig Collins, but I'm here because I want to be here, although Liam may not exactly be a volunteer."

The ceiling lay crumbled over the pews, collapsed with age and neglect. The air smelled foul, like the bottom of an unturned compost heap; the stench of rotting cadavers. It permeated the nose and saturated the skin and hair.

Liam wanted to fight Sam, to get up and run. But something held him down, even when Sam let go. He saw shimmering lights floating over the altar in the front of the church. The lights were translucent and sparkled like a sprinkling of morning dew. They formed the shapes of many people, featureless, as though they were unfinished. The ghost-boys seemed delicate and moved like waves in the ocean.

Sam laughed, opening his arms as if to embrace the ugly altar. "Why not feed the church with us rather than waste boys who are perfect? I'm disabled and you're crazy. We would die unloved. Why not give ourselves up to a better cause? Think how many lives we will save if the church takes us instead of healthy young men."

Liam found the strength to stand upright. "I'm not crazy! And neither was my father."

"Come. Let's go to our graves with some dignity. I've already started digging them."

Liam bought his foot up to kick at Sam, but the building shook as if quicksand was at its foundations. A crack ran along the floor, and opened into a chasm screaming with the dead.

Sam grabbed Liam's throat, yanking him off his feet. They wrestled, Liam catching sight of a boy with a blue face in the broken windows. *Is that me?*

He knew he was suffocating, maybe dying.

Let me do this one thing before I go. I'll do it for my father.

With his last breath, Liam reached for the blue candle in the window. He swiped at it and the candle upended. The dead were screaming as flames licked the walls like a lover's tongue.

The shock of seeing the fire made Sam let go. Liam took advantage of it and grabbed a chunk of the fallen ceiling stone. He bought it down with a mighty crack on Sam's head. Nose gushing crimson, his friend nodded furiously like he agreed with his side of an argument and dropped to his knees as if prayer.

Liam raised the stone in his hand, ready for a final blow, but stopped. He looked at the smoke generated by the fire and saw images. Some of them had faces. They were the lost boys; some dead from the plague, some dead from the flu, and some who had been kidnapped.

He could not help them. But he could help Sam.

Just as the timbers of the fallen ceiling caught fire, Liam grabbed Sam and began to drag him toward the door.

*****

In the dark bedroom, the monsters came. He wouldn't get up to go into the kitchen. No milk would help him now.

"I'm scared, Dad," Liam spoke to a man dead for four years.

Fear is false evidence appearing real. The thoughts found him, sounding like his father's voice, and he wondered from where they emanated.

"But I've seen things that no one should ever have to see."

How you process it is the difference between sanity and insanity.

"What does that mean?"

You didn't run away like I did. You acted responsibly and saved your friend.

"Dad, what do you want me to do?"

Live your life, and do the best that you can with it.

About Matthew Wilson

Matthew Wilson, 29, is a UK resident who has been writing since he was small. Recently his stories have appeared in *Beyond Centauri, Starline Poets Association* and *Carillon Magazine*.

He is currently editing his first novel.

Holodomor Girl
by Yvonne Navarro

1933: The Ukraine

Death visits Stasja in her sleep, black as a nightmare, white as the feathers on an angel's wings, red as the gaping wound in the neck of a murdered woman, things she has never seen but now somehow knows. Death is all these things and more, but it does not stay. Instead, it slips away without a sound, and when it leaves, Stasja wakes and stays that way, watches until the sky lightens with a sunrise that brings no warmth.

It is another frigid, winter morning, the cold sinking into her joints and deepening with every second. Stasja crawls out of bed and pulls on scratchy wool stockings, a much-patched long skirt, and two thin shirts beneath a hand-me-down jacket that was new long before her older brother, Yuriy, was born. Every breath sends a miniature cloud in front of her face and her fingers are numb in only a few moments. None of this matters because she can't stop her mind from replaying everything from late the night before when her father's low, strained voice and her mother's quiet sobs made her creep out of bed and crouch at the doorway to listen to her parents as they talked after they believed all their children were asleep.

"If we do not do what we must, we will not survive the month. It is the only way."

"But they say the grain shipments are on their way!"

"Perhaps...but perhaps not. These are words of hope, but they are also the words of desperate men who have said the same thing many times over these past months."

"We must have hope."

"Hope without being realistic can kill us. The bodies pile up— friends, neighbors, kinsmen. You *know* that we must do this."

Silence then, for a long time. When her mother spoke again, her voice had been filled with defeat and regret and more sorrow than any woman should ever have to endure.

"*One more day*. I beg of you...just one more."

"All right," father said after a time. "But just that. No more."

Now, in the bleak morning time, her father has rebuilt the fire that will take several hours to warm the tiny house; even so, it brings no relief from the cold that has settled into her heart. Yuriy is already outside, his jutting ribs rubbing against his shirt, his belly protruding and perpetually empty as he chops wood with weak strokes and always keeps an eye out for a rabbit or squirrel, even though they haven't seen either in weeks. The baby, Kateryna, sits quietly in her highchair at the table, too drained of energy to fuss about the hollowness in the pit of her belly. Her face is drawn but not yet skeletal, padded by a shadow of the infant fat that still remains from better times, before her mother's breast milk dried up. It is that same fading layer of fat that will send her to her doom.

The older girl turns away from the sight of her small, wan sister, then runs out the door. As it slams behind her, she gags and leans to the right to vomit, but there is nothing in her stomach but bile and fumes.

Her mother's voice—

One more day.

The hours pass, so slowly. There is nowhere to run or hide, nothing to do that will dull or distract from the constant headache of famine, the twisting in her stomach as it turns upon itself in search of sustenance, the over-emphasized thud of her own heartbeat just below her sternum. At night, when she undresses and washes before bed, she can see it pulsing there beneath the nearly translucent layer of skin, that still stubborn beat of her heart. And at the end of the day, another stretch of time during which there has been nothing to fill their bellies but wishes, it is still that phrase, those three words that have beaten out the rest of that horrible conversation and overshadowed the memory that brings a huge and horrible future:

One more day.

That night their mother helps them all into bed, tucking the bedcovers around them with fingers so thin they look as brittle and fragile as twigs. She kisses each of her children, lingering over Kateryna even though the toddler has already fallen asleep. When she straightens and turns to leave, the lamp's flame, flickering wildly in the drafty room, highlights the tear tracks on cheeks sunken by the unrelenting starvation of the Holodomor inflicted upon their people by the Soviets.

Stasja wants more than anything to stay awake, but starvation carries its own demands for sleep, for fitful, short-lived respite from a reality that has become too cruel to bear. She puts one hand on Kateryna's tiny wrist, then moves the other over the toddler's chest until she can feel the pulse of her sister's lifeblood beneath the pads of her own skinny fingers. It thumps there like a soft lullaby; soon her body surrenders, and Stasja sleeps.

But not for long.

*****

Stasja's eyes open wide in the darkness. There is no shroud of sleep to shake off, no question that she is dreaming. She can hear her parents murmuring in the other room, and she knows what they are talking about. It is only a matter of time now.

A shadow moves at the foot of the bed.

She sits up, straining to see. "Who's there?" she whispers.

The shadow is darker than the others in the room, but still visible, still *palpable*; Stasja feels it against her skin in the way a person's nerves tingle unpleasantly just after something has been touched that shouldn't have been—poison ivy, or perhaps toxic black hellebore. It moves, she's sure of it, a slight *tilt* at the top as if it were a dog trying to understand an odd sound. "Who *are* you?"

Instead of answering the shadow moves again, this time sliding around to the side of the bed. It looms above her, then a part of it extends, like an arm, and stretches toward Kateryna. It looks like a hand, reaching for her sister—

"No," Stasja hisses. Before the end of the shape can touch the baby, Stasja rolls and drapes herself protectively over the tiny girl's sleeping form. "Don't touch her!"

The voice that suddenly winds through her mind is like ink-colored blood, seeping through her consciousness and blotting out everything else, smothering all sound in her existence.

I come to mark her.

"I know who you are," Stasja says in a nearly inaudible voice. "You're Death, aren't you? But you're wrong—you can't have her. I won't let you."

It is already decided.

Stasja shakes her head and stays where she is. After a moment, the apparition leans closer. It is already chilly in the room, but suddenly she feels the cold even more, deep into her bones; she grinds her teeth together to keep them from chattering. One of her incisors moves, loosened by months of too-little sustenance.

You know this. Death's voice slides through her head again and her thoughts become painful, split by black razors. *Because you have already heard.* The shadow straightens above her. There is nothing on which she can focus, no head or face, but Stasja still feels it staring at her, paralyzing her with a gaze that promises an eternity of nothingness.

"Just go away," she manages. Her voice is a little louder and Kateryna stirs beneath her while on the other side of the bed Yuriy is stone still, sucked deep into dreams by weakness and exhaustion. Stasja drops her voice back to a whisper. "You can change it."

The black shape above her waits for a long time to see if she will say something more. When she doesn't, it waves at the air over her head. *Let me show you the future.*

Stasja tries to pull back, but it is too late—

Her father stands by the wood stove in the front room. There is a smell in the room, rich along the drafts that squeeze through the cracks around the window, some kind of broth that makes her mouth water and her stomach clench with anticipation. Her mother sits in her rocker and stares at the floor; she doesn't look up as Yuriy drags in another undersized log and pushes it into the fireplace. Yuriy pauses unsteadily before making his way to the stove and stopping next to their father. It takes a few seconds, then she realizes the two of them are staring down at the bubbling contents of the cast iron cooking pot; after a moment, the older man picks up a wooden spoon and stirs the food. Her brother takes the spoon and dips it into the pot, then puts it to his mouth for a taste. Another second and he nods approval.

Even though she is not there, cannot possibly be there because none of this has taken place yet, all of Stasja's senses suddenly explode with raw need. She can't remember the last time she had a meal, much less a soup made with meat. So much saliva fills her mouth that it leaks out one corner; her fingers find the fabric of her nightclothes and clench, hanging on with everything she has so that she doesn't reach out for the food she knows isn't in her reality. She thought she knew hunger, intimately, but now Stasja realizes that true starvation has a way of destroying control in even the strongest.

Her eyelids fly open. Has she been sleeping? Her breath hitches in her throat until beneath her Kateryna finally moves. Her parents still whisper to each other in the front room, the fire still gives decent light around the doorframe between this room and the next; not that much time has passed or the logs would have burned down and reduced the yellow glow to muddy orange.

Death still stands above her, waiting with silent, infinite patience.

Stasja starts to cry, trying her best to hold it in so as not to wake her baby sister. "I beg you." Her arms are splayed over Kateryna's small body and her hold tightens. "Take me instead."

The being that looms above her doesn't actually move, but she still feels it pause, a strange, unseen *stoppage* of movement that was never there to begin with. *You would trade?*

"Yes," Stasja says. "Me, for her."

Deep within the coils of her brain there is an oily, hideous chuckle. *It is not so simple*, Death says. *To change what has already been fated demands a fee.*

She stares up at it. "I would give anything," she says, "but I have no money, no food. I have nothing else."

There is always something, it tells her. Her skin crawls, and there is something horribly wrong with her impression that Death smiles before reaching down to stroke the top of her head.

*****

The darkness lasts forever but at the same time is over in the time it takes for a dead leaf to fall from a branch. She cannot move, she cannot speak; yet she can see through her own closed eyelids, and she can think coherently, and she can feel.

She feels—

Her mother's hands on her when she comes in to check on Kateryna, soft as she tries to push Stasja aside, then changing to rough as her oldest daughter's limp body does not respond. Her mother drags her into a sitting position and wraps her in a hug, then wails into Stasja's hair until her husband comes into the room to see what's gone wrong. Stasja's father is too weak to lift Stasja from the bed alone so he takes her shoulders and Yuriy gets up and grips her ankles; they carry her into the front room and lay her out on the table, then go back to stay with the baby so her mother can remove Stasja's clothes and wash her. After the coolness of the water, there is the sensation of smoothness as her mother carefully lays narrow strips of old silk across Stasja's chest and hips for modesty.

Before her mother stumbles from the room, Stasja feels the woman's lips brush her forehead a final time, the last warmth of breath with it, and the sting of a single, hot tear that falls onto her cheek.

She hears—

Through the silence in the house as her family prays without speaking, first for her, that her spirit be lifted to a better place, and then for themselves, that they may be forgiven.

Her father's footsteps as he returns to the kitchen and walks to the cabinet, then comes to the table to stand over her. There is nothing but the sound of his uneven breathing for a long time, then...

She feels—

The edge of the old kitchen knife, a stinging, trembling cut in the beginning, changing to soul-deep agony as his grip tightens and he forces himself to slice deeply into her flesh, to divide it into segments that will keep himself and his family alive for awhile longer, just until the grain shipments finally resume.

She cannot move.

She cannot scream.

In her tortured thoughts, Stasja hears the last words of Death, over and over over.

There is always something.

And the end is a very long time coming.

About Yvonne Navarro

Yvonne Navarro lives in southern Arizona, where by day she works on historic Fort Huachuca. She is the author of twenty-two published novels and well over a hundred short stories, and has written about everything from vampires to psychologically disturbed husbands to the end of the world. Her work has won the Horror Writers Association's Bram Stoker Award plus a number of other writing awards.

Visit her at www.yvonnenavarro.com
or www.facebook.com/yvonne.navarro.001 to keep up with slices of a crazy life that includes her husband, author Weston Ochse, three Great Danes (Goblin, Ghost and Ghoulie), a people-loving parakeet named BirdZilla, painting, and lots of ice cream, Smarties, and white zinfandel.

Her most recent novel is *Concrete Savior*, the second book in the Dark Redemption Series.

THE HUNG PREACHER
BY SCOTT NICHOLSON

Ronnie Day didn't want to believe it.

It had been four years since he'd last seen the old preacher's ghost, enough time to believe it had never happened. Ronnie and his little brother Tim still whispered about it once in a while as they were falling asleep. But ghosts were kids' stuff. Ronnie was in high school now and planning on attending Westridge University after graduation. He didn't have time for such nonsense these days.

Tim, though, was as full of it as ever.

"I seen him," Tim said, toying with his iPod. Tim was still into bubble-gum pop bands like most eighth graders, but that was fine with Ronnie. Too many of his buddies had gone for banjo music, and that stuff made him want to jump off a bridge.

"'Saw' him. I thought you were getting A's in English." Ronnie was just trying to change the subject. He didn't want to think about ghosts and monsters. Dad said to just bury all that stuff, like they'd buried the people that had died.

"I can write, I just can't speak good grammar yet. I have to see it in front of me."

"It's just the fog," Ronnie said. "Always foggy in October, there by the river."

"We come around the curve and the headlights washed over the graveyard. And I saw him hanging there plain as day."

"Except it was *night*. Shadows play tricks on your eyes. Mom didn't see anything, did she?"

"Nah. She was watching the road. You know how she is when she's driving."

"You didn't tell her, did you?"

"What, you think I'm crazy?" Tim's blue eyes flashed behind his thick glasses. He was scrawny, barely ninety pounds. If he didn't fill out before the ninth grade, the bullies would be pounding the crap out of him. Ronnie didn't want to spend his senior year playing hero.

And he didn't want to deal with ghosts and memories and legends. He had real problems, like asking Melanie Ward to the Homecoming Dance. She'd been hanging out with Bobby Eldreth a lot lately, and Bobby was the kind of competition few guys wanted to face. He was an all-conference linebacker and drove a muddy Jeep, plus he was the drummer in a garage band.

Ronnie, meanwhile, worked on the school newspaper and was one of the top students in art. Lame by pretty much anyone's standards, much less somebody's as hot as Melanie.

"Mom doesn't remember any of it," Ronnie said. "And we need to keep it that way. Especially since none of us really know what happened."

"If I saw the Hung Preacher, then we know that part is true," Tim said.

"Yeah, you got a point. Except *ghosts aren't real.*"

"Think about it, Ronnie. Ghosts are forever, right? Why would a ghost ever have to leave the churchyard?"

Ronnie was getting mad now, partly because he was afraid. "Because they all went into the river, just like the legend says. Washed them all away."

"Okay, then," Tim said, poking out his chin a little the way Mom did when she felt defiant. "If you don't believe in the Hung Preacher, then you won't have any problem going there tonight to check it out."

"To the *church*? Are you nuts?"

"Ghosts aren't real. So where's the harm?"

"I got too much to do. Some of us have lives, unlike little twerp eighth-graders."

Tim made a clucking sound deep in his adolescent throat. "Ronnie is a chiiii-cken, Ronnie is a chiiii-cken."

Ronnie picked a pillow off the bed and hurled it at Tim, knocking his glasses off. Luckily, the glasses bounced on the mattress and not the floor. Dad's carpentry jobs had dried up and they didn't have money to spare. And Ronnie didn't want to use cash from his part-time gig at the bowling alley to pay for a new pair.

Tim settled his glasses back on his nose and pushed them into place. "Okay, then. Be a chicken. But I'm going up there and have a look."

"Not in October!" The words were out before Ronnie could stop them. Everyone in Whispering Pines knew about Sheriff Littlefield's brother Samuel, who had died at the church during a freakish Halloween prank. Samuel had become just another part of the legend, and some people said you could see him hanging from the belfry just like you could see the Hung Preacher dangling from the old dogwood by a short length of rope.

Except the sheriff had cut the dogwood down years ago, shortly after his deputy drowned in the river and Archer McFall had vanished from the old red church.

For a place that isn't haunted, it's sure had its share of death and misery.

"Wow, you really are scared, aren't you?" Tim taunted.

"Get over it, dork," Ronnie said.

Tim's eyes narrowed and his lips twisted into a smirk. "Boy, I can't wait to tell Melanie you're chicken."

"Dork! I'll kill you!" Ronnie jumped toward him, but the little twerp was fast, slipping out of the bedroom they shared and hurrying down the hall. Tim ran through the kitchen and out the back door, knowing not to disturb Dad from his nightly reality shows. Ronnie followed, his sneakers booming on the floor although he tried to lighten his footsteps.

Outside, Ronnie had to look around a little before he saw Tim halfway up the driveway, just at the edge of the enveloping mist. "Get back in here. Mom will be home soon."

"So? Since when does she worry about me staying out late?"

"Get back in here."

"Okay. Right after I go to the church and see if the Hung Preacher is real."

"You can't see."

"I know the way." Tim headed up the driveway, out of the glow leaking from the house's windows, and was soon swallowed by the darkness. Ronnie cussed under his breath, reached inside the house, and found the flashlight hanging from two ten-penny nails. He switched it on, but had to bang the batteries twice against his thigh before the light poured forth.

Ronnie hadn't lied about the October nights. Moist fog hung heavy over the valley, carrying the muddy, fishy smell of the river. The flashlight did little to dispel the illusion of shapes forming along the edges of Ronnie's vision. By the time he reached the main gravel road, the house was nothing but a black block with a few yellow rectangles.

"Hey, dork!" Ronnie called ahead into the darkness. Tim was so dorky he hadn't even carried a flashlight. Or maybe he was just acting weird.

Not a good sign when weird things happen in Whispering Pines.

Ronnie started jogging, sucking wet air into his lungs. He could almost taste the darkness—it was like a solid tar of all the hidden secrets of the world. The church was barely half a mile from the house, but because of the lack of visibility, Ronnie felt as if he were traversing the same stretch of gravel over and over, like he was on a giant treadmill and the surrounding trees and roadside weeds stayed the same. The few houses in the rural area sat far back from the road or across narrow wooden bridges, so their lights were little more than soggy, distant fireflies.

Ronnie couldn't believe Tim was staying ahead. Tim was one of the biggest nerds in Whispering Pines—school chess champ, of all things— but he must have been running close to full speed, blind and frantic. By the time Ronnie reached the edge of the old graveyard, he wished he'd gotten one of Dad's rifles out of the cabinet.

A gun doesn't do any good against a ghost. You know that.

But it might have made him feel better. As it was, with nothing but a flashlight, he was afraid to enter the graveyard.

You were afraid before you left the house. You've been afraid for four years.

"Tim!" he called into the night. His voice was swallowed by the cotton of fog.

It was the first time Ronnie had been on the church property since that horrible night, and the memories flooded over him like a shroud and hugged him tight, almost suffocating him. The Reverend Archer McFall and his long-dead ancestor, the Hung Preacher, had taken the cemetery's spirits down to the river, where they'd joined him for a hellish baptism and washed themselves clean of this earth. Mom had almost gone with them, but Dad had rescued her, and everybody in Whispering Pines was smart enough to forget the whole thing.

Everybody but Tim.

Ronnie played the light over the worn tombstones. The letters had faded on many, and moss covered the names on others, but here and there he spotted a Potter, Absher, or McFall. The old, old families, the ones who had settled the valley and who had a hand in the hanging death of Reverend Wendell McFall. And it was Wendell who lived on in legend as the Hung Preacher, the one whose body was seen dangling from a rope tied to the branch of an ancient dogwood tree. But the sheriff had cut down the dogwood tree shortly after that weird night when the ghosts had risen and escaped the soil.

Which was what made Tim's story so chilling. Tim didn't claim he'd seen a ghost. He said he'd seen the Hung Preacher dangling from the old dogwood tree.

Only a dork like Tim would claim to see the ghost of a *tree*.

Ronnie called out once more, but it was more like a whisper, because he didn't want to disturb anything outside the circle of the flashlight that might be listening—dead or alive.

The grass of the old churchyard was unkempt, high weeds bending brown under the weight of autumn. The church technically still belonged to Archer McFall, who had bought the property shortly before disappearing. And even though Archer was on the books as a missing person, Ronnie knew Archer was down there in the river somewhere, chuckling and sleeping and just waiting for the right time to return.

No.

That was just a stupid old legend. What the sheriff said was true— Archer drugged the congregation, including Mom, and tried to form a cult, but then everybody wised up when they realized Archer was truly sick and evil, not a man of God at all.

"Ronnie!" Tim's voice came from somewhere above, which made it carry despite the heavy air.

Above? The dork is not in the damned steeple, is he? How could he have gotten up there? The church has been locked for years.

Ronnie swept the light above him, but the fog absorbed the beam and smothered it. "Where are you, dork? We're going to get in trouble for trespassing."

"Up here."

Ronnie staggered forward, nearly tripping over an old marble monument that jutted up like a monster's tooth. "Up *where?*"

And then he saw it—the ebony silhouette of the dogwood tree, standing withered and wild, branches thrown out like a hundred crooked arms, its few leaves curled in permanent decay.

Not real. No way. The sheriff cut it down and stacked it up and burned it. You saw the flames plain as day.

But maybe the smoke of that bonfire was just another ghost, and all ghosts carried the truth of what had gone before.

Ronnie wanted to scream at Tim, to tell him to get his scrawny ass out of that tree, but that would have acknowledged the existence of the tree, and he wasn't ready to do that. And he didn't think he could yell anyway, because his throat constricted in fear.

Instead, he wheezed, "Tim."

He didn't want to think about the church that lurked behind the tree. Something might be fluttering in the belfry, or a new preacher might be standing up at the lectern bringing a message of sin and retribution. Maybe even Archer McFall—the one who answered a calling to inflict suffering upon the guilty.

He could hear Archer's deep voice as if it were yesterday: *"And we're all guilty, aren't we, Ronnie?"*

"I told you," Tim said, loud and bold and too stupid to know he was in a haunted tree. "I told you it was real."

Ronnie found his voice, now more angry than scared. "Get down."

"Not until you admit I was right."

"I ain't admitting nothing. Get down or I'll—"

"What? Climb up and get me? Yeah, right."

"Get down. Do you want Dad to find out we've been messing around the church?"

"What, are you going to be a tattle-tale? A scaredy-cat tattle-tale?"

Ronnie moved closer to the tree, its thick, scaly bark like the skin of a prehistoric creature rising up toward the dark heavens. "I'm not scared, I just don't think it's safe around here. Plus we could get arrested for trespassing. And if Dad found out—"

"Go on home, then. I'm fine by myself. But I can't wait to tell Melanie Ward about this."

Ronnie momentarily forgot he was standing outside the red church in the middle of the night. "You wouldn't dare."

"Sure, I would."

Angry, Ronnie rushed for the thick, twisted trunk of the dogwood, planning to bust Tim a good one. He played the beam around the lower branches, then higher, and he caught a glimpse of Tim's face, glasses reflecting the light. His brother seemed to float among the eerie gauze of night twenty feet above.

Ronnie grabbed one of the twisted, gnarled lower branches, half-surprised to find it solid. He swung himself up, hooking a leg over it as he climbed. He shoved the flashlight into his back pocket so he could use both hands, and the darkness rushed him from all sides. His fingernails clawed the bark as he grappled for purchase.

"Gonna kill you," Ronnie muttered. Tim chuckled softly above him.

Ronnie clambered upward, locking his foot in the crotch of the two main branches and nearly losing his shoe. He reached above and grabbed a smaller branch, hoisting for the next handhold but then lost his grip on the moist, crenulated surface. He suffered one moment of panic as he desperately flailed on the verge of falling.

Then his hand struck something soft and damp, a dense, yielding mass that wasn't part of the tree. The contact gained him a moment to recover his balance, and he wrapped one arm around the tree trunk. With his free hand, he fished his flashlight from his pocket and shone it in the direction he'd nearly fallen.

Not five feet away, the Hung Preacher smiled at him, dark tongue protruding between swollen, cracked lips, his rounded face pale as a maggot. Above his head stretched a taut length of rope, and the noose dug into the doughy flesh around his neck.

The chuckling came again, but this time it issued from the Hung Preacher's mouth, not Tim's.

"Oh my God, Tim," Ronnie said. "It's *him*."

He expected Tim to squeal with delight and shriek, "Told ya so," but the dork had fallen silent. Maybe Tim finally had enough sense to be scared. But Ronnie couldn't afford to panic again, because he had to save his little brother.

"Come on, Tim," Ronnie yelled, easing around the trunk to put more distance between him and the ghost of Wendell McFall. He raised his voice to the foggy night. "Tim!"

"Yeah?" came Tim's voice, but it wasn't above him, it was below and far away. "Ronnie?"

Ronnie tore his gaze away from the Hung Preacher's bloated face and beetle-like eyes and scanned the foggy ground of the cemetery. A soft orb of yellow light bobbed up and down in the distance, growing larger as it neared.

Ronnie flicked his own light back to the Hung Preacher, but nothing was there but the dark-gray mist. Ronnie scrambled down the tree, keeping a tight grip on his flashlight. Once he was safely on the ground, he headed for the approaching light and Tim's plaintive summons. Tim called out once more and Ronnie located him among the tombstones.

"Tim, where the hell did you go?" Ronnie said, the anger and fear mixing into a toxic stew. "I chased you all the way to the stupid tree and you left me behind—"

"No, I didn't," he said. "You left *me*. I went back to get a flashlight and when I got to the door, you were already gone up the road."

Ronnie shook his head. That wasn't the way it happened, but it didn't matter. What mattered was that Tim had been right, the Hung Preacher was back and so was that wicked old dogwood tree.

"I saw him," Ronnie said. He spun and swept his flashlight in the direction from which he'd fled. "And the tree."

"There ain't no stupid tree," Tim said. "I was just fooling with you. I didn't think you'd be dumb enough to fall for it."

"It was right there," Ronnie said, although the spotlight of their combined beams revealed only leaning grave markers and uneven grass. Further on stood the rectangular dark bulk of the church.

"It was here," Ronnie said, his breath full of October. "I climbed it…"

His fingers ached from squeezing the wood, and bits of bark had worked under his nails, and a scrape on his wrist throbbed raw and red.

"You didn't climb anything," Tim said. "You're freaking out again, and Dad's not going to be happy about this. If he knew you were out here, he'd kill you. Good thing I came along when I did, or you might have done something really stupid like break into the church or try to climb the belfry."

"I saw the Hung Preacher," Ronnie said, almost mumbling now. In the sudden silence, the soft susurration of the nearby river rolled across the hill like hints of a long-lost language.

"Come on," Tim said, grabbing Ronnie's sleeve and pulling him away from the church. "Let's get home before we get in trouble."

Ronnie let himself be led among the dead McFalls, Abshers, Potters, and Mathesons, wondering if those graves were all unoccupied now. The river seemed to follow them, for its sinuous whispers trailed behind them.

Or maybe it wasn't the river. Maybe it was a wet length of rope snaking along high grass as the man who had died on it walked after them.

Ronnie didn't dare turn around and look, even after they hit the gravel road and headed for home. The soft slithering followed them, just at the edge of the fog, until they reached the welcoming glow of the house. Ronnie tried not to hurry inside, not wanting Tim to tease him more than he already would, but he couldn't help locking the door with a shaking hand.

The night fell silent, its breath held like an unfinished prayer. The rope lay still, as did the man who wore its strands as a reminder of ancient betrayal. Long after all the lights in the house had gone out and all sounds from within had yielded to disturbed sleep, the Hung Preacher drifted through the fog back to the graveyard of the old red church.

No need to hurry. None at all.

The Hung Preacher had forever.

About Scott Nicholson

Scott Nicholson is the author of more than thirty books, including *The Red Church, Drummer Boy, Liquid Fear*, and *Speed Dating with the Dead*.

Visit him at www.hauntedcomputer.com.

THE UNKNOWN
BY CHRIS CASTLE

A body.

This was the first thought that ran through Mike William's mind as he and his two friends ran towards the black smudge in the snow. The idea that it could be a dead body cooled the blood in his veins yet somehow made him run faster.

He had only seen a dead person once, his aunt Magenta, and the sight of her head neatly poking out of the coffin had left him with a sense of quiet terror that went with her still, papery body. It was only later at night, as his dreams were slowly swallowed up by the nightmares that he realized death was *the unknown*. His aunt had gone into the final unknown.

Yet, fear of the unknown didn't stop him from running all the same. In fact, the shame of thinking this could be death and still wanting to see more of it only made him run faster.

He skidded up to the black mound and saw, with a mixture of relief and disappointment, that it was not a dead body. It was a bag, half submerged in the snow, the handles flapping like wings. Pat fell to his left and Bryan to his right and the three of them stared, dumbfounded, at the discovery.

"God damn it!" said Bryan, who was the loudest of the three. He was hated or loved—with nothing in between—by everyone in their school. Mike loved him now but understood in the future, he may grow to hate Bryan Westerberg. He was cocky and assured and didn't hide the fact he would ruin someone just to get ahead.

"Is that it?" Pat said quietly. He was quiet, the mirror of Bryan and as a consequence, went unnoticed by most people. Mike liked him because he was straightforward and would not know how to lie if his life depended on it.

The snow began to swirl and grow heavier all around them. It was, as some old folks called it, 'a warning flurry.' As always, Bryan had huffed and puffed, Pat had stated what was in front of his nose and neither of them had done the obvious thing. It was, Mike thought, down to him, as always.

He reached down and unzipped the bag to see what was actually inside.

The first few bills fluttered away in the stiff breeze. All three of them watched dumbly as the errant bills drifted up into the air and scampered away from them.

Mike made to chase after them and then stopped. Instead, he peered back to the source and saw the bag, stuffed full of money, sitting fat in his hands, as if the ground itself had given birth to all that green. The three young boys screamed and even then, Mike wondered if he did it with fear as much as with joy.

*****

"This has got to be drug money," Bryan said, excitedly dragging on a cigarette he had stolen from his old man. They were sitting in their tree house now, in the heart of the abandoned scrap heap, where they always went on the lonely Friday nights in their town. Too young to drink, too old to acknowledge they still liked staying at home, it was a refuge of sorts. Pat had nicknamed it the Loser's Shack.

"This town doesn't have a single drug dealer and you know it, dumb-ass," Mike said. Usually, he would let Bryan ramble on but this was too important to let his friend screw it up.

Bryan sucked deeper on the cigarette, coughed and then flicked it out the window. "What, this town don't link to other, bigger places, you hick?"

Mike opened his mouth to speak and realized, for once, that Bryan was right. Luckily, he was still gagging on the smoke, which allowed Mike to look over to Pat. He nodded slowly and then looked back down to the hold-all bag of cash.

"There can't be another reason for it, not really," Pat said flatly. Ever since they'd pulled the bag back to the tree house, Pat had sat away from it, as if something inside repelled him.

"So what do we do, call the police?" Mike said and braced himself. Sure enough, Bryan immediately began to wail and even Pat screwed his nose up in a form of disgust. The only policeman in town was the deputy mayor, a man hated by all, especially by the kids. The saying went that he got fat on the two things that gave him the nickname of BB: beer and bribes.

"Okay, so BB's out, but what else is there?" Mike swallowed and tried to recall if his heart had actually slowed the entire time since this had begun. He reasoned fourteen was too young to have a heart attack, but even so, he had the idea he was close.

"We keep the money. We stash it, we pay it into a checking account over time and we guard the rest." Bryan looked from Mike to Pat. Mike again made to speak and then stopped, actually impressed by the logic of what he'd just heard. There was no lame bragging, no foolish dreams of caddies and girls. For the first time in their lives together, Bryan Westerberg actually sounded like the adult.

"This money comes from a bad place," Pat said quietly and again nervously looked back to the bag as if something were alive inside it.

"God damn it, Patty, *we* come from a bad place!" Mike's voice nearly broke as he talked and it immediately held their attention.

Bryan chimed in. "My old man's a drunk and your ma, no offense, is the same way, Patty. We both live in shacks people wouldn't piss on if they were on fire. Mike...your ma being how she is..." his voice trailed off.

Mike's dad was the original no-show and in the past three months his ma had been diagnosed with one of the illnesses that had a complicated name but a simple result. Mike thought for a moment of the money, the medical treatment it could buy his mother, and for the first time, his heart slowed.

Bryan's face drew into a pleading look and the desperation made him look like a baby, a sick infant. "Look, our lives suck, let's face it. This bag of money... it gives us an out. Not now, that's dumb, but in two or three years, when we can, this is our ticket, right?"

For a moment Mike felt sadness for his friend—and he was a friend, when all was said and done—in addition to a strong desire to help him. He finally said, "Look, Patty. You watch the news, right? You think any jobs are coming our way when we finish up at school? There's nothing now, and what, a couple of years from now, we're going to get into college ahead of the rich kids down the way? We're in a god damned procession, is what we are!"

"Recession," Pat corrected quietly, but Mike could see his brow was knitting together, like it did when he was really thinking something over. Admittedly, before this day, the questions hadn't gone deeper than which girl he like to cop a feel from and who would be the top ten best superheroes, but even so, it was the same expression.

"So we keep quiet and we keep the money?" Mike said, unable to bear the few seconds of silence that had somehow built up like a wall between them.

"We stash it here and lay low. Three ways, sworn secrecy." Bryan looked over to Pat, who was still deep in thought.

"It has to be all three, Pat," Mike said and looked over to him.

"At least," Pat finally said, "we won't have to worry about girls coming up here to steal it." For a second there was silence while Mike and Bryan processed what he had said. In the next moment, they exploded into laughter.

"That's right, Patty!" Bryan said as the three of them drew together in a hug. "Not a chance in hell of a girl coming up to the Loser's Shack!"

*****

The three of them spent the rest of the day making a makeshift hidey-hole for the money. Pat thought they should take the cash out of the bag itself and pack it like bricks around the beams and rafters. Mike smiled at the idea, both impressed and proud of his friend for coming up with a practical solution to the insane situation they found themselves in.

They worked in good-natured silence, and as they were finishing up, Mike wondered for a moment how this would affect their friendship, as well as their lives. He registered a cool chill when no answer came into his head; nothing but a sense of the unknown.

Like death, a small voice whispered in his head and made Mike Williams shudder.

For the first few days, nothing changed. Mike quietly went about checking the papers for news reports that didn't come and attended school to listen for rumors that didn't circulate. He spent the same time he always did with Pat and Bryan but none of them spoke out about what they had found.

After the third day, the vague panic Mike kept feeling at his throat downshifted into his gut, where it resided as a form of low anxiety. As he walked home one afternoon, he wondered if he would feel like this the entire time the money was in his life. He looked through the windows of the empty shops and saw pale, stressed managers. He sat with his sick mother and wondered if that was how every adult felt after they left the safety net of school. Maybe the money was simply preparing him for real life.

Once, his aunt Magenta had tried to explain to him what money meant to people in the world. "Mikey," she said through the plumes of smoke that would one day finally take her. "You've got people who spend their whole life trying to earn money and when they finally get it, they spend the rest of their lives worrying about how to keep it and how to get more of it. That," she paused dramatically and winked over to Mike, "is what folk's at your school would call a paradox."

Mike nodded good-naturedly, just to see her smile.

Now he understood what she meant.

On the following Saturday, nearly a full week after the find, Mike lay on his bed and for the first time wondered what he would spend his share of the money on. His ma would be his priority, of course, and if every penny had to be channeled over to her, then so be it.

But if there was just a little left afterwards…Mike allowed himself a grin at the thought of owning a few nice things, just a few nice things. A few clothes that would get Sally Eagles from his class to notice him, maybe. Just enough to—

The rock hit Mike's window hard enough to make the frame rattle. He jumped off his bed and ran over to the window. As he opened it, a second pebble whizzed by his ear and hit the wall behind him, taking a chunk of plaster out of the wall.

"Pat, what the *hell*?" Mike blurted out. But then his whole body chilled, as if he were in the process of being slowly poisoned.

"There are police down at Bryan's," Pat said.

Mike thought his friend's voice was fierce and scared at the same time. Mike had never heard him sound like this before and it only served to worry him more. He swallowed hard and then gripped the frame of the window harder to steady himself. "Okay, well it's Saturday night. That probably just means his old man got ripped again."

Pat's face, agitated and ramped up with fear to make him look as if he was being tortured from the inside out, put paid to that. "These are state cars, Mike! Sirens blaring outside the house, the whole thing. They don't bring out the state cars if a guy's father is drunk."

Then Pat's voice pitched up a notch. "Mike, maybe someone came for the money. Oh god, maybe Bryan's dead!"

Mike motioned to him. "Grab the key under the door and come in the back way, okay?"

Mike looked around. There was no risk of his ma coming round now that she had taken her medicine, but he worried about the neighbors, who were well on the way to being first class busybodies. Pat disappeared and Mike slipped back inside his bedroom, feeling a slow, steady thump in his temples as the blood began to rise.

Pat burst into the bedroom and began pacing as if someone had lit matches under his heels. Even though they were whispering, the sound of their voices seemed to be too much for Mike to bear. It felt as if the panic in their words was creating its own heat. Pat kept scratching his forehead until clear lines from his nails became visible on his skin. Finally, Mike stepped in front of Pat and coaxed his hands to the sides.

"Look, whatever it is, if people come to talk to you and see your hair mussed up like a mad scientist and claw marks across your head, they're going to think of you as a suspect and not a witness, okay?" Mike stared hard at Pat until he blinked. He began to push his hair down, as if he'd finally remembered who he was.

"Tell me one thing, okay, regardless," Pat said after a few seconds. He'd cooled down a little and was now looking straight at Mike. "We took the money out of the bag. You were supposed to dump the bag. Tell me you got rid of the bag."

"I—" Mike looked away, remembering how he had absent-mindedly stuffed the bag under his arm after they stashed the cash. All of them were excited and elated and too proud of themselves to remember to do the final, simple thing—dump the evidence.

Mike looked up, feeling the blood drain out of his face and he stared up to the top cupboard behind Pat.

"You didn't dump the bag," Pat said. The words were accusing but the tone was weak and quiet. Mike brushed by him and reached up frantically to the cupboard, pulled it open and the bag slipped down, skimming his cheek as it fell to the ground.

Mike watched his friend stoop down and carefully grip the hold-all bag. Pat flinched and dropped the bag back down. He looked down at his palms and then, after a long agonizing moment, lifted them up and held his hands, palms out, under the light for Mike to see.

Mike followed all this but in the back of his mind he already knew what he would see. The bag, where it had brushed his cheek, had left something on his skin, which was now crawling down at a slow, slow pace. Too slow to be melted ice, of course. The blood on his face was the same texture of the stuff that now ran down Pat's fingers.

*****

"We never should have taken the money," Pat said as they fast walked down to the ravine.

"We don't know anything for sure," Mike said, trying to keep his voice steady. As they reached the lip of the ravine, Mike got a steady footing, legs apart, securely balanced on two trunks

"It came from a bad place," Pat said darkly, repeating what he had muttered that first night when they found the money.

"God damn it, Patty, shut up!"

Mike threw the hold-all bag into the river and the two of them watched the current take it away. Mike imagined the blood mingling in the water, turning it red, but knew that was just his imagination working itself into overdrive. The bag was gone in a few seconds and he clambered down to the ground.

"Pat, I—" Mike stopped talking as his friend's face froze at something past his shoulder. Mike tried to look round but the level of fear coursing through his body stopped him from moving. Pat's face contorted into a mix of pain and disbelief, as if he'd already been struck.

Behind Mike, a twig snapped.

Another…

Mike felt his arm being gripped and for one moment didn't realize it was Pat seizing him. The two of them tore away down the mouth of the ravine, slipping and sliding but not losing their footing.

Everything about them was awkward and ungainly as they ran, while behind them, the twigs made breaking sounds with steady, brutal efficiency. Not one step was out of place, not one motion was out of sequence.

Mike willed himself not to listen to the sounds coming behind him but found he could not help it. He knew it was the sound of death, unknown but constant, moving out of sight and edging closer without effort.

The two of them staggered out of the path of the ravine and into the vague clearing on the edge of town. The sounds of their breathing had become ragged.

To the left was the town, to the right, the tree house. For a moment, they stepped apart, the unspoken idea of going different ways coming into their minds. Fear and friendship willed them back together.

Pat began to look towards town and Mike felt a stab in his chest at the thought of leading the unknown back towards his mother. Pat's expression told him he understood.

"It's all in the tree house, okay?" Pat panted. "It's all there. We found it and we stashed it there, every penny. You want it, you take it, okay? I haven't seen you, I don't know you. Deal?"

Even amongst all the rest of it, Mike understood now that Pat was the brave one out of all of them and always had been.

"Deal?" Pat screamed and then in the next flash, he was gone.

Hesitating, Mike looked back to the town, the lights, the life, and then into the pitch black of the woods. Tears falling freely from his eyes, Mike ran headlong into the darkness of the woods back towards the ravine.

The splashing of the water filled Mike's mind with the image a half-second before he reached the scene itself. The man was hunched over the water, holding Pat's body down, so just his head was submerged. The rest of his body stayed out of the water, almost delicately, as if the man was being careful to keep him dry.

Pat's feet twitched for a while and then were still. The man turned him over, checked his face and then gently pushed him down the stream, into the current. Like that, he was gone.

"The money," Mike managed to say before his voice faded. He was not brave like his friend and the truth of that hit him in the heart like a hammer blow. Even now, as the last of the three, he was a coward, shivering and whimpering and with no fight left in him, if there ever was any to begin with.

"I know about the money," the man said and rose from his haunches to look Mike over, as if readying for an interview. He was dressed in a long overcoat. His hair was grey and his eyes were clear. Even seconds after what he had done, his eyes did not blaze or show any kind of anger. Instead, he seemed kind and even handsome.

"Bryan told me everything," the man said. The way he spoke, it sounded as if he and Bryan were old acquaintances. His voice was soft, and for a second Mike had time to think, *This is not the sound of a monster.*

"You can have the money back," Mike blurted out. His voice was shattered now, the sound of a child responding to a reprimand. He thought bitterly, *Where is my rage?*

"It wasn't your money to take," the man said, his voice sounding conciliatory. He tightened the leather gloves, almost as an afterthought.

"Please…please don't hurt my ma," Mike said.

"It's only about the money and nothing else, Mike," the man said quietly and stepped forward. "It's not personal."

He was still a distance away, and for a second, Mike thought he could escape. Yet in the next moment, the man's hands shot out as if on springs and took him around the throat. He shut his eyes.

In the midst of the terror, Mike felt a pang of honor that he hadn't begged for his own life, but instead had asked for the safety of the person he loved more than anything in the world. It brought him some comfort.

He sank to his knees under the strength of the hold and his eyes snapped open. For a moment, they settled on the man, but he willed himself to look beyond to the sky and the stars. He focused on the moon as the cool leather pressed harder against his throat.

In his mind he could hear Pat's voice saying, *It came from a bad place.*

The world began to swim. The darkness began to seep into his mind and stole the moon from his sight and in the last moments, Mike Williams was plunged into the grip of the unknown.

About Chris Castle

Chris Castle is an English teacher in Greece. He has been published over 300 times, both online and in many anthologies and was Long-Listed for a Pushcart Award in 2011. His works range from horror, drama, to children's stories and he is currently working on a novel.

He can be reached at chriscastle76@hotmail.com for feedback and has a blog, 'Dunce: teaching abroad' online.

Don't Feed The Dog
By Rick McQuiston

Julia's upper lip curled into a sneer as her temper rose. She felt the tentative grip she had on her composure loosening and it threatened to spill over onto the dinner table. Her family seemed to sense this, and they shrank back into near irrelevance in the dining room.

"Samantha," Julia said sternly, her steel gaze focusing on the teenage girl sitting opposite her, "how many times have I said not to feed the dog at the table?"

The girl hunched into her polished oak chair.

Julia swung a hard look at her husband. He was a diminutive man, who despite being successful in business, was a quiet person who rarely spoke his mind. And never in the presence of his wife.

Samantha, a very pretty teenager, finally raised her head up and met her mother's gaze. Julia detected an odd expression of compassion on her daughter's face. "Mom, I was not feeding the dog under the table."

Julia straightened up, feeling angry. She was not used to anyone in her family talking back to her. "What did you say, young lady?"

Samantha looked at both her father and brother. Julia knew that she hoped to find an ally, but her daughter seemed disappointed when neither raised their heads.

Silence settled over the scene, blanketing the room with a thick uneasiness. Julia stared at Samantha, her thin painted fingernails subtly tapping on the polished oak table. Samantha, in turn, was looking at her father and brother, who were both gazing down at their laps.

"I am waiting for an answer, Samantha." Julia felt her blood pressure rising, but knew a cold, emotionless demeanor was far more effective at conveying her displeasure than a display of rage.

She saw that Samantha was becoming unhinged. Her daughter's eyes widened. Her face grew flushed. She began to sweat. And her mouth tightened into a painful grimace. She alternated her eyes between her father and brother, again and again. But still there was no response.

Finally Samantha spoke. "Dad? We can't keep this charade going on forever. Sooner or later someone has to say something to her."

Julia kept her composure. "Samantha," she said with deadly calm while setting the silver utensils back down beside her plate, "all I ask is respect. I saw you sneak table scraps to the dog under the table. Don't deny it."

"Mom," Samantha said, "we don't have a dog. We haven't had one since Dusty died two months ago. He was killed by a car, remember? He was hit as he chased a squirrel into the street."

Julie glared at her daughter. "Listen to me, young lady. I have had just about enough of your mouth. Finish your plate, and march right upstairs to—"

"Mom! You're not listening to me! We don't have a dog. Dusty died. He's dead!"

Julia stood up and abruptly pushed her chair back. With one quick snap of her fingers, both her husband and son got up from their seats and dutifully left the room.

"Samantha, I want you to clear the table."

"But Mom…"

"Enough! Clear the table. I'll inform the help that they do not need to do it." She leaned forward on the dining room table. "And after that, I want you to take the dog for a walk."

Julia left the room in a huff, and Samantha was alone.

*****

The low growl that emanated from beneath the table froze the blood in Samantha's veins. In a distant part of her mind she recognized the sound, and that recognition forced her to acknowledge the possibility of what it was.

Dusty poked his malformed head out from under the table. His eyes, mostly hidden by beige tufts of dirty fur, scanned the room for a few seconds before focusing on Samantha. A dull malevolence shone on his face.

Samantha stepped back from the table. Her mind raced to attach a rational explanation to what she was seeing, but couldn't. She steadied herself to make a run for it.

Dusty crept forward. His curved claws made unnerving sounds as they clicked against the hardwood flooring. A baleful glow churned in his hungry visage as he slowly advanced on his former owner, a trail of blackened paw prints in his wake.

This can't be happening. This is not real. I saw him die. I saw him...I saw the car coming forward...

The air in the room had grown stale and thick. The grandfather clock standing at attention in the corner ticked away the seconds in a monotonous fashion. A lone housefly buzzed erratically near the ceiling.

And Dusty advanced on Samantha.

A foggy memory sliced its way into Samantha thoughts, ushered along by her frail state of mind. *The car. Dusty ran after a squirrel, into the street.*

Samantha crouched to the floor, her arms covering her face as protection against the attack that she was sure was coming. But Dusty didn't attack. Samantha lifted her head and scanned the room.

She was alone.

She sat upright, rubbing her temples to help clear her mind, and looked everywhere for any sign of her dog. But there was nothing.

"Dusty?" She called out.

At the call, Dusty reappeared, his ragged body stepping into the room, an indifferent look on his bloodied face, clumps of dirt and gore clotting his expression. He locked his dead gaze on Samantha, and started to plod toward her.

This time Samantha stood her ground. Dusty hadn't hurt her the first time, and she felt sure the dog would not hurt her this time, either.

Dusty continued to advance. Suddenly he lunged at Samantha, leaping through the air with his mouth gaping wide open in a deadly show of force, teeth gnashing, eyes narrowed with determined resolve. But he stopped mid-leap and came back to the ground, sitting on his haunches on the floor.

The car hit Dusty. Dusty ran out into the street to chase a squirrel, and...

And suddenly, like a light switch being flipped on, Samantha remembered, and understood.

Dusty had chased a squirrel into the street, and Samantha ran after him. The car hit them both. And now Dusty was here, attempting to attack his former owner.

Why? Samantha wasn't sure. But she was certain that her dog, her dead dog, would not rest until he got what he came for.

We both died that day, Dusty and me. We were both hit by the car. I am dead. We are both dead.

A hideous, human-like expression of approval slowly spread across Dusty's bloody face. And in one split second, he sprang forward, neatly severing Samantha from what she had thought was her real life.

*****

Julia sat at the dinner table, her face frozen in a look of annoyance and impatience. Her husband and son were not eating. Instead, they merely poked and prodded the broiled fish and vegetables on their plates. The grandfather clock ticked away the seconds of the day from the corner of the room.

Julia tried her best to avoid an argument. She had supervised the preparation of the meal personally, carefully instructing the chef and his assistants as to how she wanted the food cooked and presented. And now she was watching her husband and son barely touch what she had worked so hard to make.

She made a halfhearted attempt at small talk. "They say it will be quite warm this weekend, perhaps approaching ninety degrees."

No response other than a silent nod from her husband and son.

The spectral face gleamed in the shadows of the room. A dull sneer was spread across its features. It watched Julia.

Julia fought back the growing sadness she felt. When she had reached down to remove her brush from her purse that day she had taken her eyes off of the road, just long enough to miss seeing her daughter chase Dusty out into the street in front of her car.

If only she had not gone shopping that day.

If only.

Samantha's ethereal form drifted over toward where Julia was seated. A cold aura surrounded it, exuding ill intent and a cunning capable of overcoming virtually any obstacle. It moved in complete silence.

Julia glanced over at an empty seat on the opposite side of the table. Samantha used to sit in that spot as her mother scolded her about picking up after herself and proper table manners, among other things. But now that seat was empty, vacated by a pretty young girl who met a violent end at the hands of her own mother.

"Samantha," Julia mumbled between mouthfuls of broiled fish and vegetables, "I told you not to feed the dog at the table."

Her husband and son only continued playing with the food on their plates, not looking up.

The ghostly figure drifted up behind Julia, a stark chill accompanying it as it moved. It leaned forward. "Mom," it whispered, "I forgive you."

Julia was startled by the low growl that emanated from beneath the table.

Samantha continued, "But I believe Dusty feels differently."

About Rick McQuiston

Rick McQuiston is a forty-four-year-old father of two who loves anything horror-related. He's had nearly three hundred works published so far, written two novels (*To See as a God Sees* and *Where Things Might Walk*), contributed to six anthology books, one book of novellas, and edited an anthology of Michigan authors. They are all available on Lulu and Amazon, as well as on his website many-midnights.webs.com.

Rick is also a guest author each year at Memphis Junior High School, read at various libraries, does many book/art shows, and is currently working on his third and fourth novels, in addition to more short stories.

THE CLASSMATE
BY MELANIE TEM

The classmates hooted at the door prizes—a blank book labeled *Sex after 50* and a cap emblazoned with C.R.S. for "Can't Remember Shit." Sitting by herself, not fitting in just like in high school, Vicki Gerhard tried to laugh through her headache.

A short woman in a wide-brimmed hat and ballooning ankle-length dress pulled up a lawn chair beside her. Wrinkled hands and neck made Vicki think she must have been in an earlier class, or maybe she'd had a hard life.

At first shyly pleased to be sought out, Vicki started to wonder if this was one of those adolescent pranks to make her look silly when no matter how she tried to start a conversation the woman wouldn't say a word. Finally, on the pretext of wanting another hot dog, she escaped to the other side of the bonfire, took two more ibuprofen from the bottle in her purse, and sat by herself again, lonely and relieved.

Cory Miles, the reunion host, was showing off his mint-condition 1966 Nash Rambler when he noticed someone familiar but he didn't think from school. The halogen yard light made her big hoop earrings glint blue and, when she crossed in front of it, outlined her thighs through the short thin skirt. While the guys swapped stories about vehicles they'd driven or wanted to drive in high school, she circled the Rambler, stroking the hood, leaning in the driver's door to pat the wheel. Long messy hair fell in her face. Being short himself, Cory'd have remembered any girl that tall in their class.

Out in back, George Huff was telling about his heart attacks, how he'd been taken "hot" to the hospital with sirens and lights going and the paramedics saying to stay calm. Then this lady was standing real close beside him. A lot younger, somebody's second or third wife. Small and thin, she had on spandex Capri pants and a halter top, and her hair was in a ponytail. He'd have sworn he'd never seen her before. But then he'd have sworn he'd never seen half the folks here.

On the other side of the house, Liz McMahon found herself in a situation she'd been fantasizing about for four decades. She'd been hopelessly in love with Philip Bain from the third grade all through high school with not an iota of requitement. He'd never allowed himself to be alone with her, or met her lovesick gaze, or opened the mushy Valentines she'd left on his desk every year. Although he still lived in town, he'd ignored every reunion—until this one. Liz, ever hopeful, hadn't missed one.

When tonight somebody had said, "There's Phil!" she'd felt heat rise in her face and could hardly breathe. He'd waved a hearty, generic hello to the group, either not noticing her or not admitting it, just like at all those after-game dances in the gym.

But now, amazingly, here they were, together on Cory's front porch swing like the lovers she fervently hoped it was not too late for them to be. In the mix of moonlight and porch light he was looking right at her, and he was saying her name a lot. "So, Liz, what have you been up to since the last time I saw you? Tell me about your life, Liz."

Liz was trying to decide where to start and what to emphasize about her rather complicated life when this woman materialized out of the shadows on the other side of the porch wall. Liz could make out only the glint of eyeglasses and a silhouette—on the plump side, permed hair like dandelion fluff, knee-length shorts. Politely she delayed her reply to Phil and said hi.

Phil said, "Hi," too, and Liz hoped she was detecting reluctance and disappointment to match her own. But then he added, "Join us."

The woman came up onto the porch, then sat between them on the swing. Unhappily Liz imagined the woman's ample flank pressing Phil's as he peered at her and said, "Don't tell me. It'll come to me." The woman laughed merrily and patted his arm.

Liz guessed with insincere playfulness, "Alice? Alice Frisini?" The woman did look a little like Alice—heavy eyebrows, meaty shoulders, posture angular as a T-square.

"Oh, dear," the woman said. "I'm afraid Alice Frisini is deceased."

Liz gasped. "She signed up to come, just last week. When did she—" The swing swayed and bounced as Phil shifted his weight.

"Alice and I have been in touch for years," the woman said, almost proudly. "She'd been in remission and she thought she'd be strong enough to come, but she died the day after she sent the form in."

Liz couldn't speak past the constriction of her throat. She made a mental note to ask for a moment of silence from the classmates.

The woman squirmed around on the swing to look directly at Phil, crowding Liz even more. He was preening, an easy mark for female flattery. Some things never change, Liz thought. I'm too old for this. We're all too old for this.

"Why, Philip, I'm hurt that you don't remember me," the woman was purring. "I'll give you a hint. You and I used to hang out with Freddy."

Freddy Klingensmith had been the first of their class to die, at twenty-two of a brain tumor. "Good old Freddy," Phil sighed. "But we never hung out with girls."

"You just never noticed me."

Liz got up from the swing, paused. When Phil didn't object she disappointedly went to join the group around the fire. Janie Gustafson and Mike Northrop, in separate conversations, were both talking about Viagra.

This class, even those who'd stayed in town, didn't see each other much. Except for two or three dyads among them, they couldn't really be called friends, but many of them had lightly kept up with each other from well before the non-intimate "friending" of social media. They got together every five years at least and whenever else they could come up with an excuse—the grand opening of the new high school, the year most of them turned fifty, the turn of the millennium.

At the reunions, people went out of their way to say nice things to and about each other: Mike told Vicki how desperately he'd admired her long brown hair and a particular green dress when she'd sat in front of him in history class. George and Bob Zink traded football stories, each recalling the other's glories rather than his own. Several pairs of ex-spouses were able to be civil. There was scarcely anything that could even be called gossip.

So nobody being able to identify this woman caused curiosity and consternation. Had her name been dropped from the class roster because she'd transferred schools? Had she showed up for the wrong reunion? Could they have somehow collectively put her out of their minds?

Always the most assertive of the bunch, Janie worked her way over to slip her arm around the woman's waist. "Okay, we give up. Who are you?"

The woman's straight blonde hair swung silvery. Several people thought her laugh sounded familiar, but no one could place it. "I think I'll just let you guys figure it out."

A groan went up from the people within earshot who weren't occupied with the horseshoe game, singing along with the nostalgic music blasting from Cory's pride-and-joy sound system, listening to

Bob's well-rehearsed story of his hunting accident, or involved in the game of charades.

A spontaneous twenty-questions sprang up. "Did you grow up here?"

"Among other places."

"Do you still live around here?"

"I have lots of homes. One of them is here, yes."

Those among them who'd lived long enough in big cities to have acquired a romantic-snobbish stereotype of small towns expressed surprise that everybody didn't know everybody else, annoying those who'd lived here all their lives and knew better.

Suddenly Cory thought maybe she'd worked in the nursing home when he couldn't take care of his mother after his divorce. But the sensation evaporated before he could really get hold of it. "You haven't been at any of the other reunions." It was supposed to be a declaration of fact, almost an accusation, but by the end of the sentence he wasn't so sure, and he added, "Have you?"

"Every one."

"No way!"

She shrugged. "Hey, I can't help it if you didn't realize I was there. It happens a lot."

"Who'd you have for first grade?" someone challenged.

"Mrs. Minor."

"I used to chase Phil around the playground every day in first grade." Liz tried to catch Phil's gaze. "Until finally he pushed me down and sat on me and wouldn't let me up until I promised not to kiss him anymore."

Phil added, "And I got the ruler for that." Liz wondered if she should apologize.

"Is Mrs. Minor still alive?" someone asked.

"She was ancient when we had her."

"Yeah, at least fifty." There were rueful guffaws.

"Still, that was forty-five years ago."

"Hard to believe anything happened to us forty-five years ago, isn't it?"

"Hazel Minor died in 1988," the mysterious classmate told them. "She was living with her daughter in Cincinnati. During the last couple of years she often said your name, Vicki, and Freddy's."

Vicki blushed, pleased and embarrassed.

*****

The reunion committee, Carol Lessing and Natalie Showalter, had devised a game they called "100 Things We Want to Do Before the Next

Reunion," modeled after a book they'd both loved but was probably a little too heavy for a reunion, *100 Things I Want to Do Before I Die.* Classmates had been invited to share, and the committee had spent an evening compiling a master list on poster board, which now hung on Cory's fence.

They'd expected generic things like "Lose thirty pounds" and "Quit smoking" and allusions to determined middle-age zest for life: "Learn to swing dance," "Climb a fourteener," and such that had a nice ring whether plausible or not. They'd hoped for funny ones, both off-color and silly: "Get a boob implant," "Invest in Viagra and electrolysis stock," and "Don't get suckered into answering questions like this."

They didn't know what to do with the serious ones. Morbid, actually; Carol, who was a school counselor, indignantly pronounced them inappropriate. They were all on one list, so presumably from one person, unsigned. There was no return address on the envelope and the postmark was illegible. They said "Come to terms with mortality," "Make acquaintance with Death" and "Lose fear of dying."

Offended as if by pornography, Natalie and Carol just threw the list away; no one would ever know, except the two of them and the anonymous sender.

But it made Carol muse, "When you think about it, every time we've had a reunion, somebody who was at the last one has died. First it was Freddy, and then Randy Burns, remember? He was at the tenth reunion and by the fifteenth he was dead."

Natalie gazed at her, pondering. "Who was Randy with at the tenth reunion? I don't remember her name."

"Wasn't Randy gay?"

"He was with a woman that night," Natalie insisted. "Nobody knew her."

At that long-ago tenth reunion Carol had met up again with Jimmy Eccles, whom she'd since married and divorced. She hadn't been paying much attention to anything else. In fact, Randy Burns had lived and died almost totally outside her notice.

Now she couldn't resist speculating to herself about who might be dead the next time they got together. Maybe George, from another heart attack. Maybe Janie, from fast living, or Cory, driving drunk. Maybe herself.

She'd have left then if she hadn't had responsibilities. Consoling herself that she could shop at the outlet stores tomorrow because they were open Sundays now, she laughed at some joke Cory was telling about being over the hill.

Natalie was doing her best to whip up enthusiasm for the *100 Things* game. "We'll leave the list up for a while and anybody who wants to can add things," she announced cheerily over the buzz of inattention.

"Then we'll compile a master list and make copies for everybody, and at the next reunion we'll see how many goals we reached." She didn't quite say, "Won't that be fun?"

Vicki answered, "Sounds good," but only out of pity. Never in a million years would she declare publicly what she wanted and wasn't likely to get out of life or, just as impossible, come up with some witty way not to. Her head was thudding. She ought to go home.

Liz was sorely tempted to write something up there about re-connecting with old friends, or seizing missed opportunities, or even "get it on with Philip Bain." Shocked and pleased at her own recklessness, she restrained herself.

Phil Bain was used to being chased. He mocked all those women, usually to himself, sometimes in an offhand remark or vaguely derisive tone, believing himself jaded. But practice had made him an expert at the very things that attracted them—the direct, sustained gaze implying unadulterated interest when really his mind was deliberately elsewhere; the strategic use of their names because it made them feel important and nothing said he had to remember them later; the habit of implying, by far-off gaze and small smile, some tragic secret only she could ferret out and heal, when in fact his life had been dull, and dully disappointing.

Phil enjoyed the attention from the women, but after thirty-some years, Liz Perry (her maiden name, if you could call it that) chasing him was getting tiresome. At one of these reunion things, if he remembered right, she'd been with some guy, a husband or boyfriend, and that time she'd seemed more interested in him than in anybody else, which had sort of pissed Phil off. But otherwise he could count on Liz's flirtations, the following him around while pretending not to, the fluffing of redder and redder hair, the clothes that stayed the same style while she got older so that they looked more and more ridiculously girlish on her although she did still have nice legs.

The chick nobody could place had glommed onto Phil tonight. He had the sneaking suspicion she wasn't really a classmate, had just crashed the party, such as it was. Maybe because she knew he'd be here. Sitting close enough to him that their arms brushed and occasionally their hips, she yawned and stretched and her boobs lifted. Phil wondered if she might be a lot younger than he'd thought, and naturally that piqued his interest. She looked straight at him and said quietly, "I'm ready to get out of here. How about you?"

Most women weren't quite so obvious about it. Most, in fact, never followed through. Phil didn't know if he liked this, but what the hell. "Good idea." He'd have dropped her name in right there if he'd known it.

Liz watched them go. Phil didn't even glance at her. He actually asked, "Your place or mine?" and the woman answered archly, "Oh, mine. It's always my place."

Phil's good-bye was loud and generic, making sure a lot of people saw him go. The woman, on his arm now, called, "I'll be in touch!"

Not twenty minutes later the news crackled over Cory's police scanner. Single-vehicle crash on Route 71 up by the Miles place. Car in the creek. Driver, sole occupant, middle-aged male, dead at the scene.

*****

At nine the next morning Vicki had an emergency neurologist appointment. All night the headache had waxed and waned. When it subsided she tried frantically to tell herself she didn't have to go to the doctor after all, and when it swelled again she wasn't sure she could.

On the way she stopped at the post office. At least her mail was normal—three catalogs, two pieces of junk mail, and the phone bill. Nothing personal.

Through the window she glimpsed the woman nobody'd known last night, coming across the parking lot. Her baseball cap gave her a different, jaunty air. Fleetingly, Vicki was sure she knew who she was, but couldn't quite get the name.

The woman waved and smiled. Vicki bundled her mail together and walked out to meet her. "Good morning, Vicki," the woman said, with a sort of cheerful sadness. "Isn't it something about Philip Bain? Just last night he was so alive. At least he didn't suffer. He died instantly. His neck was broken."

"Weren't you—with him?" Directness was so unlike her that Vicki looked away, but she waited for the answer.

"Yes, I was. And now I'm with you." It crossed Vicki's mind to back away, run to the car, speed off. "Would you like me to go with you to the neurologist, Vicki?"

"How do you know—" Vicki put a hand to her temple, the headwaters of the pain. The catalogs slipped out of her grasp. She didn't bother to retrieve them.

The woman said, "You told me your name last night, at the reunion."

Vicki was sure she had not. "It's nice of you, but—"

Very gently, the woman took her arm. "I want to be with you. It's an honor."

Vicki's eyes filled with tears and she whispered, "I'm scared."

The woman crooned, "You're not alone. I'll be with you the whole way," and led her to the car.

About Melanie Tem

Melanie Tem's chronicles of the terrors that haunt families and the amazing resilience of the human spirit have collected a Bram Stoker award, a British Fantasy Award, and praise both here and abroad. Stephen King said of her first novel, *Prodigal*: "Spectacular, far better than anything by new writers in the hardcover field." Dan Simmons declared it "A cry from the very heart of the heart of darkness...Melanie Tem may well be the literary successor to Shirley Jackson."

Her science fiction story *Corn Teeth* appeared in the August 2011 issue of *Asimov's Science Fiction*

Abandoned
BY Bruce Memblatt

Marty saw the sky open up like it was punched. Lightning flashed brilliantly against the night, allowing him to catch glimpses of the old buildings near the river. He could see a steel roll-up door on a run-down warehouse hanging open as if it broke off in the wind. It looked like his best bet for shelter. At least he wouldn't have to jimmy the door open.

He had enough of banging his head against walls, each one harder and meaner than the last. Everyone abandoned him, and he abandoned them in return. And then one day he just gave up.

"Fuck everything," he told himself while he maneuvered his way around the broken door that led into the warehouse.

He felt his sleeve pull and realized it was caught on a shard of steel that jutted out of the side of the doorway. It was such a blazing testament to the shithole his life had become that he almost laughed. He tugged at it with a dark hand, but too hard and his coat ripped. Marty fell and slid across the floor, which was nothing more than black tar, and on that night it was drenched black tar.

Everything seemed wet.

He'd have to travel farther into the structure to find a dry spot if he ever hoped to get any sleep that night. Lighting flashed again, setting off sparks that sprayed across the corrugated tin ceiling, allowing him to peer over the floor of the hangar-like edifice.

And then suddenly in the damp shadows, he saw what appeared to be hundreds of people, silent, sad faces; soulful, barely dressed: men, women, and children who looked like they were from another time but he couldn't sense when.

The scene startled him so much he could almost feel his skin jump. He began to slip and slide across the floor in fright; it was all he could do to keep from falling again. He didn't know if it was the hallucination of the crazy, homeless person that he was, but it seemed so real. The old warehouse was filled with people who looked like they stepped out of some drunken dream.

Another flash of lightning came and the people disappeared when the light did. Everything turned black again. He rubbed his eyes, and almost pinched himself to see if he was awake—but of course he was, he always was.

Then out of the darkness of the warehouse he heard the sounds of birds, monkeys, the airy noises of the jungle, the beat of drums, and for the briefest of instants he saw a bright day sky flash through what appeared to be trees, hundreds of branches.

And in the distance he heard screams.

In panic, Marty turned to run, but then suddenly the sounds stopped and all he could see around him was the darkness of the old warehouse, the tin walls; and he heard the rain pounding outside. He thought about the medication he had taken at the free clinic and calmed himself with the idea that none of this was real. It had been drug-induced. Although the medication had always helped him before, perhaps he was having a rare reaction to it now.

He took a deep breath, collected himself, and went back to the business of looking for dry shelter.

But in the shadows of the building's corners, he saw movement in his peripheral vision. He grabbed a lighter from his pocket; an old Zippo. The faces were back, blending into the darkness. He saw their faces everywhere, black faces like his own.

He lurched and bolted for the doorway, leaping through puddles, hoping his heart wouldn't shock to a stop. He was just about through the door when he heard someone call his name in an accented voice.

"Marty, Marty, come here. It is Ottobah."

Marty halted and didn't know why. But the voice seemed to command him. He stood, gripped in shock, and wondered if his heart had seized. Inside he began to speculate about if he'd gotten to the clinic at all that day or if, instead, he had passed out somewhere and was now trapped inside the inner reaches of a deep sleep.

Because this couldn't be real; it couldn't be happening. But again the voice came, "Marty, turn around, please. It is Ottobah and the others. We aren't going to hurt you."

We aren't going to hurt you, the words echoed in his mind. This manifestation was giving him the option of safety as if there were another possible alternative, as if they *could* hurt him. He thought they couldn't, they had to be something he created in his crazy head, and that ultimately meant he was in charge. He could destroy them. All he had to do was think it.

But as if a mind reader, the voice said, "No, Marty. It doesn't work like that. You can't think us away. We won't be forgotten. Turn around."

Obeying the command, Marty slowly turned around to see a tall black man dressed in tattered clothes, welts and scars covering his skin. The man appeared to step out of a shadow. Then he walked towards Marty, through a puddle, his hand extended.

For an instant Marty felt like he was looking at a mirror image of himself. If he could describe exactly what he was inside, that bruised man would be the result, the culmination of his own pain. He felt an intense sorrow surround him, a feeling of such extraordinary blues he was sure he was going to give way to tears. He had to touch the man. He reached for Ottobah's hand but he felt nothing, just the humid air between his fingers, and at once his eyes lit up.

He cried out, "I knew it! I knew it, you're not real. You must be ghosts!"

"We're real, very real, not precisely in the same place as you, but we are indeed very close. This is inter-dimensional, and we have crossed paths, if you will. Marty, you're with us on the ship now."

Something was deadly wrong, besides the obvious. A chill chased along the nape of his neck. "Ship? What ship?"

The man grinned and he began to laugh, "Why, the slave ship named Meermin."

A falling sensation like he'd been pushed off the edge of a cliff consumed him. Then Marty's body began to rock, and his nostrils filled with a mixture of salty sea air and a horrible stench. It was all he could do to keep from fainting. Before him, his eyes searched over what looked like the wooden hold of a ship filled with men. They were handcuffed and irons were wrapped around their feet, encased so close together he could barely tell where one started and the other ended. Black legs, arms, hands, and necks all contained wounded, scarred flesh aching for relief from a nightmare, a nightmare he had somehow fallen into.

Now Ottobah lay directly below him, bound like the rest. He heard him cry out, "Touch my hand again, Marty."

And Marty reached down through the ropes, and grazed his own black hand across the handcuffs that clenched Ottobah's skin and he felt him, he felt everything.

"See, you are completely here now, Marty."

Marty quickly pulled his hand away. His eyes traveled across the faces, the desperate eyes, hundreds of legs trapped, deprived of humanity, tears unleashed. The stench of urine and sweat and the sea burned through his nose stronger and he cried out, "No, dear God! I must have died! I went to hell!"

"Close, Marty, close."

He stood over Ottobah, trembling, "What happens now?"

"Simple, Marty, you help us, and we help you."

"How?"

"Like it happened before, except for one difference."

"Before?"

"Yes, before. You don't remember, but you were here before, Marty, and you're going to help us with the mutiny. It is our only hope for freedom."

"What?" he cried. How was he supposed to help these people? He couldn't even hold down a part-time job. If only he could run back to farthest reaches of his mind just to break free of this new reality!

He heard cries of pain all around him.

Ottobah's pupils opened wide, and Marty winced at the sight of the welts beneath his eyelids. "Now listen," Ottobah said. "At night they take us up on deck to feed us. Our women are kept on the other side of the ship. They're not chained and bound like we are. Tonight our women are supposed to start a fire, a distraction. When that happens, we will make our move, and all you have to do is bring us the weapons."

"How? Where will I get the weapons?"

"You'll know."

Then Marty heard a voice from above call his name. He asked, "Who is that?"

Ottobah whispered, "That's Johnston, your master. He uses you to help control us. You'd better go. We will see you tonight. Remember the guns. We are all counting on you."

"Those irons on your feet," Marty leaned down and looked Ottobah directly in the eye and asked, "How do they feel?"

"Like hell, Marty. Now go!"

And with that, Marty stood and grabbed onto the rail that would lead him to Johnston on the upper deck. He felt the wind hit his face as he climbed.

*****

His brave new world...his brave new world was hundreds of years in the past in a time and place for which he had no conception. Yet as Marty stepped onto the deck, there were things that caught his eyes: little snatches, sometimes just a corner of a beam of wood, or the way the light hit the glass. It was happening to him, even as he spoke with Johnston; little specks of memories, elusive things that he could almost grasp, that he recognized, that he knew, that told him he'd been there before as Ottobah had said. He even felt that his name was not really Marty, that was his name from the modern world, and not this world of the past.

There was a steely moon over the Atlantic that night, and it made the ship appear like it was haunted. It made the night seem like anything was possible. Soon Ottobah would be hoping to smell fire. Soon the masters would bring him along with all of the slaves up on deck.

Even as Marty felt changes beginning within him, there was emptiness inside his stomach he could not fight because he knew he had induced it. He felt queasy as he watched the seamen begin to assemble on the deck. Several small groups of three or four men would be armed and stationed around the slaves as they ate.

He hated thinking of Ottobah as a slave and he wondered if a new strength was growing inside him, even as he felt his heart become colder. As a black man, he naturally felt a kinship with the men enslaved on this ship, even though he knew he didn't belong here in their world.

The black man next to Marty handed him a crate, then Marty handed the crate off to the next man. They were loading the deck of the ship with yams and beans and rice. Johnston was standing about a yard away from Marty smiling at him like the cat that swallowed the canary. The sick empty feeling in Marty's stomach increased when he looked at Johnston. He hated him, he even hated his beard, the way he walked, his pompous odor, but he loathed himself more, because he gave in so easily.

Johnston shouted to a group of pale seamen standing in formation in the center of the deck, "Go and get them."

Marty watched as the white men headed down the rails. He heard muffled chatter and laughter as they descended. The wind picked up. The ship's sail stretched and pulled in the breeze. The moon made the sail appear as an apparition, but what haunted the ship that night was far worse than what any ghost could conjure up.

Johnston stepped closer to Marty and leered, "Soon you'll be up on deck with the rest of the savages. They'll carry on like children. I tell you, I can barely stand looking at them, but tonight there is one I'd be particularly happy to whip."

"Yes, sir," Marty said, biting into his tongue, knowing that Johnston meant Ottobah and that made him angry.

He thought if he could get through the next hour, he could get through anything. But what decimated him from within was that he could feel his anger toward Johnston diminishing and he couldn't stop the demise of his wrath.

He should be angry; he should be indignant and perhaps even horrified at the inhumanity he was witnessing. But those emotions took effort, and Marty was always one who ducked emotional commitment. So his anger faded.

Before he took his next breath, he could see the slaves begin to ascend and assemble on deck. The moonlight struck the perspiration on their skin and they gleamed. Marty thought they almost shimmered. Amidst their scars, their wounds, and their pain, there was beauty at the sight of them by the hundreds, lined up on the deck under the moon as if they were dancers. It became an almost magical synchronization of movement.

Johnston shouted, and the white seamen began opening the crates. Marty saw black hands, so many weary hands, reaching; yearning for sustenance. He knew what that was like in his other world where he had to find food and shelter on his own. If he could stay in this world, aboard this tragic ship, he'd never have to suffer through that again because food and shelter would be given to him.

Johnston grabbed the yams out of the crate and tossed them to the floor. In desperation, the black men ran for them, hoisting the potatoes in their mouths faster than they could chew.

Their chatter became loud. Marty even heard laughter and singing, and then suddenly a gunshot brought everything to a halt. His head quickly turned. Everyone became still as statues, silent, except for Johnston who was holding a pistol in his hand, shouting, "Quiet down, you bloody baboons!"

The silence passed. Gradually, the men began to stir again.

Marty felt Johnston tap him on his shoulder and say, "Well, which one is he?"

And it was in that moment that Marty caught Ottobah's glance on the other side of the ship. Marty whispered to Johnston, nodding his head in Ottobah's direction, "There he is, sir. That's the one you want."

"I'm going to step away. Let him come to you. Then do what we planned."

Soon Marty saw Ottobah walking towards him. He'd assumed he had waited for Johnston to leave before he made his move. The air on deck was cleaner than the stench below, and combined with the sight of Ottobah walking around freely, Marty almost forgot where he was and what he was about to do. He heard the soft sound of the ocean washing against the ship and he wished he could stay in that moment forever, not have to move forward or backward.

As he drew closer, Ottobah began to approach faster. When he was a foot away, Marty reached into his pocket and clenched the gun between his fingers.

He called out to Ottobah, "So where is the fire?"

Ottobah halted, and his eyes opened wide. "You tell me, Marty. Where are the weapons?"

A trickle of sweat seeped down Marty's brow as he pulled the gun out of his pocket. "Here is the only weapon that matters," he said, and then he wrapped his finger around the trigger and took aim.

Ottobah's hand trembled like a windblown branch as he reached for Marty and cried, "I thought this time it would be different, but you have betrayed us again! Don't you understand, Marty?"

All Marty could understand was that Ottobah was attempting to steal his new life. "Here I have position, power, and food in my mouth. I have nothing in that other world!"

Ottabah answered, "You have nothing here either, Marty, because as soon as you do this, the master will kill you. Your trust in him is misplaced. You think he believes you are special? You are a black man just like us, with one difference. You are a coward, consumed and enslaved by your own fears. You are more a slave than I am in any world."

Suddenly they heard Johnston approach, shouting, "What is going on here, Marty? Kill him!"

Then Ottobah grabbed for the gun in Marty's hand and cried, "Please! You can set us both free if you change it this time. Do it, Marty, fight for your soul!"

Tears began to well up in Marty's eyes. "I can't. I will never change. I don't like the way I am, but it is familiar. To be anything else takes me into the unknown."

His hand shook as he pulled the trigger. A shot rang out. He saw Ottobah fall onto the deck, blood pouring out from his chest.

While he watched, Marty felt something sharp dig into his spine and an intense pain seared though him.

He heard Johnston shout, "Feel my knife and die, slave!"

Then at once he felt like he was shot from a cannon. It became dark, and he found himself back on the wet floor of the warehouse, alone and hungry. His eyes searched the building for the souls that inhabited it before, but he saw nothing. Only the tin walls of the warehouse were there, and he heard nothing but the haggard sound of his own heavy breathing.

He looked toward the broken doorway and watched the rain fall under a street light. He thought if he cried, his tears could outnumber the raindrops. And so he cried, and he tugged on his tattered wet coat, and longed to smell the sea air and to hear Ottobah's voice. He knew sooner or later, he would be back there once again. If only next time could be different.

About Bruce Memblatt

Bruce Memblatt is a native New Yorker and has studied Business Administration at Pace University. In addition to writing, he runs a website devoted to theater composer Stephen Sondheim, which he's lovingly maintained since 1996.

His short story Weekend in the Country was the winner of the May 2012 short story writing contest at fablery.com.

His stories have been featured in such publications as *Aphelion, Bewildering Stories, The Horror Zine, Dark Moon Books, Post Mortem Press, Sam's Dot Publishing, Parsec Org., Strange Weird and Wonderful Magazine, Danse Macabre, The Piker Press, Midwest Literary Magazine, Freedom Fiction, Eastown Fiction, Short Story Me!, 69 Flavors of Paranoia, Necrology Shorts, Suspense Magazine, Gypsy Shadow, Black Lantern, Death Head Grin, The Cynic Online, The Feathertale Review* and *Yellow Mama*, and many more as well as in numerous anthology books.

In addition, Bruce writes a bi-monthly series for The Piker Press based on his short story *Dinner with Henry*. The first installment appeared in March of 2010.

You can catch his blog at http://sjsondheim.com/blog1

You can email him at bmemblatt@aol.com

WET BIRDS
BY ELIZABETH MASSIE

Hasn't rained for almost six weeks. The grass is brittle as old chicken bones; the air is heavy with dust and ash stirred up from the bonfire pit when a wind whips past. The sunlight is thick like pus-laced piss; it seems to soak into the earth rather than brighten it. I watch through the tiny window of the backyard shed, observing a feral cat as it sniffs the ground, gobbles up a dried cricket, and then sulks off beneath the old house trailer, its tail down, its whiskers dragging.

I'm lonely. But nobody gives a shit about that but me.

It's early August. There's a birdbath out in the dead grass, and for some reason Julie believes it is important to keep it filled with water from the nearby creek. Chickadees, goldfinches, and sparrows take turns in the water. They wait, watching, clipped around the rim like feathery decorations on a birthday cake, and then when one bird flies out another hops in. It's funny, watching them splash. Their wings shudder and flap, they dip their heads in and out. Every once in a while a blue jay comes along and they all scatter. The jay takes his time bathing, like it's a true luxury. Must feel good, to be a wet bird on a day like today.

Everything is so fucking dry. So fucking hot.

There is movement beyond the birdbath, out past the scraggly yard at the edge of the tree line. I glance in that direction, my eyes narrowing. A rustling there among the pines and sycamores, and then a flickering shadow. Could be a fox or rabbit, though we haven't seen a wild animal around for a while now. They've run off up into the mountains because they don't like the smell of death wandering in the wood.

Most likely the movement is one of the living dead sniffing around, sensing live humans nearby. Julie and Martin have a pistol in the trailer with a few bullets left. They're pretty good at shooting to kill, so if the zombie comes across to the trailer, they'll get him—or her—before the thing can reach the door.

For a while, the living dead didn't show up around here very often. We're really far out in the country. At first, they mainly hung around where bigger pockets of living food were holed up and hiding, like the cities and towns. Like Stanleyville, the town ten miles east of here. But recently, more and more have shown up at the trailer, which is why Sallie, Bucky, and I thought it might be a good idea to head up into the mountains.

Best laid plans, right?

We found the abandoned house trailer while driving the unpaved country roads almost a year ago—last September—looking for a new place to smoke our tokes and drink our beer. And there it was in all its banged-up glory, sitting on a lumpy plot of land between two thick woods, empty, just waiting for a bunch of teens like us to take it over. No electricity, of course. No running water. The thing is moldy, filled with mice, spiders. There are a couple outbuildings behind the trailer: a toolshed, smokehouse, and a splintery outhouse sitting at a tilt. But in spite of how crappy the place was—is—we thought it would be a damn good party pad. Julie, me, Martin, Bucky, Sallie, and Robin came here every weekend through the fall, winter, and early spring, bringing along our guitars, pot, and whatever beer was cheapest at the Stanleyville Sharp Shopper.

Then on the last weekend in March—it was Martin's birthday that Saturday. "Eighteen?" we chided him. "Getting old, man! We'll buy you some Viagra and a wheelchair to get you up and get you around!"—we drove out here to celebrate with a packed cooler, a Baggie of weed and papers, and a box of birthday cupcakes Julie'd baked. Sunday morning we were still there but feeling the effects of the party, sitting and lying around on the mouse-chewed sofa and chairs, sucking down the last of the beer, smoking the last of the pot, listening to Martin strum a new song he'd written, which pretty much was crap, but since it was his birthday and since Martin can teeter a bit on the edge of crazy-mad sometimes, we pretended to like it. After the song, Robin tugged on my elbow and winked. We shuffled to the back bedroom and locked the door.

"I got my black panties on for you, Lyle," she said, snuggling close against my chest. She was warm and smelled a lot better than the trailer did. Like beer, pot, and perfume. "You love me?"

I nodded. I did, kind of. As much as any girlfriend I ever had before.

But just as I was sliding my hands up under her sweatshirt, we heard a pounding on the front trailer door. I pulled my hands back and we stared at each other.

The pounding came again. My heart kicked in and started to pound, too. Nobody knew we were here. This place was out in bum-fucking-redneck nowhere where even hermits didn't live. Robin and I raced to the front room to find everybody standing, bug-eyed, in the middle of the room.

"Who's at the damn door?" I asked.

"Got to be the sheriff," whispered Julie, holding a desperate, trembling finger to her lips. "Somebody told on us, I bet!"

"I didn't hear no car engine," said Bucky.

"I wasn't paying attention," scoffed Martin. "Were you fucking paying attention? Was anybody? Damn it to hell! What's wrong with you all?"

We had our pot and beer and cigarettes—all those things us under-agers aren't supposed to have for some stupid legal reason—spread out on the coffee table and the counter that separated the kitchen from the living room. Bucky scooped up the pot and stuffed it into his shirt but the beer bottles and butts, they were everywhere. And of course, the whole place smelled of what we'd been up to.

The pounding started again, but I noted it wasn't a normal, "hello" or "let me in" pounding but a sloppy, irregular, scratchy-sounding pounding. The trailer rocked with the blows. Then we could hear a muffled, guttural grunting on the other side of the door.

"I bet it's that asshole, Pete," said Martin.

We all hated Pete. He was forty-something and had no friends and always tried to bribe us into letting him come along to our parties. We never let him but he always begged. He had a bad habit of blowing snot rockets and forgetting to zip up his pants after taking a whiz. He was drunk almost all the time and it was a wonder he could find his way from one place to another.

"Hey, Pete?" called Bucky. "That you?"

Another growl, another slam against the door.

"That don't sound like Pete or no sheriff, that's for sure," Julie said. She tiptoed to the window, pulled apart the rusted mini-blinds, and shrieked, "Holy Fuck!" She fell back, tripping over Martin's guitar case on the floor.

Everyone rushed to the window, no one pausing to help Julie up but squeezing up against each other to peek through the blinds. My head was near the bottom of the clump, my chin pressed down on the sill, but I could see who—what—was knocking on our door.

It was some dead guy.

Dead, I was sure, because part of his face was gone and a single, shattered bone protruded from his shoulder socket. Flies buzzed around his ears, touched the sticky fluids congealed there, then flew away with haste, as if tasting something so disgusting even a fly wouldn't eat it. His skin was tinted a corpse-ish yellow and green, and a few fingers were missing from his right hand. The whites of his eyes were a ghastly, putrid orange.

Bang bang bang bang.

He drove his dead, pulpy fist against the door, as if he sort of remembered how to knock, even though he didn't know why he would. He grunted, growled, slapped his bloated tongue in and out of the slit that was his mouth.

Martin jumped away from the window first. He snatched his rifle from the wall, flipped off the safety. "Get back everybody, this fucking asshole's going down!"

"Martin, don't you dare open that door!" Sallie shrieked.

But Martin, being Martin, did. The dead guy stumbled forward into the trailer and landed on his face. Black, foul-smelling spittle flew. Martin pumped two bullets in the dead guy's back but it didn't do anything but make the dead guy grunt louder. He rolled over awkwardly, his orange eyes blinking, and tried to pull himself up by grabbing the arm of the sofa.

Julie, Bucky, Sallie, and I slammed ourselves against the far wall, sweating, yelling, shaking like wet dogs in the cold as Robin, who couldn't get over to us, hopped up onto the recliner. But she is—was—a pretty big girl, and the chair folded in on her. She crashed to her ass and then bounced out onto the floor. The dead guy, still on his knees, reached out, got hold of her foot and dragged it to his mouth where he took a big bite out of her ankle.

"Lyle!" she screeched, an inhuman sound I'll never forget, but I knew if I went for her, he would get me. Damn! I didn't have a gun, did I? She couldn't blame me, really, could she?

Julie shoved me forward, "Help her, Lyle!"

But I pressed myself back against the wall again, my breath frozen in my lungs, as Martin blew another hole into the guy's back. That didn't faze him; he gulped down Robin's ankle then bit off the rest of her foot. She flopped like a fish, her stub spraying red, then went still. Not dead quite yet. I could see her chest hitching.

Martin yelled and pumped a round into the back of the dead guy's head and that's what did it. That's what killed him. He shuddered, rose up with Robin's toes clamped between his teeth, then flopped backward.

None of us moved. We stared at the dead man who was now really dead, then at Robin who was dying. I unlocked then, and fell beside her, pulling her up and shaking her to awaken her. Her eyes fluttered, popped open for a moment and closed again. Then she, too, was dead.

"Oh God oh God oh God!" said Sallie.

"What was…what is…" began Bucky, but he couldn't finish, because he'd spun around to throw up on the wall.

We were always into bonfires. There is a lot of room beside the trailer, a grass-bare, shallow pit packed hard with gravel and thick red clay. Bonfires are cool, powerful, fun.

This one wasn't going to be much fun.

Martin and I dragged the doubly-dead guy outside and put a bunch of twigs and old pallets on top of him, doused him with gasoline, and set him on fire. Robin, well, we rolled her up in a blanket and put her in the back of Martin's pickup. We figured we needed to get her back to Stanleyville and her parents' house. Tell them a bear got her or a coyote got her, anything but a dead guy got her. We knew how that would sound. They might think such an insane suggestion would mean *we* had something to do with it.

I didn't cry until I was in the passenger's seat and Martin started the truck engine. I stared out the window so he wouldn't see the tears cutting down my face. He hates shows of weakness. Pisses him off. Through the smudged glass and my blurry eyes I could see Sallie, Bucky, and Julie stirring the flaming chunks of wood and the charred pieces of the dead man around and around, like witches stirring brew.

We weren't quite half-way to town, through the forest, past fallow fields, and over a chipped concrete bridge spanning Widow's Creek, when we saw someone stumbling up the middle of the road ahead of us, coming in our direction, scuffing up gravel.

"Now just who is—?" I began.

Martin cut me off with, "Oh, fuck this shit!" He slammed on the brakes. I flew forward, almost slamming my head into the windshield.

It was another one. Another dead guy, but this dead guy was a woman. She had a long hank of matted hair on one side of her head; it swung back and forth heavily. There was no hair on the other side, but the scalp was lacerated and sticky with something dark. She was limping, as if her hip was out of joint. She wore only one shoe. Her arms swung wild like those of an ape. But it was her face, getting closer by the moment, that convinced us she was, indeed, dead. The whites of her eyes were that disgusting, deathly orange. Her jaw snapped open and closed as if on a spring.

"What the fuck is going on?" whispered Martin through his teeth. "What the hell is all this? This is just fucking wrong!"

The woman got closer, zoned in on the truck now, or on us. Her mouth began to open and close all the faster and her arms raised up, fingers clutching.

"It's like she wants to tell us something," I said. "Or she wants to eat us."

Martin jerked the steering wheel, slamming the truck around, knocking into the dead woman with the rear left end, throwing her out of her shoe and down onto the gravel. As I watched in the rearview, the woman got up and started shambling again.

When we got back to the trailer, the bonfire was leveling out. Julie had a shovel in her hands, ready to toss dirt on it when it was all done. Bucky and Sallie had their arms crossed against a cold March breeze. They glanced up at our return, their brows drawn and mouths down in tight frowns.

Martin pulled the truck up to the fire and fell out.

"There's more of 'em!" he yelled, taking Bucky by the arm and shaking it, hard. "We saw another one, another thing like that guy there!" He hitched his thumb in the direction of the fire. "A woman this time."

"Can't be," Bucky said. "This guy here, he was just some really sick dude, some insane sick dude who..."

"No!" I said. "He was a dead guy, and..."

"He wasn't!" shouted Bucky. "Dead guys don't walk around!"

"But zombies do!" said Martin.

"You've watched *Night of the Living Dead* too many times," said Bucky.

Martin's let go of Bucky's arm and his fists drew up. "That's right, freak! And it means I know what I'm talking about! It's fucking zombies! That's what that guy was. And that woman we saw on the road, too. While we been out here at the trailer, away from everybody and everything, something happened, dead people started turning into zombies and—"

"There's no such thing as zombies! That's fucking horror movie crap! That's crazy talk!" said Bucky. He shoved Martin hard. Martin punched him in return, a solid crack against Bucky's jaw. Bucky wailed and bowed over with pain.

But Bucky and the rest of us were convinced Martin was right only a moment later, when we heard noises coming from the back of the pickup. We spun about to see the rolled blanket undulating, twisting around, and then Robin's hand came out, clutching, scrabbling.

We all screamed at the same time.

Robin was buried with one of Julie's bullets in her brain. We didn't burn her like Sallie wanted, because the rest of us felt hinky about burning a friend. Even though we didn't feel too hinky about the shot to her head, being as she was trying to lunge out of the truck bed, growling and grunting, her lips curled back, her jaws open wide, her eyes glowing orange.

So we sat there in the trailer, drinking beer but not tasting it, picking at our knuckles, staring out the window—the blinds were now pulled all the way up so we could see—as the sun began to set over the wilderness.

Then Martin said, "I think we should check out how bad it is."

We knew what he meant. He wanted someone to go on reconnaissance to learn how widespread this zombie mess was. The woman who was on the road hadn't come our way; likely she'd taken another pathway off to somewhere else. Maybe there was only the two of them, only two zombies, the burned-up guy and the gray-haired woman. Oh, and Robin. Okay, three. Only three.

But maybe there were lots of others, all over the place.

Maybe we were stuck in deep shit. Maybe the whole county was. Maybe the whole country.

And we had to know.

Sallie and Bucky reluctantly volunteered. They took Sallie's car, a beat-up blue Civic, arming themselves with Martin's reloaded rifle. That left us with Julie's pistol, but I took a bit of comfort in that because she was a great shot. We double-checked to make sure the door was locked. Then we triple checked it. I drank another beer but couldn't taste it. I wasn't in the mood for a joint. I had a feeling being alert would be better than not.

They came back after midnight. The sound of the car and then the loud, crunching sound of the car striking something solid drove us to our feet and to the window, to make sure it wasn't zombies driving a car.

They shouted for us and we let them in, then watched as they sat silently on the sofa for a very long minute. At last Bucky said, "We wrecked Sallie's car. Hit that maple down by the road. Car's a goner."

Sallie nodded.

"But no matter," said Bucky, "We ain't never going back to Stanleyville."

"They're everywhere in and around town, swarmin' like bees," Sallie said. "All this in what, two days? How insane is that?"

"How'd it happen?" asked Julie. "How the hell did this happen?"

Martin glared at Julie. His eyes were small and scary. "Who ever knows? Virus? Bacteria? Space pollution? Chemicals? Radiation? Could be any of that."

Julie linked her arm through Martin's but he stalked away, moving to the counter where he stared at the floor and muttered to himself.

"There's still living people in Stanleyville," said Bucky. "We could see 'em in their upstairs windows. Went by your house, Julie, and seen your Mom peeking out her living room window. We drove by Lyle's house and Sallie's house, and lights were on so we're guessing they're okay. But we just kept driving through and out. The zombies—" (I could tell he had a hard time saying the word after the grief he'd given Martin)

"—threw themselves at the car but we floored it. Most of the stores had broken-out windows, schools, too, and churches. Sallie was damn brave. We pulled up to the Sharp Shopper just outside town and she ran in and grabbed up a big bag's worth of canned stuff. But we ain't going back there again. Too dangerous. We have to stay here."

"How long are we supposed to stay here at this trailer?" I demanded. "Are we just supposed to hope our families are okay?"

"Yeah, that's exactly what we're supposed to do," said Martin, still staring at the floor. "'Cause if they aren't dead now, they'll be dead real soon, count on it."

And as much as I hated it, I knew he was right.

I felt like such a fucking coward.

Days passed. Then weeks. Sallie's stash of canned peaches, green beans, and Spam thinned out so we—well, Julie, actually—hunted critters in the woods. They were a lot faster than dead people but she was able to snare some. We used up the rest of the gasoline from Martin's truck and Sallie's smashed Civic, siphoning it into a bucket to use to start fires to cook. The matches didn't last, either. Martin learned how to start fires with the battery from the Civic, and we all learned how to keep fires going, like people in the old days, assigning someone to always be awake to add more bark or sticks. When it rained, we tended the coals inside the old oven. We also kept a fire going in the smokehouse, where we gutted, skinned, then smoked the groundhogs and squirrels we managed to kill, using the old, crusted bags of salt that had been left there by the previous owner (thank goodness Julie had a wacky country grandma who not only taught her how to use a pistol but had also taught her how to cure meats). The meats were tough but at least they didn't spoil. Julie wouldn't let us kill birds, though. She said they were heavenly spirits and we best leave them alone.

At first we saw one zombie a week, thereabouts. Then, by early May we saw two or three a week, wandering up the road, veering off toward the trailer. Still a trickle, but clearly the live humans in and around Stanleyville were running out. Julie and Martin shot them cleanly, and we burned them. But our ammunition was down to fumes, so Martin decided to hike to the nearest house—a cabin four miles up the road to Stanleyville—and see what he could find.

There was no one there, and the cabin door was bashed open. Dried blood was splattered all over the floor and the furniture. He found an empty shotgun in the bedroom. He also found a few hanks of human hair and bits of bone on the bed. There was a box of bullets in a kitchen drawer, which he pocketed. He also pocketed the only good food he found: three cans of beets and a jar of olives. The stuff in the refrigerator was beyond spoiled.

On his way home, as it got dark, he spied a zombie out in a field, chewing on an arm. Then he saw another near the first, gnawing flesh from a head. Martin ran most of the way back to the trailer, stumbling several times in his terror, breaking his wrist in the process, and then was sick three days from all the running, his wrist splinted and making him moan even in his sleep.

There were no more animals to hunt by late May, and all the smoked meats were eaten. Now we were collecting dandelion greens and wild asparagus and berries from the edge of the forest, and trying to trap mice but they were sneaky and knew what we were up to, so rarely got caught. We were weakening from lack of food and a fear of leaving the trailer. Zombies came, were shot, burned. The stench was dreadful. Not just the zombies, but us.

The first Friday in June, Bucky, Sallie, and I had a talk. We had to get out of there. We would head into the mountains where the wild animals had gone, gather our wits and search for other foods, then move on. Zombies probably stayed away from steeper slopes, as uncoordinated as they seemed to be. We might be okay.

Martin was furious. He got up in my face, grabbed my shirt with his good hand, and swore we better stay put.

"What, and starve to death?" I asked. "Have you seen yourself in the mirror lately? Have you really looked at any of us?"

"Sure, we're starving here." Damn, but Martin's breath was sour. I tried not to make a face or turn away. Didn't want to piss him off anymore than he already was. "But here you got walls, Lyle. Look around! Walls to protect your sorry ass!"

"We got to do something."

"And if Julie and I don't go with you, you won't have guns to hunt food, neither."

"We can make snares, traps, maybe."

"Maybe? How many mice you catch with your traps here in the trailer, huh?"

"We can try harder. And we'll cross over the mountains, maybe find some other people…"

Martin's face was red, his eyes dark-rimmed, crazy, and wide. "Zombies'll get you, Lyle. You can bet your fucking ass on that. You'll fall asleep against a tree or a boulder. They'll come up on you before you know it. Bite your heads off, eat the skin like an apple peeling!"

"Martin, listen, if you come with us, you and Julie and the pistol—"

"I could have died out there!" Martin screamed. Julie reached for him but he shoved her away, his splinted arm flailing. "I realized when I was on my way back with those damned bullets that one more stumble and I would have been zombie food. Eaten alive! Or eaten partially, and then come back to life like Robin!"

"Okay, okay, we won't go," I said. Sallie and Bucky glared at me and moved to protest, but I waved them to the back bedroom as Julie helped Martin back onto the sofa and wiped his brow.

"We'll leave when he's asleep," I said once we were out of Martin's earshot. "He's messed up in the head as it is. No need to make it worse. Julie won't leave him here alone, so we'll go early in the morning, dawn, when we can see but before they're awake."

Sallie was shaking but she nodded. Bucky put his arms around her but the trembling continued. "We'll stay together, no matter what?"

Bucky nodded. "No matter what."

Dawn came after a nightmarishly long night in which I dreamed of dining on raw feet and bloated tongues. Martin was snoring on the sofa; Julie was rolled up in a blanket on the floor beside him. Sallie, Bucky, and I gathered in the hall then moved as stealthily as possible into the living room, holding our breaths, biting our cheeks. The damned front door creaked as we eased it open but neither Julie nor Martin stirred. Out we went, then around the side of the trailer where I collected the axe from beside the bonfire pit. Bucky shouldered the shovel and Sallie the rake. We looked like folks going after Frankenstein. Or three of the seven dwarfs, off to work.

Breathing as hard as if we'd run a marathon, we started off across the backyard, past Julie's birdbath, sending sparrows in a mad flutter. If nothing else, I told myself, we were trying. If nothing else, we weren't going to die in a trailer, lying on the floor in our own dried-up, mouse-chewed shit.

And then we heard Martin howling, running footsteps, and a loud *pop*! Sallie went down, cold dead, the rake flipping from her hand and red flowering on the back of her t-shirt. Bucky and I spun around. Bucky was shot in the chest and crumpled in a lifeless heap.

"Get back here!" Martin yelled. He stood at the corner of the trailer, Julie beside him, her hair caught up in her fingers, unable to make it stop.

I dropped the axe and ran.

A bullet whizzed by my ear but missed. The gun fired again, catching me in the hip, sending red-hot electricity up through my body. My legs buckled out from under me, but I pushed myself upward and kept on running.

Into the woods. Toward the mountains.

I'm not sure how long I was on my feet—seconds? hours?—but my body grew cold and my legs ceased working at some point. I dropped to my knees and then fell flat out in a patch of poison ivy and thorny greenbrier.

I lay there, panting, my breath growing shallower with each inhalation. Waiting for death, not caring anymore.

Then I heard a rustling of brush, and a grunt, and my head turned enough to see a zombie struggling through a thicket of saplings, his sights trained on me. He was one ugly motherfucker, this dead guy. Ears rotted away, ribs showing through a tattered shirt. Ticks in his beard, probably just there for the ride since there was no real blood for them to suck.

I tried to scramble away. I was ready to die, but not this way. Becoming zombie food or turning into a zombie myself? *Hell, no!* I tried to cry out but I only squeaked. This seemed to rev up the desperate hunger of the dead guy, who clacked his fuzzy green teeth and shoved himself through the saplings even as their little pointed branches tore hunks of skin from his bare arms.

Oh, shit, oh please no!

He reached down for me, grabbed my hair, hauled me up. His toxic drool splattered on my lips, in my eyes. I blinked and began to sob.

Then a bullet struck his head, splattering bone and fluid, and he let go of me. I heard Martin shout, "Die, bastard!" He could have meant me as much as the zombie. The zombie dropped away, dead for sure now. And Martin was over me, eyes twitching, fingers shoving another bullet into the pistol's chamber.

I opened my mouth to say something, I don't know what, really, and swallowed the zombie's fouled spit as Martin said, "You betrayed me, you shit!" and blew another hole in my chest.

I faded.

I died.

But then I came back. I fucking came back, sort of. Can you believe it? Damn it to hell, I'd rather have been one of the living dead wandering the roads and the forests than what I am now.

After killing me, Martin strung me up in the smokehouse along with Susie and Bucky. He and Julie stripped our bodies, scooped out our insides, stitched our mouths and eyes shut, trussed us, salted us, and then started up the fire in the firebox. Can't waste good meat, not these days.

But I came back. Not mindless like the other zombies, because I am only infected from drool, not from a bite. Funny that there are these minor details that matter. Don't think they ever talked about stuff like that in *Night of the Living Dead*, did they? I still have my mind, but it doesn't work like it used to. It won't send signals to my vocal chords or my arms and legs. As much as I want to, I can't make sounds or wriggle. I can only hang here, watching wet birds in the birdbath with the one eye that wasn't sewn tightly enough and popped loose of the threads. I can only feel the heat and the dry and loneliness.

And oh, yes, the hunger. There is that hideous, gnawing agony deep in my bowel-less gut.

There's Julie now. She's in the backyard, standing in the dead grass, one hand in the pocket of her jeans, the other holding a dull knife. She studies the birds on the birdbath from a respectable distance. They make her smile. They are life. Healthy life. Julie, on the other hand, is as far from healthy as you can get without being dead. She and Martin still scavenge dandelions and dry land cress. Asparagus season is long over. I know they've been eating insects, too. I've watched her scoop up spiders and beetles from the ground and pop them into her mouth like Skittles.

Julie leaves the birdbath, unlatches the smokehouse door, squinting against the gray smoke as it billows up around her. She steps inside, pokes at the firebox with a rake, and then adds some chunks of wood and bark. She coughs; it's hot and dry as hell in here. She comes close to me, spins me around on the hook, and frowns. Obviously I'm not ready to consume.

She moves over to Bucky, nods, and slices a long slab from his leathery, well-smoked, meaty thigh, heaves it over her shoulder, and leaves the shed.

When it comes my turn to be consumed, I hope Martin selects my head for a meal. He'll snip away the stitching on my eye and mouth, hold me up to his lips to take a bite.

And I'll bite him first. Oh, you bet. I'll bite the shit out of him. Watch him scream, see the terror in his eyes when he realizes just what lies in store for him.

I watch Julie through the tiny window. She goes to the birdbath, dips her finger in the water, rubs it on her face, and then disappears around the side of the trailer. Martin will be anxiously waiting for her inside, pacing to all the windows with her pistol, watching for movement on the road, in the trees.

I guess the movement I saw at the edge of the woods was just my imagination. Or perhaps it was the tears blurring my vision. Strange that I still can cry.

I shut my one eye. I feel the wet course down my cheek, and pretend I'm a bird in the birdbath, refreshed and ready to fly away.

About Elizabeth Massie

Elizabeth Massie is a Bram Stoker Award- and Scribe Award-winning author of horror novels, short horror fiction, media tie-ins, mainstream fiction, historical novels, poetry, and nonfiction. Recent works include *Homegrown* (a mainstream novel from Crossroad Press), *Playback: Light and Shadow* (an e-novella from Random House), and *Naked, On the Edge* (a collection of horror shorts from Crossroad Press.)

Her newest novel, *Desper Hollow*, will be released by Apex Books in 2013. She is the creator of the Skeeryvilletown slew of cartoon zombies, monsters, ghosts, and other misfits. In her "spare" time she manages Hand to Hand Vision, a fundraising project she founded to help others during these tough economic times, and Circle of Caring, an anti-bullying project.

She shares life and abode in the Shenandoah Valley with the talented illustrator/artist Cortney Skinner. Elizabeth likes snow and hates cheese.

FEARFUL SYMMETRY
BY DEVON CAREY

Was David an immortal being from another planet? I always wondered that. My half-brother from my father's first wife, he looked so calm, so happy drinking Coca Cola behind the wheel of the small pickup truck, singing along to "The Sound of Madness" by Shinedown. I thought about all the hell he'd been through—motorcycle accidents, knife fights, sinking into comas, concussions, beating cancer—it proved my theory that much more.

Of course he wasn't from another planet. He wasn't immortal. If he'd been immortal, he wouldn't have died today.

It was all thanks to this stupid trip. "To get away from the problems," he'd said. "Forget about home, okay bro?"

And the weird thing was, his words felt unreal, dreamy in the truck, like he'd been an illusion conjured from my mind. Had all this happened before? Had it happened at all? Maybe the unreality cloaked over my mind resulted from the horrid memories I tried repressing, and made the world around me feel dreamy. Waning. Gray.

Dave finished telling one of his crazy famous stories, and had me spilling my guts out by the time he'd finished. This story had been about a girl. What a surprise. *Not.* And he'd stayed the night at her house, the next day her boyfriend comes pounding on the door, Dave flies out of the house wearing only a thong because he couldn't find his clothes, and he hopped nearly five fences before he hit the woods that led to his house.

My sides hurt from laughing so hard. Cheeks ached. Eyes burned with tears. Dave smiled at my "priceless" facial expressions.

Calmer now, I asked, "Finished?"

"Finished with your mom—"

My smile waned. Anguish stormed over me.

"Oh," he said. An awkward silence filled the car. "I'm sorry. I—I forgot."

"It's fine," I told him. He'd done good taking my mind away from my mother this whole time, and the mention of Mom had been enough for my repressed emotions to come flooding back.

She died last week. I shuddered at the thought.

"So, um, how's our father doing? I haven't talked to him in a billion years."

I appreciated his change in subjects, but details about my damaged family had always been something I preferred not to share, especially seeing as how our father had been in a mental hospital with mountains of psychological problems since my first words.

"He's hanging in there, I guess," I admitted, looking out the side window, tuning out the world around me.

My mom hadn't known I'd been seeing my father behind her back, but I'd only kept it from her because she wanted to keep him from me. She looked terrified just mentioning him, though. And her fear had terrified me, even as I began seeing him. Why had I seen him in the first place, if Mom had been so afraid? I didn't know. An unseen force just drew me to him, I guessed.

*****

The first encounter I had with my father had been when I'd turned ten. On Father's Day. He wished me a happy birthday over the phone.

"Son," he'd said. "Can we meet? Please?"

"I don't know if I can find a way."

"Please find a way. I want to see you, William. But don't tell your mother, okay?"

"Okay," I agreed. "I'll spend the night at Dave's and see if his mom can take me."

"Thank you, son."

The next day, Dave's mom took me to the top floor at Cherry Point Hospital. Behind the titanium door sat my father centered in a small white room, strapped to a chair bolted to the floor. He'd been looking at the ground when I came in. He lifted his eyes, a sad man deprived of sleep. Then he smiled at me as a tear trickled into his thick beard.

"I'm glad you came, son," were the first words I'd ever heard him say in person. "I prayed you would."

I wanted to run up and hug him, but the orderlies wouldn't let me get closer, like they feared he'd break out of his shackles.

"I never meant to hurt anyone," he choked, "but the evil inside me is so strong! Son, one day you will see this evil—*my Symmetry*. You are linked to me. Promise me you will be strong when you confront my evil."

I had no idea what Symmetry even was.

"I promise," I said.

I visited him once or twice a week after that. He told me stories about mutants from other planets, and they became my favorite scary stories.

My visits became less frequent as I grew older, but Dad was fine with that. He loved me. The sad, sleepless look in his eyes told me he did. What troubled me was how such a kindhearted man felt that he harbored evil inside? And how had he ended up in this place?

So one day I asked him why he was there.

He whispered as if the walls were listening, "The evil, William."

I didn't press the issue, but I had a feeling *the evil* was something I needed to know about. I had a feeling that, whatever it was, he was trying to protect me from the truth.

Could I handle the truth?

Maybe. Maybe not. I didn't think I'd ever know.

*****

A nudge on my shoulder shattered further thoughts. I turned away from the countryside to see Dave's concerned face.

"William, if you don't cheer up, you're asking for another knee slapper. And this time I'll make sure you piss your pants. Believe it."

I chuckled softly. He always knew how to make me laugh.

"You asked for it." He told me another "Dave" story. Once finished, I was laughing my guts out. Then I let out a long yawn.

"You tired, bro?"

"No, I'm fine. Just focus on the road."

He reached into the back for the white throw pillow and handed it to me. "There, sleep on that. I'll wake you when we get to Vegas."

"Okay." I yawned, and closed my eyes.

Part of my mind lingered in the car as I drifted into slumber. Subconsciously I heard everything, as if someone had placed me in a bubble. I turned over, my mind still in a dream-like state as I looked at him through blurred vision. I blinked until his features sharpened.

How much time had passed? Thirty minutes? An hour? Three?

I saw Dave fiddling with the GPS and then he said, "Something's not right here."

The GPS screen was completely white. The sky was white as the screen. Not a single cloud. The air cooled. My skin pricked with a cold chill.

"What the hell's wrong with the sky?" I blurted hysterically. A white puff of smoke eased out of my mouth from the cold. "That's snow!"

"What?" He looked at the sky, too. "The hell."

It felt like we were driving through a snow globe. The ground was illuminated with a white blanket. Through the snow, there was enough visibility to see the street clearly.

When I looked, I couldn't believe my eyes. Strange mutant creatures appeared like ghosts, entering and exiting saloons, walking, shopping, and staring at us as we rolled through town.

This place resembled my father's stories.

The creatures had bald, moon-shaped heads and craters stretched around the craniums. Black, decayed, endless eye sockets were only inches apart above crescent teeth-filled smiles. They were skinny, and gray, and some wore vests while others wore robes or capes or dresses.

At the end of long arms, instead of hands attached to the wrists, baseball sized eyeballs blinked. Hooks protruded from the eyeballs. At the end of skinny legs, the ankles branched out into burly hands with sharp black fingernails.

The pickup truck jerked to a stop. Dave cursed under his breath as the white pillow I had been sleeping upon fell into the footwell. I could see that the pillow was splotched with blood.

Dave tried to start the ignition, but it only made a grinding noise. It coughed and coughed.

"Oh God, what the hell are those things?" I stammered, oblivious to the blood smears on my face.

"I'm not panicking!" Dave screamed suddenly.

"I didn't say you were!" I screamed back at him.

He turned toward me so hard I thought his head would fly off his shoulders. "We just need to stay calm, and let me think of a plan."

I could see his breathing quicken. My own heart climbed into my throat. My skin itched. It was cold, yet sweat trickled down my forehead.

Still trying to start the truck, Dave said, "Calmness is the key, okay? Okay. Okay?"

"Okay!" I blurted, and then I felt panicked despite my words, because suddenly one of the creatures stepped off the sidewalk and headed for the truck.

Dave stared at me hard. "Let me try to talk to this thing," he whispered. "If we can get through this without freaking out, we can get back on the road alive. Understand? We don't know what these things are or what they can do, and I'm not prepared to find out."

At a loss for words, I nodded. *Please, Dave, get us through this. I know you can. You've gotten us through worse.* Although that was a lie, I tried soothing myself to keep my fear at ease.

A hook rapped on David's window. The softball-sized eyeball on the hand blinked. The corners of the thing's lips stretched to form a sharp smile cheek-to-cheek.

Dave rolled down the window an inch. Snow swirled inside the cab of the truck.

"Welcome," it said in a tiny, high-pitched voice. "Welcome to Symmetry."

Symmetry? Why did that sound so familiar? Why couldn't I remember the meaning?

When neither of us said a word, only stared and blinked, the sexless creature said, "Shall I conduct a tour?"

"I'm sorry," Dave began with his best smile. Man, he was a good actor. "We're lost. If you can just point us in the right direction, we'll be on our way."

"Well of course." It seemed delighted. "But please, won't you stick around for a while? Why don't you roll down your window all the way? We have such sights to show you, my new friends. You are the first humans who are not afraid upon seeing us."

Oh, but we *were* afraid! Still, I had to smile, had to act normal. Nothing strange here, Officer.

"Afraid?" Dave laughed, and looked at me as if that had been the most ludicrous thing he'd ever heard. "Why would humans freak out over such beautiful fellows as yourselves?"

When he started rolling down the window, I looked at him as if to say *What the hell are you doing?* But he ignored me.

"Oh my, how flattering. I am called Nameth," the creature said, and brought its hook up to its sharp smile. If this thing had ever had a sex, it would most surely have been female. "We find it gratifying that you feel that way. Can I take you to our Lord? The One who makes Symmetry possible?"

David opened the door, and when I tried to protest, he whispered under his breath, "Just go with it."

I got out and met Dave in front of the truck, studying the snowy town. This must have been how the kids in Narnia felt when they met Mr. Tumnus.

"So how'd we get here?" Dave asked. He didn't seem surprised, or scared, but then, he had always been good at hiding his emotions.

My face probably screamed of fear. There'd be no changing that.

Nameth spoke, "Symmetry is a place for peace. To rest. To release all the negative energy from your soul into the atmosphere so it can be cleansed."

"So it's like a rest stop at a state line?"

How the hell did he get that from anything Nameth said?

"Not quite. Symmetry dwells within a dimension symmetrical to your own."

David and I jerked to a stop quicker than his truck had done earlier. Not caring if my panic showed, I blurted, "What? How did we end up driving into another dimension?"

I wanted to run, but a part of me needed to stay. Had to stay. Had to see where Nameth was taking us. Had to see where we were! Walking through this cold town felt so unreal.

"Rest assured, Lazareth will answer all questions. Come with me."

"I want to stay with the truck," I protested.

"Your truck is dead," Nameth said. "Don't worry, I won't hurt you. Neither will Lazareth. Like I told you, all will be revealed."

I didn't see any other options. And I decided that Nameth's promise we would not be hurt was sincere, or else we would have been harmed already. It felt like we walked for miles through the town. We passed other creatures, but they ignored us.

Then a dome appeared, half a mile into the white land. Black vans were parked at the front entrance. Pipes puffed smoke into the white sky. The dome sat beneath a gigantic full moon—craters, shadows and details of the lunar surface clear cut and huge. If what Nameth said didn't add up about being in another dimension, the moon, seemingly within touching distance sure did.

Just like Dad's stories. But I couldn't tell Dave.

Nameth walked beside us. What disturbing sights waited behind those doors? We stopped us at the entrance. "Lazareth, we have come."

The doors roared open to reveal pipes crawling along the orange-red tiled ceiling and walls. A cacophony of machinery heightened in the musty air. The smell of sawdust fell heavy on my nose, clinging to my lungs. Cages lined a pathway swallowed by darkness. The empty cages looked like they'd once been inhabited by savage animals. As we walked down the curving concrete path, I noticed the cells held toilets, army cots, and sinks, like in an old prison. Not something you typically kept an animal in.

My eyes widened as the light from the entrance waned. The darkness engulfed me. I didn't even realize how scared I'd been, how hard my heart was beating, how heavily I'd been breathing, until a titanium door with a single window caked with grime and murk appeared through the abyss. It stared at me, and seemed to inch its way closer the longer I stared. The machinery banged, and clanked, and thronged—and thronged—in sync with each of my pounding heartbeats.

"We're here," Nameth said and turned to look at us. "Don't be afraid. Only guidance waits behind the door."

"Guidance?" Dave inquired, his voice tense. Unsure. Through the illumination coming through the door, I saw fear dawn on his face. I realized that I had been depending on him to keep us both calm, and I wouldn't know what to do if Dave lost his cool.

"Guidance that leads to a free soul," Nameth smiled, the door creaking open.

Once inside, a suffocating aroma filled my lungs, allowing nausea to come over me. My eyes burned, watered, keeping me from seeing anything, but I didn't need eyes to sense the evil presence in the room.

Immediately I knew that Nameth had lied.

My eyes adjusted so that I regained my sight, and I stared. It was a labyrinth. Walls with intricate tribal designs crisscrossed each other throughout the maze. Directly in front of us sat a tall, sexless beast in a black throne. Not a man, nor machine, nor any creature I'd ever seen.

Its round moon face was caked with ghost-white scum. Its sockets deepened with a horrid blackness, but instead of eyes, lips and teeth stirred about in the endless pits. It had no nose, only two black holes. Deep craters ran across its scalp. Its neck looked scrawny and wrinkly, attached to a wide chest clothed in a red and gray vest. Abnormally long arms branched out to bulbous eyeballs, with hooks as long as sickles protruding from the bleeding pupils. Its legs, thick; its skin, dirty alabaster. Instead of feet, bulbous fingers curled on the dark red carpet that stretched around the room.

This had been the evil my father warned me about, but how had he known I'd one day face it? What did he know that I did not? And why now, why find this dimension *after* Mom died?

None of that mattered now. It was with that glance that I understood my father for who he was, and the evil inside him. This had been my father's insides exposed, why he acted the way he did, why he switched from one being to another as if possessed by the devil himself.

My father had dragged me into his mind. Into his dimension. *His Symmetry.*

The creature started rapping a hook on the arm of the chair, in time with the cacophony of machinery and its horrid deep cackle.

"Nameth, leave us be!" Lazareth bellowed. The rapping ceased.

Nameth ran out of the room and I could almost smell fear.

"I'm sure you have many questions," Lazareth said, sitting erect. Its closeness made my insides swish and slosh with an uncomfortable sickness. "And I shall answer each one of them. It is the least I can do considering this will be the last encounter either of you will have with the other."

David looked shocked, flabbergasted, not expecting this change. Why hadn't he realized that these creatures would back-stab him? Had he actually been so trusting and think for a second they meant no harm?

Did he actually think his charm and good looks would be of any use here?

He didn't have a real plan like he'd promised. Now we would both suffer.

This doesn't have to be the end, William, a comforting voice assured. *Remember, you promised you'd be strong.*

It was my father!

A deafening hum expanded through the room, ringing in my ears like a horde of angry buzzing bees. Lazareth stopped the humming by saying, "No, I am not going to kill you. David, William, I have brought you here to save you from your future tormentors."

"Our future tormentors?" Dave questioned. "Telling me this is the last encounter with my brother is torture in itself! I thought you were here to help us."

"I know this might be difficult for you to understand; I know how hard it is to lose someone you love, but this is the way, it is for the best. You both will accept in time that this is for the best."

"When will that be? Five, ten, fifteen years?" Dave asked, his agitation showing. "What do you really want, Lazareth?"

"Peace," Came the reply. "You two simply were not meant to meet."

"Then why did we?" Dave asked.

"So I could get my offspring back," he said, and sighed. "My offspring was murdered before you were born."

Dave said nothing, but I spoke the question I knew he'd wanted to ask. "Did you kill your child?"

"No!" Lazareth boomed, rising from its throne. Fear sank into my body. He crept toward us on bulbous hands. "That's what those fools wanted me to believe."

Just when I didn't think more unanswered questions could present themselves, a ghastly man with a mustache and dark, slicked-back hair loomed over the beast. The man had a bloody chest, wearing ripped jean shorts and white tennis shoes. It looked like my father if he had been torn apart. He spoke in unity with Lazareth, echoing each word as it was spoken.

Lazareth and the hovering man peered down at me. The air reeked of evil breath, decay and fish, but behind the beast, my dad said, "All those years I'd thought I was crazy, that I'd killed my son in a drunken rage. Inevitably, my wife couldn't stand our child, couldn't stand his deformity, couldn't stand the fact he would be tormented all his life. She hated me, and thought she was doing the world a favor by ridding us both of it."

"What in God's name are you saying?" I screamed.

"She followed the Willil, our enemy. This was the Willil's work, possessing your mother, blinding her from her evil. She had a plan. She needed help. It was just me and a couple of friends hanging around in my apartment, sharing some drinks and watching the game. Before I knew it, I fell to the floor and blacked out."

Then a man's voice interrupted, one I didn't recognize, seemingly coming from everywhere. "Do you think he'll remember anything?"

Then a woman's voice, "If he does, no one will believe him. They'll think he's like all the others."

There was a tiny hand on the man's bare chest, soaked in a pool of blood. Then a woman was screaming. Men shouting. The nightmarish crying of a baby. Doors burst, cops appeared, glass shattered, tables flipped, the wife screaming, a baby crying. Flashes of eyeless creatures with alabaster skin, and long arms, and moon heads, and distorted round faces. Eyeballs attached to wrists, hooks protruding from bleeding pupils. They followed as the man was dragged out the door, yelling, "It wasn't me, it was them!" Then thrown into the cell, so very cold; the hard icy walls burning against the skin as the man rocked in the corner.

Realization kicked in. That woman was my mom. That baby was my brother, not Dave, but my other brother.

Now I knew why Mom always ignored Dad, always ignored his pleas to come visit, always forced me to stay away. She'd done a good job hiding the truth, so good of a job that she'd never even mentioned my brother.

"So how—" I began, the taste of metal in my mouth, "how was I born, Dad, if what you say is true?"

The creature Lazareth turned, walked to its throne and sat down with an eyeball-hook-hand pressed against its cheek. "She was already pregnant with you when it happened. She wanted to recreate the child she'd destroyed, but better this time."

My father drifted away from Lazareth and came toward me to give me a long and overdue hug. "Mom meant a lot to you, and me, which was why I waited until she died to tell you the truth about who she really was."

"Dad, please, tell me what we must do to get out of here."

He frowned, and turned his back on me. "Son, this is the side of my mind I've tried to keep locked. Somehow you've unlocked my Symmetry."

"But dad, what does that even mean? What is Symmetry?"

"We all have a Symmetry, son, that chamber in our minds where we lock away evil. Knowing what you do about my Symmetry might destroy you from within. It's fatal when exposed to the conscious mind."

"Then why did you expose it to me through stories?"

"I thought knowing would keep you safe, thought that maybe you'd find a way to destroy my Symmetry before it became your reality. But I'm afraid it's too late for that now, son."

"Correct!" Lazareth laughed. "The only way to get my offspring back is if I extract the soul from a deceased human."

"There's another way, and you know it's true," my dad said.

"Yes, but this way is entertaining!" It raised its hooks toward the ceiling. "Let the game begin."

The ceiling opened. Four sickles clanked together on the carpet.

"The rules are simple," Lazareth explained. "You die, you're born again as one of us. You live, you're free to leave. This is between you and David. One of you has to kill the other. Only the victor can leave."

Dave walked forward, the only movement he'd made the entire time my father had been speaking, probably going over the unnatural evidence in his own mind. He picked up a sickle and stared at it for a while. Then turned on me.

"Excellent," Lazareth said.

"I'm so sorry, William." Dave picked another sickle up, tossed it to me.

I caught it and peered into his dark eyes. Dave spoke again, "I don't want to murder you. It has to be a fair fight."

Yes, this seemed like Dave. He never walked away from a fight, but he still found a way to remain loyal to me.

"Dave, wait," I said, shielding my face. "Just think. Please. You always have a plan, bro."

"Not this time," he said, drifting toward me as if controlled. "This time there's no escape. There is no plan."

The tears came. Dave was the only one left that mattered to me. How could he kill me? Worse, how could he want to kill me?

I dropped my sickle. It landed soundlessly on the carpet. I couldn't kill him.

"Pick it up," Dave ordered. "I'm not fighting you without your weapon."

I shook my head. "No, Dave, if you're going to kill me, you'll do it like this. I want you to go back to your family. Let's face it, I have no one, and you have a wife."

"You always have me," he said. "Listen, I don't want to kill you."

And then I could see a plan finally edge its way into Dave's eyes. Before I could react, Dave shoved the sickle deep into his stomach. He gasped, choked, and coughed up a glob of blood. He fell to his knees as I screamed and drowned out the sound of chaos unfolding around me.

I held Dave. He looked up at me, his eyes becoming hollow. He gurgled, bleeding from his mouth, and said, "I guess I'm not immortal after all, huh, bro?"

My fingers combed through his hair. I pleaded, felt like this had all been a dream. My mind spun, my stomach twisted in knots. The walls waned out of existence until I found myself in a tangible white void. Dave's lips trembled. His eyelashes fluttered. His stutters broke the dreadful silence. The smell of blood wafted in the stale air. The machinery stopped. The laughing ceased. My dad disappeared. I was nowhere now, a dimension inside a dimension.

I looked around, tried to scream. Nothing came out. I would have welcomed Nameth. Even Lazareth. The silence expanded unpleasantly, a demented torture from *my* Symmetry.

I was alone, seemingly forever in nothingness with my dying brother.

He stopped moving. He peered up at me with a dead stare. I shook him. Nothing. I shook him again. Nothing again.

"David!"

No answer. A third rapid shake. Nothing. I slapped him. Nothing!

I punched him, but his neck snapped to the side.

I felt something swoop around me in a blast of warmth. I looked around. The smell of decay filled my nose.

A cage. Dave was chained to a wall, head lowered on his chest, panting and screaming. Blood oozed from his pores as if promising to dress him in a liquefied red cloak. His eyes were blackened like onyx orbs. His head bubbled, changed to a discolored full moon. He continued to scream as the corners of his lips tore through his face to form a wide black mouth. His teeth sharpened to razor blades. His arms grew. His eyeballs rolled down long arms and replaced his hands. Legs bulged. Muscles popped. Screaming persisted.

Chained to the cage wall, his distortion laughed at me and winked. "You're a prisoner in the next room," he said.

But then everything changed.

*****

I appeared in the truck again from an aerial view on the ceiling. Dave was still singing *Sound of Madness* as my body slept on the pillow. Bleeding from my nose. My eyes.

I had died with my face on the pillow.

My dad had been linked to me. He'd visited me in my dream through the world he'd created by his own insanity, and brought that dream into reality as I'd slept. Consequently, the reality had been filled with boundless forces of evil unable to be contained inside my body.

I screamed at my corpse, tried to wake him, praying that it wasn't too late.

But it was. My body wouldn't move. Or even breathe. And I just kept bleeding and soaking the pillow red.

Dave had died. In my dimension.

And I had died in David's dimension while sleeping beside him, imprisoned within my own Fearful Symmetry.

About Devon Carey

Devon Carey is your fear. He is your horror. He is your most repressed nightmare made into a reality. He lurks in the mind of Devon Williams, and only reveals himself through tales for the disturbed.

Devon Williams came into the world in August of 1991. He is in the North Carolina National Guard as a Signal Support Systems Specialist (25 U). He is currently striving to get his degree in Screenwriting at UNC School of the Arts in Winston-Salem, North Carolina while writing novels and short stories and working at Red Robin as a Busser.

He has also written for the *Tideland News* and gets an article published every now and again. Once he gets his Bachelor's degree, he will become an Officer full time. He will continue writing novels, working on his six-book series, and, if he plays his cards right, maybe his dream will come true and he will get to see his work on the big screen some day.

You can find (Like) Devon Carey on Facebook and keep updated on current projects, book trailers, cover art, daily thoughts/quotes, and much more, here: https://www.facebook.com/devoncarey2009 or contact him directly at devon.williams2009@hotmail.com

"COME DOWN TO THE STORE, MINERVA!"

BY EARL HAMNER

She had been born here in this house. Even after her marriage she had remained to take care of her mother and father. Now she looked upon the house as a shrine to their memory and had kept it always the way they had left it. The street had once been a fashionable one, but the city had moved westward to the suburbs. People she considered less desirable as neighbors were moving in. They were the kind of people who sat on the stoops in their undershirts, who played their radios too loud at all hours of the night and day.

Minerva felt no joy in the work even though she pushed the vacuum cleaner briskly across the already spotless Oriental rug. With a look of annoyance, she glanced toward the hallway when her husband called from the front door.

"Brush your feet, Walter," she called. "I've just finished the carpet."

Walter Farmingdale attempted to appear casual when he entered the room as if it was routine for him to bring home a birdcage, its contents hidden by a cover.

"You did the carpet yesterday, Minerva," he said, holding the cage as if he already regretted bringing it.

"Some women can live with filth and dust. I'm not one of them." Minerva turned off the vacuum cleaner and glared at her husband. "What are you doing home? It's just lunchtime."

"I brought you this!" he said, lifting up the birdcage and removing the cover with a flourish.

"What would I want with a bird?" she asked wearily.

"Remember at breakfast I mentioned how quiet it is around here?"

Walter started to set the cage on the end table, but stopped when she said, "Be careful you don't scratch the table. Take it out to the kitchen."

Like the living room, the kitchen was cold, sterile and immaculate. All the appliances appeared to have come from the twenties or thirties. Minerva watched with critical eyes as Walter placed the cage on the counter.

"I thought it would cheer things up a little around here," said Walter.

"Just don't expect me to take care of it." Minerva began shining the silver service that had been left to dry on the kitchen table. "It's a known fact they carry vermin."

Walter brought his face down close to the canary. It cocked its head to one side, looking out as if taking stock of its new home.

"Oh, I'll take care of old Dickie-Boy. I guess you're thirsty by now, feller. Let's get you some water."

Minerva smacked her lips with disapproval.

"Talking to a bird. People will think you've gone soft in the head."

Walter checked the bird's water dish and found it needed filling. Hoping to divert his wife from her foul mood he tried to introduce a new subject of conversation.

"You know that little Chamberlain girl? Ben Chamberlain's daughter, pretty little blonde thing?"

"The one with the suggestive walk? I know the one she is."

"Came by the shop this morning. She's going to have a baby."

"Did she tell you she's going to have a baby?"

"No. Not in so many words. Why?"

"It just doesn't seem the kind of thing a young woman would discuss with an older man."

"We didn't discuss it, Minerva. It was just plain to see."

"If you looked close enough, you mean?"

She looked at her husband accusingly. His face flushed with guilt. Actually he had enjoyed looking at the Chamberlain girl.

"She was a customer," Walter insisted. "How can I wait on a customer without looking at her?"

"Papa ran the shop his entire life without inappropriately staring at young girls."

"I wouldn't have brought it up except I thought you'd be interested the girl's going to have a baby."

"Babies don't interest me," she said and began neatly placing each piece of silver in its proper compartment in the drawer.

"She wanted some calcium pills," said Walter.

"Who?" Minerva asked.

"The Chamberlain girl. You know she was the only customer I had this morning? Business has been awful lately."

"I'd hate to have to fall back on my savings, Walter. Papa left us enough to get by on, but we're not well-to-do by any means."

"Never mind, Min. I'm taking steps to drum up more business."

"What kind of steps, Walter?"

"It's a surprise."

"'What kind of surprise, Walter?"

"I'll tell you later, Minerva. I've got to run now. I'm meeting someone down at the store."

"Walter, I want to know about this surprise," she called, but with a quick wave Walter turned and was gone.

After her husband left, Minerva stood for a moment looking into the cage. Suddenly the canary began to sing.

"Oh, just shut up," said Minerva. But the bird ignored her and its song swelled until it filled the room. She looked at the bird distastefully, draped the cover over the cage and left the room.

Walter Farmingdale arrived at the drugstore to find Tom Rivers, a sign painter, removing a sign from his truck which read: FARMINGDALE PHARMACY.

"You want me to cover the old one with the new one, Mr. Farmingdale?" Tom asked glancing up at the faded sign over the entry that read COLEMAN DRUGS AND NOTIONS.

"No, let's tear the old one down," Walter replied. "Old Man Coleman's been dead thirteen years so I don't think he'll mind."

"You figure you'll do better business with a pharmacy than a drugstore?" Tom asked as he removed a ladder and toolbox from his truck and began tearing away the old sign.

"Got to keep up with the times!" Walter said.

Minerva slammed on the brakes, narrowly missing Tom's truck as she pulled into the space behind him. Walter had never seen her quite so angry.

"So this is the surprise you were telling me about? You come down from there and stop what you're doing!" she called to Tom.

Walter nodded and the man returned to his truck, leaned against it and crossed his arms, waiting for a decision.

"Dear," said Walter. "This is just the beginning. I'm going to modernize the place; put in all glass windows, new shelves, a cosmetic department, and a soda fountain for the kids."

"Papa always believed that a drugstore should sell drugs and fill prescriptions. He made a decent living without peddling cosmetics and running a soda fountain."

"Minerva, that was then. This is now. Your Papa's been gone a long time now."

"But his reputation is still alive. Lots of his old customers must still come here."

Tom Rivers coughed politely while he waited for further instructions, but no one paid him the least attention.

"Three old ladies who come in twice a year for smelling salts," objected Walter. "That's about all I've got left of your father's trade."

"You should have talked this over with me first, Walter," said Minerva. "After all, the store is still in my name."

"But I'm the one that does the work."

"It might make a difference," Minerva said, "if you were more conscientious. Papa never used to come home for lunch. He was down here all hours. That's why he had that bath installed in the storeroom. If there was an emergency, people knew they could find him here."

"Have it your way, Minerva. There's really no point in trying to build up the business. There's no one to take it over when we're gone, anyway."

"You always find some way to remind me of that, don't you?"

"You've lost me," said Walter.

"That I never gave you children."

"I stopped expecting children after I found out about your affliction."

"That was very decent of you, Walter."

"I've got to get to work now, Minerva. I'll see you tonight."

Minerva glared at the sign painter as she walked past, got into her car and drove away.

"Tom," Walter called to the sign painter, "We're finished here. Just send me the bill."

The following morning when Minerva came into the kitchen she found her husband intensely absorbed as he gazed into the birdcage.

"We're going to have to change Dickie-Bird's name," he announced.

"Why?" asked Minerva from the counter where she was pouring a cup of coffee.

"He's laid an egg!" Walter exclaimed with such enthusiasm that he might have laid it himself. Walter got up from the table and headed for the door.

"You haven't had your breakfast. Where are you going?"

"Down to the pet shop," he called back over his shoulder. "There's a special nesting cage I want to get for this lady bird."

"Then get a deeper food bowl while you're at it. This one's so shallow it's getting seed all over the kitchen."

"Right back," called Walter and closed the door behind him.

The bird hopped about in its cage, occasionally stopping as if to admire the new egg and then filling the room with her warbling. It paused only to scratch around in its food saucer and somehow manage to broadcast birdseed right and left.

When Minerva could stand it no longer she went to a cabinet and took down a ramekin somewhat deeper than the saucer that now held the seeds. She had to open the cage door to exchange the saucer with the ramekin, but as she did so the bird flew out into the room. In a second it was gone through the open window.

Minerva looked down at the cage. It now held only the single egg. "Good riddance," she said and took up her broom and began sweeping up the scattered birdseed.

Walter accepted his wife's explanation that the incident had been an accident. Still, he sighed sadly as he threw the little egg into the garbage and stored the cage in the garage.

It was months before Walter tried again to bring some cheer to the kitchen. This time he installed a fifteen-gallon aquarium in the place where the birdcage has stood. Even though Minerva had to admit that the colorful fish and the little lighted castle and the seascape did brighten the kitchen, she still objected to his coming home every day at lunchtime. Walter came home anyway, to enjoy watching his new pets.

"It's after one o'clock," Minerva reminded him as she removed his empty sandwich plate.

"There's something going on here," replied Walter. "I think this little female is about to have babies."

"How do you know such things?" asked his wife.

"Actually, it's very interesting. Guppies don't lay eggs, they bear their young live. Pete was telling me about it down at the fish store."

"I think it's indecent of you to watch," observed Minerva.

"See here," Walter said excitedly, "There's a baby. Come look!"

Reluctantly, Minerva peered into the tank.

"Ugly little thing. Nothing but eyes."

"Darn!" Walter exclaimed. "I'd better separate the little ones from the mother or she'll eat them."

"Disgusting," Minerva said. "I've got work to do." She turned away as the female guppy began devouring her offspring. Some of them managed to conceal themselves in the seaweed, but others swam too close to their hungry parent and were eaten.

Walter's eyes fell on an empty jelly jar. He grabbed it, filled it with water from the tank and began netting the infant guppies into the jelly jar. In his haste, he spilled a good bit of water on the counter beside the tank. Walter smiled with delight as he delivered one last infant into the jelly jar.

"Fourteen!" he said triumphantly. "I've saved fourteen of the babies. Look, Minerva. You've got to see this."

Minerva looked not at the baby fish but at the counter. She was outraged at what she saw.

"You have spilled water all over the counter, and it's smelly, filthy fish water at that." She grabbed a paper towel and began soaking up the water. In her haste she knocked over the jelly jar and sent the contents floating away.

"Oh, Walter!" she cried. "I'm so sorry. I didn't mean to do that."

"It's all right, Minerva," he replied, but somehow his response did not have the ring of truth to it. The aquarium remained there on the counter. Walter fed the fish routinely, but his interest in them was never the same.

Christmas came. There was no tree, but Minerva made the same meal that had been traditional in her family. Walter brought home a quart of eggnog and Minerva even allowed him to give it a little shove with an ounce or two of bourbon. Minerva even reminisced about the good old days when her folks were alive and theirs had been the finest house on the block.

And then the holiday was over and Walter returned to work at Coleman's Drug and Notions. One snowy night when he was closing the store he found a female dog cringing beside the door and making a whining noise. As he looked closer he could see that she was heavy with puppies.

"Hello, old girl," he said and bent to pet her head. "No night for you to be out in the cold."

The dog, a golden retriever, rose wearily and looked up at him as if pleading for his attention.

"Why don't you go home, old girl? Surely you've got a home around here somewhere. You're going to need one soon for those pups."

But even as he tried to persuade himself that the dog could fend for herself, the matted coat, the torn ear and her terrible obvious need convinced him to open the car door.

She needed no invitation to get in and made herself at home in the passenger seat, all the while looking to Walter with what he took to be gratitude.

When he reached home, Walter led the dog to the back of the building, to the cellar entrance. Once inside he found an old car robe, spread it on the floor and she was resting there when he left her.

After dinner Walter took his usual place in front of the television. Minerva was cleaning up the kitchen but he planned that, as soon as she went up to bed, he would sneak some food and water down to the dog.

In the kitchen, Minerva heard a noise and when she opened the door that led down to the basement it came again. Minerva descended cautiously. Reaching the foot of the stairway she grabbed a garden rake and advanced further into the cellar. Holding the rake to the ready she advanced toward what she could now clearly see was a sleeping dog.

She strode past it to the cellar door, opened it, then returned and slammed the rake down in front of the dog. Startled, it rose and shrieked in fear. Using the rake, she forced it closer and closer to the open door and finally it was gone into the snowy night. She was closing the door when she turned to find Walter observing her anxiously.

"What's going on down here?" he asked.

"You're getting careless, Walter," she replied. "You left the door open and a dog wandered in. I had to chase it out."

"She didn't wander in. I let her in. Minerva, that dog's going to have puppies."

"Walter, would you tell me why in the world that everything you drag into the house is about to give birth? Are you trying to tell me something?"

"Surely, you don't think I'm trying to remind you of your affliction?"

"Husband, would you like to know something about my affliction? It never existed. I could have had two dozen children if I had wanted them."

Confusion showed in his face, and then sorrow, and finally anger.

"Minerva, a little boy or girl of my own was the only thing I ever really wanted in this life. Why?"

"Because I couldn't stand for you to touch me!" she spat it out. "I couldn't stand your flesh!"

"That's the worst thing anybody ever said to me," Walter said. "If you felt that way, why did you marry me?"

"It was Papa's idea," Minerva replied. "He said once he was gone you'd be a good man to run the store."

He was not a man given to anger, and when it possessed him, did not know how to express it. He could only sputter, "I could kill you, woman."

"No, you couldn't Walter," she said. "You're not man enough!"

Neither person ever really recovered from the horror of what they had said to each other. Yet in time their relationship fell pretty much back into what it had always been.

The one marked difference was that Walter never came home to lunch again. Instead he simply closed the shop for an hour and went to the park to watch the children play, or else he would stop by Pete's Pets to show a little affection to whatever animal seemed the most needy. Walter was holding a pug puppy while Pete trimmed its nails when Pete asked about the guppies he had sold him.

"I had bad luck," said Walter. "My wife was taking care—"

"Say no more," Pete interrupted. "You can't tell me a thing about wives and pets. They'll mother them to death! You know what I mean?"

Walter nodded that he did, indeed, know.

"I guess it's just the nature of a woman," Pete continued. "My wife's the same. We've got this cocker spaniel, five years old and the size of a sheep. Sleeps in the bed right next to us."

Walter had not been paying Pete his fullest attention. He was too occupied with a sign over a nearby tank that read: MAN EATING PIRANHA.

"I saw a documentary on these things on the *National Geographic*," Walter said. "Man eaters."

"Oh," Pete said, "they'll eat women, children, dogs; anything that falls into that river down in South America. All that comes up is a skeleton."

The following day when Walter came by the pet shop he announced that he was in the market for the piranha, and even several more.

"Oh, you don't want a thing like that around the house," Pete objected. "Suppose one of the children reached his arm in the tank. You know how kids are."

"I don't have kids," said Walter.

"Well, how about the missus? Suppose one day she was feeding it and got too close? That thing would take the meat right off the bone."

"Yes it would, wouldn't it?" Walter answered.

It took a while for Walter to acquire the number of fish he wanted. Pete had to special order them, but eventually, when Walter would throw a chicken or a slab of ribs into the bathtub, the water would boil to a frothy eruption until the meat had been ripped away from the bone. Even then the fish would propel themselves around the tub like torpedoes as if they were still hungry.

When he figured he had enough fish, he went to the main storeroom and looked at the portrait of Minerva's father.

Ever since his wife had demeaned him with her remark about his manhood, Walter had attempted to adapt more manly habits. One of these was the use of profanity, which to his mind seemed a trait he associated with manliness. He had not actually said any of the words in front of anyone, but it gave him some pleasure to say them aloud when he was alone.

"Good afternoon, Mr. Coleman," he said. "I'm damn sick and tired of running your damn store, and I'm sick and tired of you looking over my damn shoulder. I'm going to give you another perch."

He took the portrait from over his desk into the storeroom and, being careful not to slip in, he hung it on the wall on the other side of the bathtub. Aware of his nearness, the piranhas in the tub thrashed around in the water in a frenzy of hunger.

"Patience, *amigos*," he said. And then he went to the phone and called his wife.

"Walter," she snapped. "What do you want?"

"Come down to the store, Minerva," he said.

"I'm cleaning the house. Why would I come down there?"

"We could have lunch."

"Well, I'm not coming down there. Who would watch the store if you go to lunch? Have you lost your mind, Walter?"

"I sure wish you'd come down to the store, Minerva," he pleaded.

Minerva hung up the phone.

A few days later, Walter and Minerva were at the kitchen table finishing a silent dinner. Suddenly Walter blurted out, "Minerva, let's go down to the store."

"What on earth for?" she asked.

"I think I forgot to lock up."

"Walter, you've been acting funnier than usual lately. I read an article the other day about people getting odd at your age. Are you having hot flashes, night sweats, anything like that?"

"No," answered Walter. "Did the article say what to do with people like that?"

"I think it said to humor them."

"All right. Humor me and come down to the store while I lock up."

"You humor *me!*" Minerva said, "And go lock the store before somebody robs us blind!"

By day Walter fed his piranhas. By night he tried every scheme he could devise to persuade his wife to come down to the store. On their way home from church he invented an excuse to stop by the store, but Minerva insisted on waiting for him in the car. Nothing he tried could convince her to come in the store.

Finally he hit upon a plan he was certain would work. He spent a day cutting out headlines from the newspaper, selecting letters and arranging them on a sheet of paper until he had a message which read:

SOMETHING FISHY IS GOING ON AT YOUR HUSBAND'S STORE. I THOUGHT YOU SHOULD KNOW. A FRIEND.

He folded the message, placed it in an envelope, addressed it to his wife and mailed it.

Minerva came down to the store immediately after she opened the mail. She came without warning, and she had no sooner entered than she began suspiciously looking around.

"Minerva, what a nice surprise," Walter said from his desk where he pretended to be going over some paper work.

"I was shopping around the corner," she said, "and thought I'd drop by."

Just then she noticed the empty space above Walter's desk where her father's portrait had hung. "What have you done with Papa's portrait?" she demanded.

"I hung it out in the storeroom," he replied. "I got tired of him looking down at me all the time."

Walter remained at his desk. Minerva gave him a displeased look then went into the storeroom. After a moment she called, "What are you doing with these perch in the bathtub?"

"They aren't perch, dear," Walter replied.

"I don't care what they are." She called. "Did it ever occur to you that if people found out you were keeping a bathtub full of fish they'd come and lock you up? Come here!"

"Minerva, I'm busy with these accounts. I can't come right now."

"I want you here, now. You've got to help me take down Papa's portrait."

"All you have to do is lift it off the wall, dear," Walter said. "You have to lean over the tub."

"I'm already leaning. If I lean any further I'll fall in."

"Just try, dear," he said. "I'm sure you can do it."

And then from the other room came the sounds of screams and a great splashing of water. Then silence.

Walter was still sitting at his desk and smiling to himself when the phone rang.

"It's Pete, down at the store. That you, Mr. Farmingdale?"

"Hi Pete," Walter answered.

"That shipment of fish food you ordered just came in," Pete said. "You want to pick it up or you want me to deliver it?"

"No hurry, Pete," replied Walter. "They've just been fed."

About Earl Hamner

Earl Hamner is best known as the creator and producer of two Emmy Award-winning series, *The Waltons* and *Falcon Crest*.

He is also the producer of many other television series and specials, and has written for *The Guild on the Air, Wagon Train, The Twilight Zone, CBS Playhouse* as well as *The Today Show*.

His short stories have been published in *The Strand, Dark Discoveries, The Twilight Zone Anthology* edited by Carol Serling, and *The Bleeding Edge* and *The Devil's Coat Tail* from the publishers of Dark Discovery Magazine.

He is the author of eight best-selling books. His latest book, *Odette, a Goose of Toulouse* was inspired by his reaction to seeing a goose who seems destined to become pate, but who becomes an opera singer instead. The book is available at Amazon.com where one reviewer called it a "minor classic."

Earl Hamner is the recipient of The Lifetime Achievement Award in Literature from the Virginia State Library.

Earl Hamner and Jane, his wife of fifty-seven years, live in Studio City and Laguna Beach, California with a bossy pug named Peaches. Their son Scott, who lives in Vermont, is Co-head writer for the daytime series *The Young and the Restless*. Their daughter Caroline is a family therapist and lives with her husband in Laguna Beach, California.

THE PEOPLE EATERS
BY CHRISTIAN A. LARSEN

"*Por favor*, be careful, *señor*," said the dark-skinned clerk behind the counter, scanning the completed documents on the clipboard like it mattered. "The Auca of Peru, these people are *muy peligroso*—very dangerous."

Silas smiled and checked his watch. "Thanks for the warning. I've been with the Waodani a few of times already, though, and the Golden Rule has always done me right. Do unto others what you would have them do to you. The rest is up to God."

"These are not the Waodani of Ecuador, *señor*. You are going to Peru, to the land of *Los Comedores de Gente*."

"The People Eaters?"

"*Sí, señor*."

"I've heard the name." Silas shrugged. "And the truer it is, the more those people need to hear God's word."

"*Sí, señor*. Your plane is waiting."

The turboprop was already humming on the runway, and wind from the propellers flung itself so hard at Silas that he had to lean into it. The Andes, struck with snow, thrust themselves into the thin, blue Peruvian sky. Their route would take them over the mountain peaks and into the selva region of the country, the vast expanse of flat terrain carpeted by the Amazon rainforest where they would find the Waodani of Peru, a people isolated even from other indigenous tribes.

"What's wrong, Silas?" asked the pilot as Silas buckled himself into the co-pilot's seat.

"Oh, nothing, Bart," answered Silas. "Just another well-meaning local trying to protect us from our work."

"What was it this time?" shouted a voice from the backseat over the noise of the engine.

Silas couldn't see around his headrest to the other three men, but he'd known them by name for years: Ted, a former pastor from Colorado who felt called from the pulpit to do mission work; George, a retired businessman who exchanged jets to European business summits for flights to the bush to work with the natives; and Jim, a spiritual writer and speaker who jumped at the chance for a change in his life—at least if it meant changing the lives of others. The question had come from Jim.

"He told me to be careful, that the Peruvian Waodani were cannibals."

"That's ridiculous," said Ted, leaning forward in his seat. Silas could hear his gap-toothed smile even if he couldn't see it. "The Waodani in Ecuador believed that all outsiders were cannibals. To them, it's the worst insult you can make to call a person that. I can't imagine they would be any different in Peru."

"That's right," said George, packing his satellite phone into his backpack. "It's probably largely owing to that belief that they're so isolated, even in the 21st Century."

"Isolated? They're practically mythic," said Bart, revving the engine as the plane taxied down the runway. He pulled back on the yoke, the plane left the earth, and the mission—the first non-indigenous contact of any kind with the Waodani of Peru—was officially underway.

Silas felt blessed that he enjoyed flying, especially in such a small aircraft. To him, it felt like floating on God's breath, but going over the mountains could be pretty dicey, and it reminded him of the scene in "Indiana Jones and the Temple of Doom" when Indy, Willie and Short Round jumped out of the plane in an inflatable raft and somehow survived. Talk about a miracle. If that ever happened to them, they would be dead, dangerous natives or not.

Bart was a capable pilot, but Silas knew that Ted always white-knuckled these flights, and there had been many. Over the past few months, the five of them made regular flights to drop gifts such as rock salt, mirrors, ribbons, and various trinkets, hoping it would make the Waodani more receptive to their eventual landing. And this time out, they planned to finally set down on and set up camp on a sandy beach of an unnamed seasonal tributary of the Marañón River.

Day became evening instantly as they crossed eastward over the mountains, so there was not enough time to circle the Waodani village and address them in their own language, or at least the language of their Ecuadorian cousins. Bart took them directly to the beach and the plane bounced heavily on the sandy beach, jostling the men in their seats and knocking a few bags loose, but giving them a landing they could not just walk away from, but fly away from if things didn't go according to plan.

*****

Silas watched the sky brighten and swallowed a mouthful of coffee, despite its being too hot and filled with gritty grounds. He had no one to blame but himself, since he brewed the pot, but as an avowed night owl, he couldn't wait for it to cool. There was simply no telling when the Waodani would come to their camp, and he was hoping and praying that it would be soon. So was everybody else in camp.

Jim had about half a dozen notebooks filled with language notes, and one big blank one that he intended to fill with his witness to the Waodani, along with a digital recorder and a satellite phone in case something really breaking happened and he wanted to check in live with America's Word Network. George prepared the assortment of gifts so carefully and enticingly that it appeared to Silas like a game show prize row. The only thing missing was a mystery box. Ted was reading scripture and praying fervently, almost nervously. Bart fiddled perpetually with the plane, making sure everything was in working order.

Silas checked the guns. There were two of them, a pistol and a scope rifle. The five of them agreed that, despite the danger the Waodani posed, they would only fire to scare them off in the event of an actual attack. The only reason the guns had real bullets at all was in case a jaguar happened by. The guns were loaded, oiled, and ready to go. He checked them again, anyway.

"I think those are okay," said Bart, rolling the wheel of the wrench with his thumb.

"Just making sure," Silas answered.

"Yeah, sure has been made," Bart replied. "The hay is in the barn, as my grandpa used to say, and now we wait."

"Not for long," said Ted, shutting the book on his lap. "Listen. Here they come!"

Bart grabbed the CB and radioed the news to their base camp. "I'll make contact again in an hour," he told headquarters, "and tell you how it went!"

Two Waodani women waved to them from across the river and called out to the missionaries. They were a people used to pain. The women removed almost all their body hair by rubbing ash on their skin and plucking it out in bunches. It made them look decidedly Western, except for their bare breasts. Silas's puritan sensibility was always rocked when he saw the bare chests of native women. They were always so comfortable. He rarely was. This time, though, no one was quite comfortable, because their mouths were smiling, but their eyes were not.

Jim, a relative expert at Waodani compared to the others, couldn't make out what they were saying, despite having studied the language somewhat. It was like a Spanish-speaker trying to understand Italian, but those eyes couldn't hide the tension shackling the women. Silas kicked off his shoes and waded into the river, knowing that it was only waist-deep toward the middle. He held out his hands palm skyward to show his innocent intentions and smiled. "Peace be with you!"

"Dear God!" screamed George. "Bart!"

Silas whipped around in time to see Bart collapse face down in the sand with a spear in his back.

Blood bubbled into the sand like oil as Waodani warriors on the near shore stepped out of the undergrowth, ruddy-skinned with clay war paint in their hair and on their faces. They carried a spear in each hand, except for the one who had hit Bart—Bart, who was either dead or suffocating in the sand.

Jim started toward him to help, but a Waodani threw his spear, hitting him in the leg and bringing him down in a puff of sand. Jim writhed in pain and tried to crawl to his satellite phone, but it was too far. He would never reach it if the Waodani didn't want him to.

Unsnapping the holster on his hip, Silas drew the pistol. *How many Waodani are over there?* he wondered. It seemed like five. Maybe seven.

He couldn't remember how many shots he had, and didn't think he could hit them from this distance. He fired into the jungle to scare them away, like they had all planned back in Lima. Birds scattered skyward, but the Waodani advanced relentlessly.

How many shots do I have left? Silas wondered, just before a dart hit him in the arm. He fell into the river, ready to meet his maker, and then everything went black.

*****

Silas woke up with a burning, biting pain in his wrists and ankles, and his shoulders felt like they were dislocated. He had the sensation of floating in the Marañón River, but he wasn't wet, except for the tears of pain streaming down his cheeks. He tried to bring his hands to his face but the attempt made the pain in his shoulder flare unbearably as he swung from side to side, his wrists and ankles tied to a pole like a wild pig. He ground his teeth and blinked his eyes, trying to remember the Waodani words for 'help' or 'please,' but he couldn't.

"What happened?" he groaned. "Who else is here?"

"Silas." That was Ted. "I was praying you weren't dead."

"Where's Bart? Jim? George?"

"I'm here," answered George. "But I'm in pretty much the same shape as you are."

"I'm here, too," Jim added. "I don't know for how much longer, though. I'm really scared. I feel kind of light headed. I'm bleeding pretty bad, but Bart…I think they killed him outright."

"Do we know where they're taking us?" asked Silas, clenching his teeth to try to bear the pain. "What they plan to do with us?"

"I don't know," answered George. "This is nothing like Operation Auca in the 1950s. Those missionaries were killed and left to rot. But Ted thinks they're bringing us back to their village for some kind of ceremonial feast."

"Is that right, Ted?"

"How should I know?" he asked. "I can barely speak Ecuadorian Waodani much less the Peruvian kind."

Silas felt a corkscrew of despair bury itself into his belly and started praying a visceral prayer. George joined him, peppering the impromptu appeals with 'Amens' and 'Yea, Gods' and it gave him some small measure of courage against whatever was coming.

Silas suddenly noticed that Jim hadn't joined in. "Jim?" No answer.

Through the branches, Silas could see a column of black smoke which made the bush smell like aviation fuel. That would be their plane. And burning with it was their radio. People knew where they were, important people with deep pockets, but no one would be coming for them until it was much too late. Silas's despair deepened, and his whispered prayers fluttered out of his mouth to die in the Peruvian jungle. But God had to have heard them, didn't he?

Jim hadn't said anything for a while. Silas stopped praying and craned his head. His friend was ashen—the only color on his body was the deep red blood stain on his thigh. He hung from the pole limply, like a dead animal. Silas had never seen a person like that before.

A few minutes later, a Waodani warrior stepped forward, cut the pole free from the body and let Jim, Silas's friend for the last seven years, roll into the undergrowth. Then the warrior stepped away, as though nothing abnormal had occurred.

"Maybe that was an accident, about Jim," said Silas hopefully. "Maybe they don't want you or me dead, or else we would be dead already."

"They don't want us dead yet," corrected George. "What do you think they plan to do with us when we get to their village? Rehabilitate us in a corrections facility? They're cannibals, *Los Comedores de Gente*, and they want us alive. For freshness."

"Oh, God, let it be quick," moaned Silas. Time seemed to be slowing down, so that even when he rocked back and forth on the pole, it seemed like he was underwater. The pain was blinding, excruciating. He couldn't stop thinking about the American businessman who was beheaded by Al-Qaeda terrorists in retribution for the mistreatment of Iraqi prisoners by the U.S. military. His head was sawed off with a hunting knife while he screamed. Would that happen to him? The forest was preternaturally quiet, but Silas couldn't get that screaming out of his ears. High-pitched, like a pig being slaughtered. Like a pig strapped to a pole. Like them.

Whether it was from nauseating fear or the poison from the dart working its way through his system for a second time, Silas grayed out, like a fever-formed doze, and he dreamed of being eaten alive, his own screaming the most terrible part of it all.

When he woke up again, he was sitting on the jungle floor, his hands still bound, but his feet were loose, and feeling much better. Even pain was better than nothing. Several Waodani warriors stood between him and George to keep them from escaping, but they didn't seem to mind that George and Ted were talking. In fact, they didn't seem to notice any more than a poultry farmer would notice turkey gobbles while he was sharpening his axe. But Silas found what his companions were saying was very interesting.

"If they're vegetarians, what do they want with us?" asked George.

"I don't know, but I'm pretty sure that's what they're saying. I remember Jim's notes," explained Ted. "And it all fits, in a weird sort of way. Do you see any bones?"

Ted noticed Silas looking at them and said, "I don't think they're going to eat us."

"I prayed that they wouldn't," Silas said with a dry throat, "and the Lord listens. But what else would they want with us? They're an isolated group that doesn't even get along with the nearby Quechua. They want to be left alone. I see that now. Why didn't they just kill us back at the plane? How does bringing us here fit with what they want at all?"

Before anyone could answer, two warriors hauled them to their feet, and Silas felt courage hit him like a thunderbolt from on high. Or maybe it was a thunderbolt of yellow cowardice, because he took off running, leaving his friends behind.

Silas ran in a panicked, chicken-from-a-fox kind of way, unable to steady himself with his arms because they were still tied behind his back. His heart in his mouth, he crossed through the center of their village and toward the outer edge before he heard them shouting. He didn't understand the words, but he knew they had a lazy, suburban feel to them, like they weren't particularly concerned that a prisoner was getting away.

"The Lord is my shepherd!" shouted Silas in-between gasps for air.

A Waodani child, naked and dirty, watched him run past with a grin so wide Silas could count his milk teeth. The child's eyes were curious, but otherwise blank. There was no pity in them. No fear. Just curiosity, with a hint of anticipation.

Silas continued screaming: "He makes me to lie down in green pastures! He leads me beside still waters!"

He was out of the village. The people were all behind him now, giving chase, no doubt, but freedom was ahead if he could just keep at it. Thoughts of how he would stay alive, even if he could escape the Waodani were vague and malformed, shushed and hidden from his conscious thoughts, while the breath bellowed in and out of him, deep and quick but even, like the quarter note strokes of a double-bass bow.

Do you even know the way back to the plane? How will anyone find you, even if you do?"My church will send a search party," said Silas. "They will."

You're more valuable as a martyr than a missionary.

Silas was running slower now, his heart pounding; his chest heaving. He panted, "He makes me to lie down in green pastures, he leads me beside the still waters. He restores my soul."

You could be running in circles for all you know.

The jungle looked thinner now; the ground was giving way to a hollow. That inner voice was wrong. Dead wrong. He had not been running in circles.

He was heading into a coulee. He could smell the water at the bottom, a fertile, almost marshy smell. "Yea, though I walk through the valley of the shadow of death—"

Silas saw the first Waodani as he was passing him. When he passed another, his stride broke and he faltered, looking for a new course to run, but the ground was clear on the slopes. There was an oasis of strange-looking trees in the middle of the bowl, but he couldn't hide there for long before he was surrounded.

Those aren't trees, Silas.

That voice of doubt wasn't lying. They were more like giant flowers. Each of the thick, wooden stalks ended in a clam-shaped leaf with jagged edges. One of the leaves opened, drooling out enzymes and detritus like a slavering dog. The insides of the leaves were pink and studded with tiny hairs, like the crotch of a woman with a slit down the middle, and that's when he realized why people called them 'Venus Flytraps.' It's also when he realized what the Waodani wanted with them, but only if they were alive.

The detritus that had fallen out of the prickled, hairy leaf was the undigested bones of a human being.

These weren't flytraps. These were people-traps. These were the people-eaters about which he had been warned. Silas had run straight into their nursery. Straight to where they wanted him in the first place.

"I will fear no evil," he said, feeling many hands clamping down on him. He had no more fight left in him. His legs felt like ribbons, and he had nowhere to run even if he could. "For you are with me; your rod and your staff they comfort me. You prepare a table before me in the presence of my enemies—"

The table was prepared, all right. In the presence of his enemies.

Hands lifted him up and carried him toward the oasis in the center of the coulee. The people-eaters couldn't see him, but they seemed to sense food coming, and the leaves opened wider, glistening with the dew that would digest him.

"You anoint my head with oil, my cup runs over," he said, wondering how much longer it would be before George and Ted would be feeling the same kind of resignation that he was. He envied Bart for his quick death, and even Jim didn't suffer like the rest of them would. He had signed on for suffering, though. He just didn't know what kind.

The hands lifted him, an offering to the people-eaters.

As the leaves closed in on him with their burning venom and their suffocating weight, Silas gathered the last of his breath and shouted: "Surely goodness and mercy shall follow me all the days of my life. And I will dwell in the house of the Lord forever!"

About Christian A. Larsen

Christian grew up in Park Ridge, Illinois and graduated from Maine South High School in 1993. He has worked as an English teacher, radio personality, newspaper reporter, and a printer's devil.

His short stories have appeared in *Chiral Mad* (Written Backwards), and *A Feast of Frights* (The Horror Zine Books) and *Fortune: Lost and Found* (Omnium Gatherum). His debut novel, *Losing Touch* (Post Mortem Press) features a foreword by *NY Times* bestselling author Piers Anthony.

He lives with his wife and two sons in the fictional town of Northport, Illinois. Follow him on Twitter @exlibrislarsen or visit exlibrislarsen.com for more information.

101 Damnations

by Carl Barker

Down at the far corner of the graveyard, dead people spoke to Jackson and he was trying his best not to listen.

He stood beneath a solitary lament of willows at the bottom of the graveyard, staring down at the morose epitaph and hoping that its sentiment still held true. The headstone was an understated thing, a tiny inconsequential chunk of rock positioned at the very end of a long row of larger grave markers like a funereal, full stop. Calvers, Foster, Nash and Kelso. Their voices slid from the earth like mist to envelop him, spiking his head with barbed opinions and sapping his resolve with their words.

"You're not real," he muttered, raising both hands to his ears in an effort to block out their words. "You're just in my head. Go away."

But the whispers persisted like angry faeries, telling Jackson over and over that anything in this world could be made real if you believed in it enough.

He looked up, peering across the barren wilderness of fields which lay beyond the cemetery's boundaries. The emptiness called to him, as it had done to those in the ground beneath him, and he steeled his mind to rigidity, struggling from the dark's embrace.

Behind him, a pair of amber suns smoldered angrily in the sky like meteors, setting beyond a tiny cluster of buildings already huddled fearfully together upon the land. The town had borne many names, depending on who was thinking about it at any one particular time, but since the others had gone, it had simply become 'Despondence' and diminished in size with every passing day.

Of late, there was often only one sun in the sky come dusk—a sign that Jackson's mental grip on that which he continually created was beginning to falter—but if he concentrated hard enough, he could still raise a second star to meet the first, for now at least.

How much longer, he wondered, *will I be able to keep this knotted and fraying ball of string theories real? How can I create an existence by force of will alone?*

Jackson shivered at the prospect of Cartesian oblivion and an icy wind gusted through the headstones in response to his apprehension, bringing with it a freshly abraded layer of topsoil that stung his eyes. He thrust his hands wearily into the worn pockets of a favorite overcoat and began to trudge back toward town. The voices of the dead screamed angrily for a moment before falling abruptly silent.

He reminded himself that the cold itself was a product of his subconscious mind, as was the clothing, and he chose to ignore the biting chill, concentrating solely on the concept of daylight. It wasn't wise to remain outside here after dark. His imagination would start to play trick or treat games on him, with his flesh as forfeit if he lost.

The narrow path that led from the graveyard through a narrow copse of trees into town had chosen to become overgrown that afternoon. Jackson tried repeatedly to empty his mind of confusion as he walked, but tumultuous thorn-covered vines erupted from the dirt on either side of the path and covered the ground in a thick mesh of living vegetation, mirroring his thoughts. The weeds snapped viciously at him as he walked by, snagging repeatedly on his boot-heels.

There was something he had been trying to remember, back there at the graveside, before the mindless wind had torn it from him. Something important that he needed if he was to survive another day.

But it was gone, swallowed into the literal abyss of disregard which surrounded the town on all sides and drew a little closer every day. Oblivion, it seemed, was the self-fulfilling elephant in the room. Given time, it would slowly reduce his sense of identity to an indivisible unit and scramble his tightly coiled psyche.

Up ahead, the twisting maze of vines parted briefly to reveal a sorry-looking post, freshly erupted from the soil. The dust-laden sign appeared faintly green beneath layers of crusted mud and filth:

DESPONDENCE
POPULATION: ~~87~~ ~~95~~ ~~100~~ 101

Jackson stared at the sign, taking in the most recent addition with an exhausted lack of alarm. The final number had been daubed erratically across the board between deep uneven claw marks gouged into the metal surface. He felt bile climb into his throat as he looked at it, disgusted by his inability to halt the steady immigration of nightmares into this hateful reality. Self-Loathing would finally be paying him a visit tonight, having moseyed on into town for a showdown.

Rounding the final bend in the path, Jackson discovered, without surprise, that the main street had already remolded itself into the layout of a deserted Wild West frontier town. Paint-flecked saloon doors hung restlessly on hinges and a barbed wire ball of tumbleweed staggered abruptly across his path like the town drunk.

He chose the saloon, and reached for the swinging double-door entrance. Pushing open the creaking batwings, he found Doubt standing behind the bar, carefully polishing tumblers with a look of intense concentration upon its face.

"Usual tipple, is it Jackson?" The voice was high-pitched and reedy, oozing from the tiny round aperture which passed for the creature's mouth like wet smoke.

Jackson slouched wearily onto the nearest stool and reached out his hand in resigned defeat. Doubt obliged with a shot of red-eye and grinned triumphantly as its customer downed the glass in one swallow.

"You know you'll go blind if you keep on knocking back the strong stuff like that."

"At least then I won't have to look at your miserable face anymore," Jackson answered without looking up.

Doubt rested its razor-sharp elbows on the bar and gazed wickedly at the town's one remaining flesh and blood inhabitant. "Maybe so, but you'll still have to listen to me just the same."

"Go away," Jackson muttered, reaching for the still full bottle beside his glass.

"Oh come on, now," Doubt said with a touch of malevolence. "Don't you know a barman is his customer's best friend?"

Jackson gulped down a second burning shot of whiskey and buried his head in his hands, massaging both temples slowly. "You're nobody's friend."

"Exactly," giggled Doubt with a gleam in its yellow eyes. "And that's exactly what you are, Jackson. Nobody."

The bottle slammed down hard on the bar top, rattling glasses and spilling whiskey across the woodwork. Jackson grunted in fury, grabbing Doubt by the throat and squeezing till he felt oily flesh squirm beneath his fingers.

And then he gave up, knowing full well how hopeless such physical reactions were. Beside him, a silky gloved hand slid across his thighs and delved down into the warm space between.

"Oh come on, baby," whispered Distraction, appearing at his side and softly flicking his earlobe with its tongue. "Don't you wanna come upstairs for a while and have some fun with me?"

Jackson turned to glower at this latest apparition, swallowing hard on the unwitting stone of desire which rose from his loins.

"You're not real," he said, reaching for the bottle once again. "Neither of you are."

Distraction smiled coquettishly at him and batted its long eyelashes suggestively. "I'm as real as you want me to be, sugar."

The label on the whiskey bottle read Anguish and Jackson gulped down two more glasses through a grimace, barely tasting a drop.

"You can't help but see us every single day of your life," Doubt said. "And you do know why that is, don't you?"

Jackson tried not to rise to it, already feeling the conversation spiraling away from him, but he couldn't help himself. "Why?"

"Because you despise yourself," Doubt said. "That means you don't trust yourself. Which gives us an opening."

Jackson felt his mind curling into a protective ball and receded from the conversation. That hand caressed his thigh again and he looked up to find Distraction's hyena face staring back at him from atop the whore's voluptuous body.

"He's right, you know," it giggled, squeezing his leg with its talons. "You're nothing but a deadbeat and come sundown you'll be nothing but a memory in this town."

Something reared itself in Jackson's head at this. A remnant shred of anger still clung stubbornly to his failing sense of identity. He stood up suddenly, sending the bar stool spiraling across the floor.

"Fuck you!" he screamed as Rage manifested itself in a leather holster on his hip. Drawing it, Jackson watched Distraction evaporate before he turned to aim the barrel squarely at the bartender and squeezed the trigger. Doubt's body exploded into a mass of squirming tentacles that leaped on the wall. Skittering vertically upwards into the ceiling, it left a dark foul-smelling stain which bubbled and burned the wallpaper.

Stabbing the smoking pistol back into its holster, Jackson picked up the bottle and hurled it against the mirror behind the bar, shattering both sets of glass into a thousand pieces.

"I do not hate myself!" he roared at the empty room, shoulders shaking.

"The new gun in town says otherwise," gibbered the thing in the ceiling as it crawled out of sight into the shadows, making a sound like dead leaves as it moved.

Jackson sank back onto the nearest upright stool, feeling hopelessness still tug at his heartstrings. He wished Kelso was still here, with her unflappable brand of logic. She'd know exactly what to say. She'd remind him that this place was simply a hologram-generated alien funhouse, constructed from the base pathways of his emotional make-up and focused into hard-light existence by a web of geostationary low-level satellites encircling the planet. She'd tell him that nothing here could hurt or endanger him in any way, unless he let it.

That was the trouble though, wasn't it? The real rub of the matter, which the five of them had realized far too late—that there was a hidden part of every person that was self-destructive.

It was an insignificant personality fraction that, though repressed, could still sprout multiple poisonous snakeheads given the right set of conditions and spread a terrible sickness through the core of a human soul. Jackson suddenly wanted to feel Kelso's arms around his waist more than anything in the world, and a great sob rocked through him at the realization.

The day Jackson found her broken body at the bottom of the ravine (her gold wedding band glinted in the sunlight as her Guilt glowered menacingly from the cliff tops) had been the beginning of the end. He had buried her in that godforsaken graveyard which added yet another inescapable, wretched voice to the others.

That was when his own demons had become bolder, slipping through the cracks in his confidence on the outskirts of existence and making their way stealthily into town. They first set up home in the drains and the sewers, living in afterthoughts and dark places. As Jackson continued to agonize over Kelso's death and whether his actions had ultimately been to blame, their number multiplied rapidly like bacteria, feeding on every morsel of emotional uncertainty he scattered on the ground, becoming emboldened by his imminent emotional collapse.

The first attacks were like *blitzkrieg*, rabid packs of hounds slavering through the streets at night, howling with glee and scratching at the shutters with their claws. Inside, his mind saw to it that there was always a bed for him to hide beneath and Jackson found himself curled beneath the bedsprings night after night; a twelve year old boy in a grown man's body, still afraid of things that go bump in the night.

The dogs were only the first to come. Later, as his vague insecurities solidified into something more substantial, he heard heavy footfalls on the ground at night. Something huge and rancid began to stalk the streets, its fetid odor unmistakable in the dark. Jackson was afraid to peek out and see what his Fear actually looked like, and that fact only made it grow larger, until the very buildings shook with its passing.

He started talking to himself about a week after he buried Kelso, just a few words of prayer at first, enough to kill the unbearable silence. That had been a mistake. Once his voice began to tremble, the manifestations had gotten inside. Materializing in the corners of the rooms, they had said nothing to begin with, only eyeing him with calculating glee. Then as his soul grew weary, they found voices and began to berate him each day.

He'd counted a dozen different demons, ranging from the short and stocky shape of Remorse, to the thing that crawled beneath the floorboards and called itself Disgust. Doubt was the worst of them, though, catching Jackson unaware whenever he felt like he was beginning to cope. It would take the form of glass and perch itself about the place, hidden from sight unless you happened to be looking at it from exactly the right angle. Its sharpened tongue had cut his resolve to ribbons, leaving him haggard and defenseless against the other creatures' attacks.

How can I fight myself? he wondered. *How can I possibly triumph against those foes who know me better than I know myself?*

The clock tower outside began to chime the hour and before Jackson could stop himself, it became midnight. Darkness flooded through the town like a wave and, cursing his lack of discipline, he shakily poured another red eye and listened to the howls of the dogs outside. A crowd was gathering and raised voices beckoned him out into the street to face them. The more he fought to ignore it, the louder the whoops and catcalls became, and by the time Jackson finally stumbled to his feet and staggered to the door, the noise was deafening.

His first footfall in the dust outside brought silence to the mob. Dog and beast, foul or fair, they all turned to look as Jackson limped wearily into the center of the street and turned to face the assembled mass of his nightmares. They were all here, he saw. Every negative thought and lapse in concentration he had ever committed; collected here to view the culmination of his downfall.

Jackson scanned the crowd for friends but found none. Courage was long gone, so was Belief, burnt to death in a slow-burning fire set by the children of Anxiety. Pride, too, had mysteriously fallen down the stairs one day and broke its neck, while Desire had simply become too corrupted to be reliable anymore; too many nights spent rutting in filthy squalor with that whore Distraction, Lust looking on.

"So you've decided to show up then?" Jackson's Subconscious called mockingly from the other end of the street. "We were all beginning to think that you didn't have it in you."

The crowd erupted into laughter at this remark, a hideous mix of piercing shrieks and animal grunting which poured over Jackson like a stampede and brought an involuntary whimper from deep in his throat. The revolver at his side was already gone, lost to Embarrassment and Mistrust. Left unarmed and vulnerable, he stared up at the colossal monster before him and trembled.

Reading his mind, Guilt called, "Oh, it's no good thinking of Kelso, since you're the one who killed her."

Self-Loathing added, "We all know she only went with you because you were the last man alive. She couldn't possibly love a pathetic little parasite like you. I mean, why would she?"

The image of Kelso in his head became twisted by the demons' words, her sweet face contorting into an elongated grimace, fingers pointing accusingly at him as she began to wail like a banshee. The voices of the crowd rose to meet it, and Jackson opened his mouth in a silent scream, falling on his knees in the dust. His diminished resolve created a vacuum and the demons surged gleefully forward; the whole town becoming instantly smaller as it contracted around the shriveled kernel of his self-belief.

Jackson looked up to find Self-Loathing now only a few feet away, black smoke belching from the glowering sockets of its eyes. Many of the crowd now bore weapons, cudgels and batons, some with steel nails and jagged implements protruding from the tips, eager to have their fun.

"Not yet," Hatred crooned. "We haven't yet finished our sport."

Jackson's eyes narrowed into slits and he gazed at Hatred, uncontrolled anger seething beneath the surface of his skin. Climbing to his feet with a roar, his hand went instinctively to his side for the pistol that rematerialized there.

But suddenly Self-Loathing dragged one mammoth six-shooter from the holster at its side and hauled back on the enormous trigger.

Two bullets tore through Jackson's left leg, blowing away the majority of his kneecap and sending him pirouetting onto the ground. He clutched the shattered bones of his leg and stared up into the black abyss of the barrel now aimed at his head.

Jackson wrapped both palms round the flesh of his leg in an attempt to hold it together. Blood spurted from the wound, oozing down into the dust and covering the exposed skin with a warm sticky blanket of red. He stared at the blood in disbelief.

He could feel the collected breath of his demons, panting spittle down on him as they crowded around their supper, hungrily licking their lips. The warmth of the blood was spreading, rising up through his legs and into the rest of his body. It felt strangely pleasant and he smiled weakly, the action producing a sensation which stirred something in his head.

And suddenly he remembered what had evaded him before. The thought returned, the one wrenched away by the wind in the graveyard.

It came to him now as he stared down at his blood-soaked hands and watched his own blood pouring out onto the ground. His blood covered everything, drowning the dust and the earth, until the only thing that existed was him.

Subconscious stiffened slightly and then frowned in confusion, scuttling backwards. Raising his blood-soaked hands, Jackson held them out in curiosity to his captors and watched in fascination as they stepped warily back from him.

"I," he said quietly, watching in amazement as Self-Loathing noticeably flinched. The smaller creatures quickly moved to stand behind it, cowering behind its massive body and peering out at him between its legs.

"I," Jackson repeated, more firmly this time, suddenly finding he had the strength to clamber to his feet. The mob of creatures seemed to grow smaller, shrinking both in stature and confidence as he hobbled towards them with palms outstretched. The sight of his blood seemed to scare them, a symbol of his id, which blazed fresh confidence into Jackson's broken body.

Self-Loathing tried again. "You cannot deny that you still hate yourself, Captain William Jackson."

"Of course I still hate myself. I always will for what I have let happen here. But I'm not going to let the mistakes of my past destroy what remains of my soul."

Self-Loathing opened its mouth to scream but the rest of its head had already dissociated, the space created by the movement swelling outwards until nothing remained of the whole but an outline, which fell lifeless to the ground.

Jackson took a deep breath and carefully focused his growing confidence into something inwardly corporeal. Glancing down, he noted with satisfaction that his leg had healed itself. Another intense burst of concentration and the cowering mob vanished from his sight, taking the rest of the town with them as they went.

"No more," murmured Jackson as he turned to find the crashed remains of his spacecraft waiting for him in the dust.

The graves remained: four identically filled holes in the dirt, lying parallel to the crippled wing of the ship. He wished they'd been stronger in the end. Especially Kelso. It hadn't been his fault that she died; it had been the collective decision of the crew to land here.

Moving to stand beside his departed crew, Jackson planted his hands determinedly on his hips and stared, business-like, up at the craft's deformed wing. The idea of self-repair was forming in his mind.

"Now, time to imagine a way off this planet," he said softly, as the ship began to put itself back together again.

About Carl Barker

Carl Barker is currently living in hiding in a small village on the Scottish Border, where he hopes that the ramshackle personifications of his own personal demons won't be able to find him. He'd tell you exactly where, but then of course he'd have to kill you.

His fiction has previously appeared in magazines such as *Midnight Street*, *Dark Horizons* and *Title Goes Here*, as well as various anthologies over the last few years.

For more information about Carl and his work, please visit www.holeinthepage.co.uk.

THE TIN HOUSE
BY SIMON CLARK

The young detective looked out of the window. The killing happened right there in front of him. He watched the stoat chase the rabbit across the meadow—the gold-colored predator appeared tiny in comparison to what seemed almost a behemoth of a rabbit. The stoat ran alongside its fleeing prey before burying its teeth into the rabbit's neck. From here, in the Chief's office, the young detective heard the agonized scream of the rabbit as it fell to the ground kicking and dying.

The Chief studied a computer screen so Mark Newton had ample time to consider this undeniable fact: life and death battles are constantly being fought just a few yards away from us: whether it's the stoat slaying the rabbit, or a neighbor struggling with terminal illness, or entire armies of bacteria waging war beneath a single fingernail. *Life vs. Death. Forever and ever, amen.*

After closing the computer file, the Chief took a swallow of coffee, and said, "The Tin House. Heard of it?"

"It's before my time with this squad, but I remember it from the news. The owner of the Tin House went missing." *Too light on detail,* Mark warned himself; he still wanted to impress his new boss, so he dug deeper into his memory. "A man in his seventies by the name of Lord Alfred Kirkwood lived alone at the house. His neighbour found the lights out, a rear door open, and a bowl of tomato soup on the kitchen table. It was still warm."

"You'll go far," grunted the Chief, "or you'll go insane. There's only so many details of a case that a policeman should memorize, you know? Particularly if it's not their case."

"It's an old habit from when I was a boy. I loved mysteries. Probably even quite a bit obsessed by them."

"Well, you better not admit to your colleagues that you have obsessions; they'll get the wrong idea entirely."

"Yes sir."

"Anyway, back to business. The Tin House case is unsolved. Lord Kirkwood never turned up, either dead or alive. Seeing as six months have gone by since he vanished I'm putting the case into deepfreeze. When there's a legal presumption of death Kirkwood's nephew will inherit everything. What I want you to do is take these keys—one will open up the Tin House—I want you to photograph every room. And I mean every room, no matter how small."

Mark frowned. "Surely we've a detailed photographic record of the house already?"

"We have—from six months ago, but it's a requirement of the police authority's insurance company that we photograph houses, cars, livestock, every blessed thing that we hand back to owners, just in case the owner decides we've damaged their property in some way and hits us with a compensation claim: believe me, it happens. Once you've done that, give the keys to Kirkwood's nephew. Jeremy Kirkwood is meeting you at the house."

Mark had a suggestion. "I could show the nephew that the house is in good order. After all, don't we trust him?"

"No. We do not." The Chief spoke with feeling. "The Kirkwood family is famous for suing people." He shot Mark a telling look. "I also learned that the first Lord Kirkwood, back in the eighteenth century, made a fortune from the slave trade."

"Really?"

"Kirkwood shipped thousands of Africans to the Caribbean where he sold them to plantation owners. With the proceeds he bought twenty thousand acres of land near the coast and built a mansion."

As a new detective Mark was conscious that he should question his own superior, to prove he was listening—that and thinking analytically. "The Kirkwood trade in slaves must have been over two hundred years ago. That can't be relevant to a man going missing six months ago, surely?"

"Can you immediately assess what is relevant to a case?"

"It's ancient history."

"Ancient history or not, the Kirkwood family are, at this present time, still living on proceeds earned from selling slaves. All that capital generated from kidnapping African men, women and babies was invested here in Britain. The man you will meet..." He glanced at his watch. "...forty minutes from now enjoys a luxurious life-style as a result of one of the most barbaric commercial enterprises in the history of the human race. Okay, detective…time you went to the Tin House."

*****

The drive from town to the coast took thirty minutes. Mark Newton went alone. He remembered the route from childhood when his family spent two weeks here every August. The only thing markedly different from back then was the weather. Today, fine snowflakes tumbled from a November sky, and even though it was only mid-afternoon he drove with the headlights burning into a gloomy landscape.

As a child, Mark had loved his time at the coast; in his imagination, the vast sandy beaches became transformed into mysterious deserts that contained secret castles and hidden treasure. The real mystery occurred there when he was ten years old; his mother asked him to bring her glasses from a drawer. That's where he discovered a letter from his mother's sister. The letter clearly revealed that they'd had a major falling out, and the letter closed with a stark PS in capital letters: SO YOU'RE FINALLY GOING TO LEAVE *YOUR MARK* ON THE WORLD. He interpreted YOUR MARK as referring to him. The comment was clearly designed to hurt his mother. Though he loved solving mysteries, the ten year old Mark Newton decided not to delve into this particular one. He had a lurking sense of dread that some family disaster would happen if he ever discovered the truth behind that letter's bitter postscript.

Satnav efficiently directed him to the Tin House. The building stood on a narrow coastal road with its back to the beach and the sea. There were no other houses within half a mile—so the neighbor who discovered that Lord Kirkwood had vanished, leaving a still warm bowl of soup, must have happened by due to sheer good chance. With no sign of the Lord's nephew, Mark decided to start work immediately and photograph the building's interior as his superior had ordered. Photographs would prove that while under the protection of the police the property hadn't been burgled or vandalized, so no claims could be lodged by the next of kin.

After parking at the side of the road, which seemed to be one of those quiet, backwater ones, he headed up the drive. A plaque above the front door announced: THE TIN HOUSE.

"And, yes," he murmured, "the house is actually made of tin."

The two-story house had been clad in corrugated tin sheets, which were green in color. They even covered the roof. At some point after Kirkwood's disappearance the windows had been covered with mesh security screens. From the outside, anyway, the house looked in a perfectly good state.

As he tapped his knuckles on a tin wall, he imagined what the din would be like inside during a fierce hailstorm. Meanwhile, he breathed deeply, enjoying the tang of salt air. From the distance, came the forceful hiss of surf. He pictured himself on that very beach twenty years ago: an adventurous child with senses tuned for the next mystery that came his way.

"Hey you, get out of there; it's private property."

Mark saw a man striding through the drive gates. Aged about forty, he wore a bulky jacket in brown leather; he also wore an expression several degrees nearer anger than irritation.

"Mr. Kirkwood?" Mark asked pleasantly.

"Who are you?"

"I'm Detective Mark Newton. You are Mr. Jeremy Kirkwood?"

"Of course, I am. Who else would be hanging around this Godforsaken hole?"

"I'm here to photograph the house; then I'll give you back the keys."

"Photograph the house? Whatever for?"

Mark explained that taking photographs before handing over keys to next-of-kin was standard procedure.

"Police rules and regulations, eh?" snorted Kirkwood. "You'd think taxpayers' cash would be better spent on catching murderers."

Mark's professionalism dictated that he would neither like nor dislike the man, although he suspected Kirkwood's face probably always wore an expression of bad temper. This gentleman had been born with angry bones. For some reason, Kirkwood didn't approach Mark, and he remained near the driveway gates, hunching his shoulders against the cold.

The man shot Mark a sour look. "So this is it, you're closing the case on my uncle?"

"Lord Kirkwood is still listed as missing."

"But scaling things back, eh? Taking things easy on the investigation?"

The Chief had told Mark that the case would be going in the deepfreeze, seeing as investigations had reached a dead end; however, the case wouldn't be officially closed. After Mark Newton politely stated that the investigation would continue, he pulled the keys from his pocket and nodded in the direction of the front door.

"I'll take the photographs," Mark told him. "You might want to check inside for yourself."

"No, thank you." Jeremy Kirkwood spoke primly. "I'm staying out here."

"It's starting to snow again."

"If I go in there, I'll be sneezing all night." He scratched his throat as if he'd started to itch. "My family used that shack as a beach house. Whenever I stayed here I'd have a violent allergic reaction to the place: spores, or dust, or something. Wild horses wouldn't drag me in there."

"It'll probably take me about ten minutes."

"Go and take your ten minutes, then." The man visibly shuddered as he gazed up at the bedroom windows. "What a God-awful box it is. Being in there's like being in a tin coffin. The place scared me half to death when I was a boy. I'd lie in bed at night and hear the entire house squealing, tapping, clicking, moaning. That God-awful racket kept me awake for hours." He permitted his stone-hard features to soften into something near a smile. "I didn't realize back then that the sounds were caused by all those tin sheets contracting as they cooled after the heat of the day. Ergo: contraction of metal, not noisy ghosts." He briskly cleared his throat. "My sisters tried to convince me it was haunted. Nothing like siblings to tease one, eh? Especially at the witching hour."

"What made your uncle choose to live out here?"

"Pardon?"

"After all, he'd have been an extremely wealthy man, so what made him want to spend his time in a small beach house made from tin?"

"Well, detective, that's none of your business, is it?" Jeremy Kirkwood thrust his clenched fists into his jacket pockets. "Didn't you say ten minutes?"

*****

People often describe a haunted house as an Unquiet House. The Tin House wasn't the least bit quiet—though whether that suggested this quirky building was actually haunted wasn't, he decided, for him to judge one way or the other. As Mark Newton walked along the hallway toward the kitchen he heard a series of clicking sounds, together with squeaks, loud popping noises and the creak of timbers under pressure. Mark recalled Jeremy Kirkwood talking about the racket the tin cladding made during the night as it cooled.

"This is November," Mark told himself. "It's been cold all day. This can't be the metal contracting."

He rested his palm on the kitchen doorframe. The woodwork trembled as it might do if the house was hit by a storm. But outside was relatively still. Just a few snowflakes drifted by. This is a mystery. He loved mysteries—he'd love to spend time investigating the popping noises and the sharp tapping coming from upstairs, but he'd been ordered to take the photographs then hand the keys to Jeremy Kirkwood. Perhaps there were rats in the walls—however, rodent infestation wouldn't be a police matter.

Mark switched on the kitchen light. The place had been left tidy by the forensic team. Of course, the bowl of soup that the missing man had abandoned had gone, no doubt for fingerprint and DNA testing. He photographed the old fashioned stove, the Belfast sink, then moved onto the lounge. Again, tidied, vacuumed and untouched by man or rat. At least, untouched in the last six months anyway. After taking photographs of the 1950s era armchairs, he worked his way through the ground floor rooms. Meanwhile, the scratching, tip-tapping and popping continued. Dear God. Who'd live in a house made of tin?

Upstairs, he photographed tidy bedrooms and a trim bathroom. Mark had been ready to head back downstairs when he recalled the Chief's order, *'I want you to photograph every room. And I mean every room, no matter how small.'*

Mark checked the master bedroom. Straightaway, he realized he'd missed a narrow door in the corner. As he walked toward it he glanced out through a window that was covered by steel mesh. From up here he could see the dark expanse of ocean. While on the driveway stood Lord Kirkwood's nephew, and heir to his fortune. A man with a motive. Though no doubt the Chief's team would have scrutinized that angle already: *greedy, impatient nephew murdering rich uncle* would top the list of suspects. Jeremy Kirkwood had retreated to the driveway gates where he stood, glaring at the house. The man's expression was strange. He looked as if he expected the building to lunge forward and bite him. Kirkwood appeared decidedly scared of the Tin House.

Detective Mark Newton took a moment to scrutinize details of the master bedroom. Several framed photographs of Lord Alfred Kirkwood hung from the wall. The missing man clearly preferred to see photographs of himself when he woke in the morning. On a table beside the window was a hairbrush. Mark noticed long, white hairs sticking to the bristles. When he glanced back at photographs of the elderly Lord he saw the same white, shoulder-length hair. In his youth, the man must have been an aristocratic dandy.

Mark opened the narrow door in the bedroom to discover a small antechamber. Perhaps four feet by eight feet, the vestibule might have been used for storage, although now it was completely empty.

After taking the single photograph he'd have walked away, if it wasn't for a sudden, frantic clatter from the far end of the room, which formed part of an outside wall. There was a rapid, metallic popping, as if tiny, bone-hard fists rapped on the tin sheet at the far side. For some reason he felt compelled to rest his palm against that part of the wall. This was the only section to be covered in wallpaper; the paper itself had a furiously busy pattern of tiny red roses peeping out from green leaves.

The wall vibrated powerfully against his hand. A mystery all right; however, a mystery he wasn't ordered or paid to solve, and one hardly relevant to the case of the missing lord.

As he walked away, the metallic popping changed. The sound morphed from pell-mell clattering to a unified rhythm: whatever objects or vermin that attacked the metal cladding had now begun to strike it at the same time; pretty much in the same way a dozen different drummers in a percussion band would strike the same beat.

The door swung shut behind; immediately the room crashed to darkness. He could see nothing. The pounding on the wall intensified, growing louder as it did so. Maybe it was Kirkwood's claim that he was allergic to the house that caused the effect. But suddenly Mark's skin began to itch. His chest tightened and breathing in that dark, little chamber became difficult. Quickly, he tugged open the door. The light from the bedroom spilled in. He quickly strode back along the narrow room to where the sound seemed to emanate from the rose-covered wallpaper. He balled his fist and slammed it against the wall. The drumming sound irritated him. For a moment, he even told himself that the metallic popping coming from the other side made his skin itch. His fingernails scratched at his face, making the looser parts of the skin slide over the jawbone.

The clatter from the other side grew louder.

"Shut up."

He pounded the side of his fist against the wall again. If there were rats in there they'd get a nasty shock. But the rodents or whatever made the noise didn't scarper; instead the rapping grew louder. The sound goaded him. It demanded to know if Mark HAD LEFT *HIS MARK* ON THE WORLD.

Remembering that line in his aunt's letter twisted a nerve to the point he felt a blaze of fury. As the metallic drumbeat reached a crescendo, he stood back then delivered such a hell of a kick to the wall. His police training had taken over. He used that particular kick he'd practiced so often to kick down some drug peddler's front door. The loud drumming against the metalwork had stopped at least. Now he could hear nothing but his own heartbeat.

When he looked down he saw, to his surprise, that he'd managed to slam the toe of his shoe through not only the wallpaper with its blood red roses, but the plywood panel. Damn it. Now he'd have to photograph the damage he'd inflicted on the house. Cop turns vandal. Mark imagined the Chief's anger when Jeremy Kirkwood submitted the repair bill.

Mark crouched down before the hole he'd made—a gaping one at that, almost a foot wide. Outside, Jeremy Kirkwood must have clearly heard the crash, so no use in pretending this injury to the house had happened a long time ago. Duty and honesty dictated that Mark would report truthfully that he'd inflicted the damage.

The hole, large though it was, revealed nothing but shadow. No rats, no vermin of any kind. He raised the camera, centered the yawning black void on the screen, and took the picture. The brilliant flash dazzled him, however, a moment later his vision had returned to normal, and he could check that he'd accurately recorded the effects of his violence against the Tin House.

Mark studied the photograph on the camera's screen. A second later he scrambled to his feet and was running for the door. The image of what had been revealed behind the wall had fixed itself as firmly in his mind as it had been fixed into the camera's memory card. Mark Newton had not only photographed broken plywood, he'd also taken a photograph of a face. A human face.

*****

Snow was falling again. November gloom crept in from the ocean so that the house resembled a block of shadow.

Mark Newton hurtled outside through the front door. He raced past Jeremy Kirkwood at the driveway gates.

"Hey! What's wrong?" bellowed Kirkwood. "Hey! Answer me!"

Mark threw himself into the driver's seat, started the engine and slammed the car into reverse. Jeremy pounded on the car's roof as Mark hit the accelerator pedal.

The man yelled, "What are you running away from? What's in there?"

Mark glanced up at Kirkwood's stark, white face. There wasn't just anger in his eyes, there was dread, too. Mark felt a huge lightning bolt of fear, because he remembered seeing the photograph of the face he'd just taken—the face in the wall.

He punched the vehicle forwards across the road, through the driveway gates, and across the lawn. When the headlamps blazed fully on that forlorn building, he braked, leaped out, and a moment later he pulled a crowbar from the back of the car. Before Kirkwood had time to react, Mark Newton attacked the front of the house. He jammed the sharp end of the crowbar between where two sheets of tin cladding overlapped; once he'd done that, he began to lever them apart with a furious strength.

"Hey you!" Kirkwood actually screamed the words. "Hey! Leave that alone! Stop that!"

Mark put his foot against the wall to brace himself and heaved. Nails that fixed the tin cladding to the wooden frame began to snap with brittle-sounding bangs.

"Stop that!" Kirkwood bellowed from the end of the driveway, but he didn't come any closer. "What the hell do you think you're doing, you little bastard! Stop it, or I'll report you!"

"Who to? The police?"

A section of corrugated tin flapped loose. Mark gripped one side of it before ripping away an entire six by four sheet. That's when the car's powerful headlamps revealed the secret of the grim house.

"You're insane!" screamed Kirkwood.

"I'm not the one who's insane." Mark stared at what had been stretched tightly over the building's timber skeleton. "It's one of your damned ancestors that was insane. See! He went and covered the framework in skin...human skin...the skin of men, women and children."

"What!" Kirkwood gaped; his eyes bulged. "What did you say?"

"I kicked a hole in the wall upstairs. There's a face on the other side...at least, the skin from a face."

"You *are* insane."

"See for yourself."

This time the man did gingerly approach the house. He gazed at what had been illuminated by the car's lights.

Mark Newton gazed, too, with emotions that flashed from astonishment to absolute revulsion. There, nailed across the timbers, were the skins of human beings. They'd been scraped clean of meat, blood, hair and subcutaneous matter. Clearly, they'd be treated too; some form of hide tanning process had been applied.

The tightly stretched-out skins were dark red in color. Originally, the skins must have been black but the tanner's chemicals had reddened the flesh. Mark found himself thinking that the skins resembled sheets of red plastic. They were glossy, even wet looking. The headlights shone through them, casting a blood-red glow on the vertical plywood boards behind.

Both men stared in silence. The spectacle was horrific. It was distressing, too. The skins had been cut away from each body in a single piece. Each skin, or 'hide,' contained a face—a stretched-out face, like a leather mask. Eye sockets formed gaping holes. Lips had dried into hard circles. Nostrils, too.

One of the most noticeable and unsettling features were the fingernails; these were at the ends of strips of skin that had once covered fingers. Each fingernail was white—a gleaming, pearl white, as if it had somehow being carved from an oyster shell. Mark knew that was hardly a rational comparison. Right now, however, he found it hard to stay rational, or calm.

Jeremy Kirkwood repeatedly swallowed; he was close to vomiting. "Who are they?"

"Your ancestors traded in slaves. Your family still lives on slave money today."

"These are the skins of slaves? But…why do this?"

"In the past, books were sometimes bound in human skin. So why not a house bound in human skin?"

"No, you're lying!"

Mark spoke with cold certainty. "Picture this: Two hundred years ago, your ancestors kidnapped thousands of men, women and children from their homes in Africa. They were chained together, and they were transported in ships without adequate ventilation, food or clean water. Hundreds would have died on the way. Those that survived faced a harrowing life of forced labor until they died."

Kirkwood stared at the dried-out face of a young child. A split in the skin ran from the corner of its mouth to the distorted opening of an eye. "But why on earth would anyone cover a house in human skin?"

"Undoubtedly, your ancestors were superstitious. They were terrified that the ghosts of slaves would come looking for revenge. Superstitious people have been doing something like this to protect themselves from vengeful spirits for thousands of years. In some cultures they make shrunken heads from their victims, or even eat part of their bodies. In the case of your ancestors, they decided to adopt elements from voodoo cults and incorporate the skin from a number of slaves into the fabric of the house."

Despite his fear, Jeremy Kirkwood moved closer. "If they're stretched over the entire frame of the building, there must be dozens and dozens."

"And dozens of your ancestors must have been involved with this barbaric ritual."

"What do you mean?"

"Even after the abolition of slavery, your ancestors continued to be wealthy because of the money they made from selling human beings. They also continued to believe that the slaves could somehow come back from the dead and hurt them, so they made sure they still kept these talismans for protection."

"This house… I knew this house wasn't right…even as a child, I knew something was wrong…"

"Your uncle knew, too. That's why he rarely left what he believed to be the magic protection of this building. But he left in the end—"

At that moment, the wind started to blow from the sea. Mark thought he could hear those grim diaphragms made from tightly-stretched human skin softly hum as they began to vibrate. When the breeze quickened, the strips of finger skin fluttered. The white fingernails attached to the ends struck the tin sheets, making a popping and clicking sound. This is must have been what he'd heard earlier. Like tiny bone-hard fists hammering at the metal.

Jeremy Kirkwood gave a shriek. "Cover them up! Cover them!"

He seized the corrugated section of metal that Mark had pried off, and tried to push it back over those tremulous skins.

The fingernails tapped against that piece of tin as Kirkwood tried to shove it back into place. Instantly, the tapping became a furious clatter. In the glare of the headlights, Mark noticed filaments attached to one of those dead fingernails.

"Wait." He pushed Kirkwood away.

"I'll sue you! I'll sue the entire police force! You'll pay for this!"

After silencing the man with an angry glare, Mark turned his attention to the pearlescent fingernail. Between finger and thumb, he carefully removed the filament from the nail then held it in front of the headlamp. A single long, white hair. Straightaway, he remembered photographs in the master bedroom of Lord Alfred Kirkwood, the white-haired man who'd lived on the wealth generated by the slave trade. And Mark pictured the fine white hair still adhering to the hairbrush.

He fixed his eyes on the lord's nephew, who stood there panting, with the tin sheet in his hands. Mark held up the hair for him to see. "I'm certain a DNA test will prove this belonged to your uncle."

"How did it get stuck to one of those disgusting things?" He threw a frightened glance at the red material stretched tight over the woodwork. The distorted faces pulsated as the breeze played upon them. The lips tightened and slackened as if mouthing words. "And why did my uncle disappear?"

"Perhaps the magic doesn't work anymore. Occult protection doesn't last forever."

The skins billowed as the winds blew harder. Fingernails rapped louder on the walls of the Tin House.

Jeremy Kirkwood appeared to freeze, his muscles locked tight. "My God, I'm the next of kin. I inherit everything. All the slave money. They'll try and kill me, too!" His eyes blazed with terror. "You're a policeman, you've got to protect me. It's your job, you bastard!"

The man that Mark had judged to have been born with angry bones swung the six foot by four foot tin panel. It struck the side of the detective's face. That heavy piece of metal cut him down as if it were an axe. Its sharp edge sliced open his jaw, blood sprayed—an aerosol of crimson in the car's light.

He must have passed out for a moment, because when he opened his eyes he realized he lay on the lawn, looking up at both Jeremy Kirkwood and the front of the house.

The human skins were melting. That's what it looked like. Those skins that were almost the size of bed sheets slipped downward from the building's timber skeleton. Jeremy stared at what was happening. He appeared fixed there. Hypnotized.

The skins continued to slide downward. Mark saw something dripping down through the narrow gap between the tin cladding and the frame at the bottom of the wall. The dripping effect resembled dark treacle being poured from a jar. Thick and continuous. These were yet more leathery remains sliding down from behind the intact panels. He realized he should try and stop his wound from bleeding, only he found he couldn't move, either. He lay there on the grass propped up on one elbow. He watched the skins, and he realized they weren't melting after all, they were sloughing from the woodwork. Detaching themselves from the house. Breaking free.

The car's headlamps not only illuminated the dark red hides, but shone through them.

Mark could only compare those relics as something that resembled outstretched sheets on a washing line, except they moved into the wind. The mask-like faces at the top of the hides contained distorted holes where the eyes and mouths had once been. He caught sight of the whorl of navels in the centre of the hides. He saw the black discs that were the nipples.

When the detached skins reached the inheritor of the Kirkwood's bloody fortune they enclosed him. Sheets of human wrapping paper. They formed a parcel of Jeremy Kirkwood. His silhouette struggled inside for a while…but as time passed the struggles stopped…then even the silhouette was gone. Dissolved away. Dissipated. Broken down into slime and hair.

Detective Mark Newton managed to follow the paper-thin human remains that billowed and flapped across the dunes to the sea. He glimpsed peeled faces that formed part of those rippling sheets of skin. Although his senses still reeled after being struck by a section of the Tin House, he knew deep down that those skins that had once housed the bones of men, women and children were truly free. Now they were heading for the ocean. Mark Newton wondered if, given the right tides, favorable currents and enough time, the waters from which all life once emerged would finally carry its precious cargo back home.

About Simon Clark

Simon Clark has been writing full-time for almost twenty years and his novels have been published worldwide; these include *The Tower, Blood Crazy, Vengeance Child*, and the award-winning *The Night of the Triffids*.

His latest novel is *His Vampyrrhic Bride*, which draws on Norse mythology, and features a romance that threatens to be thwarted by a Viking curse and a dragon-like creature that prowls the forests of a remote quarter of England.

THE CELLAR
BY TIM JEFFREYS

"I heard something," Rose said, sitting up in the dark. "Peter, wake up. It's happening again."

Peter rolled over in bed, reached out, and turned on the bedside lamp. Blinking against the light, he put on his glasses and read the time from the clock on his night table. "It's half-past three in the morning."

"There was a noise. Outside, I think it was." Rose's voice had dropped to a whisper. She stared, wide-eyed, at her husband as they both fell silent and listened.

After a few moments, from somewhere below, there came the unmistakable sound of breaking glass. Rose uttered a small yelp and covered her mouth. Peter felt his heart pick up. Drawing back the duvet, he threw his legs over the side of the bed.

"Someone's trying to get in," he said, at the same time thinking: *Oh no. Not again!*

"It's that man!" Rose said. "I saw him again yesterday. He was standing by the gate looking up at the house. I stood in the window looking straight at him, holding the phone, pretending I was calling the police, and he went away."

"I wonder if it's starting again."

Before his wife could answer, the light went off, plunging them back into darkness. Even the digital clock on his night table had gone black. "Someone's cut the electrics."

Rose uttered another yelp. "What're they doing?" There was a note of hysteria in Rose's voice. "What've they done that for, Peter? No one ever did that before."

"It's all right," he said to calm her. "I'll go and see."

Feeling his way in the dark, he located his bureau and opened the bottom drawer where he kept a flashlight. Once he found it, he switched it on and turned it on Rose. She was sitting up in bed, clutching the duvet in her two hands, her face startled and afraid like some poor animal caught in the headlights of a car.

"Don't Peter," she said. "Don't go down there."

"I have to, Rose. You know I do. We can't call the police."

"Just be careful, okay? Just be careful. And don't let anyone—"

"It's all right. I'll be careful. We've been through this before, haven't we?"

Putting on his slippers, he opened the door and crept out into the hallway. He went first to the banister and looked over, shining the flashlight beam all the way down the stairs to check no one was coming up.

Perhaps it's only burglars, he thought. *Or some madman come to murder us in our bed.* But no, he told himself, he knew better than that.

Seeing nothing, he made his way downstairs. Though he tried to be quiet, the floorboards creaked and groaned under his every movement.

At the foot of the stairs, he found that the small window next to the front door and been smashed. Someone had knocked all the glass out of it, probably so they could climb through. Glancing out into the night, he saw only blackness. Turning, he shined the flashlight for a moment over the mess of broken glass littering the carpet.

He could hear his heart beating in his ears. *I should be used to this by now. I shouldn't be so afraid. I know the drill.* He turned towards the downstairs rooms.

The living room door was closed. He opened it and flashed his torch light about inside. Seeing nothing untoward, he closed the door again and turned to another further along the hall. He wondered why he had bothered looking in the living room. The intruder would be in the kitchen. They always went straight there. They always knew exactly where they were going, what they were looking for. Knowing this didn't make Peter feel calmer.

He started forwards then stopped, hearing a sound. It was a muffled bang. Another muffled bang followed and there was no mistaking it. *Who is it? Who are we dealing with this time?*

Could it be the man both he and Rose had seen on separate occasions hanging around the house recently? Peter had been the first to see him, one day when he was driving home from the market in the village. It had been raining and the man stood across from the house under the shelter of the trees. He had a hood covering most of his face, and he simply stood looking at the house until, seeing Peter's car, he turned and ran.

Whoever it was in there, Peter thought the only thing to do was to move quickly and surprise him. This he did, flashing his flashlight around the walls as though it were a weapon.

At first he saw nothing. Then he caught sight of something in the far corner of the room by the cellar door. A pair of legs. He raised the flashlight and pinned the man who was standing there looking back at him with it.

The two men only looked at each other for a long moment. Peter had time to register that the other man was large: tall and broad. He was dressed in what looked like army fatigues. He also wore a black hat and had what appeared to be smears on his face, like a soldier's camouflage. He was holding something in his hands, holding it towards the cellar door.

"I know why you've come here—" Peter began. Before he could finish, the intruder moved quickly forward and lunged at him, knocking him off his feet.

They rolled and wrestled for a few moments. The flashlight, having fallen out of Peter's hand, tumbled onto the kitchen tiles, its light skittering about all over the walls. The other man was strong, easily overpowering Peter, but because he thought of his wife alone and unguarded upstairs, he struggled on.

One of the man's hands had fastened around his neck, making it hard to breathe. A thought went through his head: *That's it. He's got me. I'm too old and too weak to fight him off.*

Then there was a dull thud and the stranger made a squawking sound and slumped forward over him. Peter, pushing him aside, rolled out from under and fought to find his feet. He was panting.

"Are you all right, Peter? Are you all right?"

The flashlight was turned away from him, but in the dim light he saw Rose. She was holding a hockey stick. She must have taken it from their daughter's room upstairs. Peter had been telling her for years to clear that room, but Rose wouldn't listen. *They're Danni's things*, she would say. *I'm not going to get rid of them.* And Peter would say: *Danielle doesn't need those things anymore, does she, Rose?*

And now look. The hockey stick had saved them.

Hearing a groan from the body on the floor, Peter glanced around, then said to Rose, "Go quick. Go to the switch box. You know where it is. Get the lights back on."

He saw the uncertainty in Rose's face, but she turned and left the kitchen. Then, stepping over the prone body, Peter retrieved the flashlight and began a hurried search of the kitchen drawers. He eventually came across some washing line cord. Using this, he tied the man's feet and hands just as the man started to come to life. He turned the body on its side and saw that the man was awake and watching him.

"You're...you're *monsters*," the man said, his voice gruff. "How can you do that to her?"

Peter paused a moment. *Her?*

"This is our home. You've no right to be here."

"I know you're not gonna call the cops."

Peter felt a jolt. He stared at the man's face.

The intruder smiled wanly. "I know your secret, old man."

"You know nothing about us."

Peter heard Rose enter the kitchen behind him. At once the room was stark with light. "I found the switches, Peter."

"Yes, Rose. I can see that."

"How can you do it?" the man on the floor said, becoming angry and struggling against his bindings. "How can you do that to your own *daughter?*"

Daughter? So that was it.

"Now, listen," Peter said. With some effort, he turned the man onto his back so he could look him in the face. The man was wearing army fatigues and he had camouflage smudges on his face. Peter guessed that he was in his mid-thirties.

"Where are you from?" Peter asked. "Did you come from the village? We've had people here from the village before, although we thought we were far enough away to..."

The man glanced away, struggled a moment against his bindings, then looked back at Peter. His expression had softened a little. He spoke matter-of-factly. "I'm not from the village. I'm not from anywhere around here. I'm with an army squadron doing training exercises in the woods. Every night, asleep in my tent, I've been dreaming about this house. Really vivid dreams. It's to the point where I can't rest. The dreams are so real."

Peter nodded.

Rose had moved closer behind him to look down at the man. In a small voice she asked, "What did you dream of?"

"Of a little girl locked in a cellar. Chained up like an animal. I don't know how but she reached out to me in my dreams; she called out to me. She began to show me things. The cellar. This house. *You*, her so-called parents."

"Look," Peter said to the man, "I'm going to talk honestly with you."

He motioned for Rose to help him lift the man so that he was sitting up against the cupboards, his bound hands resting in his lap, his legs stuck out in front of him.

"We did have a daughter," Peter began. "Her name was Danielle. But she died more than twenty years ago, just after we first moved to this house."

As he talked, Peter stood and walked over to the cellar door. On the floor he saw the crowbar the man had dropped before leaping at him when he entered the kitchen. On the edge of the cellar door, just above the keyhole, there were splintered notches.

"No," the man said. "I've seen her. I've seen her in my dreams. She's down there. Down in that cellar. She reached out to me. She called out to me for help."

Peter returned holding the crowbar and crouched down beside the man, looking into his face. He had not noticed before a thin trickle of blood running down the man's temple from his hairline.

"Yes, well," Peter said, "Danielle had dreams too."

"She dreamed about a baby crying!" Rose put in suddenly, her voice wild. "She said it was her little brother. She said he was in the cellar. We told her she didn't have a brother, but she said the dreams were so real."

Rose turned away, stifling a sob.

"I know the dreams must have seemed very real to you, too," Peter said calmly, looking the man in the face. "But believe me, you're wrong. Our daughter...she's dead."

"Let me go down in the cellar and have a look then," the man said.

"Oh, I can't do that, I'm afraid."

"Why not, if there's nothing to hide?"

"There's no point. There's nothing down there."

The man's face turned scarlet. "You're a liar!"

Suddenly Peter realized that the intruder had worked his hand free of the binds. He swung a punch at Peter that knocked him sideways.

Peter fell against the floor tiles, his head ringing from the blow. By the time he was able to lift himself, the man was also out of the binds on his feet and then he leaped up.

Peter saw the man grasp Rose from behind. He had plucked a large knife from the rack on the wall and he held it at Rose's throat. Rose's face was stricken, her eyes wide.

"Did you think those pathetic knots could hold a man of my training?" the man shouted at Peter. "Get the key, you old bastard, and get that cellar door open! We're getting that little girl out of there!"

Peter climbed groggily to his feet. He faced the man with his palms raised. "There's something I need to explain."

"Explain? Explain what? I've had enough of your lies."

Peter spoke quickly. "No, listen. We inherited this house from an uncle of Rose's. A strange old man, living up here all alone, keeping to himself. He had no wife or children. He left no will, but he wrote Rose a letter before he died saying he wanted the house to be burned when he was gone. We thought he'd lost his marbles. When he died, we decided to move here instead. We thought it'd be perfect, and we needed the space for Danni and—well, anyway—when we moved here the cellar was locked and we hadn't been given a key. Then Danielle starting having these funny dreams about a baby crying. One night she got up while we were asleep. She came down here. She must've found the key to the cellar, somewhere, somehow, or perhaps she was shown where it was in…"

"What the hell are you talking about?" the man cried. "What are you saying?"

"There's no little girl down there. Our daughter's dead. We thought she'd run away, then over time, after other people came here, people who'd had dreams, we put two and two together—"

"That's it!" the man shouted. "Shut up! No more stories! Just get the key and open that door over there!"

"You're not listening to me. What's down there is not our daughter. There's something down there that calls out to people. It gets into their dreams. It lures them. And when they come, it—"

"Shut up!"

"—it feeds on them. Do you hear me? It *feeds*."

Rose gave a loud sob. The man was still holding the knife at her neck. "I said shut up!"

Peter realized he was losing time. The man was not listening to him. No one that came here ever did. The dreams had cast such a spell over them.

He kept on spilling out words, hoping that something would catch in the man's mind to convince him that he was wrong. "The thing down there. We've never seen it. We think it hides in the daytime, sleeps, somehow. Rose's uncle had been keeping watch over it all his life. Now we have to do it. Sometimes I wish we'd just burned the house like he wanted, but we were afraid."

"Stop it!"

Peter ignored the man's protest. "Now and then, people come. Lured here, trying to get in the cellar. One of them had dreamed that his missing wife was being held prisoner down there, another dreamed of—"

"Listen!" said the man through gritted teeth. "If you don't shut your mouth and get that cellar door open, I'm going to slit your wife's throat. So just stop talking and do what I say!"

Peter was silent, looking into the man's face for a long moment. Finally he asked, "If you thought we'd locked our daughter in the cellar, why didn't you go to the police?"

The intruder said, "And tell them what? That I saw it all in a dream?"

"So you thought you'd be a hero and come here alone instead?"

"You've got ten seconds, mister. One…two…"

Peter waved his hands. "All right. All right. But the key's upstairs in our bedroom."

"Go then," the man said. "And don't try any funny business. Don't bother trying to call anyone either. You old people always have landlines, never cell phones. Makes it easy. I cut the phone wires."

"I'll be quick."

As Peter left the kitchen, Rose called after him. "No, Peter! No, you can't let him down there!"

But Peter ignored her. He went quickly up the stairs and to their bedroom. He was out of breath by the time he got there, and had to pause for a moment, leaning against the doorframe. Then, going to his bedside table, he took a key from the drawer. He went to the wardrobe and found a locked metal box. He used the key to open the box and inside was an older, rusted key. This key he carried with him downstairs.

Rose began to plead and sob again when he entered the kitchen, but he said to her in a soft voice, "It's what he wants, Rose. He won't listen to me."

Peter's hands trembled as he fitted the key in the lock on the cellar door and turned it. Opening the door, he turned to the man who still held a knife to his wife's throat. "Go do what you think you have to do," he said.

The man hesitated a moment, staring hard into Peter's face as if he were trying to decipher the truth. But Peter, out of words, only looked back at him. Then the man released Rose and as he crossed the kitchen, he grabbed the flashlight from the floor.

"You're coming with me."

"No," Peter said. "No way."

"Give me the key then. I don't want you locking me in with her."

Peter handed the man the large key.

As the man stepped onto the first step down into the cellar, Peter stopped him by saying, "I don't know how long it's lived down there."

The man looked hard at him again. "Do you think a ridiculous story like that's going to get you off the hook? Once I get her out of there, I'm going to tell the world about what you did. She called to me. *Me*, no one else. And I'm not going to let her suffer down there a moment longer."

Before Peter could answer the man turned, and directing the flashlight forward, he began hurrying down the cellar steps. "Little girl!" he called. "I'm coming! I'm coming to get you out, okay?"

Peter closed the cellar door. Glancing around, he met his wife's wide staring eyes.

For a few long minutes there was only silence.

Then from below, slightly muffled, they heard the man's awful, horrified screams. Accompanying the screams was another sound, a sound Peter had heard before but which never failed to chill him to the bone. It was another scream, thin and shrill, like the sound of the wind when it whistled sometimes around the side of the house.

It was not the sound of something in fear. It was the sound of something on the attack.

"Help him, Peter!" Rose said, suddenly. "Open the door!"

Wincing against the sounds from below, Peter replied, "It's too late for that."

"He might have had a family!"

"It wasn't our fault, Rose. What else could we do?"

Screams still emanated up from below. Then, all at once, they were cut off. There was silence.

Rose turned away and began to weep.

"Tomorrow we can have the lock changed again and another key made," Peter said with a sigh. "Have to keep this door locked." He walked calmly forward and picked up the hockey stick Rose had left propped against the table. Returning to the door, he jammed it under the doorknob. "That will have to do for now."

The only sound now was Rose's weeping.

"Do you think someone will come looking for him," she said, between sobs.

"Who knows?" He put an arm around her. "Who knows if he told anyone about his dreams, or where he was going tonight? Let's go back to bed."

"I won't sleep."

"I know. But we've had an ordeal. Both of us need to rest."

Together they climbed the stairs. At the top, Rose moved ahead of Peter and he saw that she was heading for Danni's room. He wanted to tell her no, but the word died on his lips. Instead, he followed her into the room and found her standing by the bed with her arms folded around herself.

She hadn't turned on the light. The light from the hallway picked things out of the gloom: a row of doll's faces on a shelf, their eyes fixed and glassy; the pillow on the bed that even after all these years still looked to show the imprint of a head; a pile of exercise books on the desk; a poster of some long-forgotten pop star half-hanging from the wall.

Rose was still weeping. Peter took her in his arms.

"We should never have brought her here," she sobbed.

"We didn't know."

"Uncle could've warned us."

"Maybe. And probably we would have looked at him the way that man down there looked at me, like I was out of my mind."

"I miss her, Peter."

"I know. Come on. To bed."

They left their daughter's room, went to their own, got in bed and held each other. To his own surprise, overcome by the night's exertions,

Peter soon fell asleep. When he woke, gasping from a dream, it was still dark. He lay for a few moments staring into the blackness, then, as carefully as he could, he got up from the bed.

Rose lay still. He crept towards the bedroom door, but—though she still hadn't moved—Rose's voice stopped him. It had a note of authority.

"Have you been dreaming, Peter?"

He was silent a moment. Then he said, "Yes, dear."

"It's not her. You know it's not her, don't you?"

"Yes, dear."

"Get back in bed."

For a moment he remained by the door. Then he crossed the room again and climbed back into bed beside his wife. She still lay turned away from him, not moving.

"Peter?"

"Yes, dear."

"Let's do what Uncle wanted. Let's burn the house."

Peter closed his eyes. At length he answered, his voice barely a whisper, "Yes, dear."

About Tim Jeffreys

Tim Jeffreys writes horror, fantasy, and 'weird' fiction. To date he has authored three collections of short stories, *The Garden Where Black Flowers Grow, The Scenery of Dreams*, and *The Haunted Grove*, as well as the first book of his Thief saga: *Thief's Return.*

His short fiction has appeared in international anthologies, magazines and on-line e-zines. To sample more of his writing, visit him online at www.timjeffreyswriter.webs.com

Pig
BY MICHAEL THOMAS-KNIGHT

Some undetermined influence pulled Vicki from the dream world into the opaque blanket of her lightless bedroom. Her eyelids parted like velvet curtains, slow and laborious. Clunky silhouetted shapes materialized. Some she recognized immediately as her dresser, night table and lampshade.

As her eyes continued to adjust, it became evident that a different black shape stood before her, clearly not one of the furnishings. It had round, soft edges and a nondescript lumpiness. Only inches from the bedside, it blocked her view of the bedroom doorway.

Control your imagination, she thought. The bedside lamp, which was within easy reach, would give her answers once she turned it on.

She distinctly heard the metal base of the lamp slide away from her across the tabletop, and felt the rush of air from its motion. Her breath caught in her throat and chills crawled up her spine like icy spiders.

She sat up, found the lamp and flicked the switch.

A child's costume of a pig, stained with time and dirt, loomed before her. Although small, she feared the entity inside was not a child at all. The pig-eared hood shrouded the mystery within it.

Eyes reflected from inside the hood like twin spheres of dull glass. A glossy shine in vertical lines flashed from the jagged, pointy teeth. A smoky breath, acrid like a deep burning fire, passed through the mouth and filled the air with unpleasant heaviness that seemed to scorch Vicki's lungs.

She screamed, and pulled her bed covers tight to her neck. Her pulse raced and she fought the dizziness that threatened to make her pass out.

She could hear her heart thumping in her ears, and she began to hyperventilate.

Suddenly she felt a piercing jolt of pain in her leg. Shock waves raced through her calf and up her thigh. She saw the creature's mouth locked down on her leg, teeth embedded into her flesh. She screamed again, this time in a short guttural bark.

Vicki kicked with her left foot, three times, to the side of the beast's head and it let go. It snickered at her and ran off, scrambling into the hallway. Vicki pulled her legs up to her gut. Her quick and harsh breaths halted after each exhale as she watched the doorway where the creature had exited. She half expected the creature to come racing back in for another attack.

But the room was quiet and still; the costumed creature didn't come back.

She thrust her leg from out of the covers. Seeing the bloody teeth marks on her leg made her queasy. She felt an anxiety that was rising to panic, and she fought her fear with all her might. Silent tears fell from her eyes as she asked herself, *Is any of this real? How can this be happening?*

She pulled the casing off her pillow and wrapped it tight around her calf and shin to stop the blood flow. Her hands were trembling as she tied a knot. The question *how* gave her some strength to get up from the bed. It pushed her forward in the face of fear.

Vicki limped to her dresser and opened one of the drawers. She pulled on a pair of khaki shorts and a light shirt, and then hobbled into the hallway.

She proceeded to inspect every corner of her apartment, turning on lights in every room. She checked all the windows and doors. All were locked from the inside, which told her the creature had clearly not left the dwelling. It was still in the apartment somewhere.

She went to the landline phone in the kitchen, held the receiver to her ear and began dialing 911. Then she stopped. How could she report a creature in a child's pig costume?

But wasn't her wound evidence that she had been bitten? Yes, but evidence of being bitten by what? Slowly she put the phone back on its cradle.

Maybe she should make sure of her facts before she brought in the authorities. She had a gun in her bedroom drawer. She could go on the hunt inside her own apartment.

She got the gun.

Only one place remained that Vicki had not searched, the crawlspace storage compartment above the ceiling of her living room. She approached the crawlspace with her Sig Sauer in her hand, her legs wobbling with each step, and she pulled outward on the three-foot-high, barn-like doors. The gun felt cold and comforting in her grasp.

The stench of hot attic space and dust hit her in the face. A brown house-spider, disturbed by the movement, crawled away as webbing drifted to the floor. She hesitated, not wanting to stomp the spider with her bare foot, and it scurried into hiding. She switched on the single-bulb fixture but most of the glow seemed absorbed by the dark and dust.

She squirmed into the dimly lighted crawlspace, maneuvering around assorted boxes, holiday decorations and unused furniture, still grasping the gun. She moved deep into the long triangular space created by the angle of the roof and truncated walls of her top floor apartment. It was tight and claustrophobic.

She looked back at the door space where she had come in. The entrance seemed a long way off, a small, insignificant rectangle of light in an otherwise dim world. A sound emanated from the gloomy space ahead of her and she looked forward, catching something that moved. For a brief second she saw something pink, and then it became hidden behind boxed items.

Vicki's breath became shallow as she listened for any further movement. When no other sound made itself evident, she resumed creeping forward. She climbed over a mound of winter blankets wrapped in clear plastic, pushing them down as she inched forward.

She heard her personal items being ripped and torn as the demon creature scraped and clawed its way toward her.

It was coming for her. She was no longer the hunter. She was the hunted.

She lifted her Sig Sauer, trying to aim at the sounds.

Suddenly the creature was behind her, and before she could turn her gun around, it grabbed a handful of her hair and yanked her head backward. She dropped the gun and it tumbled away, making sounds like measured knocks on the wooden floor.

The creature seemed energized as though, somehow, it knew she was now defenseless. It grabbed her hair with its other clawed hand and leaned back with all its weight, intending to drag her further into the depths of the crawlspace. To her surprise and horror, she slid several inches, and digging her heels into the wooden floor didn't stop her from being dragged.

"No!" Vicki screamed.

She tried to fight the beast off with one of her hands. She felt around for the gun with the other hand as she squirmed to get away.

Now lying on her back, she hooked her foot around a wooden beam as the demon pulled again with tremendous force. The top of her bare foot ground against the old stanchion, splintered edges of its surface cutting into her flesh. She held her hair with her hands to relieve some of the pressure on her head. It felt like her scalp was going to be ripped off.

The creature stopped pulling. It began to scamper back into the dark of the attic space, grabbing a white box. Vicki threw her arm forward, snatching a fistful of the pink costume's soft material. The beast screamed and squealed like an actual pig, struggling to get away.

She repositioned herself onto her knees, still gripping the costume, and found the gun with her other hand. She tried to aim the gun just as the demon creature turned to look at her and its face filled with light.

She pulled the trigger and nothing happened. Panic rushed through her. Had she grabbed an unloaded gun?

The creature seemed angered. It dropped the box and screeched painfully. It slashed with its claws, catching Vicki in the face; its sharp talons gouged lines in Vicki's cheek. The scratches burned as if acid had been thrown in her face.

She let go of the costume and the beast scampered away, taking refuge in the deep, dark space of the attic. The crawl space settled to an eerie quiet.

The scratches on her face stung and the bite on her leg hurt. She needed to escape. But first she took up the white box that the pig-creature had seemed so interested in. Vicki climbed out of the storage space with the white box in hand.

She brought the box into her bedroom. Somehow, she knew it held the clue to what the pig was all about.

She took a deep breath, opened the box and looked at the top pictures on the pile. Three loose pictures stood out, one of her childhood home, the second a family portrait, and the last a photo of her brother. Vicki had been raised by her grandmother since she was young, when her parents and her brother passed away.

It had been a terrible tragedy. The fire had consumed their little house in minutes. As a child, Vicki was lucky to escape through her bedroom window, jumping to safety into the arms of neighbors. Grandma raised her and helped her to cope with the tragedy.

Is that why these pictures are so important? Vicki wondered. *Because Grandma saved them for me?*

"When you are ready to look at these photos, then you can look," Vicki's grandmother had said. "But be sure you are ready. Otherwise, you might not like what you see."

Vicki picked up a stack of photos to take a closer look. Something caught her eye in the right side of the top photo, the one depicting her childhood kitchen. Way in the back, near the darkness of the kitchen counter, she saw—pink. Vicki's heart skipped a beat, her eyes widened and she put the photo close to her face. In the dark area of the photo, a pink blotch smeared the blackness. Shapeless, unclear and indeterminate, it hid there.

Vicki moved to the next picture, her brother Joey Jr. kissing Mom. Again on the right side of frame, a pink blotch stood near the edge of the darkened kitchen. She checked the next picture. To her shock and amazement, the kitchen light was brighter in this photo, so she could see that the pink blotch was clearly the shape of a pig. Little ears, big hood, rounded bottom, curly tail, there was no denying it. The pig was there. This thing had followed her since childhood, had been around her family perhaps her whole life.

She tossed the photo aside and scanned the next photo, Joey Jr., the favorite child, hugging Dad. The pig, clearly defined in this picture, stood in the kitchen. It seemed to be retrieving something from the table next to Joey's birthday cake.

In the next picture, the pig could be seen even more clearly. It peered around the corner, glaring at Joey Jr. Vicki put the photo closer to her face, not believing what she was seeing. Strands of straight blonde hair flowed out of the bottom of the hood.

"It's me.Vicki," she stammered. Her jaw dropped open and her head began to swim with vertigo.

In the photo, the hard glare of jealousy burned in the pig's eyes, the gleam of disdain for her brother.

She heard a noise in the apartment that startled her, perhaps the creaking hinges of the doors to the crawlspace. She listened a few moments in a daze. The pig was still here, inside the apartment. It had always been here.

Vicki remembered. *They called me "Pig."*

Her mother and father had referred to her as Pig, always. "Pig will clean the dishes. Pig will get little Joey his bottle. Why didn't Pig do her chores? Pig will be punished!"

They had purchased the pig costume to degrade her. They made her wear it often, even when company came over. Pig sat in the corner most nights, crying her eyes out as her parents yelled, "Shut up, Pig."

Yes, Pig! *She* was the pig. She dropped the photos back in the box and kicked it away with her feet. Tears streamed down her face and she hugged her knees, pulling them close.

The pig creature peered around the corner of the doorway and into the bedroom. It snickered at her, a nasty little laugh that seemed elated over her misery. As its head bobbed, the piggy ears bounced with awkward motions, as if they were individual entities themselves trying to poke and taunt her. Then the pig scurried back into the hallway. Vicki wiped the tears from her eyes.

She was no longer afraid of the thing in the costume. Now she understood what was happening.

Vicki stood and followed it to the kitchen and stood in the doorway. The creature in the pig costume looked up at her. In a way, it looked like a carnival mirror image, an evil version of Vicki herself, with nasty teeth and sharp nails. Blond hair flowed out of the bottom of the hood area. Vicki could see its eyes. Although they were sunken in and surrounded by dark circles, its eyes were blue-green, just like hers. *Little Vicki.*

The pig had something in its hands, something of importance. The pig held a book of matches. Vicki faintly heard the hiss that she had been aware of for quite some time as it whispered through the apartment. A displeasing odor invaded her nostrils, a smell like rotten eggs. *Was it? Yes, it was. The smell of gas.*

The pig smiled at Vicki, a sad smile but filled with malevolence. Vicki smiled back and she understood. Little Vicki lit the match.

About Michael Thomas-Knight

Michael Thomas-Knight lives in Long Island, New York, down the block from a famous Amityville house and just east of Joel Rifkin's lovely home. Growing up, his family lived in a real haunted house and his childhood babysitter was shot by Son of Sam. No doubt, these strange events influence his tales.

His first chapbook of horror titled *The Clock Tower Black* was published by Goblin Press in 2007. Since that time, Goblin Press has gone out of business. "Oh, the humanity…"

Michael can be found on the web at his blog:
http://parlorofhorror.wordpress.com

DREAM HOUSE
BY CHERYL KAYE TARDIF

The day we moved into our dream house was the beginning of our nightmare. And it all started with five fortuitous words...

"I want my dream house," I told my husband.

We stood in the poor excuse of a kitchen in our rundown Boston bi-level. I was stuck between the open oven door and a cupboard on the other side, while Ray unloaded the dishwasher and tried not to bump into me.

"This kitchen is ridiculous," I said. "Whoever designed it must have been a size zero anorexic who lived on her own."

I was neither a size zero, nor an anorexic. I wasn't willing to give up my bacon cheeseburgers and DQ Blizzards. So the scale tipped a little further—*not* in my favor. Oh well.

"Two weeks, Christine," Ray said. Then his psychiatric training kicked in. "Are you sure you're not substituting the new house for something else?"

"I just want space. If that makes me crazy, then..." I shrugged, "so be it."

Fact is, I'd fallen in love with the idea of buying and renovating an old home. You know, one of those period mansions with hefty wooden doors and arched hallways. Where the ceilings are ornate and massive chandeliers hang suspended high above your head.

My dream became reality when we found a stately-looking manor in Danvers, Massachusetts, not far from Boston.

"A perfect reno project," I'd told Ray when I'd spotted the manor in a real estate magazine.

Ray hadn't been too thrilled with my plans. He was a city guy. Give him smog, traffic and a condo on the twelfth floor, and he'd be happy as a pig in mud.

Speaking of pigs in mud...

Our six-year-old sons bounded into the room. They wore identical outfits—not the 'norm' for my boys even though they were twins—and almost identical dirt marks from head to toe.

"Oh jeez," I said, shaking my head. "What did you two get into this time?"

Danny and Nicky were quite the handful, always playing pranks on people and confusing them. The boys thought it was hilarious for one of them to answer the door dressed as a pirate, then close the door and reopen it so the other could stand there dressed as a policeman. To the person on the other side, it was as if the boy had changed clothes in the blink of an eye.

And before you think I'm a rotten mother letting my young children open the door to complete strangers, let me tell you that we have that front door rigged up like Fort Knox. Yes, those little—uh, *angels* of mine always seem to figure out how to unlock it. Even the lock at the very top.

I called Nicky and Danny my 'lucky boys.' They'd been born a minute after midnight on Friday the Thirteenth. Full moon and all.

"We planted trees," they said in unison.

I glanced out the back window and saw fresh footprints around the daisies I'd planted. I squinted. The boys' 'trees' looked suspiciously like last night's broccoli.

"Dream...house," I enunciated to Ray. "Where the trees *aren't* vegetables."

My husband groaned. "I'll get the boys cleaned up."

"My dream house will be *perfect!*" I said as he herded the boys upstairs.

*****

Danvers was a quaint, charming town located on the Danvers River, and our new home was located on the south edge of Putnamville Reservoir. When I first saw the house, it took my breath away.

My dream house was situated at the end of a winding road guarded by high steel gates that were operated by remote control. The house towered over us as we parked the car. A balcony on the second floor overlooked the circular driveway that swept past the front door. There were arches, columns and carved wooden accents, all remnants from another era. Imposing and regal, with castle-like turrets on both ends and a peaked roof between them, our new home almost pulsated with imperceptible power.

"It's spectacular," I said, stepping from our minivan.

Danny and Nicky jumped from the van and headed for the steps.

"Careful," I warned as Nicky stumbled. I turned to Ray. "Is the inside as beautiful as the pictures?"

He grinned. "Even better."

We navigated the wide stone steps and I waited for Ray to unlock the door. I noticed it had one of those hefty brass doorknockers with a cherub face on it. I touched it, snatching my hand back as an icy chill spread through my fingertips.

Ray grabbed the knocker and banged it twice. We could hear the sound echo inside the house.

"Shall we, madam?" he asked me, one brow raised.

"Fine, sir," I said, playing along. "Will you carry me over the threshold?"

My husband swept me up and I giggled, wrapping my arms around his neck. The boys stared at us as if we had lost our marbles.

Ray nudged the door open with one shoulder.

Then we entered our new home.

With wide eyes, I took in the spacious foyer and double staircase that rose on either side to the second floor. Peaceful cherubs perched on the ends of the handrails, again made of brass that was blackish green with age.

"Angels are watching over us," I muttered as Ray set me down.

A five-layer chandelier hung above the center of the foyer. Beneath it was a round table in burnished cherry finish. In the center sat a crystal vase filled with a rainbow bouquet of roses, irises and other fragrant blooms.

"We want to see our room," Nicky said, tugging on my sleeve.

With a deafening roar, the boys went charging upstairs.

"Is it safe?" I asked Ray.

"Perfectly. It passed the inspection with flying colors. All this place needs," he hugged me, "is a little TLC. And I'm sure you're going to give it that."

"*We're* going to give it that," I corrected. "Don't you dare think I'm going to do all the work while you play with your patients."

He cocked his head. "Play? Is that what you think I do?"

I saw the warning in his eyes and let out a shriek. Then I raced up the stairs, with Ray not far behind me. Laughing, I ran down the hallway until I came to a door at the end. I opened it, stepped inside and shut the door, leaning on it, breathless.

"Okay," I shouted. "I know you don't play at work."

There was no answer behind the door.

"I was joking." Well, not really. Sometimes Ray told me he'd have a chess match with a patient. That was playing, wasn't it?

Again, no answer.

"Ray?"

I slowly turned the doorknob and inched the door open a crack.

The hall was empty.

Where the hell did you go?

"Boo!" a voice said.

I shrieked and nearly jumped out of my skin.

Turning, I saw Ray. He was leaning against a door frame across the room.

"There's a connecting doorway from this room to the next," he said.

"Jesus!" I slowed my breathing and leaned down, putting my hands on my knees. "You took ten years off my life."

"And you'll still outlive me."

"Ha ha. Very funny."

"I thought so."

"Let me guess," I said. "These are the boys' rooms."

Ray nodded. "I'm not sure they'll want to be separated, though."

"They can choose. At least now we have room to expand." I followed him into the hallway. "So where's our room? I think I need a nap."

When I entered the bedroom at the opposite end of the hall, I gasped in shock. The room consisted of a sitting area with a fireplace and a raised pedestal where our king-sized bed reigned supreme. Two doors led to a balcony that overlooked the tree-lined backyard, another door led to an en suite bathroom and the final door in our room revealed a walk-in closet so big Ray and I could get lost in it.

"I need to buy more clothes," I said, mesmerized by the rows of hangers and empty floor-to-ceiling shelves.

"As long as you don't turn into a hoarder," Ray teased.

"Stop bringing your work home with you," I said, grinning at him. "Doctor."

Ray crossed the room, closed the hallway door and turned the antique key in the lock. In his best Sigmund Freud impression, he said, "Come lie down und tell me all about your obsession vis clothes."

"Nope. No time for *that*, mister."

Ray pouted. "Gee, first I was *doctor* and now I've been demoted to *mister*. That sucks."

"I'll give you a promotion later." I heaved a sigh and turned slowly in the center of the room. "Right now I just want to take in this...ah...space."

Freedom...

Our lives had changed drastically in the past two weeks. Ray had secured a position at the Danvers State Hospital, one of the oldest psych hospitals in Massachusetts. He'd enrolled the boys in Plumfield Academy, an expensive private school. And I'd found a part-time job in the town's library.

Life was perfect.

Until it wasn't.

*****

The first peculiar event happened early Sunday morning of the third week. I awoke at 6:06 AM to a bloodcurdling scream. Ray and I jumped from the bed and raced down the hall. "Danny! Nicky?"

Ray flung open the door to Nicky's room. It was empty.

"Nicky!" I cried.

I ran to the other door and opened it.

The boys were sitting in the single bed at the end of the room, their arms clenching each other, fear etched in their eyes so palpable that it made me freeze in my tracks. The twins weren't looking at us. They were staring at the far corner of the room, at a shadow that flickered rapidly like a static-filled television.

I blinked and the shadow vanished.

"R-Ray?" My voice squeaked. "Did you see that?"

Ray was already reaching for our sons, gathering them into his strong arms. "Just a bad dream, boys. Relax and close your eyes. Everything's fine."

Without a word, they obeyed and settled back to sleep.

I hesitated by the door. "D-didn't you see it?"

"See what?" Ray asked, confusion etched on his face.

"The shadow. In the corner."

He chuckled. "Don't tell me you're seeing ghosts now. The boys had a nightmare. You know how it is with twins. One has a bad dream, so does the other."

My mouth gaped for a second. I closed it and shook my head. "Obviously I'm overtired." I glanced at the empty corner. "Yeah, I need sleep."

Minutes later, Ray and I climbed back into bed. He fell asleep immediately, but I stayed awake until his alarm rang. Then I clambered out of bed and headed for the shower, trying hard not to think of the flickering shadow in Danny's room.

Just my imagination. That's all. Nothing more.

The second incident occurred two days later. I was dusting the living room. No small feat, I must add. That one room was bigger than the first floor of our Boston bi-level.

The manor had come with some original artwork, paintings I was sure must be worth a few pennies. According to the realtor, none of the previous owners wanted to remove them, so the paintings had been passed down with each sale of the house. I thought that was weird, but who can argue with free décor?

The paintings weren't my taste so I decided to replace some with our family photos. I took down a gray-brown monotone of a husband and wife, both with serious, unsmiling faces. "Time for you to say goodbye," I said. "This is our home now." I placed the painting face down.

After digging through two boxes of mostly junk, I found our oversized family photo taken last year at Christmas. As I reached out to hang it, a slight movement caught my attention. In the detailed wood panel that lined the walls of the living room, a hole had been drilled.

An eye stared out at me.

Startled, I cried out and dropped the family photo. The glass in the frame shattered. I stepped back, my bare foot catching one of the splintered glass pieces. "Ow! Ow! Ow!"

Ray ran into the room. "Christine, you're bleeding. Sit down. I'll get a cloth." He disappeared for a moment, then returned with cloth in hand.

"Someone…was…watching…me," I said between deep breaths.

He squinted at the nearest window.

"Not from outside. From the wall." I pointed.

He smiled at me. "Honey, how can anyone watch you from a wall?"

"There's a hole." I grabbed at my chest. "I saw an eye."

Ray strode to the wall. "Here?"

"Just below the nail for the picture."

He touched the wall. "There *is* a hole here, but it's awfully small." He leaned forward, pressing his face against the wall. "I can't see a thing, Christine."

"Don't do that," I said, my stomach churning with dread. I was terrified that he'd pull away, screaming and flailing at his face, his eye gouged by a sharp object. "Get away from the hole."

"No more horror movies for you," he said, turning toward me, his eye intact. "You have an overactive imagination, honey."

"B-but I-I saw…" Hell, I didn't know what I'd seen. Maybe Ray was right. I'd let my imagination get the better of me. "I'm going to lie down."

After a short nap, I returned to the living room. Ray had cleaned up the glass and rehung the eerie monotone painting of the couple.

"We'll take it down as soon as we replace the glass in our family photo," he promised.

I studied the couple in the painting. *My house. Not yours.*

Their expressions seemed to mock me.

*****

Over the next few weeks I noticed more bizarre incidents. At times I swore I heard someone whisper my name. Then objects began to go missing, only to be found much later in the weirdest of places. I found more holes—I came to call them 'peepholes'—camouflaged in the ornate paneling of the walls. They were everywhere. Ray said they were most likely old nail holes, but I didn't believe that. I'd seen the eye in the wall twice in the past week. Of course, my husband thought I was being silly.

"I'm going to get started on some of the renos while you're at work," I told Ray one evening.

We'd decided to tear down some walls, which were rotted near the baseboards.

"Just wait 'til the workers come," he said. "They'll be here next week. Seven days."

But I had to know what was behind those walls.

When he left the next morning, I took a small sledgehammer into the living room. Removing the monotone, I glanced at the small hole where I'd first seen the eye. "The moment of truth."

It took a few good whacks before the wood collapsed. When it did, it dissolved into the space behind the wall. I poked my head inside, the barrel of a thin flashlight pressed against my cheek. "I knew it."

A narrow, *secret* hallway ran into the shadows at either end.

Before Ray came home, I rehung the painting and cleaned up.

What should I do?

If I told Ray what I'd found, he'd shrug it off as just part of the old manor. He was already giving me his 'shrink look,' the one he gave others when he thought they were 'out to lunch.'

That evening, Ray noticed the painting on the wall was crooked. He went to straighten it, frowned, lifted it down and gazed at the head-sized hole in the wall. "Christine? Something you want to tell me?"

"Uh…I hit the nail too hard?"

He flicked a mocking look over his shoulder. "Really. You expect me to believe *that*."

"I was right, Ray. There's a hallway behind the wall."

He scrunched his brow, then poked his head into the hole. "Not much of a hall. It's just an empty space. Probably to eliminate drafts or circulate stale air."

"Big enough for someone to hide in."

"Nobody is hiding in our walls." With a huff, he left the room.

I rehung the painting. "I know you're in there," I whispered.

Am I losing it?

I had the intense feeling I was being watched. The hairs on the back of my neck and arms stood up. A deep shiver slithered up my spine.

I peered over my shoulder, my eyes locking with one of the cherubs at the bottom of the stairs. I could swear he moved. And wasn't he supposed to be smiling, not leering at me with an evil scowl?

I blinked and his smile was back, all innocent and serene.

Am I going crazy?

*****

Later I drove to the library, sat through a boring speech on categorizing books and found myself standing in the stacks in the history section.

"Can I help you?" Mary Kendall, the head librarian, peered at me over horn-rimmed glasses.

"I-I'm not sure." And I wasn't. I had no idea why I was standing there.

"Are you doing research?"

Research. "Uh, yeah. I was curious about…our house. About the former owners."

Mary pushed her glasses up the bridge of her nose and turned toward the bookshelves. "This way."

"We live at—"

"Oh, I know where you live, Mrs. Kingston. The old Burroughs house. Reverend Charles Burroughs had it built for his wife Ursula." She looked at me. "What do you know about Danvers?"

"Not much. We lived in Boston for five years. Before that we were in New York."

Mary leaned close and lowered her voice. "You heard about the Salem witch trials, right?"

I nodded.

"Well, honey, this here is Salem."

I laughed. "This is Danvers."

"Used to be called Salem Village."

My smile dropped. "For real?"

"Can't get any *more* real."

I chewed on this information for a few minutes. *Salem, Massachusetts. Famous for the witch trials in the late 1600s.* That was about all I could remember from high school.

"I guess it's a good thing there aren't any witches around anymore," I said with a grin.

Mary's eyes widened, but she said nothing. A second later she handed me a thick leather-wrapped book. "This will give you an idea of the history of the town."

"Thank you." I signed the book out.

Once back at home, I made a cup of chamomile tea, settled into a chair and began to read.

Salem Village. 1692-1693. The Salem witch trials...families torn asunder by wild accusations of dark magic.

I read for hours, haunted by horrific images from the past. It had been a brutal time, one filled with suspicion, misperception and mass hysteria. If a woman had any abnormal affliction, she was thought to be a witch. If she'd experienced any sort of bad luck, she was marked. If she consorted with a known witch, she was suspect and guilty by association.

I read countless cases of friends turning on friends, and husbands turning on wives. Some were brought to trial, found guilty and condemned to prison where many starved to death. Others were hung.

Then I saw a familiar name. *Reverend Charles Burroughs.*

"Charles and his young wife Ursula were to oversee the parish," I read, "and in exchange were given two acres of land to build their dream home. Charles preached that God had no tolerance for witchcraft, and the hunt was on. It was his mission in life to lure out those practicing the dark arts."

I paused, taking in this vital piece of the town's history.

Then I continued to read aloud. "Unfortunately, Charles had no idea Ursula had fallen prey to a coven. Out of loneliness, she'd turned to witchcraft and used their manor for meetings. Since her husband had left her in charge of overseeing the building of their home, she took it upon herself to hire contractors who built secret passageways in the walls so that she and her 'sisters' could come and go as they pleased, unbeknownst to Charles."

I glanced up at the family portrait, knowing that behind the wall were Ursula's secret passageways. *Should I tell Ray? Show him the book?*

Logic suggested that my husband wouldn't care if there were passageways behind the walls or not. After all, what difference would that make? It wasn't as if I were planning to take up the dark arts, or anything.

*****

Ray went to work the next morning and I spent most of the day reading the book from the library and checking over my shoulder. With each passing hour, I was feeling more certain that someone—or some*thing*—was in our house.

Now before you roll your eyes and berate me for not just grabbing my family and moving out, you have to understand something. This was our first real home. We owned it. Every square inch of rotted wood, every nail hole, every peephole, every secret hallway. We had every penny we owned tied up in that house.

Plus, I had to prove to Ray that I wasn't going insane. Last night when he'd found me tapping the walls in the upstairs hallway by the boys' rooms, he'd given me a look that screamed, *What the hell's wrong with you?*

Of course I know I probably looked a little deranged, but all I could think of was, *What if something behind the walls wants to hurt my family?*

When Ray returned home that evening, I showed him the book.

"Okay," he said. "So you're right. There *are* passageways behind the walls. But we're the only ones here now. You, me and the boys."

"Can't you feel it?" I lowered my voice. "A presence. Something strong and...evil."

"Come on, Christine. Enough of this."

I picked up the book. "Listen to this. In August 1692, Rebecca Morrow, five years old, was found dead in the woods near the Burroughs Estate. All of her blood had been drained and a silver chalice was found in the bushes nearby."

"You really have to stop reading this stuff," Ray said, shaking his head. "No wonder you're seeing things."

"During the investigation," I continued, ignoring him, "many of the townswomen were brought forward to confess their sins. Most were innocent. Later, it was discovered that the coven in which Ursula belonged believed that if they drank the blood of a child no older than seven, they would remain forever young and beautiful."

"That's horrible. Put the book away."

"When Charles discovered his wife's betrayal, he ordered her to be hanged with the other witches. To be made an example of. Ursula cursed him right before she was hanged. She told him their home would become his prison. He could never leave. Unless he did one thing."

"What?"

"Charles could escape his fate and lift the curse," I stared at Ray, "only if he killed seven children before they each turned seven."

"So what did he do?" Ray ran an impatient hand through his hair.

"He hung himself. In the attic. He thought he could avoid the curse this way."

"I guess he did."

"No. The curse remained in place and his spirit suffered, according to another witch who was hung the following day."

Ray rolled his eyes. I could almost hear him mentally ticking off all the illnesses he was sure I had. *Depression, delusions, paranoia, maybe schizophrenia...*

I turned a page in the book. "The manor remained closed for many years and was finally reopened and sold to out-of-towners. They had no children. They lived there for over twenty years, until 1713. It was sold again in 1714 to an older couple whose kids were grown. They lived there from 1714 to 1762. The house was then sold to a family with one child—a son. He went missing about six months later and the couple sold the house in 1767 and moved to New York."

A chill engulfed me. "The house remained empty for the next six years. The townspeople thought it haunted." I gave Ray an 'I told you so' look. "Finally in 1773, a family with teens moved in. In 1837 the manor was passed onto the oldest son, who lived alone until 1885 when he died in his sleep."

Ray let out a soft sigh. "Christine…none of this is all that strange. It was the times. Things happened. They do in our era, too."

"But don't you find it weird that things have gone missing and turned up in places we *know* we never left them? And I know I saw an eye in that hole. And what about the shadow in Danny's room? I *saw* it." I surveyed the room and took a deep breath. "It's Charles. He's still in the house."

"For Christ's sake!" Ray snapped. "You're not thinking clearly, maybe coming down with something. Whatever is wrong, it's not the house. It's *you*."

I held up the book. "I didn't imagine the history of this place."

"This was Salem Village, honey. Everyone knows about the witch trials."

"Well, I didn't. Not until Mary at the library told me." I opened the book again. "You want to know the history of our *dream* house? In 1887 it was sold to a wealthy widow and her sister. When the widow passed away in 1926, the sister sold the house. This is where everything gets twisted." I took a deep breath, waiting for my husband to stop me.

He didn't.

"In 1926," I said, "the Morgan family moved in—husband, wife and three kids aged eight to fourteen. The wife became pregnant and she was warned by the townspeople that the house wasn't safe for her baby. She didn't believe them. When her baby was four, she found him at the bottom of the well on their property. Another *accident*." My heart raced almost as quickly as the words streaming from my mouth. "Grief struck, she blamed her husband and a rift was created in their marriage. She left a year later, in 1932, with the other kids. The husband stayed behind for the next five years until 1937."

"Keep going," Ray said, his voice flat.

"In 1940 the townspeople tried to turn the house into a museum, but no one wanted to step foot inside, so it was left empty for another four years. In 1944 a couple from New Jersey bought the house and began to restore it. They lived in the house and their daughter was born in 1947. When the daughter was almost seven, she went missing and was never seen again. In 1956 they had a second child, Victor. In 1960, at four, Victor was crushed during another round of renos, when the ceiling of a room caved in. The couple moved away in 1961."

I was on a roll and nothing could stop me. Ray *had* to see where I was going with all this, why I was so terrified of this house.

"The house was empty until 1963 when Linda and Scott Huntington from Toronto, Canada, bought the place. They had three sons—eight, nine and eleven. They lived there for forty-seven years. Their kids, who had their own families later on, stopped visiting because too many 'odd things' happened in the house and their own kids were terrified."

"Chris—"

"One of the grandchildren fell down the stairs." I pointed. "Right there, Ray. He broke his back and was paralyzed. In a wheelchair for the rest of his life. He had to live in a group home for the disabled. He was six years old. And in 2010 the oldest son accepted his inheritance and moved his family into this house. His kids were older so their time was uneventful—until his daughter got pregnant and fell down the stairs, miscarrying."

"Coincidences!" Ray yelled. "All coincidences." He moved toward me, took one of my hands and kissed it. "Just plain rotten luck. But it's *our* house now. And we'll make our own luck—*good* luck. I promise."

My eyes watered. "Can't you see what's happening, Ray? Something is going after the children. Before they turn seven."

He dropped my hand. "So you're saying that because Nicky and Danny are almost seven, we should pack up and go?"

"No, I—"

"Then what the hell *are* you saying?" Ray clenched his teeth. "I don't understand you. You wanted your dream house, a renovation project. You got that. Why are you trying to ruin it? Do you want to go back to Boston?"

"No, I don't want to go back."

"Then what *do* you want?"

"It's not what *I* want that matters, Ray. It's what the *house* wants."

Without a word, my husband stormed upstairs. I flinched when I heard a door slam.

*****

Ray was gone by the time I awoke the next morning. My thoughts were consumed with the book. I needed answers. I read while Danny and Nicky cleaned up their rooms.

After lunch I dropped the boys off at my sister Angela's house. She lived in Beverly, not far from Danvers, and she'd called me that morning to ask if the boys could stay for the weekend. To tell the truth, I was relieved that they weren't going to be in the house.

Back at home, I sat on the swing on the porch, the book in my lap. I think I must have fallen asleep because the next thing I knew the telephone was ringing and it was four o'clock.

"Hey," Ray said, the phone line a bit muffled. "I thought I'd pick up some pizza...taco for us...pineapple for the boys."

"The boys aren't here this weekend."

"What?" The line crackled. "Sorry, Christine, the line's cutting out. Sounded like you said they boys weren't there."

"They're not. They went to Angela's."

"Sorry, honey, you're cutting out."

"Nicky and Danny are at my sister's."

Silence.

"Ray? Did you hear me?"

"This line's really bad." I heard him chuckle. "Sounded like you said the boys were at your sister's."

"Yes." I sighed with frustration. "They're at Angela's. They'll be back Sunday night."

Another long pause greeted me.

"Did you hear what I said?" I asked.

"You said the boys are at Angela's."

I let out a huff. "So you *are* listening."

"I'll be home in about twenty minutes," he said, his voice so intense that it filled me with dread. "Promise me you won't go anywhere."

"What's going on, Ray?"

"Just promise me you'll stay where you are."

I swallowed hard. "Okay, I promise."

I heard the car door slam about eighteen minutes later. Record time for Ray.

"Christine?"

"I'm in the living room."

Ray rounded the corner, his face flushed, sweat beading down his forehead.

"You look terrible," I said, moving to his side. "What's wrong?"

His eyes wild, he ran upstairs. "Danny! Nicky!"

"They're at Angela's," I hollered.

Now I was pissed. Ray was acting bizarre.

"What the hell's going on?" I shouted.

Footsteps thundered down the stairs.

When Ray entered the living room, he walked slowly toward me, hands clenched at his side. "Where are they?"

"Jesus Christ! Don't you listen? Nicky and Danny are at Angela's. My sister took them for the weekend."

"Your *sister*," he said between clenched teeth, "is *dead*."

Time stopped.

I heard nothing but my own breathing.

"Angela is dead?"

Ray glared at me. "Yes."

"W-what happened?" A sob caught at the back of my throat.

"There was a fire."

"Oh God…" I began to cry. "Are the boys okay?"

"I don't know." Ray grabbed my shoulders. "The fire was four years ago."

I batted away a tear and struggled to smile. "But…but I saw Angela this morning. When she took the boys."

"Angela didn't take the boys anywhere."

"Yes, she did! She drove them to her house."

Ray gritted his teeth. "Angela couldn't have taken the boys today. She died in that fire four years ago."

I slapped his hands away. "Then where the hell are Danny and Nicky? Don't you think I'd know?"

Ray surveyed the room, his gaze resting abruptly on the wall behind the sofa. Our family portrait stared back at him. "You fixed the wall."

I blinked. "I did."

He strode toward the sofa and shoved it out of the way.

"What are you doing?" I cried.

"You taped and mudded every piece together. And then painted it. Why?"

"Because it needed to be fixed."

"All this talk about someone living in the—" His eyes flared.

With a roar, he grabbed the sledgehammer and swung it. The photo crashed to the floor, glass flying everywhere.

"Stop it!" I shouted. "What are you doing?"

"And that godforsaken book!"

Another hit and the wall panel began to crumble.

"And this fucking house!"

He swung one more time and the wall exploded.

"Ray!"

When the dust cleared, I saw my husband's face. He was as broken as the wall.

"Oh God," he sobbed, tears streaming from his eyes. "Oh my God, *nooo*…"

I moved beside him, took his hand. "Ray, what have you done?"

"What have *I* done?" He looked at me with pity. "No. What have *you* done, Christine?"

He stepped aside so I could see what the gaping hole in the wall revealed.

My boys. My beautiful boys. Their bodies pale and still, and their eyes empty...*dead.*

"They're my lucky boys," I said.

Ray gasped. "Lucky?"

"I saved them, Ray. That's why they're lucky."

"Saved them from what?"

I walked to the coffee table and picked up the old painting that had once hung on the wall. "Reverend Charles was going to kill them so he could join Ursula. He'd already killed five children. He only needed two more." I smiled. "But I saved our boys. Now they can never be used to reunite such evil as Charles and Ursula Burroughs."

We stood in silence for a long moment.

Then Ray led me to the sofa, made a phone call and returned to my side.

Somewhere deep in the house I heard laughter.

"They're happy," I said.

"Who?"

"Nicky and Danny. Can't you hear them laughing?"

I heard sirens in the distance.

"It's time to go," Ray said.

"Where are we going?"

"I'm taking you to a safe place."

I followed him to the front door. "To my dream house?"

Ray turned away, but not before I saw tears in his eyes.

"Sure, honey," he said in a hoarse voice. "To your dream house."

About Cheryl Kaye Tardif

Cheryl Kaye Tardif is an award-winning, international bestselling suspense author from Edmonton, Canada. Her novels include *Divine Justice, Children of the Fog, The River, Divine Intervention*, and *Whale Song*, which New York Times bestselling author Luanne Rice calls "a compelling story of love and family and the mysteries of the human heart...a beautiful, haunting novel."

Cheryl also enjoys writing short stories inspired mainly by her author idol Stephen King, and this has resulted in *Skeletons in the Closet & Other Creepy Stories* (ebook) and *Remote Control* (novelette ebook). In 2010 Cheryl detoured into the romance genre with her contemporary romantic suspense debut, *Lancelot's Lady*, written under the pen name of Cherish D'Angelo.

In 2012, she penned the nonfiction marketing book, *How I Made Over $42,000 in 1 Month Selling My Kindle eBooks*.

Booklist raves, "Tardif, already a big hit in Canada…a name to reckon with south of the border."

Visit Cheryl Kaye Tardif at http://www.cherylktardif.com or at http://www.cherylktardif.blogspot.com

The Last Memory
by Dominick Nole

Rick heard the familiar sound of rubber scraping off of concrete and the popping of pebbles as his father parked their work van too close to the curb. There would be another grey scar to go on the side of the tires now, the seventeen-year-old thought as he rolled his eyes.

"What?" his father said, looking at him with his thin eyebrows raised.

"Do you always have to park so close? You're gonna ruin the tires again."

His father snatched at a clipboard lying on the dashboard and began flipping through invoices with a grease-darkened finger, leaving smears on the corners of the pages. "I pay the bills on this damn thing. I'll drive it how I want. When you pay the bills and have your own van, you can drive it how *you* want."

Rick rolled his eyes again as he turned his head and looked out the window, his breath fogging the glass. "You say the same thing every time you roll through a stop sign, too. Won't be a van to pay for when somebody T-bones ya."

The emaciated sound of a scratching pencil filled the van as his father jotted something down. "Quit complaining. We've got work to do." He opened the door and stepped outside, looking in at Rick.

Rick felt a moment of pity as he looked at his father's face: the hanging cheeks, the dark and hollow eyes, the work-roughened skin, the way his thin hair rose and fell in the wind, and wearing his thirty-five years of tough plumbing work like an old, beaten jacket. He hadn't always been like this. There used to be a light in his eyes no matter how hard the job was, and there was always a smile to give. But that had all changed when Rick's mother died a year ago, and jobs became increasingly harder to come by.

"Grab the pipe machine and the other stuff, all right? I'm gonna go talk to this guy." His father slammed the door and walked off, lighting a cigarette.

Rick opened his door and stepped out into a cold, overcast December afternoon, his feet kicking empty potato chip bags and soda cans from the grimy floor of the van into the street, his breath shooting from his mouth like the fumes of a fire extinguisher as he sighed and threw the trash back into the van. He looked up and down the street. A few specks of snow danced in the wind as thick, low-hanging storm clouds threatened to come their way on the horizon, making the street full of ramshackle, low-income houses feel even more desolate.

He walked to the back of the blue van, not even glancing at the sign on the side that said "Scott Johansson Plumbing & Heating, Inc." He opened the large windowless door like the door of a hearse, though instead of pulling a casket out, he pulled out the tripod base of the heavy pipe cutting machine, slick oil staining his hands and sweatshirt as he laid it against the bumper. He looked inside.

There were rolled up coils of red and yellow and green extension cords hanging from the wall on the right side, large and small pipe wrenches; some new, some peppered with rust. All were dangling and clanking from the nails pounded into the ends of the shelves on the right side. Hammer drills, regular drills, reciprocating saws, saw blades, nails, screws, gas cocks, hammers, and screw drivers were all gunked up with years of accumulated dirt, pipe dope, and anger.

Rick shook his head, reminding himself for the umpteenth time that the van needed to be cleaned. The way the disheveled innards of the van mirrored their disheveled lives hurt him and made him feel a little sick. His thin arms strained as he picked up the pipe cutter and shut the back door of the van with his shoulder, shuddering as the wind blew over his head.

He looked at the rundown house he and his father were going to be working in, the broken porch and tattered screens hanging from the windows. He shrugged and continued walking along the side of the house into the back yard. He could hear arguing voices as he placed the pipe machine on the hard, frozen dirt.

His father's voice floated out of the open basement door at the back of the house like a vengeful spirit. "This is how the boiler has to be put in! That's the city code! If I don't follow it and the plumbing inspector sees it, I'll lose my license!"

Rick trotted over and went down the steps. *Here we go again,* he thought.

The basement had a low ceiling, causing his tall father to hunch over as he argued with the old man. A single low-watt bulb highlighted the cobwebs that dangled from the joints in the ceiling, white, long-dead spiders in some of them. There were clusters of cardboard boxes, most of them with beer labels on them, stacked into every corner. There were dusty old chairs and tables, and the dirt floor was strewn with dead insects and a couple mouse traps with the dead mice still occupying them.

"I doan like having the boiler there!" yelled the old man in a thick Italian accent, his breath heavy with cheap beer and liquor, "Thass where I keepa my beer!"

"Well you're gonna have to park your beer somewhere else, because that's the code! That's where the boiler has to go, and this is where I have to run the gas and water lines!" His father pointed here and there along the ceiling, walls, and floor.

Rick noticed with some alarm that a vein was poking out of his father's reddened neck, and another in his forehead above his bugged-out eyes. His father was a nice, friendly man who would have thirty minute conversations with complete strangers in the middle of the street, yet there was a terrible temper that ran underneath the pleasant façade like lava. His old man usually kept it in check but with the recent recession, customers trying to skimp out on what they agreed to pay, and the death of his wife, his father had been steadily going over the deep end.

Just last week Rick had to pull his father's vice-like hands off of another plumber's neck. They had both been bidding on the same job, and his father was going to get it, but then the other guy had undercut him by dropping his bid by six-hundred dollars. His father had been squeezing the man's neck so hard that yesterday, when Rick had seen the guy in a mini-mart buying a soda, he could still see the cruel purple markings of his father's fingers.

The Italian flapped his hands at Rick's father. "Ah, you gonna do what you want anyway! Put the damn thing in!" He snagged a beer from an open case and stumbled upstairs, cursing under his breath.

His father turned to Rick, one eyeball twitching. "You get the pipe machine?"

"Yeah, it's out back."

"All right, go get the rest of the stuff." His father pointed outside. "I need a ninety, a gas cock, about twenty feet of pipe . . ."

Rick nodded and walked up the shoddy wooden stairs as his father continued to talk. The snow began to come down a little harder and he heard a crow caw as he unstrapped the long lengths of pipe from the top of the van and slid them off.

He was making his third trip back to the truck when the guys from the supply warehouse showed up in their truck with the boiler. They hefted it out of the back of the truck and left it on the sidewalk.

"Tell yer dad he's gotta have the money for this by tomorrow," said one of the men, a large man with a big, blubbery belly peeking out from under his jacket. "We can't give him credit on this one, he's already behind on what he owes."

"All right Harry, I'll let him know," Rick said as he loaded the boiler onto a hand dolly, his heart filling with a sorrowful love for his desperate father. "Take it easy."

Rick grunted and groaned as he yanked the boiler up over the curb, the wheels wobbling and crunching the dead grass as he wheeled it into the back yard. He left the metal hulk in the yard and walked into the basement to deliver the bad news to his father.

"Harry from the warehouse said you gotta have the money for the boiler by tomorrow, dad. They can't give you no more credit."

His father was on all fours, a pipe wrench screeching away as he removed a fitting that was connecting two water lines. Rick had to gulp back a sob as he saw his father stop what he was doing and drop his forehead to a tented hand and his face scrunched up with emotion. Was his father going to cry?

"When did it come to this, Rick? When did it get this bad?" He started turning the pipe wrench again, slowly, like the gears that had begun turning in his mind, the teeth worn and slipping out of the notches. His eyes remained dry. "Used to be, no one stiffed us on our pay, the jobs were plentiful, we had good credit, and there was more than three day old pizza waiting for us when we got home because your ma cooked for us."

"Ay, whatsa going on down there?" the old Italian man's voice came down the stairs.

Suddenly Rick's father screamed, "Shut up and let me do my job!"

Silence followed.

Rick's father went back to work on the water line. "Get the boiler down here, then go back up and start cutting some pipe."

Rick went out into the back yard where the snow was really starting to come down, coating the ground like a mortuary sheet. He hauled the dolly over to the basement, then slowly bounced it from stair to stair until he got it inside.

"Thanks," his father said, a little calmer, as he slid the dolly from under the boiler and handed it to him.

Rick spent the next fifteen minutes cutting the pipe in the cold while his father put the boiler together. He could almost hear the memories of his mother being carried on the wind. He remembered how the snow reflected on her white face as the coroner lifted the sheet so he and his father could identify her.

Things had been better when she was around. But after she died, their lives had become a steady decline down a slope oiled with anger and depression. Now his father's eyes were always worried, as if somewhere inside, he knew he was beginning to slip through the cracks...but didn't care.

Rick brought the cut pipe down and slathered the white dope over the threaded ends as he handed them to his father, who connected them to the boiler and to the other pipes via nineties and T's. It wasn't that bad of a job because the boiler was small and they didn't have to re-pipe the entire basement.

"Hey, we're done!" his father called up the stairs. He looked at Rick and gestured at the floor. "Take all this crap back to the truck."

Rick bent, his spine aching a little bit, and went about his task.

He had to pull hard to open the van's back door, the wind had started getting serious as it ushered the incoming blizzard. He and his father were going to have one slippery ride home. Rick thought he heard screaming voices, but it was hard to tell over the battering wind.

As he walked along the side of the house to get to the last of their stuff, he heard voices again. They were definitely angry voices.

He walked over to the pipe cutter and picked it up, nervousness stamped on his face. His father and the old Italian man were arguing, though he still couldn't make out anything specific.

The wooden steps creaked as Rick stepped down into the dim basement. "Dad?" he called out when he reached the bottom of the steps. The basement was empty. He heard some scuffling noises from the floor above, and a strange, choked gargling noise.

Gawwkk!

It sounded like rust-clogged water spurting from an old pipe.

"Dad!" Rick called again as he rushed up the stairs into the house, the noises growing louder.

He ran through the doorway into a trashy kitchen. Empty beer and liquor bottles lined crumb-littered linoleum counters, and the smell of burning meat entered his nose.

He stopped in shock at what he saw.

On the filthy floor next to the table was an overturned chair, and next to the overturned chair were the Italian man and his father. His father was pressing his thumbs into the old man's windpipe, whose legs were kicking up and down erratically as he tried to pry the hands away, spittle foaming over his blue-tinted lips.

"Dad, stop!" Rick ran over and grabbed his father's shoulders, trying to pull him off. His father shrugged him away, and Rick bounced against the counter, the empty bottles clinking and clanking, some of them falling and smashing on the floor.

"This is taking too long," his father said in a calm voice. He pulled one hand away from the old man's throat and grabbed a large brown shard from a broken beer bottle. He placed it roughly against the old man's jugular vein, which popped from his neck like a thick, wormy cable.

He sliced once, with precision, and the blood squirted from the opening like an over pressured ketchup bottle, painting a red stream across Rick's shocked, white face as he braced his hands on the counter.

"That's better," his father said as he stood up, looking down at the old Italian man as if he were a water heater he had just installed. The Italian homeowner clapped a hand over the sputtering wound, his mouth working like a dying fish as he took in great gasps of air. He gave one great breath and began to let out a scream, but it was cut off when Rick's father planted a worn boot on the man's chest.

"Rick, go get a drop cloth out of the van. We've got some work to do."

Rick was staring at the blood pouring from between the dying man's fingers, cascading like a thick red waterfall.

His father grabbed his chin and turned his face. "Don't worry about him. Just go get the drop cloth."

Habit caused him to obey his father. Stunned, Rick exited the front door of the house like the lone survivor of a catastrophe, pale-faced and shaking, his eyes scanning the streets. He opened the back of the van and grabbed the grease stained drop cloth, bundling it up under his arm as snow pelted him, melting and dying on his face as the old Italian man lay dying inside the house.

He stood facing the front door for several minutes, freezing, terrified and confused. He knew what his father had done was wrong on so many levels, a ghastly deed. But it was *his father*. This was the man who had raised him alongside his mother, the man who had loved him unconditionally.

Could he really turn his back on him?

He pushed the door open as he decided he couldn't.

"Had me worried for a minute there, bud," his father said. He was seated at the kitchen table, a cigarette bouncing from between his lips as he talked. "Thought you slipped out on me."

"I...I couldn't." Rick dropped the cloth next to the homeowner, who was moaning weakly and reaching at him with a shaky hand. "He's still alive?" Rick backed away, retching and holding his stomach as his mouth flooded with saliva, the sticky, acidic taste of bile coming up his throat. He ran to the sink and vomited.

"Yeah, them Italians are stubborn bastards, even when it comes to dying," his father said in a spray of smoky laughter. He rose from the chair and patted Rick on the back as he continued to heave, same as he used to when Rick was a young boy and had gotten sick in the middle of the night. "Get it all out now, we're not done yet." He paused. "There's going to be quite a lot more blood I'd say."

The pipes chugged as Rick turned the cold water on, taking great mouthfuls of icy water and spitting it back into the sink. He splashed some over his face, and then looked up at his father. "He's already gonna die, dad, what else can you do?"

"Oh, send a little message I guess." His father snatched the drop cloth and flapped it hard, letting it go as it opened up and floated to the floor. He grabbed the chair he had been sitting in and placed it in the middle of the cloth. Then he kneeled and pried the old man's hand away from his neck, the last of his blood flowing slowly and smoothly out from the vein. There was an intake of air, and it was exhaled in a long sigh as the old man's eyes locked onto his tormentor.

"That's right," Rick's father said, smiling, "get an eye full. You won't be back talking to anyone anymore, my Italian friend, all thanks to me."

"Dad, let's call 911. Let's get an ambulance," Rick pleaded, staring in horror as his father pulled a box cutter from his back pocket.

His father said, "Too late. I killed the sumbitch. He's dead. Now it's time to finish the job."

The box cutter flashed in the kitchen light as Rick's father propped the dead man in the chair and cut his buttoned flannel shirt open, exposing a grey-haired beer belly. There was a thick sound like Velcro tearing apart as he took the box cutter and cut into the stomach in an upward slicing motion like he was gutting a fish. He grabbed the wound with two hands and ripped it the rest of the way open.

Rick grimaced and looked away.

"What?" his father asked with his eyebrows raised.

"Dad...what in God's name are you *doing*?"

"I'm a plumber, ain't I?" He began pulling out the man's organs and dropping them onto the cloth, where they plopped and bounced, leaving red smears and splatters. "He's got something wrong with his plumbing. I'm going to fix it. Go in the basement and get my tools and whatever spare pipe is left." He turned away and plunged his dripping red hands back into the man's innards.

Rick vomited again while he was in the basement, making harsh choking noises as nothing came up but mucous strings. Before, he had wondered if they were going to roll the man up into the drop cloth like a grisly burrito and find some place to dump the body. But now he was starting to suspect that the final outcome would be much worse.

Once upstairs, he watched in both disgust and morbid curiosity for an hour as his father worked on the man, whistling and smoking, nodding here and there as the pieces came together just like he wanted them to.

"There, all done!" His father stood up and wiped his hands on the seat of his jeans, leaving dark maroon stains. He clapped Rick on his back and looked at him with pride. "Were you paying attention? I hope so, since you're going to be taking over the business some day."

Rick hoped to forget what he had just watched, but inside he knew it would be impossible. Shock therapy wouldn't make him forget; hell, Alzheimer's disease couldn't even make him forget this.

"That's it for today," his father said when Rick didn't reply. "I'm gonna go warm the van up. Roll those parts up into the cloth and toss em in the van, all right?"

Rick gulped and nodded weakly. He heard the front door slam as he began to fold up the drop cloth, the organs inside like little plump, squishy packages in his hands as he picked it up, his nose wrinkling at the foul smell of intestine and bowel. He took one last look at the dead man in the chair before he left, still unbelieving.

With the gruesome bundle tucked under one arm, Rick exited the house. In his haste, he skidded and fell on the top step of the porch, and a dark lumpy object that may have been the dead homeowner's liver fell from the rolled up cloth. It bounced down the stairs, granules of dirty snow and chips of grey paint sticking to it like sprinkles on a scoop of ice cream. Rick wrinkled his nose and looked away as he grabbed the organ and stuffed it back into the cloth with the others.

He was grateful for the rusty smell of the van's exhaust as he opened the back and tossed in the bundle. He peered at the sign on the side of the truck for a moment, wondering how his father could think there would be any business after what had just happened. They might as well drive right to the jail.

"You know, Rick," his father began as Rick entered the van, "You probably think I've flipped my lid, but what I did was a good thing."

His father turned the headlights on, fat flakes of snow swirling about in the beams of light. It wasn't quite a blizzard outside, but there was about three inches of slushy snow covering the roads, and the van slid this way and that as his father drove, the bald tires finding almost no purchase. "I had a revelation in there."

Rick said nothing. He rocked in his seat as his father turned onto the highway.

His father seemed undaunted. "What was this revelation, you ask? Well, I'll tell you. I went upstairs to tell that guy I was finished, and there he was, drunker than all hell, his car keys dangling from his fingers. And what does he say? He says, 'I burnt my dinner, gotta go get something from the store.' Remember how your mother used to burn dinner sometimes, and I'd tease her about it?" He reached over and grabbed Rick's shoulder, squeezing it in painful urgency. "Remember?"

"Yeah, I remember. Where are we going? Why are we on the highway?"

Rick's father ignored him. "It was a sign, Rick. A sign from your mother. 'Don't let this drunk leave the house and kill someone like I was killed' is what she told me. I heard her. So I killed him before he could kill someone else. It was a preventative measure. Your mother is looking down at us from Heaven, and she's proud."

"Dad, where are we going?" Rick was getting scared, even more than he already was. He didn't think his father would hurt him, but he didn't know what his father had planned, and the van was sliding all over the highway, tractor trailers and cars blaring their horns as they passed.

"We're gonna stop and see your mother at the cemetery, so I can talk to her before we move on."

Rick looked at his father with a cocked eyebrow. "Move on? Move on where?"

"Oh, wherever she tells us to go." His father lit a cigarette, "You see, we're starting up a new business. Plumbing is out, killing drunks is in. We're gonna cruise from town to town, take care of them idiots."

Rick looked out the window and he remembered how his mother had been run off the road all those years the ago by a drunk driver, a cross planted on the inside of the guardrail marking the spot. "Dad, this is insane."

He was rocked forward as his father clipped him on the back of the head and pointed a blood-crusted finger at him. "You mind me and your mother. You're gonna help me whether you like it or not."

All the great memories of how his father taught him to ride a bike, the first time they went fishing, the first beer they shared, the way his father looked at him with pride when he graduated high school, and the way they comforted each other in the wake of his mother's death... had been obliterated by the dead Italian man in the chair.

There was nothing good anymore, nothing pure; and hadn't been since his mother died. The smiles and laughter and sunny days were now always being replaced by angry red faces and screams.

Rick made up his mind as they passed mile marker 426.8; only another quarter of a mile to go before they reached the cemetery.

And now he understood. He knew the way things were. He couldn't leave his father, abandon him to his madness, but he also couldn't go on to be an accessory to any of this. The thought of killing people sickened him.

"What the hell are you doing?" his father screamed as Rick grabbed the wheel and jerked it hard to the right. The speeding van fishtailed, spun around, then smashed through the guard rail in a shower of sparks and screeching metal, his mother's remembrance cross splintering in a spray of wood as the front of the van plowed through the rail and careened over the steep embankment.

The van flipped over and over, the roof crunching in violently and compacting Rick's head down into his shoulders, shattering his spine. And the final image before his eyes wasn't the spinning world around him, or his father's agonized face, but an old dead Italian man in a chair, his organs replaced with empty beer bottles connected by a series of pipes and fittings, and the words 'NEVER AGAIN' carved into his wrinkled forehead with jagged letters.

About Dominick Nole

Dominick Nole was born in 1984 and lives in Dunmore, Pennsylvania. Aside from writing, he also enjoys playing the guitar, drawing, taking care of his cat Skellington and bearded dragon Bonnie, and watching as many horror movies as he possibly can.

His other stories have appeared in *SNM Horror Magazine*.

The Wood Witch
By Jonathan Chapman

I am a forty-six-year old man now. I work as a social worker in Waterstown, New York. I rescue little girls from the type of situations from which no one had rescued Carin.

Who is Carin?

You never forget your first love. She was mine.

It amazes me how vividly I can still visualize in my mind the moment I first saw her, as if it happened yesterday. I am thinking of Carin, pretending it really did happen yesterday, and deceiving myself that I still had time to rescue her; that I would be her knight, her hero.

The Marley Woods was where I went as a thirteen-year-old to have a quiet, deserted place to be alone. It was up a little hill just at the edge of town. There was a trail from the little pre-war homes and streets down below, leading up to the edge of the thick pine and elm woods that stood dense and silent at the top and stretching away for miles. That day the snow was falling heavily as I ran and huffed to the top.

She was sitting on a little log in a space obviously hand-cleared of snow, looking prim and proper with her knees together and her hands on top. She was wearing an odd purple coat, too small and torn, maybe a hand-me-down—no girl my age would be caught dead in it—and worn jeans with boots that looked too water logged to be worn on that snowy day. A poor girl, without doubt. Still, there was something pretty about her as she looked up at me, her red hair falling all down behind her, green eyes peering at me, quick and alert.

"Hi," I said. I didn't know what else to say; the whole "talking to girls" thing was entirely new to me. And I had never seen a girl up there at the edge of the woods before. Girls didn't go to most creepy places like deep woods and creeks by themselves, as I could recall.

"If you're going to make fun of my clothes, just go away," she said.

I patted my jacket with the patches and the holes and the stains. "I wouldn't make fun of anyone who dresses like I do."

"Thank you." She smiled and looked me over less defensively. "Let me see—you're the smallest boy in your class, your family is poor and you get bullied a lot. You come up here to forget and to dream about life."

I stared at her. "Um—wow. You don't hold back any punches. And you're?"

"A girl version."

"My name's Jack," I said, feeling lame. Was this banter? She was better at it.

"Hello, Jack. I'm Carin. With a 'C'."

"They should have named you Lilith," I said, "because of the red hair and green eyes, like in the books."

"Maybe I can read your mind like Lilith can," she said with a wry smile. "If I could, what would I see?"

"My baseball card collection," I said. I was nervous; I was actually talking to a girl. The last time I had talked with girls had been far back in the mists of sixth grade. Then, of course, the goal was to get them as mad as possible. This felt different.

Then I realized that I was much too old to be talking about baseball cards. That was kid stuff. To change the subject, I motioned towards the Marley Woods. "What are you doing up here? They say there's a witch far back in the woods."

"Maybe there is," she said. "Maybe it's Lilith. Have you seen the witch?"

"No, but I don't go past the creek."

"Oh! So, if there is one, will you protect me?"

I threw my chest out in play-action fashion. She was fun. "I would! As best I could. But why *are* you here, really?"

She pointed down the hill at the rows of homes on the little street leading to that hill. The one closest to the woods sat like a squatting toad, broken down and crumbling. Old cars rested in the yard, where a pit bull prowled. The grass was shoulder high; the shutters hung limply, if they were attached at all, and the paint was coming off in flakes.

I knew the house; on the way up the hill I had skirted past it by a wide margin, staying clear of that dog. Within, I heard a woman screaming curses and a man's drunken retort. The home had been like a black thing on the white street.

She lived there?

"Oh," I said. "Oh. I get it."

She nodded gravely. "Maybe I will go into the woods and find the witch. Live with her. It can't be worse than home."

"Do you have anyone to go to? Besides a witch, I mean. An aunt, a grandma?"

"No…we're all alone. I'm all alone."

I sat down next to her. "Well, we can be friends."

"I don't want you to just feel sorry for me, Jack."

"I…um…I…"

"What?"

"I'm here…out here, now…because my dad left. A year ago. And mom comes home and yells at me and then drinks vodka in a little cup until she falls asleep on the couch. So I've got no one either. I can't have company or go to things…" I trailed off in the way a thirteen-year-old does.

Carin put a hand on my knee. It was shocking in its warmth, and even more shocking that she did it at all.

"It's okay," She said. "I understand."

And then we talked for hours. We talked until the dark fell and the bone chilling cold made our hands and feet numb and we might have talked all night except her dad was suddenly a few feet away, huffing and puffing up that hill.

"Caaaaaaarr-innnnnn! Get your ass over here right *now*!"

Carin stood and walked meekly back towards the towering monolith that was her father. He glared at me from the top of his bull neck.

"Stay away from my daughter, boy."

I heard Carin suck in air as he grabbed her by the arm and squeezed. He yanked her hard, so that her whole body shook, but she didn't say anything. She looked back over her shoulder, waved bleakly and was gone, back into that little war zone, while I ran home to mine.

But the deal was done, the way it is when you are thirteen. A secret, unspoken pact had been made.

We were pals.

The next day I went back up that hill—not to see Carin, I told myself. Only to go explore the woods.

She wasn't there. The little log we'd sat on still had the little cleared spot, but no Carin. I stood at the edge, looking into the forest. Had she gone in there? Or was she home? There was no way I was going to her house.

And then something moved in the forest.

I stared into the darkness of the thicker branches. The woods became denser as they went, with great deadfalls of branches and fallen limbs. The land itself fell away into a big creek that made a natural barrier. No one I knew had ever crossed that creek, or climbed the high bank on the other side. It was full of nettles and brambles, we'd say. Not worth the trouble.

There! A dark shape.

I turned and ran. I ran down the hill and back to the street, back by Carin's house. I slid to a stop, ashamed of my fear, of my running, of my mooning around for her. I could hear yelling inside; the rumble of a man's loud voice; someone crying. Who was crying? Carin? Her mom? I stood a long time, but when you're thirteen you don't know what to do at those times. So I did nothing. After a while, I went home.

*****

"Happy birthday!" I said. We were sitting huddled in the big public library, on "our" bench far in the back. It was that special time of freedom after three in the afternoon, with school out and her father not home yet. We found our shelter in the library, bus station and the park when it was warm.

"Thank you, good sir," she said. She took the Twinkie package I handed her.

"Happy sweet fourteen."

"Well, it's not a fancy party really since you're the only guest, but I'm having a literate birthday, anyway. Oh! Shhh! Grab a book!"

We took up our props and sat still, eyes glued to pages.

Ms. Kanipe rolled her cart around the corner, stared at us skeptically and almost said something. I looked out of the corner of my eye to see that Carin had swept the Twinkies under her book bag.

"Why do I find you two here so much?" Mrs. Kanipe grated.

"We're study partners," I said. "Carin is going to the same school as me now."

Ms. Kanipe shook her head. "I don't care where you go to school. I do care about how you behave in my library."

I looked back at my book. I had learned if I stared at it long enough she went away.

"She's gone," Carin whispered. She leaned over, just as I was leaning over to tell her the same thing, and we were suddenly inches apart.

And kissing.

I don't know how long. How long is a kiss at fourteen?

"I knew it!" Ms. Kanipe stormed back around the bookshelves. "Out! Get out of here!"

We gathered our things and left, giggling but also aware we'd lost our main place to be in the cold winter afternoons. And we were also aware that something had happened. Something new.

"Where should we go?" I asked, huddling up with Carin.

"Let's go into the woods."

We walked to the edge of the forest. I glanced into the woods. They still made me nervous. Scared, even, though I would never say that out loud.

"Are you going to kiss me again?" Carin asked.

"I...um..."

Carin leaned on my chest, and we made an awkward embrace.

And something moved in those woods. I jumped, making a little hop and intake of air.

"Carin! Did you see that?"

"It's okay," she said. She looked into the woods calmly. "I've seen it a few times."

"What?"

"Maybe it's time I told you. It's not an *it*, it's a *she*. She lives far back there. She's called me to visit her. I haven't, yet. But I think she comes out after I sit here a while, even if I can't see her."

"Carin, you need to stay away from whatever it is. It's evil."

"Don't say *it*; I told you she's a *she*." And then Carin shrugged. "What's evil? She wants to spend time with me. She wants to teach me. What are my own parents? Tell me she can be worse than them? She isn't evil. She likes broken things. Like me."

"You don't know that she wants good things for you."

"Okay, let me prove it!" Carin was laughing. She turned to the woods, teasing me, waving her hands at the dark underbrush. "Here! Hello there! Hello!"

There was motion in the forest. On the edge of sight, the edge of vision, the edge of knowing. It was the thing you see in the corner of your eye and walk away from, quickly. It was the shadow you see in the hall at three in the morning and explain to yourself as nothing at all because to think otherwise would be impossible.

"If you want to help us, do something about Ms. Kanipe!" Carin called to the forest. I grabbed her and pulled her away from the hill front. I had turned it to imagination; I would not believe. It was a trick of the light, no more.

The next day Ms. Kanipe was gone.

They never found her, although there were searches. Not a body, not a trail of blood...nothing. She was just—gone.

We huddled in the library that next day, whispering of it. Carin seemed awed, struck with the power of it, and the immediate response. I wasn't sure if she felt guilty at all; I did. And yet, it might still all be a coincidence, a strange thing that had happened randomly. Or so I kept thinking. Hoping.

A week later I was on my way home from my first job shoveling snow off a driveway for a neighbor. This time of year night came early, so the sun had already set, even though it was only seven o'clock.

I was "high" on too many Diet Cokes and working and I walked by Carin's house, maybe to think of her or see her walk by the blinds. It was terribly romantic to be walking by her house in the snow, thinking of her so close. I thought of Romeo throwing a stone at her window, but shuddered. Her father would kill us both if he caught us. I walked by ever so slowly—

I heard her screaming.

It was her, without a doubt. She was there, in that house; around her piercing screams her father's shouts, his loud bursts of anger, rage; it was a drunken rage.

But I was not thirteen this time, now I was a whole year older. Fourteen was old enough to do something.

I ran to the door, relieved that the big black dog was still chained to the tree. I was surprised and pleased to find that the door was unlocked. I ran inside, rushing down the hall.

There, in the living room were Carin and her father. He had her down on the floor, fist raised. She was tear stained, streaked, red faced. I was on him in a moment. I jumped on his back.

We wrestled. The old man was strong as a bull, while I was still a boy, really. But he was fat, tired and drunk, and I wriggled my way around him this way and that. I was fresh from those forced PE wrestling classes. In a second he was off her.

"Run!" I screamed.

And she did.

"You're a dead man, you little shit! Oh, I know you've been dragging around after my daughter, you little pervert! And now you break into *my* house? You're going to jail, you filthy shit!"

I pushed the man off me and backed down the hallway.

"I'm calling the police, punk! I'm getting my gun!"

I ignored him and ran outside as well. I could see Carin's tracks in the snow, even as I ran to the street. To my surprise her footprints did not turn left, towards town, they turned the other direction.

Into the woods.

I ran up the hill, following her tracks, calling for her. Behind me, the red and blue lights of the sheriff moved up the street. How could they have come so quickly?

I ran to the edge of the woods; it was too dark to go further. But she could not have gone far, I told myself; not in the night. No one would go into the woods at night.

There was a whoosh from somewhere in the trees. I felt it as much as heard it. Something was moving in the dark. Motion mixed with feeling, deep within. The message was simple and final: *Go away. She's mine now.*

"No!" I screamed into the black forest, plumes of steam from my breath casting out into the night. It was all blackness before me, but in the snow the faintest light reflected. I could see the steps Carin had taken as she ran into the trees.

I had to make a decision. I could go home now, and be fourteen, or I could go into the abyss of the woods and be a man.

Ahead of me a tree branch broke loudly with a sharp *Crack!* I jumped and fell into a crouch, heart thundering in my chest. The big branch whacked and crashed its way down to the ground. My mind raced; if she could knock that branch down there, couldn't she do that to my head?

And then I was so frightened again that I felt all the bravado of a minute before disappear. What was I thinking, to challenge some…creature?

But this was *Carin.* Dear God, this was the girl I loved. The thought of her there, with that *thing*, and all the hurt that was her life and I was supposed to rescue her—

"Carin!" I yelled. "Carin, come back! You're just going from one wrong thing to another! It's the same! The witch doesn't care about you!"

There was a whistling, almost howling sound in the dark and something went by my ear—*fast!*—and I ducked again. What had that been? I heard it smacking through the brush behind me, then out of the woods. By the sound, I knew that if it had struck me, I'd be dead.

But I had no choice. I had to save Carin. I stepped in the blacker dots of her tracks, racing now and crashing through the brambles. I could hear the creek up ahead, rushing with winter water. Had she crossed there?

I ran to the bank. My eyes were adjusting to the inky black depths of the forest. I could make out the water below, the trees against the sky above me, and the snow in the trees across the little chasm. A fallen ash lay across the water, the snow disturbed by something that had crossed there. Carin?

I stepped onto the log. It was slick; below me, the waters rushed on in the blackness, only the white water visible. I inched forward, one step at a time, and then I looked up.

There was Carin, across the creek, standing in the little snowy clearing, fifty yards away. She stood still, head down, hands clasped in front of her.

"Carin!" I shouted in relief. She was alive!

And then something stepped in front of her. It was a thing of total blackness, a wave of dark that blotted her out entirely. I realized I was panting in terror, my heart actually hurting as it pounded in my chest.

The blackness before Carin turned. Slowly, it rotated around, and a face materialized in the gloom: a long, sickly white form, the length of her head grossly exaggerated, too long, almost two feet long, unnatural and monstrous. The eyes were horrible sagging holes that held back a glimmering reddish-black glow, like old embers when the fire has gone out but still smolders hotly. The mouth was a hawkish gape, the nose too long, hanging bulbous and insanely hooked, a cartoon image, true…but dear Heaven, so much more than comedy. Instead, a terrible reality.

I was drawn back to those terrible eyes that glared hatred at me like a burning brand. I imagined it was the way Satan would look as he threw you into the pit, laughing at your pain.

And then the thing moved. One black arm began to rise and a white finger emerged from the cowl that she wore, and the finger pointed at me, the finger of death on a winter's night, the bony finger of the reaper.

Carin was disappearing into the folds of that thing's cloak, and I knew—felt it, was sure of it—that if this night ended with Carin and that thing together, she would never rejoin my world, the world of light. No one could exist in the presence of such terrible blackness and not be changed and lost forever in some way.

I kept moving forward, and I realized that I was almost to the other side. The bony finger snapped, making a sickening dry sound.

And the log beneath me cracked and broke, and after a dizzy, wild second I fell into the water below, a sudden shocking fall, the water instantly numbing my arms, shoving me along and around, my feet above my head. I was drowning in freezing darkness and the rushing water bounced me off the banks and along the bottom.

There is no terror as complete as being underwater in the dark, in a freezing flood, certain of your death, certain you would drown alone at night and be lost forever. So I fought the water viciously for my life; I couldn't tell which way to swim because I was thrown around the rocky bottom and was disoriented, but I swam anyway.

Suddenly I found myself at the top of the water, and my head broke through. Lungs aching, I gasped for air before propelling myself to the side. I tumbled along the bank, dragged by the flooded creek, too fast to catch, my body bouncing along and being clawed by branches and rocks, rolling over and over. Ahead in the black, the creek met with another storm-swollen river, and if I reached that I was dead without doubt.

I made one last effort, throwing myself onto the bank and digging my hands into the dirt, clawing at it, grasping mud and roots and stones, unaware that my fingers were cut and bleeding.

I pulled myself up and out of the water.

I lay on the little shore, shivering in great spasmodic waves, the front of my body torn open in a hundred places, left leg broken, snapped between knee and ankle, coughing water out and throwing up in fear and terror.

But no pain was as great as the realization that I had failed Carin. I thought I could rescue her, and instead I was witness to a terrible entity that absorbed her...an entity that Carin didn't fear. I knew that the Wood Witch offered her a safer place than that of her own home.

But I also knew that the offer was a lie. Children can grow up and leave their parents. But Carin would forever be a prisoner of the Marley Wood Witch.

*****

The search party formed to look for Carin that night, but found me instead. It was luck; I should have probably frozen. The man who found me said he heard a girl calling, and that led him to me.

The authorities looked for Carin and I was questioned. I told them the truth, part of it, anyway. I had followed Carin into the woods and I had gotten as far as the creek when I fell in. But about the witch...there are such moments in life; things of which we never speak.

The authorities noted that her bare footprints ran a hundred yards into the Woods to the creek and then stopped. They supposed that she ran and jumped into the icy water and was swept into the Great Lakes. They did not find her footprints on the far side of the creek, where I'd seen her standing. The incident was listed as "probable suicide."

I never accepted that. I sat at the edge of the woods, staring into the blackness, calling out to her. She had been my best friend; the girl I loved. And she had gone—somewhere. I was sure she was still there, in those woods—with that thing. I went there every day for three years. On her birthday I left flowers on our sitting place.

I graduated high school and went away to college. I lived my life. But one day I came back to Waterstown.

Marley Woods had changed. An old hobo was found dead there one winter's night with a crow stuffed down his throat. It was the first murder in Waterstown in thirty years, and particularly gruesome. I was the only one to notice that he looked like Carin's dad.

I did not see Carin again. To this day I have not seen her.

But I see drunken parents beating their children. I see others neglecting their children. And still others think it is okay to allow their children to wander into the woods.

As a social worker, now I can do something about it. Now I don't have to fall into storm-swollen creeks to save a young girl. Now I don't have to face the Wood Witch, only the demons of dysfunctional families that I try to help.

And that's how I rescue Carin today. I decided to stay in Waterstown, because there just seems to be so many Carins here.

About Jonathan Chapman

Jonathan Chapman is a Social worker and child abuse investigator in Contra Costa County. He has an MA from St. Mary's and three wonderful daughters.

You can frequently find him in the woods and forests of Contra Costa County. He doesn't mention what he's looking for out there.

THE HOUSEWARMING
BY RONALD MALFI

Mark and Lisa Schoenfield spent the afternoon preparing for the party.

They scurried about their spacious new home, making sure the floors were spotless and the large bay windows were free from smudges. Lisa prepared guacamole, miniature tacos (chicken, beef, and vegetarian), cocktail wieners wrapped in flaky croissants, fruit salad, a Caesar salad, and a variety of cookies fanned out like playing cards on a gorgeous Wedgwood serving tray. Mark made the liquor store run, and returned with a carton of assorted bottles and several cases of low-calorie beer. They squabbled playfully over what playlist to select on their shared iPod, with Lisa preferring classical selections to Mark's more modern pop sensibilities. In the end, they settled on a rotation of up-tempo jazz numbers, and finished preparing for the event amidst the brassy intonations of Coltrane and Davis.

Mark was forty-two years old, in good shape, and had all his hair and teeth. He was a musician by trade, having once toured the East Coast with a group who played original Americana in the styles of Springsteen, Mellencamp, and Seger, though for the past decade or so he had found a comfortable little niche composing and recording the scores for independent studio films. This afforded him the luxury of working from home, which made the soundproofed basement the biggest selling point of the new house, at least as far as he was concerned.

Lisa was thirty-eight and was in equally good shape as her husband. She maintained her figure with a steadfast regiment of aerobic exercises, proper dieting, and an overall positive outlook. She was an attorney who specialized in contract law, and she had recently taken a position with a downtown firm who lured her away from her previous employers with promises of partnership in the not-too-distant future. The new job was the reason for the relocation, and for the new house.

And the house itself? It was a neoclassical Victorian with great flow and four bedrooms at the end of a quaint suburban cul-de-sac. The lawns were blindingly green, the driveway like a black satin ribbon winding in serpentine fashion up the gradual incline of the property toward the two-car garage with the carriage-house lights. At the topmost roof, a weathervane fashioned in the shape of an archer's arrow spiraled lazily in the cool summer breeze. It was the first house the Schoenfields visited, and they had made their offer—quite a generous offer—the very next day.

Now, two weeks after they had moved in, the place had begun taking on some semblance of home. In tandem, Mark and Lisa had spent much of the previous week visiting their nearest neighbors, introducing themselves in their cheerful and overzealous way. The neighbors all seemed friendly enough, and pleased to have a seemingly normal-looking couple move into the neighborhood.

"We're having a housewarming party this weekend," Mark and Lisa would take turns saying, "and we'd love it if you'd come by."

Nearly everyone on the block agreed, and seemed enchanted by the prospect.

The first guests arrived that night at precisely eight o'clock. They were a young couple named Baum, the man in spectacles and the woman in a swoopy floral sundress.

"Hey," Mark said, fervently shaking the man's hand while grinning to beat the band. "Great! You guys are the first to arrive. Can I get you a drink?"

Mark fixed a vodka tonic for Mr. Baum and a glass of merlot for Mrs. Baum, which he handed off to the respective guests with his smile still firmly in place. In the parlor, Lisa raised the volume of the iPod in an effort to make the atmosphere livelier.

Soon after, more guests arrived. Mark immediately made no promises to himself that he would remember all the names of his visitors, though he did intend to conclude the evening having memorized the names of at least three of the couples. The Tohts, the Nancers, the O'Learys, the Smiths, the Barrows—they were all young and handsome and well-groomed and cheerful. Each time the doorbell went off—a plangent *cling-clong!* that sounded to the Schoenfields like a church bell—a new wave of bright faces filed into the foyer. Lisa was pleased to see that many of the women brought food. Mark was pleased to find that a number of the men brought liquor.

As is the custom at such events, the men eventually gravitated toward one end of the house and remained huddled in a tight little group away from the women. They clutched cans of beer or rocks glasses and spoke of the neighborhood's comings and goings with a sense of pride and stewardship Mark Schoenfield admired. They were straight enough to be proper but loose enough to laugh at the occasional crass joke, which endeared them all the more to Mark. When one of the wives swooped by, the respective husband would slip an arm around her waist and plant a quick little peck on her check.

Lisa led an expedition of inquisitive women through the house—up and down the stairs, in and out of all the rooms. Closet doors were opened and bathroom shower stalls were subjected to intrusive scrutiny. One woman even possessed the audacity to peer under the bed in the master bedroom. A few women marveled over what the Schoenfields had managed to do with the place in such a short amount of time.

"We've hardly begun," informed Lisa.

"Nonsense!" said a woman named Tracy Birch. "The place is lovely!"

"Hadn't any of you been in the house before, when the previous owners had lived here?" Lisa asked the gaggle of women.

"Of course, dear," said Sandy O'Leary, "but they had gotten so *old,* and their tastes were so *old.* It's good to have fresh young blood back on the street."

Downstairs, the men had become garrulous in the absence of women. Mark was pleased to fetch them drinks and returned to the parlor at one point balancing a bowl of guacamole in one hand, drinks in the other, and a bag of Tostitos wedged under one arm. The men applauded his foresight then tore into the bag of chips like a pride of lions descending on a carcass.

"Do you play golf?" asked Bob O'Leary.

"On occasion," Mark said.

Bob O'Leary beamed and clapped him on the forearm. "Brilliant! There's an exceptional course less that fifteen miles from here. It's right on the bay. Gorgeous!"

"Gorgeous," echoed Milton Underland, who stood close by, his mouth full of guacamole. He held a beer in each hand.

The doorbell stopped ringing, yet the guests continued to arrive. The Nevins, the Copelands, the Wintermeyers, the Joneses, the de Filippos. Mark took snapshot photos of each of their faces by blinking his eyes. *Gotcha.* Heavily perfumed women kissed him wetly on the cheek, their scents floral and fecund and delightful. Each man shook his hand while gripping his upper arm in a familiar but not unwelcomed embrace. Mark realized that it had been a long time—since college, maybe—that he'd had a group of male friends with which he could so casually bond.

At one point during the evening, Mark and Lisa bumped into each other in the hallway. The rooms were choked with people and there were more walking up the flagstone path, but they didn't care: they kissed, and it wasn't a brief and perfunctory act. It was meaningful. The stress of the move sloughed from Mark's flesh; the anxiety of switching jobs seemed to burn off Lisa's shoulders like steam off hot blacktop.

The Quindlands, the Hamms, the Dovers, the MacDonalds, the Kellers, a second pair of Smiths—they kept coming. In the kitchen, fresh plates of food replaced old ones. Beer coolers were replenished with new cans and bottles then covered in a shower of ice cubes.

"What is it that you do?" Ted Hamm asked him.

"I'm a musician," Mark explained. "I compose and record the soundtracks for indie films."

"Fantastic! Any films I would know?"

"The most recent was called *Oglethorpe and Company*," Mark said, though he confessed that it had had only minimal distribution. "The most popular is probably the *Sledge* series of films."

"You mean those over-the-top horror movies where all those nubile young waifs get clobbered by the masked maniac wielding a sledgehammer?" Ted Hamm's eyes blazed with what Mark interpreted as pure enchantment.

"Yes," Mark said. "Those films."

"I *love* them! I go hog-wild for those movies! They're so ridiculously bloody, I don't know whether to laugh or scream in terror."

"Thank you," Mark said, unsure if such a comment should be taken as a compliment or not, "but I didn't make the movies. Just the soundtracks."

Another man—someone Mark hadn't yet met—appeared beside Ted Hamm and began humming the discordant title theme from the *Sledge* series of films. Ted grinned, nodding like an imbecile at the man, then turned his blank and grinning face back to Mark.

"Yeah," Mark said. "That's it, all right."

One of the wives also appeared before him. She was a slim brunette in a stunning red dress. She addressed the small upright piano toward the rear of the parlor with beautifully manicured fingernails. "You must play it," she told him. "Oh, please?"

"Yes!" boomed Ted Hamm. "You must!"

It seemed that he was carried toward the piano on a wave of arms. Before being deposited onto the piano bench, some invisible pair of fingers administered a sharp pinch to his midsection. The keyboard cover was thrust open, revealing a mouthful of grinning alabaster teeth. Temporarily disoriented, Mark did not begin to play until some of the guests began humming the theme song. He came in midway through the second bar, his fingers first fumbling over the keys before finding their rhythm.

"There it is!" one of the men shouted. "You've got it now!"

Mark laughed and continued to play. It was all minor chord progressions and jangly high keys—a simple but recognizable melody that had helped secure the *Sledge* franchise some status among horror movie aficionados.

When he finished, the room applauded. Yet when he tried to get up, hands appeared on his back and shoulders, forcing him back down onto the piano bench.

"Please," a woman's voice pleaded. "Once more around the mulberry bush, Mark."

So he cracked his knuckles and played the piece again.

Meanwhile, in the kitchen, Lisa found herself listening to the neighborhood gossip with mild voyeuristic pleasure. Which husband was sleeping with which wife; whose children were just *awful brutes;* what local restaurants were known swingers' joints.

"Is it something you've ever done?" one of the women asked Lisa.

"You mean Mark and me?" Lisa said, hearing Mark at the piano in the next room the instant she spoke his name. "Have we ever…?"

"Not even once?" another woman asked. She was meatier than the others, with great silver streaks in her otherwise raven-colored hair.

"No," Lisa confessed. "Not even once."

"This is so distasteful," said a third woman. Lisa thought her name was Betsy. "Such talk. Who are we, anyway? This isn't *Desperate Housewives*, you know."

A few of the women chided Betsy, though good-naturedly.

Lisa heard the piano stop again…then start up a third time. The same tune. She recognized it as the theme from those horror movies Mark had composed.

The patio door off the kitchen slid open and two good-looking couples came in. They ignored Lisa, and went to embrace some of the other women gathered around the kitchen. All of a sudden, Lisa felt like a stranger in her own house, and in her own life.

"The house is beautiful!" said one of the new women. "We love what you've done with the place. Show us around?"

"Yes," said the other woman. "We'd love the grand tour."

Again, Lisa took the women in and out of rooms, down hallways, opened closet doors. One of the women seemed to take exceptional interest in the cleanliness of the toilets, stopping to peer down at her reflection simmering on the surface of the water in each bowl.

After a while, Lisa packed away the food, leaving only the desserts on the counter. She brewed some Sumatran coffee and decided to forgo her good china cups in favor of the Styrofoam ones Mark had picked up yesterday at the grocery store. There were too many people and she didn't have enough china to go around. As she handed out coffee to extended hands, her guests smiled warmly at her.

"We love what you and Mark have done with the house," Sheila Duggan said.

"Your taste is exquisite," Sallyanne Monroe said.

"Oh," Lisa said, "we've hardly had a chance to do a thing."

The Bostons, the Daleys, the Fritzes, the Loans filed into the house, cheery-faced and smelling of colognes, perfumes, deodorants.

In the parlor, Mark struggled up off the piano bench. More hands gripped him and tried to force him back onto the bench, but he slid sideways and marshaled decisively through the crowd. Several of the guests issued boos at his departure, until someone else claimed the piano bench and began playing a fairly commendable rendition of Joplin's "Maple Leaf Rag."

Mark found Lisa in the doorway between the parlor and the kitchen, her back toward him. He sighed into her hair and muttered, "My fingers are burning."

Lisa turned…and it wasn't Lisa at all. Another woman in the same dress, her hair done up in a similar fashion. The strangeness of her appearance caused Mark to utter a small cry.

"Hello," she said, smiling prettily at him.

"I'm sorry. I thought you were my wife."

"She's delightful," said the woman. "You both are. Was that you on the piano just a moment ago?"

"It was."

"You play so well. You are a professional?"

"Yes, I am."

"So wonderful to have such a talented new couple join the community."

In the kitchen, Lisa waved to him over a sea of bobbing heads and grinning faces. Mark excused himself and navigated through the crowd until he reached his wife. She looked tired.

"Coffee?" she asked him.

"I'm too tired for coffee," he said, "if that makes any sense."

"They keep coming," she said.

"They love us," he responded, though without the satisfaction expected with such a sentiment.

In the parlor, "Maple Leaf Rag" segued into "The Entertainer." Voices boomed in pleasure. A few of the women in the kitchen began dancing with each other, their coffee cups held up above their heads while they twirled each other around with their free hands.

A perky redhead approached the Schoenfields dragging behind her a man in a pressed oxford shirt and pleated khakis. "My husband Michael and I missed the tour of the house," she said in a nasally, almost pleading voice. "Is it too late for us? We'd love to see all the work you've been doing."

"We really would," Michael added.

"We haven't done any work," Mark advised the couple.

"Everyone is bragging about the upstairs," said the woman, as if she hadn't heard him.

"It's nothing," Lisa cut in.

The redheaded woman cheered with glee, clasping her hands together. "I bet it's outstanding!"

Mark and Lisa exchanged a look. "I'll take them," he offered, then led the couple up the stairs. The three of them wandered around the hallway, dipping in and out of unfinished bedrooms, bathrooms, closets. The redhead paused before one bathroom mirror to examine her reflection, then—astoundingly—she readjusted her cleavage while Mark stood gaping at her in the bathroom doorway. The woman's husband didn't seem to notice; he was too preoccupied examining the grout in the shower stall.

A few minutes later, as Mark led them back down the stairs, he noticed that the pianist had abandoned Joplin in favor of plucking out random sour notes on the keyboard. It was as if the piano player had suffered a stroke while on the bench. Nonetheless, the guests still cheered on the abysmal playing.

Exhausted, Mark looked around the kitchen for Lisa, but could not find her. It seemed more people had showed up while he had been upstairs, which was strange because it was awfully late for new arrivals. He glanced at the wall clock above the sink and saw that the clock had ceased working at 8:39 PM. He then glanced at his wrist before realizing he hadn't worn his wristwatch.

Someone began playing "Chopsticks" on the piano. Badly.

Mark shouted, "Lisa?" but doubted she could hear him over the cacophony of their guests, the piano, and the muddled jazz coming from the detachable iPod speakers. His head throbbed. "Excuse me, excuse me," he mumbled, cutting through the crowd. When he reached the parlor, he saw men dancing with men, women dancing with women, and a huddle of striped polo shirts standing around the piano. "Chopsticks" ended abruptly and the guests began haranguing the pianist. Mark saw the pianist try to stand, catching a glimpse of the familiar hairdo and dress, and thought, *Lisa*.

It was. She sat before the piano, several hands on her shoulders as if to hold her in place, while her hands sat now in her lap. A terrified expression was etched across her face. She did not know how to play the piano—barring, apparently, a rudimentary rendition of "Chopsticks"— and when she met Mark's eyes, he could see all the fear bottled up inside her. He reached out and she grasped his hand...but then *other* hands shoved him down onto the piano bench beside her.

"Play 'Heart and Soul,'" someone shouted.

"I want to get up," Lisa uttered very close to Mark's ear.

"Lean on my shoulder and I'll play," he told her.

After he had played "Heart and Soul" twice, he grasped Lisa's hand and tugged her up off the bench. Hands tried to shove them back down but Mark swatted them away as he dragged Lisa toward the kitchen. There were so many people in the parlor now it was becoming difficult to breathe.

"I'm so tired," Lisa said. "I don't think a single person has gone home yet."

"They just—" He was about to say *keep coming* when the patio door swooshed open again and another bright-eyed, pleasant-smelling couple appeared in the doorway.

"Hello!" boomed the man.

"So *nice* to finally meet you both!" cried the woman.

Lisa smiled at them wearily. Mark paused to shake their hands. To his surprise, the woman leaned in and kissed him on the corner of his mouth. The kiss lasted longer than it should have, and although it was dry and unobtrusive, she exhaled into his nostrils before pulling away. It was like tasting her breath. Instantaneously, Mark felt an erection threaten the front of his pants.

"I'd love to see the upstairs," the woman said to him, her stare hanging between then like cabling.

"In just a minute," he said, excusing himself, and dragging Lisa into the kitchen.

"Do you mind if we put on another pot of coffee, Lisa, dear?" said Betsy, coming up and breathing in Lisa's face.

"Well," Lisa said, her eyes skirting the room. "Do you think people will—"

"You're a peach!" said Betsy, then twirled away to address the coffee pot on the kitchen counter.

"I'm exhausted," Lisa moaned to Mark again. "It's got to be close to midnight."

"The clock is dead," he told her, glancing up at it again. Only now, it read 8:42 PM. As he stared, he could see the second hand moving at nearly imperceptible increments. "Or," he amended, "it's *nearly* dead."

"Excuse me," Lisa said to Betsy. She pointed to the woman's sparkly gold wristwatch. "What time do you have?"

"Oh!" Betsy cooed. "Don't tell me you two are bushed already!" The woman glanced at her wristwatch. "Why, it's not even nine yet!"

Lisa said, "I'm sorry—did you just say it's not even *nine* yet? Nine o'clock?"

"This coffee smells so *good*," Betsy said with a wink, then turned back to the coffee pot. She began shoveling spoonsful of coffee into the percolator.

From the parlor, someone shouted Mark's name. When Mark turned, he saw a man he did not know waving him into the room. "I hear you're a regular Liberace!"

Mark just shook his head, a drawn expression on his face.

A woman in a dark blue beret appeared in front of Mark and Lisa and said, "I think you were a bit premature putting the food away. Do you mind if I break it back out? The Wilsons haven't even shown up yet, and they'll be ravenous!"

Lisa just blinked at the woman dumbly.

"Have at it," Mark interjected, then dragged Lisa out into the hallway.

Yet the hallway was cluttered with people, too. Hands extended to shake theirs, to pat their backs, to congratulate them and welcome them to the neighborhood. Again, those invisible fingers gave Mark's abdomen a pinch. This time he whirled around to address the culprit...but found himself staring at a wall of tightly-packed people, any of who could have been the violator.

Claustrophobia tightening around his neck, he pulled Lisa toward the staircase. Together, they bounded up the stairs to the second floor...yet froze at the top of the stairs as they saw the queue of people standing in the upstairs hallway. Wide eyes peered into the bedrooms. People murmured as they examined the bathrooms, the hall closets. A man in a tweed sports coat and a corduroy necktie stood before one open closet door, one of their bath towels in his hands. As Mark and Lisa watched, the man brought the towel to his nose and sniffed it.

"Enough," Mark called out. "It's getting late. We're going to have to ask that we at least keep the party downstairs. We'd appreciate it if—" But he cut himself off when he realized no one was listening to him.

"Mark," Lisa said, and touched his arm.

Angry, he stormed back downstairs—

"Mark!"

—and shoved through the guests in the hallway on his way to the front door. It took nearly a full minute for him to reach the door, grasp the knob, yank it open.

A man and a woman stood on the stoop, a platter of cookies in the woman's hands. They both smiled warmly at Mark, their teeth big and bright. Mark could see lipstick on some of the woman's teeth.

"Ah," said the man. "You must be Mark Schoenfield. Welcome to the neighborhood, old sailor."

Hands grabbed Mark around the forearms. Fingers snatched at his shirt and the legs of his pants. He craned his neck around to see the ghoulishly smiling faces of the men from the parlor breathing down his neck.

"You're quite the virtuoso," said Bob O'Leary. There was spinach dip stuck in his teeth. "Come play us that horror theme again, will you?"

Mark yanked one of his arms free.

"Aw, come on, now," Bob said, frowning playfully. "Don't be a spoiled sport." Bob checked his wristwatch. "It's early yet."

Lisa appeared on the stairwell. Mark met her eyes. She opened her mouth to say something to him, but was immediately approached by the young couple who had come through the patio door and requested a tour of the house. Mark saw Lisa shake her head. Nonetheless, the couple advanced on her, ascending the stairs. Lisa slowly backed away from them, moving up the stairs herself. She glanced one last time at Mark before her head disappeared beyond the ceiling. He watched her legs move backward up the stairs as the couple continued to advance on her.

Bob O'Leary and some of the other men dragged him through the kitchen toward the parlor.

"Seriously," Mark said, trying to shrug them all off. "I'm in no mood to play. It's late. Everyone needs to go home now."

"Coffee's on!" Betsy trilled from the counter. A wave of people flowed toward her.

"Late?" Bob O'Leary said. Then he pointed to the clock above the kitchen sink. "What's the matter with you, Mark?"

The clock read 8:50 PM.

"That clock is wrong," Mark said. He gripped the countertop and kicked at some of the more aggressive hands. They let him go. "It's late," he said, his breath coming in labored gasps now. "That clock is wrong."

Bob O'Leary's face seemed to crease down the middle with frustration and, Mark thought, something akin to anger, too. He thrust his wristwatch in Mark's face. Mark stared at the digital numbers. "Is *my* watch wrong?" Bob O'Leary wanted to know. "Is it, Mark?"

Bob O'Leary's watch read 8:50 PM. As Mark stared at it, he saw the dual numbers indicating the seconds hang on 32. As he watched, the seconds did not change…did not change…did not change…until *finally* the 2 turned into a 3. It took what felt like a full minute for one second to tick by.

Mark shook his head.

"So," Bob O'Leary started up again, that cheerful smile back in place, "how about regaling us with some tickling of the ivories?"

"Oh, yes!" chirped a woman in a houndstooth scarf. "That would be lovely!"

The hands returned, gripping him high up on the forearms, at the wrists, around the waist. Someone clenched him hard high on the thigh.

Bob O'Leary winked at him...then reached down and tweaked Mark's penis through the front of his pants.

Upstairs, something heavy tipped over and smashed to the floor. A moment later, someone cranked the volume on the iPod.

"No!" Mark shouted as his guests dragged him toward the parlor and the piano. "No! Leave me alone! Let me go!"

"It's so early, Mark," Bob O'Leary said.

"We've got all the time in the world," said another man.

"All the time in the world," the woman in the houndstooth scarf echoed.

Mark Schoenfield screamed.

"Party pooper," Bob O'Leary said, laughing.

About Ronald Malfi

Ronald Malfi is the award-winning author of eleven novels, to include *Snow, The Ascent, Passenger, Cradle Lake, The Narrows*, and many others. Most recently, his novel *Floating Staircase* was awarded a Gold IPPY Award for best Horror Novel and was nominated for a Bram Stoker Award for best novel of 2011. In 2009, *Shamrock Alley* received a Silver IPPY Award for best Thriller/Suspense novel. Malfi's short fiction has appeared in various print and online magazines.

He lives in Maryland with his wife and daughter where he is currently at work on his next book. He can be reached online at: http://www.ronmalfi.com.

I AM THE FEEDER
BY CHRISTOPHER HIVNER

The light came through the wall like a laser, pointing ominously at Justin Pfaff's nose. He had pulled the tack out of the corkboard to use the sharp end to dig dirt from under his thumb nail, and now there was a thin beam of light emanating from the pin hole it left behind.

He mumbled, "What the hell?" as his head cocked to the side, his face tightening. He put his index finger over the hole, closing off the beam and felt a buffet of warm air on his skin. When he slid his finger away, the stream of light poked him in the forehead. Then he looked at the tack. It had a white plastic head with a slightly bent metal point, like every other pushpin he had ever seen.

He looked up again and wondered, "How long had the pin been there?" His wall was covered in them, some holding up schedules or meeting notes, others supporting cartoons that took the edge off the dull days. Then there was the herd of unused pins, a rainbow of colored heads. The whole lot of them had already been hanging there when he got his desk assignment last year. Had he ever used this particular white one?

"Yes, Justin," he whispered to himself in the stodgy voice of his boss. "Don't you have a spreadsheet on your tack usage?" He laughed at his inside joke, but soon the slight heat from the light drew his attention once again. It had interrupted his thoughts of Jolene in her shimmery dress and high heels which had in turn demolished the chances of his getting any work done that afternoon.

I'll bet Jolene could help me burn off the last few hours, he thought. But in reality, he knew things with Jolene would go nowhere. She liked athletes, which Justin was not. Besides, even if he were on the cover of Sports Illustrated as the world's greatest everything, he was too shy to ask out a woman with legs like hers. She was a fantasy. The light, as it stuck to the tip of his nose, was real. He set the tack down on his desk.

Standing up, he stretched out his tall, lean frame, taking a surreptitious look around the office. Only two others were in the wide room with him, and they were engrossed in playing solitaire on their laptops. Justin quietly walked out the door and down the hall. He came to the adjoining room which had been empty since Mr. Peters had been laid off months ago. He stepped into the darkness, closing the door behind him.

Justin gasped. The thin beam of light cut through the middle of the office from the wall Justin shared into the other wall which joined a large conference room. Walking up to it carefully, he stared down the length of the light shaft. He stuck his hand into the beam but it remained uninterrupted, meeting his palm and continuing from the back of his hand. He walked up to the conference room wall, and there was a tiny pin prick hole. Justin backed away again to get a wider view.

The light sliced through the room in a perfectly straight line. The hole in the conference room wall was in the same position as the hole in the office wall twenty feet away.

"That's not possible," he said out loud, continuing to study the length of the beam. "Where the hell is this light coming from?"

He left the office and stumbled into the conference room, stopping abruptly just inside the doorway. The beam traversed the entire length of the seventy foot long room, perfectly straight, and disappeared into a hole in the far wall—a hole which matched the positioning of the others. Dumbfounded, he shook his head.

He bumped into the door while scrambling out of the room to run down the hall, his ungainly legs propelling him forward. When he came to the end of the conference room, the hallway angled to the left. Justin stopped and stared, jaw agape, at the beam of light exiting the wall and continuing down the corridor, through the lobby and piercing the glass window to the outside.

Running to the lobby, Justin stopped abruptly at the sight of two clients walking through the front door. The heavy-set man and tiny older woman continued to the welcome desk. They had passed the light as though it wasn't there, but when he looked out the window, he could see it continued across the parking lot. He took a few steps back into the hallway, leaning against the wall, crossing his arms over his chest.

Mesmerized and confused, he stared at the light. It went through the lobby glass, through the atrium and the outside glass. The beam continued on a straight line between two rows of cars, then disappeared into a copse of trees that bordered the lot. Justin peered around the corner, watching Judy, the receptionist, lead the clients to their meeting. When they entered room seven, Justin strode across the lobby and out the door.

It was bright outside, the cloudless sky allowing the sun to envelope everything. Justin immediately felt a slap of heat on his face. He loosened his tie as he tripped across the entrance into the parking lot, following the beam. It took a moment for him to realize there was a woman in a dark blue skirt and blazer walking toward him. She nodded politely. He smiled, turning to watch her walk in a diagonal path into the light.

Like the others, she didn't seem to notice it. Frustrated, Justin started to call out to the woman, "Don't you see the beam?" As she turned toward him, her body crossed the light, and she screamed.

Justin jerked backward; he put his hands to his head to dull the woman's piercing cries. The laser entered her left arm just below the shoulder, and when she lurched forward, it sliced through her chest and back like a heated blade. The top of her torso from mid-breast to the head shifted and hung in the air for a paralyzing second as blood sprayed out in all directions. Then the lower half of her body fell backward, landing on the macadam with a wet thump while the weight of her head pulled the top half face-first to the ground. A dark red pool quickly spread out from under her body.

Justin still held his hands to his head although they were now shaking. His mouth hung open; droplets of the woman's blood had landed on his lips and tongue. His mind was numb; he couldn't think. He watched the blue-suited woman's fingers and legs twitch as though they were drumming out a tune.

"OhmyGodohmyGodohmyGod," he mumbled quietly, his eyes darting away from the corpse. He took a step toward the building but then backed up. Tears rolled down his cheeks. He had no idea what to do. With his head spinning and his legs on the verge of collapse, the light sang to him.

The beam vibrated at a low intensity which produced a pleasant, rhythmic noise. Justin looked over. The light particles rolled in a shallow wave now. Still caught between running away, screaming, and seeking help, he ambled around the parking lot like he was drunk. His hands remained pinned to his ears as if pressing hard enough would make the entire horrific tableau around him disappear.

He leaned down and lay across the hood of an SUV, trying to breathe. The volume of the beam's humming increased, violently invading his brain. Reluctantly turning his head, he saw the light wave had grown in size, the amplitude now measuring several feet. He grabbed onto the vehicle's fender to support his bandy legs and watched as the wave split apart, sending dozens of wildly vacillating beams of lights through the walls of the LuJack Corporation's office building. Windows exploded outward, showering the ground with glass. In a hallway on the second floor, Justin saw what looked like lightning followed by a charred human body falling through the window.

Justin sat on the pavement and leaned against one of the truck's tires, watching the wave break into ever-smaller tributaries. The beams buzzed, giving off a smoky heat that left behind the smell of burning wood. After a moment, the offshoots of the beam began to coalesce into once light source once again. The shaking slowed, as if the laser was suddenly pulled taut by invisible hands. The humming stopped.

Although his legs trembled, Justin rose up because he saw the far end of the beam, which had been hidden in the trees. It moved slowly, in a steady straight line. He followed it as it inched toward the building. He skirted far around the dead woman. The beam cut through the glass of the lobby, and continued to move on the same trajectory as when he had first discovered it.

He pushed the front door open, entered the lobby, and nearly stumbled over Judy's remains. Her torso rested on the back of an overstuffed, forest green chair while her were flung almost casually on the floor just inside the door. She looked like a mannequin that had come apart. Justin stared hard at the scene, thinking it had only been a few hours since he had greeted her with a sleepy "Morning, Judy. Glad it's almost the weekend?"

Able to finally tear his gaze away, Justin saw the beam was gone. He remembered what had started this nightmare. The pushpin. He had to go back to his office.

Walking on the right side of the lobby, he passed two small rooms. Instinctively he glanced in as he walked by. Each contained a body, one a man, the other an older woman. The man's shoulders were still hunched over his computer keyboard while the rest of his body stayed sitting in his chair. The woman had been decapitated, and the neck stump was still pumping out a weak stream of blood. Justin felt like he was going to vomit, so he hurried down the hallway toward his office.

Mouthing a childhood prayer as he ran, he was thankful that he saw no more dead co-workers. When he reached his door, however, he hesitated. He shared his office with three other people. Two of them were sitting at their desks when he had left. Justin palmed the doorknob but couldn't turn it. He rested his forehead on the door.

"Come on, Justin," he whispered. "Everyone is dead except you. You have to find out why." He pounded his free hand against the door, trying to release his anguish so he could go on.

"Lionel? Peggy?" he called out. His answer was silence. "Li, Peggy!" Nothing.

He spoke his thoughts out loud. "Maybe they got out." Then he took a deep breath to gather himself because he recognized the truth. "No, they're all dead."

He opened the door and walked in, almost stumbling over his own feet. He stopped abruptly. Peggy's laptop was dinging madly because her head was lying on the keyboard. The beam had punched a gaping hole in the back of her neck, and she had collapsed forward. Lionel must have turned around to talk to her because he was facing Justin, slumped in his chair, a charred golf ball-sized hole in his chest that went out his back through his chair and through the wall.

Justin had worked with Lionel and Peggy for almost two years and liked them both quite a bit. Peggy treated him like a little brother, trying to solve his problems with girls and teach him to save his money. Even though Lionel had been passed over for a promotion he deserved and was languishing in a job that bored the life out of him, he never took it out on other people. Justin was a fountain of questions, and Lionel had always taught him the right way to do something. Now they were both dead, and Justin felt like it was his fault. He looked over at his own desk.

The white pushpin still lay where he left it next to his notepad. He glanced up at his corkboard. Even from a few feet away he could see the glow in the tiny hole. The beam had receded and now sat in its entirety in a hole that was only a fraction of a fraction of an inch.

What the hell is it? he thought. What had he done when he removed the pushpin from the wall?

"What did I do?" he shouted incredulously. "What did I do? I pulled a tack from the wall! That's all I did. I couldn't have caused all of this!" He held his face in his hands as he sobbed. He walked over to Peggy and stroked her hair. "Peggy, I'm sorry."

He sat on the edge of Peggy's desk looking across the room at the pushpin hole. The light was still there, waiting for him. He was certain of it the same way he knew when his friend Jordan was bluffing during a hand of poker. The light was waiting for him.

Justin pulled his chair out and sat down at his desk. Initially he aimed his gaze down at his keyboard. The letters jumped out at him, and he found himself mentally writing a plea for help. Finally he shifted his eyes up. He looked directly at the hole, into the light.

What if I just put the pushpin back? he thought.

Then the light exploded outward. It broke into two beams which entered Justin's body through his eyes. He jumped in his seat, his body going limp momentarily, then his legs and arms went rigid.

Inside his head, the light bounced about in his skull, rewiring his brain. Images flashed in bands of white and black. His eyes and lips twitched as the deep crevices of his brain were invaded by thoughts from a thousand minds. Electricity buzzed inside Justin's head as it encased his brain in waxy filaments. His body started to relax, arms falling to his sides, and his ankles rolled so his feet lay sideways. Justin blinked several times before his eyes opened wide, staring straight ahead.

The beam had been on a mission to find a savior. Justin Pfaff, the twenty-four year old intern who had been daydreaming about the girl on the second floor who smelled like lilacs, had been the first to physically encounter the light. The collective had chosen its deliverer by random as it does every century when the need arises within its weakened flesh.

And so Justin stood up, now knowing what to do.

"The hive is in danger," he said flatly. He stood directly in front of Lionel, whose eyes were still staring up into the flickering ceiling lights.

"The hive is in danger. I am the feeder," Justin said before opening his mouth as wide as he could. The light beam shot out from his throat into Lionel's body. The corpse shook violently as the beam spread out into every organ, blood vessel, muscle and bone. It took apart Lionel's body cell by cell, absorbed everything and transferred it to Justin.

Every cell of every kind was taken by the light and fed into Justin's waiting mouth. From there they dispersed to mate with Justin's own cells. When it was over, all that was left was an empty chair and a pile of Lionel's clothing on the floor.

Justin turned to Peggy and repeated the gathering process. The light broke into smaller and smaller beams until one photon was absorbing one body cell, then rejoining the main beam and carrying them to Justin's body for storage. The light worked with such speed that each body took only a few minutes to disintegrate.

When he was done with Peggy, Justin moved through the entire LuJack building absorbing each dead employee's cells, leaving behind disheveled clothing as the only evidence they had existed.

Trillions and trillions of cells were now packed into Justin's body. As he walked through the lobby to the front door, he moved with some difficulty. The extra material inside his skin had caused him to grow larger and thicker. He was several inches taller and his muscles were bulging and as hard as concrete. The extra cells were squeezed so tightly together that he was one spectacular human mass. His clothing tore and fell away so that, as he crashed through the front door, he was naked. His skin began to rip from the strain of the increased tissue, muscle, bone, and tendon underneath.

Justin stepped, stiff-legged, into the parking lot when he heard the sound of a car approaching. A gray sedan pulled up next to him. A man leaned his head out the window of the passenger side and began to say something. Then the man saw Justin clearly.

"Holy shit!" the man yelled. The female driver screamed and stepped on the gas. Justin reached a gargantuan arm into the air, and as the rear end of the car passed, he brought a mammoth fist down on the trunk of the vehicle. The punch was so powerful that his fist drove through the body of the car, and into the rear axle, snapping it in two. The sedan careened away and smashed into the side of the LuJack building.

Justin strode over and dropped to his knees. Both occupants were stunned, lying behind deployed air bags. He opened his mouth, releasing the light beam. It pierced the head of the man, exited the other side, and shot into the woman. Justin shook as their cells were added to his body. The skin of his thighs and back split open as it could no longer rein in his mass. Muscle and tendon were exposed. Blood poured down his legs.

With the two visitors absorbed, the light retreated back inside of its host. Justin turned toward the woods at the end of the parking lot.

"The hive is in danger," he said, his voice now a wet, bass-toned gargle. "I am the feeder."

Walking was now blindingly painful. The voices in his mind pushed him on, urging him to finish his mission, imploring him to save the hive. With each step he took, he felt the love of the hive. He roared as the skin continued to flay off of his body, but he would not stop.

Once inside the grove of trees, he crashed through the brambles, breaking off several saplings in his way. After a hundred tortuous yards, Justin came to a clearing with an irregular-shaped, twenty foot diameter pond at the center. He looked into the brackish water and heard the hive calling to him.

Justin dove in, sinking down about ten feet before seeing the tunnel. He swam through, and after another twenty feet, came up into a small chamber. He climbed out of the water, looking around. Tunnels were dug in every direction, even up high on the walls. There were tunnels on top of tunnels. The largest one was to his right. A figure emerged from the darkness.

The hive's Master was six feet tall, twice the height of the drones. His pale white body was a globular corpus of skin and soft gray fur. Blind, milky orbs sat in twin eye sockets, bobbing side to side. Thin, translucent wings protruded from his shoulders while stubby arms and legs allowed him to carve new tunnels in his world with ease. The Master's mouth was two slits connected by a bit of tissue, and when he greeted Justin, it came out as a toneless hiss. Then Justin could hear all the voices of the hive in his mind as they welcomed him.

The Master turned and re-entered the large tunnel, and Justin followed, needing to hunch over and turn sideways to get his bulk through. The Master led him deep underground. When he emerged from the snaking tunnel, Justin found himself in a large, excavated cavern. Drones clung to the walls by the thousands, their mouth slits hissing in anticipation.

In the middle of the cavern was an indentation in the dirt large enough for Justin to lie down in. He dragged his exhausted body over and collapsed into the bed, rolling onto his back. The hissing in the chamber slid over the walls wrapping all the creatures in a cocoon.

With a signal from the Master, the drones lifted up a flap of skin on their bellies, revealing six small holes lined side by side in two columns. Justin opened his mouth.

The light beam rocketed from his body, splitting into thousands of striations. Each one found an open hole in the drones' bodies, and they all began to feed simultaneously. The hissing slowly stopped as the creatures fell into a coma-like state to absorb the human cells to nourish themselves.

Justin knew that he would be eaten as well, and he would cease to exist as all the others had. But, he reasoned, he would get to die knowing he was part of something greater than himself. He had saved the hive. As he lay in the cool dirt feeling the cells swim from his body, Justin was at peace.

I am the feeder, he thought.

About Christopher Hivner

Christopher Hivner writes from a small town in Pennsylvania surrounded by books and the echoes of music. His work has recently appeared in *The Carnage Conservatory* and *Thrillers, Killers 'n' Chillers*. A collection of short stories, *The Spaces Between Your Screams* was published in 2008.

He can be visited at www.chrishivner.com.

RED INK
BY LISA MORTON

This is how it began:

The Lightning Struck Twice.

It entered the Hardcover Best-seller List at Number Twelve, and although it peaked at Six it was nonetheless an auspicious debut for a first-time novelist. The book was also well-reviewed, and so its author, Garson Anders, had respectability. The movie rights were sold for six figures, and so he had wealth. The talk-shows booked appearances, and so he had fame. Garson was still young and reasonably attractive and now successful, and so he had women.

He also had a best friend named Neal Darvin, and *The Lightning Struck Twice* had almost as great an effect on Neal as it did on Garson. Outwardly, Neal celebrated with Garson; but in his secret heart—the one that knew *he* was the better writer—he wondered why.

It was for Neal's thirtieth birthday that Garson presented him with the pen. They had left Garson's latest ingénue girlfriend in his new home in the Hollywood Hills, and gone to dinner at a restaurant where Garson had waited tables a year before. As soon as the wine was brought, Garson handed across the small package badly wrapped in a *Lightning* dust jacket.

"Let me guess," Neal ventured, as he pried the newsprint away, "you did it yourself."

"For that personal touch," Garson countered.

Inside the oblong box was an exquisite antique fountain pen. It was large, heavy, dark red, rubbed to richness by years of other fingers. Like a Mont Blanc "writing instrument," it featured a gold nib inlaid with platinum and bands of other precious metals. It glittered with caught light, and when Neal picked it up its weight surprised him; it felt good in his hand, as if it was perfectly counterbalanced to its tip when placed to paper.

Garson watched expectantly. "What do you think, bro?"

"Gar, it's—it's beautiful. I mean it. Just gorgeous. A work of art. And old. It must've cost a fortune."

"Probably," then, to Neal's expression of curiosity, "it was a gift to me from Bob Markson."

Neal nodded, remembering. Bob Markson, the legendary author of the 1965 classic *Phobic*, had taken a shine to Garson shortly before he'd passed away at the age of 92. "So this was Markson's pen?"

Garson nodded. "Go ahead, try it."

Neal looked around, but didn't see any paper.

"Use a napkin," Garson suggested.

"They're linen—"

"They can add it to my bill."

Neal laughed, shrugged, spread out the napkin and uncapped the pen. The nib skated across the white cloth and Neal was shocked to see a red line there, coursing thickly through the material.

"It's always been filled with red ink."

Neal eyed his friend. "Always?"

"As far as I know. I wrote *The Lightning Struck Twice* with that pen, in red ink. I figure it was good luck for me, so maybe it'll work for you."

"Do I need good luck?"

Garson exhaled, leaned forward, spoke urgently. "You're thirty today, so I'm laying the facts of life on you. There's only one reason I can afford to doodle on a linen napkin and you can't, and that's because I have no illusions about winning major fiction prizes and going to cocktail parties with this year's Booker Prize winner. And with the way publishing is changing…you may not have much time left to make your mark."

Neal stared down, realizing he was doodling with the red pen, leaving big bloody spirals on the napkin. "So I'm deluding myself?"

"Neal, you are a motherfucker of a writer, but who cares, if you're not writing anything that people want to read?"

"What should I be writing?"

Garson grinned at his own response. "What I'm in a position to help you sell."

"The thrill ride."

"Bingo." When Neal didn't respond, Garson went on. "Look, bro, take that pen, get yourself a clean white notebook and write something that'll make everybody who reads it wet their pants. Then I'll sell it for you, and *you* will be buying *me* the expensive meals. Will you at least think about it?"

Neal did more than think about it. Two months later he handed Garson a 400-page manuscript written longhand in red ink.

"With your pen," he added.

The Crimson Thread startled even Garson. Certainly no one could accuse it of being either too literary or too tame.

"Christ, it turned my stomach, Neal. I mean, it's great, but—it's so far beyond what I expected."

Neal smiled and blamed the pen.

A month after the book was typed, Neal got an agent and almost immediately sold *The Crimson Thread*. He quit his job teaching English to illiterates at a community college. He put aside the red pen and took a year to complete a novel about a man trapped in a stifling middle-class despair (which he refused to label "horror"). He was dismayed when his publishers read it and told him they wanted to wait to see how *The Crimson Thread* did first.

The Crimson Thread was released a month later. Although critics decried its graphic murders, mutilations, eviscerations and dismemberments, it shot to Number Four. It sold equally well in print and in e-book.

It was the subject of a heated debate on the floor of Congress when an elderly Senator mistakenly denounced the book during a debate on public funding for the arts (it had received no such funding). Neal went on radio interviews, wherein he was castigated by feminist callers. He did signings across the country, using the red pen, and enjoying the gasps of admiration it always drew. He was propositioned on several occasions. He accepted once. It was a bad experience.

The worst, though, was one night when Neal was home from the tour, relaxing with someone else's book, and Garson called.

"Turn on the TV right now, CNN," he insisted.

Neal did. They were running a story about a serial killer who had been apprehended in Detroit. Adam Durst had eviscerated at least seven of his victims. When police went through his apartment, they found a broken-backed copy of *The Crimson Thread* with various slaying sequences heavily underlined.

Garson was saying something on the other end of the phone, but Neal couldn't hear it. He was staring, paralyzed, at the screen. He didn't hear his call-waiting beep for attention. He couldn't move. He felt sick. He wanted to laugh. He was simultaneously full of rage and emptied. When he could move, he hung up, walked to the kitchen, and threw the phone into the trashcan.

The police talked to him the next day. Of course he wasn't "suspected of anything, Mr. Darvin, we just wondered if Durst might ever have tried to contact you, or…?"

Neal knew they did suspect him of something. He could see it in their eyes. They suspected him of being even sicker than Durst.

Neal wasn't so sure they were wrong.

Next week *The Crimson Thread* was Number One.

Neal's publisher called to congratulate him. Neal asked if there were any plans to pull *The Crimson Thread*. They roared at that one.

Then they asked him for his next novel. Neal told them they'd already read his next novel.

"We meant your next thriller," they politely clarified.

Neal was aghast. They told him they'd talk about "the serious thing" after one more book like *The Crimson Thread*. They tried to fly him to New York for a face-to-face. He refused. They sent him a contract and a check with far too many zeros on the amount lines. They didn't even care what it was about, as long as it delivered the bad goods.

Neal thought and paced and talked and sweated. Garson assured him he wasn't responsible for the actions of every Adam Durst, that the guy was a nut who would've killed anyway.

"But would he have killed them like *that*?"

"You are not—I repeat, *not*—responsible."

"Funny. There's a senator in Washington who thinks I am."

Garson snorted. "Are we talking the same nitwit who thinks we should be teaching Intelligent Design in science classes?"

Neal shook his head. "He's a nitwit that a lot of people listen to, Gar."

Garson laughed. "Good, more power to him. *Crimson Thread* will be at Number One as long as people listen to him. And so will anything else you write."

"I'm not sure I can write anything else."

"Why?" Garson demanded, "Because some crotchety old fucks want to ban your book?"

"Because," Neal replied, his voice barely above a whisper, "what if they're right? What if it happens again?"

"Yeah, well, think about this, bro: For every nutcase creepo who reads your stuff and considers living it out, there are probably a hundred-thousand readers who have been entertained and grossed out and scared shitless, and you've made them feel alive for a few hours. It's a sacred calling."

Neal wasn't convinced…

…but two nights later he picked up the red pen again.

He couldn't explain why, except that he'd thought a lot about what he felt while writing *The Crimson Thread*. Yes, the acts contained in its pages were terrible, but in committing them to paper he'd felt a sort of delirious purging, as if his own soul had been partly relieved of its burden.

He wanted to feel that again now. Badly.

At first he just held the pen, feeling its cool length, studying the glittering gold and silver of its point. He knew as soon as he put that nib against a blank sheet and let the red ink flow that he was taking a risk...but he also knew that not to do so would be as good as admitting guilt, compliance. No, he would defy responsibility. He would write.

Once the decision was made, the pen began to move. His ears were filled with the glorious sound of nib scratching paper. His mind was so teeming with images that the work transcended effort. The pen, although gripped by his fingers, seemed to move of its own accord.

The red ink flowed.

*****

By the time Adam Durst came to trial, Neal had written his next book. He was surprised at how easily, how naturally it had come forth.

When the jury found Durst guilty and a judge sentenced him to six consecutive life sentences, Neal was finishing up the third book. It hadn't just come easily, it had exploded out of him, his control surrendered to it.

As Adam Durst faded into yesterday's news, Neal was working on the fourth.

Now he had no choice.

He no longer wrote; he obsessed. He had no friends; even Garson stopped trying to contact him after he had his phone disconnected. He didn't want the intrusions. He moved into an expansive new house and left no forwarding instructions. He had an accountant who handled all his bills, and an agent to deal with the offers. He only went out for food, and then only to the nearest market. He bought bread and crackers and fruit, he wouldn't eat anything he had to take the time to cook.

Because his time was no longer his own. Neal belonged entirely to the red pen now, and the images it stroked and provoked from him. Images: Disasters, deformations, dystopias in which dwelt devils both human and superhuman. His mind raced with unnatural storms that carved holes in the quilt of reality, madmen who mauled each other in mausoleums, far-flung outreaches of hell where harbors held black-sailed slave ships. The tarantella in his head whirled with fears, of spiders and snakes and spaces too big or small, of heights and houses, blood and women, violence and men, death and afterlife. In his dreams he saw misshapen beasts with massive wounds, diseases that consumed more than flesh and bone, sorcerers who could raise the dead but not master them.

After a while Neal realized he was no longer dreaming; that he had in fact stopped sleeping some time ago. There was no separation for him now; between day and night, in somnolence and slumber, ego and id and subconscious. He began to dread his trips outside, not so much because they distracted him as what they provided for him—grist, the stuff of waking nightmares.

At a stoplight, a street person begging change was a thinly disguised descendent of an infamous tyrant, a new incarnation awaiting the signal to begin a fresh reign of terror. At the market, the aisles were teeming with well-groomed zombies, kept walking only by the metal carts that tugged them along. The coins the killer at the cash register handed to him were carrying microscopic cybernauts that could infect with inorganic viruses.

Neal stopped going out, made arrangements to have his simple necessities delivered, but it wasn't enough. Sounds filtered in: A car engine, a distant siren, a squealing child. His own body became suggestive of horrors, vile plots...

Neal wanted it to stop. He wanted to halt the red ink, to walk out into a world he could again understand...but he couldn't go back. Oh, he tried. He realized it wasn't enough simply to stop writing—in fact, it was worse, because then the things in his head just piled up there, dammed without release. He drank, and it helped until the liquor erupted, and his sickness splattered around him in physical form—and he wrote about it. He took drugs, but found he lost any last ability to distinguish between what was really happening and what was only generated under the red pen. He tried both angry and lovely music, the volume spun to deafening levels—and heard voices beneath, whispering new obscenities to him. He even had an expensive workout machine installed, but realized the thing itself terrified him so much he had it taken out again. He tried moving to a custom-built house in the Mojave Desert, far from any urban disturbances, but he only wrote more about the dread of alienation.

Alone in the wasteland, he was stunned one hot day to realize the book he was halfway through writing was about a murderer named Neal Durst who slew to stop the pictures in his head.

That was when Neal stumbled back from his notebook, dropped the red pen and screamed. He screamed for a long time. It didn't matter, because there was no one to hear him. After a while he cried instead; great choking, gasping sobs.

Finally he took an unfilled page from the ream and found his checkbook. With the red pen he scribbled his signature on a check, and an amount that he thought represented the sum of his holdings. He left the payee blank, and put the check in an envelope addressed to his accountant, accompanied by a note instructing him to use the check to set up a fund for the families of victims and survivors of Adam Durst.

That done, he gathered all the manuscripts he hadn't yet sent off, took a lighter and the red pen and walked out the door of his house forever.

Neal walked a long time, through one sunrise and one dusk. He didn't see anyone else in that time, only sand and cactus and Joshua tree. He saw a few lizards, some birds high overhead, the twisting trail of a snake long gone by.

When he could stagger on no more through the desert night, he fell to his knees. He dropped his burden of filled pages, thousands of them, careful not to let any escape. He found deadwood and placed it around and atop the pile, then set fire to it all. He watched it burn until he was satisfied that it was all smoldering, then he uncapped the red pen and stabbed himself with it three times. He'd planned then to snap the pen in two and toss the pieces onto his fire of words, but as he grasped the pen firmly in both hands, applying pressure, he saw them: Phantoms, but with the authenticity of memory.

They stood before Neal, looking at him impassively. In front was a young girl, dressed in a 19th Century gown, holding the hand of a stitched-together dead man. Behind her was a bearded Irishman oozing blood from twin punctures in his neck. Next, a lantern-jawed man in a prim 1930s suit, but his skin had an unnatural, alien glow to it. There were others, and Neal even saw Bob Markson, standing in back, an oversized spider seated on his right shoulder while a snake slid around his left arm. Somehow, Neal could make out all of their hands perfectly, and he saw the red ink stains on their fingers, and he knew they'd all possessed this pen before he had. The pen was horror, and it was history. He couldn't break it.

He let the pen fall to the desert sand, and the visitors vanished. Neal lay back to die. The last thing he saw was the scarlet smear on his hands. In the firelight he couldn't tell if it was ink or blood.

*****

They found him towards dawn. A plane working for the Highway Patrol had spotted the fire in the middle of the black expanse and sent a sheriff out to check on it. The fire had died by the time they arrived...

...but Neal was still alive.

They called a MedEvac and 'coptered him out to the nearest hospital. He was still bleeding from his three wounds, but they were small and he wasn't even listed in critical condition.

He was unconscious for several days. When he awoke, the attending nurse was surprised to see him smiling. She asked how he felt. He grinned. She asked if he was really Neal Darvin the famous horror author. Saliva burbled down his chin.

Despite the fact that Neal's accountant actually complied with his request to set up the fund for Durst's victims, Neal had seriously underestimated the amount of his own worth, and so he still had a great deal of money left. This money bought him the best psychiatric care in the world. Once he recovered from his attempted suicide, he was placed in the finest of clinics, watched over twenty-four hours a day, but nothing changed. He never spoke, he never wrote, he never watched a movie or read a book. Garson, who continued to write and sell adequately done dark mysteries, came to see him twice, then shook his head sadly and never returned.

Neal lived for many years, thinking happy idiot thoughts. He didn't notice when the youthful intern—the boy with the piercings and the dark eyes—found the red pen and discretely slid it into a pocket. The boy would eventually sell it online, for a fair amount of money, because he wasn't a writer. But the girl who bought it was.

And the red ink flowed.

About Lisa Morton

Lisa Morton is a screenwriter, a novelist, a short story writer, and a world-renowned Halloween expert. Her fiction works include *The Castle of Los Angeles* (winner of the Bram Stoker Award for First Novel), *The Lucid Dreaming,* and *Monsters of L.A.*

She has recently released two new non-fiction books: *Witch Hunts: A Graphic History of the Burning Times* (with Rocky Wood and Greg Chapman) and *Trick or Treat: A History of Halloween.* She lives in North Hollywood, California, and online at www.lisamorton.com.

Sassafras
by John T. Biggs

Smell is the simplest sense. Awareness enters through the nose without an invitation, an unwelcome guest with a master key. An injured brain needs only a few molecules to remember everything there is to know about disinfectant, urine and adhesive tape.

Sound comes next: distant conversations, wheels with bad bearings, compressed air hissing at regular intervals. Fifteen times a minute, but who's counting.

Then vision. Two of everything—separate images that won't come together without a struggle. The first thing is acoustic tile on a ceiling a thousand miles away.

Then a pair of faces merge into one as my double vision clears. A man I recognize but don't remember. A lover? A brother? Something else entirely?

His face is friendly, but not handsome. Eyes the color of violets, slightly too far apart. They're partially hidden under a shock of unruly blond hair that matches his Scandinavian complexion but not his African lips.

Those full lips move when he says, "Morning Cinderella." It sounds slightly out of sync, like a poorly dubbed foreign movie.

No one calls me Cinderella anymore. Too childish. Too many syllables. What do people call me now? I want to say a name or two—hear them spoken in my own voice, but there's a tube going down my throat, and a headache where my memory used to be.

I try to sit up, but every movement brings new pains in places that never hurt before.

The man I can't remember backs up a step. Comfortably distant, but still close enough to tell me things I need to know.

"You've been gone a while, Cinderella, but now you're back," he says. "A fresh start in a new world where everything is possible."

He kisses me on the cheek, hard enough to wake the headache that slipped away while my mind was occupied with other things, like who I am and what I'm doing here.

In a hospital.

Badly injured—my head hurts the most—with a man I knew a long time ago, whose name is full of S's and A's. It sounds fun and a little naughty, and I'll know it when I hear it.

"Sassafras," he says, reading my mind. "My name is Sassafras." He is sliding backward with no apparent effort, getting smaller as someone else enters the room.

"Cindy, can you hear me?" A doctor's voice this time, androgynous behind his paper mask, but definitely male. Too arrogant to be a woman. Too much in charge. Too eager to poke me in tender places without warning or permission. And I smell his aftershave—Old Spice. "I'm Dr. Bergstrom, Cindy."

Good-looking, even behind the paper mask, and he knows it. "You've been hurt, but we're taking good care of you." He proves that by shining a bright light into my eyes, holding it there long enough to leave yellow spots.

Dr. Bergstrom says something reassuring about a bullet passing through my brain. Those usually kill you, according to the doctor, but when they don't, victims recover "with only minor deficits."

Deficits? Like not remembering who I am, why someone shot me, or anything about myself?

I can't talk, so I ask with my eyes, indicating the hospital. If I could say something, it would be, "How long have I been here…with, well, deficits?"

Dr. Bergstrom hesitates. I can tell he knows my question. Then he says, "A while."

Husband?

Family?

Mental status?

I'd ask those things if I didn't have a breathing tube.

"Your husband's name is William," Sassafras tells me from across the room, as though he'd read my mind. "One decade of wedded bliss."

Sassafras moves closer. He talks over Dr. Bergstrom's shoulder loud enough to make himself heard over lists of medications and descriptions of what my life will be like with a hole in my brain. "Will and your sister Emily are your only family."

"No unsightly scars; everything will be hidden when your hair comes back," Dr. Bergstrom is saying.

Sassafras holds a mirror so I can see the damage.

Dreadful. Two black eyes, like an addled raccoon. Bandages on my head, shaved as slick as a Gypsy's crystal ball. The tube in my mouth is held in place by an X made of adhesive tape that has caused a rash on my lips and chin.

"The police will want to talk with you," Dr. Bergstrom says, as if Sassafras' mirror isn't between us. "I'll send someone to remove the tube."

He looks at his watch, a Rolex, to prove his time is valuable. Too valuable to spare another second. Too valuable to bother with goodbyes.

*****

The cop wears a blue polyester suit and a wide yellow tie. His shoes are brown, his socks don't match, and his smile is insincere. A woman notices these things when her breathing tube is out and she can sit up, even if she has a headache that won't go away.

Bullet Headache.

"I can't remember anything," I tell the cop.

"It may come to you later on," officer what's-his-name says. He puts his card on the tray that slides over my bed so hospital food will be more convenient. His name is upside down but I can see it's something Polish or Russian. A string of letters, ending in 'ski.'

Officer What's-his-name-ski doesn't seem to mind when husband, Will, and my sister Emily enter the room.

"Visitors," I say.

"Suspects," Sassafras says. "He's a detective, Cinderella. He wants to watch you interact."

Emily walks in like a fashion model, or maybe a prostitute; pretends she is younger and thinner and prettier than she is. Even though I don't remember her, I suspect Emily is good at that; she always knows exactly what men want—at least from girls like her. The look on the policeman's face proves she got it right.

Emily extends her hand, like a princess. Like Detective what's-his-name-ski should kiss it, and he thinks about it for a second—I can tell.

"Charmed," she says with a fake English accent. She turns her gaze on everyone in the room but Sassafras, and holds it long enough to make us squirm. She winks at Will, and then she kisses me.

Still smoking. Now, how do I know she smokes if I don't remember her? I think I do remember things about Emily. Oh yes.

Will doesn't kiss me, but he puts a hand on my forearm, just above the IV line. He talks like a New Jersey gangster. "How you doin' Cindy?"

I remember some things about Will as well. We were married in Las Vegas by a minister who looked like Johnny Cash, and Emily was the maid of honor. Everything after that is gone—like Dr. Bergstrom. Maybe I don't need those ten years of marriage anymore—like I don't need Dr. Bergstrom.

Does Will have a favorite song? Does he want children? Does he like Emily as much as I think he does right now? He doesn't step back when she *accidentally* brushes her hip against him.

I clear my throat instead. I say, "Whore," under my breath, not loud enough for anyone to hear but Sassafras.

"Careful, Cinderella." Sassafras pretends to lock his lips and throw away the key. "Wait until the time is right."

The same advice he had when I was twelve years old. By then most kids have given up invisible companions, but Sassafras was still around. Protecting me from my older sister who did mean things right from the start.

"Emily stole my Barbie Doll," I say. Out loud, like it was one of those involuntary things brought on by bullets through the brain.

"Are you still going on about that?" Emily rolls her eyes at the detective and stands a little closer to Will.

"She put Barbie in the garbage disposal," I tell the cop. "Emailed pictures to me."

"After you showed dad where I kept my ecstasy." Emily covers her mouth a second too late. She steps behind Will and peers at the detective over his shoulder.

"Ecstasy, huh?" The cop spends a studious minute punching keys on his Blackberry. Getting a search warrant for Emily's apartment? I can only hope.

But instead the cop gets up. "Got to go," he says. "Call me if you remember anything," He smiles at me, shakes hands with Will, tries to keep from checking Emily out but can't quite manage it. He waves at us over his shoulder as he leaves.

Emily walks to the door of my private hospital room that doesn't feel so private any more. She looks both ways before she comes back into my room and says, "Really Cindy, I can't believe you brought that up."

"Don't mind me," I tell her. "I'm just the little sister with the brain injury."

Will puts an arm around Emily's shoulders. She leans into his embrace as if it's something that happens all the time. I can't remember much about my marriage, but maybe I don't want to.

"We'd better come back when you're feeling better," Will says.

"When the cops aren't around," Emily says. "To take notes on my childhood indiscretions."

"Barbie Annihilator," Sassafras says. "Drug user."

"Slut." I can't resist adding to the list. "Didn't mean to say that out loud," I say. "Brain injuries—you know."

"He's screwing her," Sassafras says as they walk away, arm in arm, like high school sweethearts on prom night.

"I know. I'm not *that* brain-damaged," I say. But maybe I am.

Then I study him. "I haven't seen you in a long time," I tell Sassafras. "Are you something from my childhood churned to the surface by a bullet?"

"Like butter," Sassafras says. "Or am I margarine? I can't be sure. Can you?"

I know this much about Sassafras: He used to be my best friend ever. Now he's back. I'm the only one who sees or hears him, but people hear me speaking to him just fine. Too bad about that.

"We don't need words," he tells me. "I can hear your thoughts."

But here I am, a head shot victim with a damaged memory and God knows what other limitations, so naturally a word or two slips out.

"Do you know who shot me?"

Sassafras smiles as enigmatically as Mona Lisa. I can't hear his thoughts at all, but it's pretty clear he knows.

"It'll come to you," Sassafras says. "Everything will come to you at exactly the right time."

Like the emails Emily sent me to tell me how much better it would be if I were out of the picture. Right before the shooting. Could that be a coincidence?

Sassafras punches Detective What's-his-name-ski's number into the hospital telephone so I can tell him what a bitch my sister is.

"The emails are in my laptop." I tell him where to find it, but all he wants is access to my email account. My user name and password. I remember all those things—no problem—as crisp and clear as Sassafras.

"Go for it," I tell the detective whose name I can't remember even though I just looked at his card.

"Chartoryiski," Sassafras tells me, but I can't say it. That means Sassafras must be at least a little real, doesn't it?

The detective says to call him anytime. "Night or day. It's all the same to me."

I start to hang up, but Sassafras reminds me about Will's nine-millimeter pistol.

"It's a Glock." I repeat Sassafras's words, like the star puppet in a puppet show about woman who grows up and starts her own dysfunctional family, with a husband who sleeps with her sister, who sleeps with almost anybody, and isn't nearly as pretty as she thinks.

I ask the detective, "Which one do you think did it? The one with the poison emails or the one with the gun?"

"Too soon to tell," the cop says. "Call me anytime you remember anything. Day or night."

It's all the same to Detective Chartoryiski, and it's all the same to me.

*****

The search warrants don't make me popular with Will and Emily, but I suspect I haven't been popular with them for a long time.

"I warned you not to marry him," Sassafras tells me, "but you wouldn't listen."

"Maybe I couldn't listen," I say, "with you being an imaginary companion and all."

But I'm listening now, because Sassafras loves me even though I ignored him for a long time after I met Will. Getting shot was a blessing—sort of. The bullet wiped out the part of my brain that separated Sassafras and me like that ugly metal wall between the United States and Mexico.

"Nothing important about your brain was disturbed," Sassafras says. "Perfect marksmanship."

It almost makes me believe in God again, but I'm already busy with one invisible companion.

*****

The chaplain drops by almost every day to talk about my soul. "Personal walk with Jesus," he says because everybody who hears me talking with Sassafras thinks I'm praying. I try to keep the words from getting out, and I'm getting better. Now I mostly just move my lips, the way I do when I watch a foreign film with subtitles. Mexican magical realism is my favorite.

I walk all around the trauma ward now, almost ready to be moved onto a floor that will charge my health insurance company a lot less money—the rehabilitation floor. In my case, that means social workers and psychologists will assess and re-establish my cognitive skills.

That means pretending Sassafras is God won't work much longer, because psychologists don't want you to be on speaking terms with any invisible companions even if their names are in the *Pledge of Allegiance*.

The nurses on the floor all talk to me when I'm out and about. They pretend to care about me and I pretend to believe they care.

They say, "Way to go Cindy," when I pass the nurses' station, encouraging me to walk the halls in spite of my hospital gown that ties in the back and my bald head and my two black eyes.

They say, "Poor thing," when they think I can't hear. "Her husband tried to kill her."

They find out before I do that Will has been arrested.

"His 9mm Glock is missing," detective Chartoryiski tells me. "We think Emily was involved, but we haven't got enough to arrest her."

"Not even with the emails?" I remember them being pretty nasty, but my memory is questionable, and Detective Chartoryiski says they aren't nasty enough.

"No direct threats," he says. "No mention of murder. Almost like she was encouraging you to kill yourself."

"That's pretty bad." I rub the exit wound on the back of my head to make a point.

"Not criminal," Detective Chartoryiski says. I wish he had a simpler name. "Your husband will probably get out on bond, because our case is very weak."

He doesn't look too happy about that.

"You'd think screwing my sister and having a missing gun would be enough," I say.

"You'd think." Detective Chartoryiski's cognitive abilities are right on track with mine.

*****

CNN is my favorite news channel, because they have a really handsome news reader on at 10:00 AM who seems to look right at me when he talks.

"He knows all about you, Cinderella." Sassafras turns the TV on so the good looking man can catch me up with current events.

I am interested in what the handsome newscaster tells me. A lot has happened since Cindy went away, and Cinderella came back.

Like the Russians hate Americans and the French hate Americans, and the Iranians hate Americans, and we elected a black president. A lot happened, but not much has really changed except for the black president, and even that hasn't made as much difference as everyone expected, according to the good looking man who reads the news.

TV cameras zoom in on a Wal-Mart parking lot in Bartlesville, Oklahoma.

Showing is better than telling, but the news reader likes to talk so he tells us to, "Watch this parking lot security camera video closely."

Something small and black falls out of the sky into a crowd of shoppers, and explodes when it hits the macadam.

"Looks sort of like an act of God," Sassafras says.

The good looking news reader thinks so too, but he can't put it quite that way because of pretending to be unbiased. So he says, "It was a nine millimeter Glock semiautomatic pistol that fell out of the sky," like that kind of thing happens all the time. "It fired when it hit the ground and a passerby was injured."

I listen as the newscaster continues, "The serial number matches that of a pistol believed to have been used in the attempted murder of an Oklahoma City woman early last week."

"It's all about you, Cinderella," Sassafras tells me.

"But how did the pistol get into the sky?"

He shrugs and smiles. The shrug looks like he doesn't know, but the smile looks like he does.

*****

My new room in the rehab center is private, thanks to Detective Chartoryiski. Will managed to make bail—probably with Emily's help—and even though no one thinks he'll try to kill me again, nobody is sure enough to be my roommate.

"Guys like Will aren't all that determined," Detective Chartoryiski says.

"You can say that again." I tell him how Will isn't even determined enough to stay married to me and not sleep with my slutty sister.

But Will is clever, according to the detective.

"No one can figure out what he did with the gun…whether it was an accident to drop it on the shoppers in the Wal-Mart parking lot, or part of some larger plan."

Sassafras says, "God's plan."

And then Detective Chartoryiski says, "That's possible," like he can hear my invisible companion's voice. "But usually God doesn't engage in murder."

The detective looks right at me as though I'd made the suggestion instead of Sassafras. And maybe I did. Sometimes invisible friends borrow your voice when they want other people to hear.

Sassafras uses my voice again while Detective Chartoryiski makes an entry on his Blackberry.

"I remember something else."

And when the detective looks my way, I don't have the slightest idea what I'll say next. But I keep talking.

"I remember Will shooting me." Sassafras uses my lips and vocal chords and air from my lungs and he gives my face a really sincere expression, which must look pretty convincing, with my bald-head and two black eyes.

One tear rolls down my left cheek, like when I was ten years old and might be in trouble. Ordinary crying won't get me anywhere with a cop, but the single tear effect is special.

Detective Chartoryiski puts down his Blackberry and hands me a generic hospital tissue. He's totally convinced, and all it took was a single drop of salt water teased down my cheek by Sassafras, the invisible tear wrangler.

"That's all I remember." Sassafras and I did this all the time, way back before the doubting age. He'd tell lies though my lips, and they'd be much more convincing than anything I could think of. He hadn't lost the knack.

It's easier when Detective Chartoryiski isn't looking at me, so I wait until he's punching information into his Blackberry so fast he might break the little keys.

"Just Will's face, and his hand holding the gun, and him telling me I had to die so he could be with Emily. So it was kind of Emily's fault. Don't you think?" I say that with no help from Sassafras, because a quiet room just screams to be filled with words.

Sassafras says, "Easy, Cinderella. A fish who keeps her mouth shut never gets caught."

Detective Chartoryiski does something with his Blackberry, and it plays the 911 call I made just before the shooting.

"I'm in my back yard." My voice is distant and metallic because of the little speaker. "Someone's trying to kill me." Then bang, a gunshot, and the sound of the phone dropping to the ground, left on so emergency services could use the GPS to find me.

How convenient. That's what I think, so the detective must think it too. Sassafras is getting me into trouble with his lies, just the way he did when I was a child.

"Will's the one who shot me." I say before Detective Chartoryiski has a chance to ask questions. "I don't know why I didn't tell the 911 operator."

"You've got to die, bitch, so Emily and I can be together," I say, in my best Will imitation.

"He said it really low, so you couldn't hear in on the telephone. How could anyone forget a thing like that?" I don't care whether Detective Chartoryiski answers, because now I remember the incident clearly—as if it really happened.

Detective Chartoryiski will make a phone call any minute and share this startling new evidence with the assistant district attorney assigned to my case. "What did he do with the gun?"

"I don't have a clue." I push the call button on my bed and asked the nurse if I can have an ibuprofen. The six hundred milligram tablets get rid of my headache completely and they don't make it hard to lie.

"I hate narcotics," I tell the detective. "Don't you?"

*****

Birthdays happen whether you're in the hospital or not. Your husband might not remember, because he's got other things on his mind, like being a bad man's girlfriend in prison. But your older sister always remembers, because her life changed when you were born.

"I was five years old when Mom and Dad brought you home." It doesn't sound like the happiest day of Emily's life. She stands beside my bed holding years of pent up hostility and a dozen helium balloons. She tries to smile, but doesn't quite make it.

"I'll never forget that day." She gives the balloons an involuntary jerk. Most of them are ordinary latex, but two are some kind of foil with printed words in big fancy calligraphy.

Sassafras turns one of the foil balloons so the message faces me. "Happy Birthday," he reads. "In *Lucida Handwriting* font. Nice touch, Cinderella."

Fonts are something I used to know, but now I have to let Sassafras remember for me. I can tell when he's remembering because he gets three little furrows across his usually smooth-as-silk forehead, and I get a little headache right below my exit wound.

"Something I need to tell you, Cinderella." Sassafras hasn't quite figured out how to tell me what he's remembering, and he'll keep it to himself until he's got it exactly right.

"Maybe I don't want to know," I tell him, loud enough to stop Emily from ruminating on the unfortunate day I came into the world, but not quite loud enough for her to understand what I said.

"How's Will?" I say that a little louder, so she'll think I'm repeating myself. "I hear he's going to wear one of those house arrest leg bracelets like rap stars get after they shoot someone."

Emily doesn't say a word. She doesn't sing happy birthday, or wish me many more, or even give me a sisterly smile—the kind that says we're friends even though she'd be better off without me. I know she bought the balloons in the hospital gift shop, because Sassafras turns the other foil balloon around and it says *Get Well Soon,* in the same *Lucida Handwriting* letters.

"Will didn't do this." Emily lets the balloon strings go and puts her hands on the sidebar of my hospital bed. The balloons separate and bounce against the acoustic tile, caught in the draft of the air conditioner, on their way to somewhere else.

"People used to ride balloons around the world," I tell Emily. "Hot air, hydrogen, but these are helium. Pumped out of the ground in Amarillo, Texas. Nobody knows how it got there." Why can I remember so much about helium and so little about the last ten years of my life?

"You were so unhappy, Cinderella." Sassafras says, and his remembering furrows are really deep. It's a lot of responsibility, knowing everything.

"You did this to yourself," Emily says. "I don't know how, but you did it!"

She watches the *Get Well Soon* balloon drift under my hospital room door and into the hallway, looking for a more peaceful atmosphere, where the mood is easier to lift.

"One cubic foot of helium will lift an ounce," I say.

"Careful Cinderella." Sassafras pinches one of the latex balloons until it pops.

Emily jumps, like she's been shot, and I tell her, "You actually do hear the one that gets you. Take it from the birthday girl."

She watches the remaining balloons follow the first one out the door, floating off with her chance of living the good life with poor old Will.

Helium balloons can lift a lot of things: hopes and dreams, birthday wishes, and a fully loaded 9 mm pistol.

"I didn't shoot myself, Emily. I don't know anything about guns."

But Sassafras knows everything, like where the bullets go, and how many balloons it takes to carry a pistol into the sky after the shot is fired, and how a slutty sister is not an acceptable alibi for an unfaithful husband. Sassafras has perfect aim, and he loves me more than anyone else in the whole world.

A single tear rolls down Emily's left cheek. Very convincing. I wonder if she has an invisible companion, too.

About John T. Biggs

John Biggs has about twenty published pieces of short fiction in a variety of genres. His darker stories have appeared in *Pravic, Midwestern Gothic, The Storyteller Magazine, Litro, Rampillian,* and *Glimpses of Insanity.*

In 2011, he won the grand prize in the *Writer's Digest* annual competition with a piece called "Boy Witch," and third prize in the annual Lorian Hemingway short story contest with "Soul Kiss." Pen-L Publishing will be releasing a collection of his stories along with his first novel, *Owl Dreams.*

Tommy Boy
by JM Cozzoli

With great effort, Frank hoisted himself off the treehouse floor and up to the glassless window. The sun would be up soon so he had to be ready this time. He had only one chance left and the steady leak of blood from the deep, jagged, rip along his right leg was making him woozy. Duct tape could only go so far.

He knew this time he couldn't miss and with more light he wouldn't. He was sure of that.

The pain made him vomit. Again. He wiped his lips as best he could with whatever clean space he could still find on his sleeve, and steadied himself by grabbing the windowsill tight, although the growing numbness in his hands made that difficult. He leaned over the sill, biting his lower lip hard, making it bleed as he concentrated all his remaining strength on getting a long, good look. The cool morning air fanning across the sweat on his face helped clear the nausea growing in his stomach. But only a little.

In the fluorescent glow from the porch lights sixty feet away, he could see Tommy was still pinned under his BMX bike. With its chrome handlebars caught in the slats of the picket fence, Tommy didn't have any leverage to free himself. Even if his small arms weren't chewed to the bone in spots, they'd still be useless to help him. They kept flopping mechanically, back and forth, like he was at a baseball game doing the wave. *Tommy loved baseball*, thought Frank.

A bright orange pillowcase with the word "Booty," written in big black letters with a magic marker, hung loosely from one of his wrists, its hoard of candy spilled on the ground in a neat arcing line that followed his useless back and forth motion. A badly aimed, yellow steel-tipped, crossbow bolt was stuck fast through Tommy's wrist, pinning the pillowcase to it.

Frank turned to look at the pistol crossbow. It was supposed to be Tommy's Christmas present. With all the goddamn push and rush for holiday shopping, Frank couldn't resist. He'd wanted some playtime with it anyway. His eyes dropped to the beat up, dried up, flat-top leather steamer trunk it rested on. They had found the trunk at a yard sale. It was the only furniture in the treehouse. It was Tommy's pirate treasure chest. Frank still wondered how he ever managed to carry it up the rickety ladder, let alone fit it through the narrow trap door in the treehouse floor.

Damn it caught in Frank's throat as he looked back at Tommy, now more visible in the growing morning light, and tallied his misses. Two yellow bolts were stuck deep in the picket fence close to the boy's constantly bobbing head and another had flattened the BMX's front tire, and another bolt stuck out of Mr. Wilson's back, a neighbor.

Shitty shot, murmured Frank. He stared with fascination at Mr. Wilson's eyeballs, bouncing from their sockets like bungee jumpers while the old man stumbled back and forth, first bumping into the picket fence, then into the telephone pole, then back again, around and around, like that damned yellow rubber duckie at a shooting arcade.

No, not any arcade, but Funfair's. I was how old?

Frank's heart raced. His palms sweated more. He was known as Frankie then. His memory skimmed shallow, then plunged deep, drowning him again with how shitty it felt to keep missing every time he tried knocking down that one stupid yellow duckie, smudged with grease, coming around and around, each of his shots hitting everywhere else. His dad had laughed at him, it was so funny. Eventually the scabby grunt agent running the arcade joint pulled the Duckie Shoot rifle out of his hands—*Sonny, start smoking and grow a pair, will ya, then come back*—coughing up sputum and tobacco with each word puffed over his hand-rolled cigarette. Frankie endured it. No different than being piss-soaked and frustrated, egged by name-calling—*By my friends? My birthday friends? But I invited you…it wasn't my fault I couldn't hold it anymore, I lost control and…*

Frankie. Shorts get a little wet? Get a little sticky and warm? You wuss up good, you never get to forget. Right, Frankie? Frankie boy, you sucked bad. Baby boy, you sucked it really bad. Bet you suck now.

Shitty duckie, said Frankie through Frank's lips. For a moment he could feel the small Duckie Shoot arcade rifle being yanked from his hands. *Stupid duckie*, he thought and wiped his palms on his pants. His eyes fell on Mr. Wilson, again. *Poor stupid duckie*, he whispered, then changed his mind when he realized they were all poor stupid duckies, including him. Frankie and duckie and those dead duckies and Mr. Wilson and... *Tommy.* Tears welled in his eyes and he screamed so loud it hurt his throat. The pain shut his mind down, enough to bring him back to what he had to do.

The sun was tipping over the horizon a little more now. The light he needed was coming harder and brighter. It looked like it was going to be a beautiful fall day. He had one bolt left. He couldn't miss now. He wouldn't miss now. He repeated to himself, *Don't you miss, don't you miss, don't you—*

The arm reaching through the window for his throat didn't miss. He suddenly realized those poor stupid dead duckies could climb trees, especially when your scream sounds like a dinner bell. The stubby, mottled fingers choking and ripping his throat tightened, but one bitten-off pinkie and a split thumb gave him the leverage he needed. This chewed-up dead duckie was going down.

Frank slammed the invading arm against the window edge again and again until it cracked and the fingers let go. He gulped air, staggered back on his bum leg, screamed again to get through the stars, and reached around for Tommy's Maple-solid Louisville Slugger bat. Tommy liked the feel of a solid wood bat. To Frank, the bat in his hands felt almost like the Duckie Shoot arcade rifle. This time, though, he wasn't letting go.

He got into his batting stance and waited until a partially chewed head, minus one eye and both ears, poked through the window. He swung the bat up and out, going for a homerun. It felt good.

It also knocked him off his good leg and sent him rolling, nearly plunging him through the open trapdoor. *Crap, I thought I closed that,* he almost said out loud, but the thought flashed quicker than his tumbling. His bum leg dipped through the opening before he stopped rolling. Another dead duckie grabbed the opportunity.

Out of breath, aching in places that already were aching, and sprawled like some dumbass softball rookie, Frank couldn't put enough energy into his ground-out swing and the bat only bounced off the dead duckie's beak, breaking it. The duct tape on his leg tore away as the hand tightening on it pulled downward, letting his blood seep out, egging the dead duckie on even more. *Okay, Mr. Thick-Nasty-Head-Dead-Duckie, it's now or never.*

Coming through the trapdoor, pulling itself up with the help of Frank's leg, Mr. Thick-Nasty-Head lunged forward with broken teeth clicking. Frank flipped the bat end over end and jammed its handle tip into Mr. Thick-Nasty-Head's left eye socket until it tapped the back of its skull.

Hey, I found a new sweet spot on the bat, thought Frank.

Mr. Thick-Nasty-Head slumped down, blocking the trapdoor opening, blocking any further distractions for the moment; but the dead weight kept Frank from slamming the trapdoor shut. He was running out of time anyway. He had more important things to worry about.

The sun was shining golden light into the treehouse when Frank picked up the pistol crossbow and loaded the last yellow bolt. He barely made it back to the window, crawling as much as he could, and when he tried to stand up, he vomited. This time he didn't wipe his mouth.

What really bothered him more than anything was he couldn't hold his pee anymore. He'd been dying to piss for hours. *Oh, what the Hell. Not like anyone'd notice.* As his pants leg got warm, he thought about the arcade and the yellow rubber duckie and his ruined birthday and his stupid friends...

...And now another dead duckie was tugging on Mr. Thick-Nasty-Head from below, and inch by inch, the body would soon be free of the opening, allowing more dead duckies to go around and around, too many for Frank to handle. Frankie, the pissing kid, started screaming out of frustration. Again. He almost threw the pistol crossbow out the window before he realized what he was doing. What stopped him were the Almond Joy candy bars on the floor. They had fallen out of his coat pocket. They were Tommy's favorite candy.

Tommy.

Both Frank and Frankie stopped screaming. They ignored the pain. They ignored the sticky blood and warm piss dripping down their leg. They looked at the yellow bolt cocked in the pistol crossbow, spit on it for good luck, and looked at the pirate treasure chest. They crawled over to it and pulled on its handle with one hand while the other one helped drag them and the chest to the window, inch by inch, until they reached it. They pulled themselves up, using the trunk as support, then sat on the lid.

Frank held his breath as Frankie took aim. Shaking hands braced against the window's edge. The sound of Mr. Thick-Nasty-Head sliding free of the trapdoor didn't make them turn around. They waited for that grease-smudged rubber duckie to swing around again into firing range. This time, they were leaving the arcade a winner.

Once more, for no more, thought Frank. Warmth pumped through his arms.

Screw you, duckie, thought Frankie.

The yellow bolt fired. It went through Tommy's right eye as it should have done before. Tommy stopped doing the wave. Zombies could only be stopped by a head shot.

Frank slumped, sliding off the steamer trunk. Frankie screamed with joy. Both of them reached for the fallen Almond Joys, lying there in the golden light of morning on a beautiful fall day.

"And for the rest of you yellow duckies," said Frank out loud while Frankie unwrapped a bar, "no Almond Joys for you. They're all mine. Man, I do love coconut."

About JM Cozzoli

Tired of being a corpse-orate zombie, John M. Cozzoli traded in the sharp needles and voodoo doll effigies of his coworkers for the more rewarding pleasure of writing his blog, *Zombos' Closet*, where he reviews and views the pop culture of horror, the genre people love to fear. Growing up as a monster-kid in the 1960s and having two theaters within walking distance in his neighborhood, it was bound to happen sooner or later.

He lives in Westbury, New York with his wife and son, and dreams of one day owning an old-styled movie theatre serving steamy hot popcorn smothered in real butter, ice-cold Bonbons, and lots of horror movies, old and new.

WILLARD JUNCTION
BY CHRISTOPHER NADEAU

Coyle gazed about the desolate patch of Arizona desert. He knew Lenny was right but he had come too far to admit it out loud. He'd already made an ass out of himself on several occasions, so any credibility he'd gained as an "amateur historian" was long gone. He hadn't been able to find Willard Junction despite repeated attempts.

But Coyle had a feeling about this particular place; the voice told him it was correct and the voice never misled him.

"Even if it is a red herring," he said, "this will be the last place we ever look. If this isn't it, we're done."

Lenny glanced away, clearly displeased to hear his shared crusade was coming to an end. "Guess we'd best get to it, then," he said.

Avoiding eye contact, Coyle sighed and headed back for the SUV. Perhaps this time the dreams would stop.

Lenny called after him, "What if it *is* a myth?"

Coyle stopped walking and shook his head. Skepticism came with the territory but he'd never expected it to come from Lenny. He turned around. "It's not, dammit. Too many people talked about Willard Junction."

"Then why didn't more than a few people ever agree on where it was?" Lenny's eyebrow shot up in expectation. "I mean, if we're gonna say this is our last search, shouldn't we at least be ready for the possibility that it was all bullshit?"

Coyle had never told Lenny about the dreams. He came close a few times but never had the courage to let the words escape the tip of his tongue. That goddam voice always told him it was a bad idea to tell.

He'd grown to dread the voice even more than his dreams.

Lenny remarked that the sun was going down and soon it would be too dark to see anything out here. Coyle nodded absently and got to work making a campsite. He decided they would set up their tents here and drive to the area on the map the old woman had given him.

He thought about the old woman.

*****

She'd come to him during a moment of total collapse, when Coyle finally decided he was a fool who'd dedicated his life to stupidity and pointlessness in equal measure. Perhaps he'd been lied to or laughed at one too many times but one day he simply fell over in the middle of his hotel room and started weeping uncontrollably. He remained that way for quite some time, barely noticing the passage of time as everything he had ever held inside leaked out onto the floor of that unfamiliar place.

When he'd finally run out of tears and dissolved into occasional bouts of dry heaving, someone knocked on the door to his hotel room. He glanced up at the Sharper Image alarm clock on the mantle and frowned. It was awfully late for someone on the hotel's staff to come and see him. Perhaps he'd been too loud with his sobbing and attracted the attention of the other guests. It was the only explanation that made sense considering the fact no one else knew he was staying here.

He opened the door, blinking in mild surprise when he saw who stood in the doorway.

"Not what you were expecting?" the old lady said.

Coyle shrugged. "Didn't really know what to expect."

"I brought you something that will change your life."

Coyle snorted. "Credibility?"

The old lady returned the grin. "Better." She handed him a rumpled piece of paper and raised an expectant eyebrow.

"Did you just slip me your phone number?" Coyle asked incredulously.

The old lady chuckled. "That's a map."

*****

"What tree?" Lenny said, upper lip curled.

Coyle, behind the wheel of the SUV, glanced over at him as they headed deeper into unknown desert. "It's on the map. A tree out in the middle of nowhere."

Lenny chuckled. "Right next to the Fountain of Youth, eh?"

Coyle muttered under his breath while swerving the vehicle to the left to avoid a sharp row of jagged rocks. "Scoff all you want. I had a dream."

"I know. I've been following your dreams for more years than I'd care to admit."

"Just need to find that damn tree."

"There's no tree, boss. This is the desert!"

Coyle brought the SUV to a screeching halt that forced Lenny's head to strike the dashboard. Panting like a distressed animal, Coyle released his own seatbelt and slowly opened the driver side door. "This here's where it happened."

Rubbing his bruised forehead, Lenny blinked and squinted in Coyle's direction. "Come again?"

Coyle exited the vehicle and stood a few feet away, eyes closed and head back. "Right here," he muttered. "Right...*here.*"

He knew because the dream had told him.

*****

"Right here is good enough, boys." Clem can't keep the excitement out of his voice. "Now go get the horse."

Coyle's blurry vision barely registers the fact that one of the men walks away to do Clem's bidding. He can barely stand upright and if not for the other man holding him, he would most likely fall flat on his ass again. He didn't expect it to end like this but he supposed it had always been heading this way. The days when a man could do as he pleased were long over. There was too much law nowadays and men like him were seen as things to be gotten out of the way in the name of progress.

Clem's man brings the horse back and stands off to the side, awaiting further instructions. Coyle wishes he had a pistol right now because the big dumb bastard is wide open for a shot to the chest.

"Get that rope around his fool neck."

Coyle hears Clem's heavy breathing and hates him even more. How is he any better than Coyle? Unlike Clem, he never once took pleasure in watching another man die. Maybe that's why it was always so easy.

Within moments, Coyle is picked up and unceremoniously dumped on the horse's saddle. He cries out from the pain as his balls are pushed up from the force if impact. One of the big fellas puts the noose around his neck and snorts.

"I hear a man shits his pants when the rope gets tight," he says.

Coyle grins. "I'll make sure to aim for you when I do."

He isn't surprised by the gut punch he receives but that doesn't mean it hurts any less. What does surprise him, however, is who it comes from.

Clem rubs his fist and shakes his head. "You wanna know the funny thing about you, Coyle? There ain't nobody gonna remember a shit-kickin' killer like you. There ain't gonna be no books or stories or nothin'. It'll be like you was never here."

Coyle doesn't bother telling him that's exactly what he wants. He never wanted to be famous for being an outlaw. He just wanted to disappear into some other life far away from all this shit.

"Any final words, Coyle?"

Coyle glances around Clem and his two meaty helpers and cocks an eyebrow at the new arrival. "It's about goddam time."

Without hesitation, Clem slaps the horse on its rump and it lunges forward, leaving Coyle dangling from the rope as it slowly squeezes the life out of him.

*****

Lenny limped over to where Coyle stood and stared at him for a long moment before speaking. "Boss, I think I need to go to a hospital. You made me bang my head on the dash when you stopped so short. My head really hurts."

Ignoring him, Coyle said, "Where it all began. She knew where to send me."

Lenny tried to follow Coyle's gaze and nearly passed out from the effort. "There's nothing here. I think I have a concussion."

Again Coyle ignored him. The hot sun spoke to him without words, its merciless assault both familiar and enlightening. He heard something coming, something far off but moving fast, and smiled because he knew Lenny had no idea what it was.

"I'm going to take the SUV and drive back into town," Lenny said. "I don't want to leave you here, but I need to see a doctor."

"No."

Lenny halted in mid-stride. "Good. I'd prefer it if you drove."

Coyle shook his head. "Nobody's leaving. It'll be here soon."

Lenny frowned. "What's coming?"

Coyle smiled as he looked up into the receding sun. "You'll see."

"Boss, you're really starting to creep me the hell out."

Coyle blinked and looked away from the sky. "Do you see it?"

Lenny waved his hand in dismissal. "If I could see anything, I'd be seeing two of them. I'm out of here, boss."

"No, you're not," Coyle said through gritted teeth. "I told you, nobody leaves."

Lenny started jogging towards the SUV, occasionally glancing over his shoulder as he went. "I knew this would happen," he said. "You've finally lost it!"

"Sounds like you were always expectin' me to."

"What's with the accent? You're from fucking Lansing, Michigan."

Coyle grinned and spat a large gob of yellowish saliva onto the ground. "I come from a lot of places, boy."

"Tell you what, Clint Eastwood. You keep up whatever *High Noon* shit you're doing while I go to the hospital to make sure my brain is still where I left it."

"I said *nobody* leaves."

Lenny's eyes widened as he stared at his employer's hands. "Where'd you get a gun?"

Coyle sneered and cocked the hammer. "Same place that tree come from."

Lenny chanced a glimpse off in the direction Coyle was looking and gasped. "That wasn't...I know there wasn't anything..."

Coyle placed his finger to his lips. "Hush now," he said gently. "The voice has finally stopped."

*****

"This ain't how it was supposed to happen," Clem screams with increasing hysteria. *"You were supposed to die!"*

Coyle swings back and forth from the noose, his eyelids hooded. He hears a far away rasping sound and assumes it's coming from him, considering the condition of Clem's foolish helpers fidgeting and rupturing like over-filled balloons on the ground.

"Where's my reckoning?" Clem said. *"We had us a deal!"*

"Indeed we did."

Coyle forces his eyelids to open at the sound of a new voice, a female voice. He isn't sure why but he feels heavier as she arrives, as if she brings the weight of things unknown and best forgotten.

"I gave you what you wanted most," the woman said evenly.

"He don't look dead to me!" Clem yelled.

Coyle had to give him that one; he sure as shit did not feel dead plus he was still breathing. But maybe that was more out of habit than necessity.

"You asked that Mike Coyle be erased from the memory of the world," she said.

Coyle feels the rope snap loose, dumping him without ceremony onto the dusty desert floor. He gets to his feet and dusts himself off. His vision clears enough for him to see the old woman gazing at him with what appears to be an amused fondness.

"You weren't the only one who made a deal," she says.

*****

Coyle motioned for Lenny to start walking toward the tree which had not been there moments before. Reluctantly, his assistant did as ordered, the whole time glancing over his shoulder as if expecting to be shot.

"You ain't got a thing to worry about whilst walkin' away from me. Mike Coyle never shot an unarmed man in the back."

Lenny forced a laugh that came out sharp and high-pitched. "I'm hallucinating. It's the goddam concussion. All thanks to your shitty driving!"

If he received that last part as an insult, Coyle gave no indication. "Yer about to look on somethin' most folks never get to see. A real miracle."

"Yes, I see the tree. Can we go now?"

Coyle shook his head. "Not the tree." He motioned for Lenny to keep walking, past the tree and over a ridge, where he halted, fell to his knees and screamed.

Coyle walked up behind him. "Ain't it beautiful?"

He watched Lenny weep as Willard Junction manifested itself before him. After all the endless searching, they had finally found it. He knew Lenny would forgive him now for what he was about to do.

Lenny kept covering his eyes with his hands and lowering them as if he couldn't commit to the supposed reality revealing itself in the Arizona desert. At times he would laugh crazily, cackling like a drunkard many decades older, the occasional *"Whoop"* coming from him whenever something new was added to the town; he was a child experiencing his fantasy world coming to life, appearing totally oblivious to the fact of Coyle's pistol was still at the back of his head.

"We found it," Lenny said between sobs.

Coyle shook his head. "It found *us*."

"Wait until we tell all those stupid sons of bitches who thought we were crazy!"

Coyle fingered the gun and glanced over Lenny's head as the buildings started unfolding from thin air. He recognized the saloon and the livery stable but there were new ones as well; there always were. Willard Junction was a living town and it was always growing.

"Should we go down there?" Lenny said. "I want to! Don't you?"

Coyle frowned; He knew part of him longed to step foot in town but some other, older part of him knew it was a terrible idea. Yet, he'd labored so long and lost so much to reach this point. And why the hell did he hold a gun to the head of his assistant and good friend? It seemed that ever since the voice stopped communicating with him, he'd started losing it. Wasn't it supposed to be the other way around?

"I...I'm not sure," he said.

Lenny jumped to his feet, pausing at the sight of the pistol held limply at his boss's side. He looked in Coyle eyes and shook his head. "The Mike Coyle I know wouldn't even hesitate."

Coyle frowned. "Yeah, but which Mike Coyle am I?"

"There's only one Mike Coyle, boss," Lenny said. "The guy who gave up everything to find the place we're looking at right now."

Coyle nodded. "Maybe…"

Lenny emitted a loud, unintelligible cry of incredulity. "What the hell is wrong with you? First you stop the car so hard that you made me bang my head. Then you bring out a gun. All the years we spent together finding this place, all the shit we put up with, and suddenly we really find it and you go batshit. You don't know if you want to—"

The shot to Lenny's right kneecap happened so quickly that he was already lying on the ground before he started screaming and rocking back and forth. Coyle merely stood in place, his expression unreadable, wondering again why he was here and what he was supposed to do next. Behind him, the sun had nearly set yet he could feel Willard Junction's arrival on the breeze. Although it had no voice, it spoke to him in other ways, expressing a need, a desire, to be appeased. It did not appear without reason and it would not disappear without satisfaction.

The town's desire drowned out the sound of Lenny's cries of pain and anger.

Coyle nodded to himself, thinking he finally got the gist of what he needed to do. "I'm ready," he said.

In his head, Coyle heard the old woman reply, *Well, it's about time.*

Lenny looked up from his bloodied knee, eyes widened in shock. Coyle walked toward him with the deliberate slowness of someone recovering from a rather large dosage of narcotics, his mouth twitching involuntarily. But despite whatever odd behavior he exhibited, his gun hand remained steady.

"I wanted to thank you," Coyle said.

"Thank me? What the fuck for?"

"You need to understand. I needed a fresh start."

Lenny stared at him through slitted eyes. "Why are you doing this, Mike? Why?"

Coyle shrugged. "Town needs people." He raised the pistol and fired once between Lenny's eyes.

Suddenly, there she was. The old woman walked around him and cocked her head upward in his direction. "You almost forgot this time, didn't you?"

Coyle wiped tears from his eyes. "Yes, ma'am."

Nodding, the old woman walked over to Lenny's carcass. "Help me roll him to the edge of town."

"What happens to them once they're inside?"

The woman turned her head in his direction and chuckled. "Only one way to find out."

Coyle shivered. He knew what was coming next and he was not ready for it, not this time. The old woman seemed to sense his reluctance. Once the two of them had moved Lenny's body to the edge of the still arriving town, she sat on a nearby rock and stared at him for a long time before speaking.

"Any time you think you're finished with all this," she said, "just set foot over that line."

He looked at the town and shook his head; once you were in Willard Junction that was where you stayed. No more fresh starts. No more hiding. Only the old woman got to leave and even she only did so in service to the town.

"Where will I end up this time?" Coyle said.

"How should I know?" She pushed herself off the rock and walked to him. "Maybe this time you'll forget. Maybe this is the last time we'll ever see each other."

Coyle closed his eyes to halt the tears and sucked in a deep breath an instant before the familiar sensation of the noose around his neck filled him with agony.

"Sleep now," she said into his ear as he slid to the desert floor. "Sleep now."

He dreams of faraway places, of adventure and a life that is thrilling and filled with wonder. Sometimes he feels like his life is a lie. He swears he will strike out and do something everybody will remember.

Being remembered is all that matters.

Otherwise, it would be as if Mike Coyle was never here.

He can't think of anything worse than being erased.

About Christopher Nadeau

Christopher Nadeau is the author of *Dreamers at Infinity's Core* through *COM Publishing* as well as over two dozen published short stories in such august publications as *Sci-Fi Short Story Magazine, Ghostlight Magazine* and more anthologies than one could take out with the toss of a single hand grenade.

He was interviewed as part of Suspense Radio's up and coming authors program and collaborated on two "machinima" films with UK animator Celestial Elf called *The Gift*, and *The Deerhunter's Tale*, both of which can be viewed on YouTube.

He received positive mention from Ramsey Campbell for his short story *Always Say Treat*, which was compared to the work of Ray Bradbury and has received positive reviews from *SFRevue* and *Zombie Coffee Press*.

His newest novel is titled *Echoes of Infinity's Core*.

An active member of the Great Lakes Association of Horror Writers, Chris resides in Southeastern Michigan with his wife Lorie and two petulant long-haired Chihuahuas.

SUKA: THE WHITE WOLF
(BASED ON A TRUE STORY)
BY JEFF BENNINGTON

Mick Dawson drove his 1980 Pontiac Trans Am through Amarillo, Texas on his way to another job. As he cruised down the Texas interstate, a fury of wind swirled through the T-top and Mick lifted both hands high, holding the steering wheel with his knees, enjoying the freedom and fresh air.

He turned up the radio when the number one song of the year, "Centerfold" by the J. Geils Band started playing. It was a big year for J. Geils. In fact, Mick always thought 1982 was a good year for music. Like a fine wine, 1982 had brewed so many classics it could make you drunk just thinking about it. Songs like "I Love Rock-n-Roll" by Joan Jett, "Rosanna" by Toto, "Eye of the Tiger" by Survivor, "Abracadabra" by The Steve Miller Band, and the list goes on and on. Mick loved music and being single—he was a free bird—just like the song.

His peers, often gruff, bearded tradesmen who seemed more like Appalachian mountain men than craftsman, criticized Mick for his taste in music. The preferred music on the job site was country or heavy metal. Mick didn't mind Ozzy or Black Sabbath or even Kenny Rogers. He liked what he liked. Music wasn't about being cool to him. It was about filling the gap that he knew existed in his soul. Women couldn't fix it for longer than fifteen minutes or so. His working buddies couldn't fix it beyond a few laughs, and God knows his family couldn't fill more than a hairline crack worth of the emptiness. But music had a way of filling him up. If he couldn't play the radio, he could sing. If he couldn't sing, he could hear whatever song fit his mood in his mind. Music was his medicine, his drug, his addiction.

As he practically floated down the freeway listening to "Who Can It Be Now" by Men at Work, something caught his eye. Along the dry and dreary highway, just past a dusty cattle ranch, an old woman stood at the edge of the road attempting to hammer a sign into the dirt. The wood on the post had become frayed and split. The earth was thick and hard and he could see that she was struggling, alone, surrounded by barren fields meant for grazing.

Mick thought she must've walked a long way since there weren't any side roads nearby. Maybe she needed a lift? Maybe she needed a hand? He considered stopping as he approached, but the thought was brief. He had to be in Albuquerque by morning and it was already mid afternoon. The local foreman expected him at seven in the morning.

Then, as he passed, he turned his head to the right and caught a glimpse of the sad figure on the side of the road. She had a dark complexion with long silver hair peppered with strands of black throughout. She wore blue jeans and a long-sleeved plaid shirt with her sleeves rolled up to her biceps.

When Mick drove by, she stared with brilliant eyes that penetrated his easy-going feelings. Her eyes looked as black as a skillet and seemed just as hard. She glared and squared her jaw as he passed. She seemed to speak to him directly. He didn't know how to explain it, or if the feeling was real, but her face had immediately imprinted into his brain.

He drove on but she continued to stare within his thoughts. He turned down the radio. He needed to think, or rather, listen to what she was saying, as strange as that sounds. Thoughts swirled through his head but they didn't belong to him. He concentrated so hard that his foot lifted from the accelerator and he started to drift without realizing it. He saw her eyes dark and deep, then felt compelled to stop and turn around. The words were as simple as that—stop and turnaround. He did.

The highway stood as lonely and dry as the land that surrounded it, so Mick hit the brake and zipped through the median. He thought about Albuquerque, work, and the foreman, but the voice in his head spoke much louder, far more convincing. He circled back and stopped about fifteen yards from where the woman pounded on the stake. A cloud of dust billowed around and over and past her. He stepped out of the car and she quit hammering, waving the airborne grit away.

*****

Mick took a deep breath, thinking he'd rather drink a sun-warmed can of Pabst Blue Ribbon than take time to stop. But as he drew closer to the woman he began to feel sorry for her. She looked much older up close. Her skin looked tough as dried leather. She wore multiple layers of plaid shirts covering her frail bones. She squinted, studying the visitor, and the wrinkles on her face rippled like water on a windy day.

He reached out and said, "Here, let me help you with that."

She covered her eyes from the glare of the sun, and one eye barely managed to stay open. She handed him the hammer, but said nothing.

The dirt was hard and rocky so Mick walked back to the car and grabbed a milk carton filled with water that he kept for emergencies and poured it down the hole to loosen the dirt. He hammered some more until the sign stood strong, somewhat leaning, but secure.

"That should do it," he said as he cocked his head to read the sign.

The letters were barely legible and painted with a substandard paintbrush, but he could still read it: "White wolf for sale."

Mick looked at the woman curiously. He had never heard of a white wolf and he couldn't imagine how an old woman could care for such a creature. He thought about the song "Hungry Like the Wolf" by Duran Duran and pictured the old woman feeding the dog, imagining it gnawing away at her hand, gobbling up her flesh all the way to her elbow. He had never seen a white wolf before but he pictured a gruesome white beast, with sharp teeth and a blood-red mouth dripping with fluid and loose flesh.

"You own a wolf?"

She smiled, revealing her crooked yellow teeth—the two in the front were missing.

"And you're selling it?"

She nodded happily and began walking briskly toward a path that was barely visible. She waved her arm, directing him to follow.

"Whoa. Whoa. Whoa," Mick said, stopping the lady with a gentle tap on her shoulder. "I don't want a wolf, I was just asking. Just curious, that's all."

She waved some more, lifting her eyebrows, still smiling.

"No, really. I have to get back on the road. I've got a job to—"

The woman performed her own style of sign language that Mick interpreted as eating, drinking, and something about an animal playing. She pinched her fingers together and playfully bounced them up and down. She seemed so desperate.

Mick looked at his watch and sighed. He wasn't one to abandon his work, but there was something about her, something that compelled him to follow. Mick learned to respect his elders back when he was a kid. His father was a forestry worker in Michigan's Upper Peninsula back in the fifties. A hard man with hard principles, he used his belt often and without shame on all of his children, including Mick's younger sisters. He didn't know the meaning of grace and didn't play favorites. In fact, one would be hard pressed to find any evidence that he favored his children at all.

But that was a different time. That's the way men thought back then; beat 'em good and beat 'em often and they'll be strong enough to handle life when life gets hard. Funny thing is, it worked; they grew hard all right, but they didn't have a hope worth more than a nickel of having any kind of decent relationships. Mick and his six siblings were hard by design, and distant, and loners and dysfunctional, but not in any particular order. Mick favored the loner quality while the others favored the features that caused some of them to lose their children thanks to the watchful eye of family services.

So without further argument, Mick followed the woman down the long walk that led to a tiny ranch nestled on a hill that must have been a mile away. They walked in silence and Mick could barely keep up. His shirt dripped with sweat and his forehead collected bits of dust.

When they approached her humble property, Mick took in his first glimpse of Native American poverty. From a distance, the structure looked cozy, a pleasant cabin on a hill. But upon closer inspection it was actually a single room hut. The outer walls were made of dry-rotted plywood, the tin roof pieced together and rusted. The front door hung on one hinge, held together by a small latch that kept it from falling to the ground or blowing off at the slightest gust of wind.

There were no cars, no electricity, and probably no indoor plumbing either. She had a windmill out back, trash bags piled high about fifty yards to the east, and the property was littered with junk; stupid stuff that didn't make any sense, like tires and tree stumps and metal crates. The only material object on her property that had any value was a metal fence that stood directly beside the hut. The sides must have been twelve feet by twelve feet long. It was a bright, galvanized fence at least eight feet tall, constructed plumb and level with obvious quality that included four-inch metal posts and a reinforced chain link fence. Mick knew right away where her priorities stood.

She turned for the first time in a mile and waved her hands again, bending her frail little fingers, encouraging Mick to come closer. She smiled, again revealing the dark hole between her teeth and pulled a shiny key out of her pants pocket. She dangled the key in front of Mick as if it were a magic bean, some kind of supernatural tool to unlock a gift from God.

She gestured for him to take it and pointed him toward the fencing. Her sign language directed him to turn hard when using the key on the lock.

He looked at the cage and noticed a big doghouse inside, much larger than normal. There were several white puffy balls walking outside of the house, tripping on each other and chewing on the few weeds that remained, biting with their sharp puppy teeth. For the first time in a long while, Mick felt his heart melt. I can't believe I'm getting all mushy over these stupid puppies, he thought.

"Those are white wolves?"

She nodded, her eyes exuberant.

"How much?"

She flashed all eight of her fingers twelve times, and then flashed four more fingers one time. Her right pinky and ring finger looked like mangled nubs. Mick felt nauseated by the sight but didn't make the connection until years later.

"A hundred dollars? Damn. For a dog?"

She nodded her head, irritated. She threw her hands up in the air and spread her fingers, a universal symbol for the stars or heaven that even Mick recognized. Then she mouthed more words with her eyes glowing.

"The white wolf."

Mick understood what her lips were saying, or doing, to be more accurate.

She directed Mick to open the gate. He did so and she let out a muted whistle that blew through the gap in her teeth.

The puppies came scampering to the door and a Siberian husky stepped out of the house. The dog's eyes were as blue as the summer sky, and its coat a mix of white and gray, but mostly white. Her belly hung low, with nipples drooping. She was obviously the mother and still nursing. She stood still and kept a watchful eye on the humans. The mother let her pups run free to frolic as they pleased.

Mick was intrigued by the notion of mixing a husky with a wolf, so he bent down to play with his new friends, wondering about the father.

His lonesome self felt good. He felt warm toward the pups and enjoyed the feeling of the little critters snuggling against his face; an experience he was denied as a child; a feeling he wanted to recoup for his lost childhood's sake. They nibbled on his sandy blonde hair and fingers and Mick just laughed, never thinking about the time.

In their play, he noticed one of the pups, a female, traipsing outside of the perimeter, circling the other puppies. It had a thin gray line on the top of each paw and a gray diamond between its eyes. All of the marks were barely visible. One eye was blue and one was dark brown. He picked it up and it whimpered a sad little cry that Mick couldn't resist. They played and rolled around for a few minutes until Mick stood up, holding the pup close. He told the woman he'd take it. She smiled, pursed her lips and opened them again. Her mouth made a cracking noise that sounded like a "k." She repeated this a few times but Mick couldn't make out what she was saying. All he heard was, "K—K—K—K."

Her eyes narrowed in frustration and she bent down and wrote in the dirt with her finger. Her letters were just as messy as those on the for sale sign: *Suka*

"Is that her name? Suka?"

The woman nodded and mouthed her word one last time.

"K."

Mick looked at the pup and grinned. "I'll take her."

Not sure how he'd care for the thing, he knew this was an impulse buy that he might regret, but as always, he couldn't resist filling the hole in his heart, and the puppy seemed to do the trick.

He reached into his wallet, but only found about fifty bucks. He offered to go back to the car and get the rest. But the woman refused. It was then that Mick understood how desperate she really was. He realized that she probably lived off of the meager income she made breeding her dogs.

When they scooted the pups back into the cage, Mick noticed a shadow from the corner of his eye. He looked toward the doghouse and watched a very large, majestic, white creature take heavy steps into the bright sun. This animal was much bigger than a husky. Its legs were long and thick with fur, strong and narrow, much larger than the South American and legendary white wolf. It was one of the biggest dogs he had ever set eyes on…or rather the only wolf he had ever seen outside of the movies.

"Is that the father?" asked Mick, humbled by its awe-inspiring and terrifying mien.

The woman nodded, throwing her star hands back into the air, mouthing, "White wolf."

The wolf's appearance left Mick feeling heavy, concerned. Knowing that his little puppy was crossbred with that beast gave him little comfort. But still, he couldn't resist the puppy. After all, who could resist a fluffy little snowball?

As he walked back to the Trans Am, he heard a howl resonating from the ranch. Soon other howls joined in harmony, each animal taking on a different note. It sounded beautiful and primeval and frightening. He felt bad taking the pup from the family but figured the howl was the family's way of saying goodbye.

*****

Months and years passed and the little pup grew older and larger and hungrier. Mick settled down after taking a permanent job with a power company just north of Lansing, Michigan. This brought him closer to his surviving brothers and sisters and provided a healthier climate for

Suka. The dog loved the winter and snow and played frequently with other dogs that lived on the same country road.

With each passing year the marks on Suka's paws faded. In the first six months, while playing with the pup, Mick noticed that her left front paw had become a brilliant white. He ran his fingers through her coat but couldn't find the patch of gray. He thought little of the markings after that.

When the crops were ready, the local farmers hired migrant workers to harvest the fields of cherry tomatoes, hay, and corn. And each year a little Mexican boy would walk from the across the street, leaving his family, and knock on Mick's door. The first year, he offered Mick five dollars for his dog. He couldn't speak English at the time, so he handed Mick the money and pointed to Suka, speaking his native tongue. With no intention of selling, Mick graciously gave the boy a drink and sent him on his way.

The dog became the center of Mick's life. He spent all of his free time with Suka, playing tug-of-war, catch, and tag. And in the harsh Michigan winters, Mick rigged a sled so that Suka could pull some of the children who lived nearby. Suka was happy and friendly. She played well with the neighbor's dogs, and to Mick, she was family. They were a pack all their own. They ate together, slept together, and traveled together. They even ended each day with a kiss. Mick never went to sleep without saying, "I love ya, pup. You're one helluva good dog."

Then at harvest time, the migrant worker paid Mick a visit. He, too, was growing. As always, Mick refused the money and sent the boy back to the fields. But each year he returned with a bigger wad of cash that eventually grew to two hundred dollars. Still, Mick could not sell his faithful friend.

As Suka grew older, Mick had begun to see two different personalities in his pet. Most of the time she was cheerful and content. But sometimes, she displayed a hint of stubbornness, occasionally challenging Mick's authority. On one particular day, Frank, Mick's neighbor, a hay farmer that lived a half mile down the road, called him on the phone.

"The damn thing's all but ready to kill Barker and the other dogs. Hurry up!"

"No way," said Mick, chuckling. "That dog wouldn't hurt a flea. Well maybe a flea, but she loves your dogs. Plays with 'em all the time, you know that."

"Not today," said Frank. "She's growling and showing her teeth. I know it ain't like her, but if you don't get over here and do something about it, I will."

Mick wanted to reach through the phone and wring his neck. Nobody's going to call me a liar, he thought, and nobody's going to accuse my dog of being belligerent.

"All right, Frank, I'll be right there," said Mick, hiding his disbelief.

Mick stormed out of the house and jumped into his '77 Chevy Cheyenne. He had to give up the sports car now that he owned a home in the country. He drove to the neighbor's house, hopped out of the truck and followed the sound of barking dogs. Frank stood near his barn door with a rifle in one hand and waving with the other. His face was pale and his eyes glistened with terror.

"Come on, Mick. They're in the barn."

Mick hustled to the barn holding a leather leash. The barking grew louder and furious, echoing throughout the large wooden structure. Frank and Mick ran through a maze of shadowy corridors, past a huge wagon loaded with hay bales and piles of scattered forage. They stopped at a stall in the back used for cows giving birth. Suka stood at the door, growling, her legs crouched and ready to strike. The other dogs were backed into a corner, some bleeding near their noses and necks, barking and yelping. They too had a look of terror in their eyes.

Mick took pause, staring at Suka's appearance. Her hair stood tall on her back. He had never seen her like that before. His first reaction was to grab her by the collar and yank her away, but she was obviously wound up tight, full of hormones, or had rabies. He knew he'd have to approach her with caution.

Mick signaled the farmer to step back and then gripped the leash tight, ready to latch her or whip her, whichever was needed. He took a step closer, whistled and called her by name.

"Suka."

She kept barking but turned her head, acknowledging his voice.

"Suka!" He whistled again. "Come here girl. It's okay." Mick made a popping noise with his tongue. That usually got her attention. Suka stopped barking, still watching the other dogs, quickly turning to see her master.

"Suka. What are you doing? Get over here!"

She heard one of the dogs move and snapped again.

Mick was getting pissed. He took several powerful steps in her direct and reached for her collar but Suka spun her head around and snapped at him, showing her teeth and gums, snapping over and over. Mick jumped back, startled by her grisly appearance.

He approached her again and she snapped again. Mick smacked her nose with the fold of the leash. He figured that would get her attention and it did, but she hunched down, forgetting about the other dogs and let out an intense growl that came from the deepest part of her gut, snarling and baring her teeth.

That didn't work, he thought. Damn dog.

"Hey now. Come on. Calm down, girl," said Mick, thinking he'd have to try the comforting approach instead, sensing his legs shaking. "Those dogs aren't gonna hurt ya, girl." He smacked his leg, another gesture Suka usually obeyed. But she didn't budge.

"Mick," said Frank, standing near the wagon. "Here." He threw a bone and Mick caught the slimy thing. "We just slaughtered Millie yesterday."

"Good idea."

Mick reached his hands out, tempting Suka with the slab of cow femur, still cold and frozen and bloody. "Hey, girl. Hey, Suka. Come and get it." He popped his tongue again—snap, snap, snap. "Come on, Suka."

Her growl dissipated and she turned slow and apprehensive. Mick continued to walk backwards, leading Suka away from the other dogs. Frank gathered up his pets and rushed them inside, where they all stared through a picture window, watching like frightened, curious children.

Suka's breathing slowed and Mick threw the bone in the back of his Chevy. The dog jumped in and started gnawing at the marrow. By the time they returned home, Suka had returned to her happy self. Mick stayed with her throughout the night, stroking her fur as they sat on his front porch staring at the stars. While shaking her paw as Mick often did, he noticed that a third mark had lost its gray stripe and the fourth was nearly faded, too. He took this as a sign that she was growing up. Mick wondered what had gotten in to her. But since there was no way of knowing, he brushed it off as hormones, pack instincts, or a fluke. But it wasn't a fluke.

*****

Two weeks later, Mick came home from work and immediately knew something was wrong. Suka usually met him at the start of his driveway and raced him all the way back to the house. They did this daily and Mick took great pride in the devotion and consistency that Suka displayed. So when she didn't show up that day, he sensed that something had gone awry.

Mick parked the truck and found Frank sitting on his front-porch swing, resting his rifle on his lap. As he walked closer, he could see blood smeared on Frank's hands, bib-overalls and face.

Mick picked up his pace.

"What the hell'd you do to my dog, Frank?"

Mick could feel his insides tense and twist into knots. The sight of Suka's blood on another man's hands sickened him. No one had the right to put his pet down. He thought of poor old Candy from John Steinbeck's *Of Mice and Men* and how broken hearted he was after Carlson shot his dog. The thought infuriated him and so he stormed the front porch only to be met with the butt of Frank's gun in his gut. He tumbled down the steps and rolled to the ground, gripping his stomach.

"What the hell was that for?"

Frank stepped down from the porch and said, "That was for killing Daisy." He then swung his foot under Mick's jaw. Mick twisted with the momentum of the blow, feeling a dull pain in his neck and a stinging in his tongue. His mouth and lip started bleeding before he knew what hit him.

"And that's for killing Barker."

Mick tried to overcome the pain and gather his thoughts. "But I didn't—"

Before another word flew off his tongue, Frank's fist reached down and landed a heavy uppercut to Mick's jaw, sending him tumbling back deeper into his front yard.

"And that's for killing, Otis!" Frank exhaled and gritted his teeth, his chest throbbing and eyes raging. He stared at Mick, who was stunned and bleeding badly now. "Lucky I don't do you in myself."

Mick felt a numb sensation in his lower lip and could tell it was swelling up. "I didn't kill your dogs."

"Yeah ya did," responded Frank. "You let that wild animal loose. I told you to keep it locked up. I told you to keep it away from my..." Frank started to choke up, holding back tears and stiffening his jaw. "You know—you know how long it took to train those dogs?" He stepped closer to Mick and raised his voice. "You know how much time I spent with them, teachin' 'em to hunt?"

Mick said nothing. He just sat there bleeding and throbbing, wondering what the hell happened to Suka.

"No, you don't, do you? Those dogs was family to me, too, Mick."

Mick lifted his head and asked, "Where's Suka?"

Frank looked out into the open field across the street. "She ran off. And it's a damn good thing, because if I ever see that beast again I *will* shoot it, and I won't hesitate for one second."

Mick followed Frank's eyes and peered into the orange pasture, covered by the glow of the setting sun. Frank gripped the bill of his baseball cap, adjusted it, revealing his straggly hair beneath, and turned back, angry and severe.

"That thing's wild, Mick. You need to put it down." His tone grew deeper with each syllable. "I'll give you one night. But if you ain't done it by mornin', I'm going after it." Frank locked the safety on his gun and walked through the meadow between the two properties. Mick looked at his watch. It was seven-thirty. He had two hours until the sun went down.

*****

After packing his rifle, ammo, binoculars, and a flashlight, Mick hopped into his truck to begin the search. Before he closed the door he heard a familiar howl to the east, deep into a patch of woods that lined the field that Frank had pointed out. The howl sounded creepy and sent an icy chill down Mick's back. He knew Frank was right, but he never wanted this day to come. He remembered when he bought the pup, watching her father, thinking how untamed and dangerous he looked. He also remembered how he brushed off his fear and plunged into his longing for companionship.

He started the truck and it rumbled and sputtered as he drove into the field. He drove slowly toward the trees, looking through his binoculars, occasionally pulling them away to get a closer look at the path in front of him. With his window down and the sky growing darker by the minute, he heard Suka howl again, and he knew he was getting closer. When he arrived at the edge of the woods, he grabbed his gear and tucked everything into the pouches attached to his hunting jacket, and then began his search on foot.

He heard another howl and lifted his binoculars, looking in the direction of the noise. Suka sat atop a crest deep in the woods, her snout covered in blood, her eyes wild and ferocious. The sight saddened Mick. She had become exactly what he feared she would the day he brought her home. He remembered the vision he had of the old woman being devoured and eaten alive. And then he thought of one of the hottest songs of the era, "Maneater," by Daryl Hall and John Oates:

> She only comes out at night...the lean and hungry type.
> Nothing is new...I've seen her here before.
> Oooh here she comes...Watch out boy, she'll chew you up.
> Oooh here she comes...she's a maneater.

The dog had obviously become a danger to others and herself. The chase was on. He headed for the hill, but when he arrived she had disappeared. The only evidence of her presence was a small puddle of blood that had pooled on a sycamore leaf. He followed the drips that trailed and the sun fell behind the hills to his right.

The night erased the track, leaving nothing but shadows and dark tree trunks in his path. He heard another howl and human voices that echoed in the same direction, about a hundred yards away. Although he couldn't tell for certain, there appeared to be an orange glow rising through the trees. It had to be a fire, and where there was fire, there were people.

He hurried through the dark, occasionally tripping over fallen timbers and root systems. The glowing grew brighter and the voices were no longer jabbering; they were screaming. He could hear barking and growling and the swoosh of a swinging stick. Mick ran faster and faster, his feet barely touching the underbrush beneath them.

When he came upon the ridge, he looked down into the valley. Suka had bit down on one of two young campers. She had his left calf in her mouth, shaking violently and tearing into his flesh. The young boy, no older than twelve, let out a high-pitched shriek, kicking and thrashing, beating the dog with a burning stick, unaware that he was inciting a survival instinct in the dog. The other camper, a freckled face redhead, whose hair burned as orange as the fire, had a much larger stick and was charging toward the dog.

"Haaah! Get outta here!" he said, jabbing the branch at the dog's face.

"Kill it," shouted the wounded boy. "Hurry! Hurry! Hurry!" he cried.

The boy screamed as he swung the stick. "Aaaah! Aaaah!"

"No!" said Mick, running down the hill. He cocked his rifle and prepared to shoot the dog, but Suka dodged the limb, grabbed hold of it with her sharp teeth and starting shaking it, moving the redhead into Mick's line of fire.

The limb broke and the boy lost control, falling backwards near the edge of the campfire. The dog's angry teeth glimmered in the kid's enlarged pupils. The frightened boy crawled back and burned his hand on a hot rock. Suka took advantage of the moment and attacked her attacker, leaping upon him. The kid tried to grab her throat and push her away, but he was no match for Suka's speed and agility. She tore into his throat, ripping his neck to shreds, tearing muscles and veins with ease, removing chunks of flesh with the predatory instincts of exactly what she was, a wild wolf.

Mick shot his gun into the air, hoping to at least save the boy and scare Suka away. The gun boomed, but the dog didn't move; something strange happened instead. He noticed that a third boy had entered the campground, the same Mexican boy who came knocking on his door every summer. He looked older but Mick knew it was him.

The boy held a bundle of sticks in his arms. He set the wood on the ground with care and made a gentle whistling sound with his hands and mouth. He started walking very slowly toward the bloodied beast.

Suka pulled her lips back and growled and snarled and snapped at the boy, but she never moved forward. She held her ground, paws dug in deep, claws outstretched. The boy continued moving. He was cautious and never took his eyes off of Suka.

With a clear shot, Mick cocked his rifle and aimed, preparing to fire. He stood close enough that the boy heard the click from the gun. He turned slowly in Mick's direction and shook his head, silently warning Mick not to move. He put his index finger to his mouth, directing Mick to remain silent.

Mick watched in wonder.

Suka sat down. She continued growling, but closed her mouth and stepped back. She had somehow subjected herself to the boy's authority. Mick lowered his gun and his jaw dropped. The boy with the leg injury crawled toward the kid whose neck was mangled, and tried to stop the bleeding with his shirt.

The dark-skinned teen walked closer still, reached out his hand, and Suka, now lying on her belly, took slow and cautious steps toward him with her head slightly tilted down. He had a connection with the dog that Mick didn't understand.

When Suka had crawled to the boy's feet, she began licking and rubbing against his legs. The kid bent down and started petting her. Mick couldn't believe how quickly she returned to her usual self. She panted in exhaustion, nuzzling her snout into the boys lap. Mick kept his gun at his side, just in case, and began walking toward the gruesome scene.

Suka noticed her master coming but ignored his presence, keeping near the teenager. Mick made his way to the redhead and checked for a pulse, but he felt nothing. The kid was dead. He moved on to the other boy who was clinching his leg in agony, hyperventilating and in shock. Mick tore his shirt, creating a tourniquet, and wrapped it tight under the boy's knee. He used the rest of his shirt to clean the wound with water the boys kept in a canteen, and then pressed hard on the shirt, slowing the blood flow.

"Hold the shirt here," he directed the teen, and then turned to the Mexican boy.

"What did you do?" asked Mick.

The teen, answered in a soft voice. "She was scared. I calmed her down."

"How?"

"By not being afraid. She knew their fear. The wolf is like that."

"But she's a mix breed," said Rick. "She's part husky."

"Yes," agreed the young man. "But wolf, too. When she's a husky, she doesn't know fear like she does when she's a wolf. She feels deep," he said, beating his chest with his fist. "Look." He pointed at Suka's face. "Her marks are gone. The dog is away… and the wolf has come." The boy smiled and began petting her, speaking in Spanish.

"Why are you smiling?" asked Mick.

"Because she's mine now."

"What do you mean, she's yours? I have to put her down."

"No!" said the teen, shaking his head, disapproving. "Never. You can't."

Mick pointed at the dead boy by the fire, "Do you see what she's done? She just killed a boy! And she killed three other dogs earlier today."

The kid shook his head. "She's scared. She needs to be free."

"Oh, I'm gonna free her all right," said Mick lifting his gun to shoot.

The boy moved in front of Suka. "No! Not what I mean. She's a protector, a guide. She's a white wolf. She has the spirit of the gods, guiding only those who look into her eyes without fear. That's why she loved you. But now you're afraid and she won't submit to you anymore. Her work is done."

"Pfft. What work? Killing?"

The boy turned toward Suka. He held her face with both of his hands. Suka sat still, exhausted, panting. The boy narrowed his eyes, peering deep into the soul of the dog. Mick and the wounded boy watched in silence. The only sound that could be heard was the snap and crackle of the burning embers and the injured boy's whimpering.

"She gave you love," said the boy, still staring at the dog. Mick cocked his head, disbelieving. "She gave love when you didn't have it. She gave a gift, and you did the best you could, but you didn't understand her. You didn't know what she needed—freedom. Then when she wanted to break free, she found fear." The boy scratched behind her ears. "Fear threatens her. That's why she killed. "

Rick approached the boy and Suka growled deep in her throat.

"She has to die," he said. "I can't let her go with you."

The boy laid his forehead on Suka's nose. "Please," he said, pleading. "She's my guide now. I need her, and she needs me."

Mick turned and paced in circles. He thought of the consequences; he was the adult and owner of a murderous dog. How would he ever explain setting his dog free when she killed a human? He would be liable, and maybe charged with murder or some type of associative crime. He couldn't do it. The dog had to be put down.

"No," said Mick. His voice had never been so stern. "She's killed, so she has to be killed in return. It's a legal matter." Mick handed the boy the gun. "If she's yours, you have to do it. It's only right."

The teen shook his head, crying. "No."

Mick bent down, his eyes connecting with the young man. "If you don't do it, someone else will. Trust me, they'll find her and kill her."

The kid gave Suka a hard squeeze around her neck. "And...her spirit...will leave without me?"

"Yes."

The young Mexican reached out his hand and took the gun.

*****

Mick discovered that the two boys in the woods were brothers, wards of the state. Their mother had abandoned them and they had run away from many foster homes.

Mick may have been motivated by guilt, but for whatever reason, he took an interest in the surviving kid. And after several months of tests and background checks and inspections, Mick was awarded custody of the young teen. He took the boy in, as his own, and became the father the boy never had. The boy's name was Anderson. As the years passed, he grew to be kind and intelligent, but he never got over his fear of dogs.

One summer, while taking Anderson on a road trip to the Grand Canyon, Mick decided to return to the small ranch just outside of Amarillo to show his adopted son where he found Suka, and to tell him of the good times he had with his pup, a story Mick never shared until then. The hut was still there and the fence still glistened.

Together, Mick and Anderson walked the long stretch to the dusty ranch and knocked on the dilapidated plywood. Dishes rattled and Mick heard footsteps inside. When the door creaked opened, there stood a dark-skinned young man, no older than twenty years old. Mick looked at the young man with amazement and the look was returned. Without a word, they embraced, and laughed. The man, the same Mexican boy from long ago, invited the two visitors inside and they shared their stories of fate, stories that came full circle. And when Mick walked out of that hut, there had been no doubt in his mind that his life was still guided by the spirit of Suka, the white wolf.

About Jeff Bennington

Jeff Bennington is the author of *Reunion*, *Twisted Vengeance* and the *Creepy* series, a collection of scary stories. He blogs at The Writing Bomb and The Kindle Book Review.

When Jeff isn't writing and blogging, he's busy raising and homeschooling his four children with his wife near Indianapolis, Indiana.

SEEING THE LIGHT
BY WILLIAM C. RASMUSSEN

Staring up at the Tybee Island Lighthouse, Mike Parker felt a strange sense of unease mixed with awe over its magnificent presence. His disquiet had a lot to do with the lighthouse's checkered past. During the past hundred years, a dozen people had turned up missing in and around the structure. Most of the disappearances had gone unsolved, but in each instance there had been a possible logical theory, at least.

Aside from that sobering statistic, however, the lighthouse was truly a remarkable creation: 154 feet tall, 178 total steps, and it had withstood everything that nature had thrown at it for close to three hundred years. Built on Tybee Island in the early 1700s, it cast its powerful light miles out across the Atlantic at night, still guiding vessels safely up the Savannah River in Georgia to this day. Mike chuckled and thought it could probably survive another three hundred years easily.

"What are you laughing about?" Jessica asked. She was making her way back from the Tybee Island Museum, which sat just a short distance from the lighthouse.

"Nothing," he said with a smile. Proudly, he watched his fifty-one-year old wife approach, still beautiful to him after all these years. Jess stood around five-three, wore her frosted blonde hair shoulder-length, and had barely added ten pounds to her college cheerleading figure. He wished the same could be said about himself. At the age of fifty-seven, he had been forced to retire from his law enforcement position with the federal government because of health issues, which Mike felt were entirely due to stress. Most of the time he felt just fine.

"Did you know," he said when his wife caught up, "that most lighthouses throughout the country have a history of spooky stories associated with them?"

"Hmm, that doesn't surprise me at all. People are always saying that they're haunted. I don't care. I just like them because they're so pretty."

He snickered softly, latching onto her arm. "Well, are you ready to climb to the top?" He tipped his head in the direction of the majestic, 154-foot monument.

"Of course I am. Let's go."

As they passed through the entrance door, a pleasant, elderly man stationed like a sentinel just inside the building reminded them that the lighthouse would be closing promptly at 5:30 PM. Mike glanced at his watch and saw they had a little over thirty minutes left to make it to the top and back down.

They made it to the third landing before Mike succumbed to fatigue.

"I told you I could go farther than you without stopping," Jess said.

"Yeah, well..." he trailed off, gazing out the window at the beautiful scenery and trying to catch a breath that seemed quite elusive at the moment. "You know my health sometimes stumbles a bit. So, at least I have an excuse."

"You *are* an old man...but at least you're *my* old man," Jess said, laughing.

"I'll show you who's an old man," Mike said, starting up the fourth set of steps with renewed energy. Jess tagged along close behind him.

As they wound their way up to the top of the lighthouse, Mike gave his surroundings a cursory inspection, noting the weathered brick walls where the surface desperately cried out for a coat of paint though no one was listening. He brushed his fingertips lightly over the rough, rusting railings lining each side of the stairway. They both agreed on a rest stop at the sixth landing, choosing to be more refreshed once they made their final push to the top.

Once they finally reached the last landing, a few more steps brought them almost to within a reach of the huge Fresnel lens, whose sole purpose was to magnify the much smaller light bulb also located in the Lantern Room. Retreating to the last landing area, they carefully pushed through a heavy metal door which deposited them on an outside platform that circled the topmost part of the lighthouse, and sat roughly 140 feet above the ground.

"Oh, no," Mike muttered as he followed his wife onto the platform, vertigo settling in, his legs turning to spaghetti. A brisk wind pummeled him, carrying a strong, salty tang to his nostrils.

"What are we doing up here?" he asked, chuckling nervously and hugging the outside of the lighthouse, one sweaty hand braced on the structure's exterior, the other hand palming his cell phone.

"I want a photo of the view," Jess said. She crept up to the railing and gradually positioned her digital camera in front of her eyes before snapping off a picture. "Relax, hon, you'll get used to it."

"I'm not so sure. Geezus, we're up high!"

Like an inchworm, Mike traipsed slowly behind his wife as they circumnavigated the lighthouse, trying to enjoy the scenery from their lofty perch. Apparently they were alone on the platform, and for that, he was glad—at least he wouldn't be embarrassing himself in front of others.

"Are you okay, hon?" Jess asked, her face a mask of concern.

"Whew, I guess so…just feel a little light-headed, that's all. Maybe that leisurely hike up 178 steps took a little more out of me than I'd thought." He fabricated a weak smile for her benefit.

"Maybe we should start back down."

"You stay up here, get some more photos and enjoy yourself. I'll head back down, take my time, and see you at the bottom in a little while. I'll be fine."

Jess stared at him doubtfully, studying him before relenting. "All right. Go on ahead, but be careful. I'll be down shortly."

With a sly wink, Mike retraced his steps south, passing no one on the way up and pausing for a moment or two at most of the rest stops. During his descent, with the swiftly failing sunlight causing lengthening shadows to drape the stairwell, he noticed numerous nooks and crannies and hidey-holes that, in his mind, only served to further reinforce the haunted lighthouse legends. When he finally reached the ground floor, his strained thigh muscles quivering like harp strings, he unselfconsciously exhaled a huge sigh of relief.

A bit out of breath, he maneuvered through the small entry and stepped outside. The fresh, briny breeze felt good on his face after the somewhat musty confines of the narrow, cramped lighthouse. A slight chill now cut the air. His dizziness diminished and, as he peered around the swiftly-darkening grounds from which visitors were fleeing like felons, a peek at his watch indicated it was almost 5:25. He squinted up at the now-shaded Tybee Lighthouse platform, but couldn't see Jess. She should be down soon, he thought.

With a few minutes to kill, he ambled over to the beautifully-restored lighthouse keeper's dwelling and saw the old gentleman who had greeted them on their journey up into the lighthouse. Mike continued over to him and, affable as always, engaged the man in conversation.

After several minutes of friendly banter, Mike again glanced at his watch.

"Whoa," he said. "I better go find my wife. It's after 5:30." Scanning the shadow-swathed grounds and not seeing anybody, a frown tugged at his face.

"Yep," said the older man, whose name was Griffith, "time to check the lighthouse. I need to lock up."

"I wonder if my wife is still up there..."

"Well, let's go see," Griffith said, and the two of them hastily made their way back to the lighthouse entrance.

But Jess wasn't in the lighthouse showroom, or anywhere nearby, he realized, after quickly surveying the grounds.

"Hmm," Mike said to Griffith. A finger of unease traced a cold, ragged line up his spine. "Should I yell up to the top? See if she's still up there?"

"Not sure anyone at the top could hear you, unless you really bellow. But she's probably still straggling around the place, maybe even in the restroom."

Mike nodded, then sprinted a dozen steps up the stairwell and hollered as loud as he could for his wife. After several tries, he gave up.

"I'm gonna check around outside—the restroom, like you said—and our car." He fished out his cellphone and punched in Jess' cell number. "Be right back."

Ten minutes later, after he had canvassed the women's restroom, searched the grounds, and checked their car, Mike hurried back to the lighthouse doorway, where Griffith was huddled up against the wind.

"Can't find her anywhere," Mike said, voice quavering nervously. The chill onshore breeze wound through the grounds like a slippery serpent; the salty bouquet that accompanied it was beginning to make him feel sick. "And she won't answer her cell. It must be turned off. It goes straight to voice mail. I'm starting to panic a bit. Where the hell is she?"

Mike felt his heartbeat racing, nervous sweat trickling like a leaking faucet down his forehead and the back of his neck, and realized that this reaction to stress was the very reason why he lost his law enforcement job. "I'm gonna climb back up to the top of the lighthouse and see if she's still up there."

"Now, hold on a second, Mike," Griffith said, reaching out and laying a hand on his arm. "Let me go with you. It's darker out now and the lighthouse should be switching on automatically any second. It'll be a lot more dangerous going up those steps than it was a half hour ago."

Mike twitched and fidgeted in the dank, early evening air as if he needed a dose of Ritalin. "Fine."

And even as they turned to enter the doorway, the photo-electric relay that governed the lighthouse lamp switched the powerful beam on, its miles-long ray flashing and probing the distant, dark horizon over the Atlantic Ocean, once again providing safe passage for skippers piloting their vessels up the Savannah River.

Mike fell behind at the fourth landing, his head swimming again with light-headedness, his vision impeded by the falling dark outside. Small flashlight in hand, Griffith stepped in the lead and soldiered on, his stamina belying his advancing years. Mike trailed in his wake.

When Griffith finally reached the top landing and began clearing the area in his quest for the missing woman, Mike was still laboring upward some twenty-five or thirty steps below. But Mike thought both his body and mind had toppled over the edge into delirium when he suddenly heard Jess's faint, distorted voice calling out to him from somewhere, but he couldn't tell where.

"S…me, Mike, s…me!"

What the hell? he thought. *Is she saying save me, save me?*

"Jess, where are you? I'm here, honey, I'm coming. Where are you?"

Scrambling up the remaining dozen steps, Mike vaulted onto the top landing, face flushed and heart pounding like a bass drum inside the cage of his chest. Head reeling from his efforts, he continued to cry out for his missing wife, but her muffled voice had abruptly gone silent.

"What's going on? Did you find her?" Griffith said, flashlight leading the way as he edged back in through the narrow doorway that led to the outside platform.

"No, I just—thought I heard—" he panted, trying to catch his breath. "Did you hear anything?"

"No, I was outside checking the viewing platform. What did you hear?"

Mike shook his head. How could he tell Griffith he'd heard a voice out of nowhere? "Nothing," he said, erring on the side of caution. "Must've been the wind or something, I guess…Listen, I'm going outside to the platform."

As Mike cautiously made his circuit of the platform, the chilly, gusting onshore wind prickled his face and raised goose bumps along his neck and shoulders. Just above him, the powerful lighthouse beam swept the area, flashing brighter every few seconds like a slow motion strobe light.

Jess wasn't on the viewing platform.

Mike pushed back through the door to the lighthouse interior, his downcast eyes finding Griffith's.

"She's not up here, so we can rule this out," Griffith said. "Let's head back down. See if she turned up somewhere else."

With Mike leading the way, they began their descent. But they hadn't gone more than a half-dozen steps when Mike accidentally kicked something located near the vertical metal pole, from which the individual steps were connected like spokes.

"Griffith, shine that light at my feet."

The older man complied, his feeble flashlight beam penetrating the darkness just enough to highlight what appeared to be a camera. Mike bent down to retrieve it; Griffith focused the light on Mike's find.

"It's a Sony...Jess's camera," Mike said somberly, examining it in the wan light as if it were a family heirloom.

"That doesn't necessarily mean anything, Mike. She could have simply dropped it on her way down. With all the racket that footsteps make on these old, metal stairs, she probably didn't even hear it fall."

"Sure," he said, not believing it one bit. "Let's get out of here."

The rest of the way down, Mike continued to cradle the camera in his hands as if it were the last remaining link to his wife.

Once they made it to the ground floor and the showroom area, Griffith stepped outside to corral a few cohorts working the grounds and determine if they had found Mike's wife or any clue to her whereabouts. Within minutes, Griffith learned that they had come up empty as well. He trudged over to give Mike the bad news.

"I think it's time we called the police," Griffith said.

Sweaty and exhausted, Mike was bent over a display case like a man twenty years his senior as he attempted to reach his wife over and over by cellphone. He sighed, tears trickling from the corners of his eyes.

"You're right," he said, and resignedly punched in 9-1-1.

A few minutes later, an officer from the Tybee Island Police Department pulled up in a dark, late model Dodge Charger, gunning the engine once before shutting it down and exiting the vehicle. He quickly made his way over to where Mike was sequestered like a juror with Griffith and several of the employees, the lighthouse and its flashing beam framed behind them like a postcard.

"You know," the officer, whose name was Donnelly, said, "your wife could have simply gone elsewhere of her own accord."

"But I can't reach her on her cell!" Mike said, desperately trying to convince the officer of the severity of the situation.

"Battery could be dead," Donnelly replied, squinting at Mike.

"And I found her camera on the steps at the top of the lighthouse," Mike added, displaying the Sony like indisputable evidence.

Donnelly grasped the proffered camera and examined it briefly before returning it to its owner. "Mr. Parker, normally we don't actively investigate missing person cases immediately, but this lighthouse gives me the creeps. I'm gonna head back to my office and file this report. And I'm not gonna promise anything, but I'll talk to my supervisor and see what we can do."

"Thanks," Mike said.

"Now, I suggest you head back to your hotel and try to get some rest, maybe get something to eat. Who knows? Your wife may even be there already." He paused for a moment, ensuring he covered all bases. "If you find her there, be sure to call me right away."

"I think you should listen to him and go to your hotel room," Griffith said, as they watched the officer walk away.

Mike shook his head. "I can't leave...not yet. I'd feel like I was abandoning her."

"Well, you know, my shift's over and I want to go home."

"I understand. I can take a look around the grounds and the facilities myself. See if I can turn up anything."

Griffith sighed. "You do what you gotta do, but I need to lock up the lighthouse."

Mike watched Griffith leave. It was fully dark now. No moon brightened the scenery in between the swoops of the lighthouse orb. The salt-tinged breeze whistled in off the ocean like the wail of the banshee. Guided by the slowly strobing lighthouse beam high overhead, Mike began his trek. But after twenty minutes of fruitless searching, he gazed at the camera still clasped tightly in his hand and felt scared and hopeless.

Did I really hear you in the lighthouse? he wondered. *Was it really you, Jess?*

He stared up at the top of the lighthouse, its wide beam windmilling around every five or six seconds, splashing the distant ocean with white light, and oblivious to the fear and agony he was mired in.

I can't go up there again, Jess. I'm sorry. I'm tired and my legs are exhausted. And besides, Griffith locked it.

Feeling like a coward, he turned away with his head tucked between his shoulders, and trudged back to his car. He unlocked the door, fired up the engine, and peeled off in a spray of loose gravel. He first checked the hotel, but as he figured, Jess had never made it there. Getting back into his car, he had no idea where he was going—maybe grab a bite somewhere, or just keep driving till he ran out of gas—but after ten minutes he pulled into the parking lot of a fast-food restaurant and killed the engine.

Alone with his thoughts in the pervasive darkness of the car's interior, Mike picked up Jess's camera, rotating it in his hands. Out of curiosity, he turned it on and began thumbing through the shots she had taken at the top of the lighthouse. There were several of them, mostly from when she was standing outside on the viewing platform.

They were taken near the Lantern Room, showcasing the huge Fresnel lens...and something else. As he looked carefully at the shots, flipping from one to the other, magnifying the images for closer inspection, he realized his wife might have unwittingly stumbled upon something she wished she hadn't.

"Oh, my God!" he whispered, his eyes glued to the tiny camera screen.

One of the snapshots displayed the Fresnel lens to near perfection—its multiple, fly-like lenses captured exquisitely by the camera—along with several bleached, figure-like distortions creeping onto the side of the pictures and looking almost human…but not quite.

Ghosts?

Cursing, he tossed the camera aside and restarted the car engine, toying briefly with the idea of calling Griffith and Officer Donnelly and asking them to meet him back at the lighthouse before dismissing the notion. Instead he decided that he'd rather investigate this on his own before calling in the cavalry.

Thrusting the car into gear, he burned rubber in his haste to return to the inscrutable lighthouse. He made it back in well under ten minutes, bringing his car to a skidding halt in the empty sand-and-gravel-covered parking lot, as close as he could get to the main entrance. He didn't jump out immediately, choosing instead to wait in the shadowy interior of his car for a while and confirm that all of the employees had left for the evening.

After a few minutes, he glanced at his watch and saw that it was fast approaching 8PM. He climbed out of the car, a small flashlight in hand and his wife's camera secreted in his jacket pocket, and eased the door shut.

Like a thief, he crept along the side of the car to the trunk, where he rummaged around inside for a moment before retrieving a lug wrench from alongside his spare tire. Earlier, he had noticed a latch on the lighthouse door and a padlock hanging from a hook on the outside door jamb, and knew he'd need a tool that would grant him sufficient leverage to enable him to break in. Now armed for battle, he moved stealthily across the grass toward the lighthouse entrance as the intense beam swirled overhead, monitoring his progress.

Reaching the lighthouse door without incident, Mike took stock of his surroundings before pocketing his mini-flashlight. With the cool onshore breeze battering against him as if he were in a wind tunnel, he levered the prying tip of the lug wrench between the latch and the door and pressed down with his entire weight. Nothing happened the first or second time, but on the third try the latch ripped free of the salt air-blasted door with a shrill squeal, the screws catapulting onto the grass.

He peered cautiously behind him once again, and then carefully pulled the damaged door open and snuck inside the showroom. He tugged the door almost to the closed position, leaving it slightly ajar in case he had to exit quickly. Plucking the flashlight from his jacket pocket, he thumbed it on and slowly chased the slender, dancing beam to the foot of the circular staircase.

Plodding purposefully up the steps, he knew this would be his third summit in a little more than three hours, but he was determined to find Jess this time or die trying. A little past the fourth landing, his breath was rushing in and out of him like a bellows, and perspiration coursed down his forehead and the back of his neck despite the cool temperature.

Suddenly he thought he heard Jess's voice once again, resonating softly down the stairs.

"S…me, Mike, please s…me!"

"I'm coming, Jess, hang on! I'm coming!"

And with a burst of energy he never thought he could muster, Mike shifted gears and rushed upward, pursuing an elusive voice and the wonderful memories attached to it.

When he finally gained the seventh, and final, landing, he thought he was going to pass out. Gasping for breath like a lifelong smoker, legs overdosing on lactic acid, he lunged for the stair railing to support himself. The flashlight and lug wrench he brandished nearly dragged him down. But his wife's pleas urged him on.

Staggering like a drunk around the corner toward the few steps leading to the Lantern Room, the powerful beam's absence every four or five seconds as it swept by like a carnival merry-go-round revealed a terrifyingly surreal sight.

And then he saw them.

Floating in the pale, ambient light left in the wake of the slowly-spinning beam were the indistinct shapes of several people in widely different styles of clothing, their figures leached of color and substance.

Oh my God! he thought, transfixed by the images, his acute fatigue forgotten.

As the beam swept by again, it passed effortlessly through the lighthouse ghosts, limning each one with an incandescence that only served to heighten their spectral appearance.

He spotted his wife suspended in their midst, her face contorted, her appeals falling on his ears more clearly now.

"Stay away from me, Mike, stay away from me!" her cries repeated until Mike thought his head was going to burst under the onslaught.

"Oh shit," he mumbled, cold fear worming its way into his stomach while icy prickles spider walked down his spine.

She had never been calling at him to save her. She had actually been warning him to stay away! There would be no saving Jess now; he knew she was gone.

Suddenly, all of the apparitions trapped within the lighthouse turned to him as one, their faces radiating pure malice. Leaving Jess behind, they swarmed toward him like bees, abandoning their haven in the Lantern Room.

Momentarily frozen in place by their approach, Mike broke free of his bonds and stumbled to the top of the stairs, his flashlight and lug wrench unceremoniously cast aside in the process. Beginning the descent for the third time, he barely heard his wife's foreboding cries above the wailing and rustling of the malevolent spirits, like hounds out for blood, sniffing at his heels.

As he veered by the second landing in his frenetic flight, he caught the distinct thud of what could only have been the lighthouse entrance door slamming shut below. Pausing momentarily, breath hitching in his chest, he knew he had nowhere else to go. With the vengeful spirits from the past literally breathing down his neck, he barreled down the remaining steps and onto the ground floor.

The entrance door was shut. Whether from the howling wind or his pursuers, he didn't know, and didn't care: he had to get out. Charging up to the door, he gripped the handle with sweat-slicked hands and twisted.

Nothing.

He tried again, but the door wouldn't move. He risked a glance behind him, heard the horde approaching the ground floor, and leaned into the door with his right shoulder. Finally it flew open, rebounding off the outside wall and smacking him in the same shoulder as he made good his escape.

He stumbled away from the lighthouse, hoping that the spirits within were trapped in a dimension limited to the structure. His quads and hamstrings burned and cramped. Staggering across the grass, crying out for help to a crowd of none, the strong, salty onshore winds tearing apart and shredding his words, his legs finally gave out some thirty or forty yards from the base of the lighthouse. He tumbled to the ground, and heard a loud *whooshing* sound behind him.

Lying there, he realized he couldn't get up. He looked over his shoulder and saw various colors like the northern lights. Somehow the wraiths were able to leave the lighthouse, their faces now lit with a demonic glow. They surged and pulsed through the lighthouse door, swirling into the air, and closed in on him. He had to get up. He *had* to.

Tearing himself free from his rigor, he pulled himself to his feet, his wind almost gone. Glancing at the entrance to the lighthouse grounds, he spotted his Honda CR-V twinkling like a beacon beneath one of the lights in the parking lot. The car was his only chance, he realized. Anxiously fumbling for the keys in his pants pocket, with the howling spirits playing together in the wind as they came for him, Mike made for his car, perhaps a hundred yards away, his last sanctuary.

But even before he had traveled half the distance to his goal, his old body once again failed him. The lactic acid accumulating in his strained leg muscles proved too much, and he fell yet again on the grassy grounds.

"Shit!" he mumbled on hands and knees, and peeked over his shoulder, releasing a high-pitched scream at the sight. The malevolent specters had surrounded him at the edge of the lighthouse grounds, and their furious passes, like swooping birds of prey, now froze him in place.

The spirits continued their manic assault, swooping close by him, sometimes right *through* him, as he lay there helpless on the ground, batting his arms futilely at ethereal forms. He realized it was suicide to remain there any longer.

Mustering strength from a reserve he wasn't aware he had, he struggled to his feet once again and blundered the rest of the way to his car, all the while swatting his hands through the air as if he were fighting off a colony of bats. Digging into his pocket, he was relieved to find his keys.

Time seemed unnaturally slowed, but somehow he managed to reach his car, triggering the car key's automatic door opener and diving into the driver's seat. He plunged the key into the ignition, fired up the engine, and reversed out of his parking spot in a spray of sand, dirt and gravel. He jammed the gear shift into drive and stomped on the gas pedal.

But something slammed into the front of the car, causing the side of his head to slam into the steering wheel. He blacked out.

*****

Later—whether it was seconds, minutes or hours, he didn't know— he groggily came around to the sensation of warm, gentle hands cradling and caressing his face and head. He suddenly realized he was lying in someone's lap. He sensed it was his wife and she was talking to him softly.

"I'm here, honey," Jess said. "Everything's fine. You're gonna be all right."

"Oh, God, Jess," he said, slowly regaining his faculties, "I thought I'd lost you. I'm so glad you're back. We got away! We're safe now, right?"

"Oh, honey…" she said as she looked away.

And as he also looked away, he realized he was no longer sitting in the driver's seat of his car, but floating in the middle of the Lantern Room, the lighthouse's powerful beam sweeping around beneath the two of them, illuminating the grounds and the ocean.

He stared at his arms in disbelief, jerking involuntarily as his gaze pierced through his now transparent body. Moving effortlessly to the side of the Lantern Room, he peered down at the lighthouse grounds and spotted, so far below, his car that was stalled haphazardly in the parking lot.

He—*they*—hadn't gotten away after all.

Gazing back at his wife, he found her floating next to him and smiling. He gathered her lovingly in his arms and just held her. He realized the other wraiths were gone for the moment, but surely they would be back. And he also realized that although he and Jessica would never return to the world of the living, they would at least be together…and now he would never lose her again. Their love would last forever.

About William C. Rasmussen

A native of Hawaii, William "Bill" Rasmussen spent over thirty years in the islands before being transferred to New York City as a Special Agent for the FBI. After eleven years in "The Big Apple," he was then transferred to Memphis, Tennessee, where he retired in 2004, and currently lives on its outskirts with his loving wife.

Since March of 2010, when he returned for the first time in over twenty years to his passion for writing horror fiction, he has had short tales of horror accepted/published in the following magazines: *Sounds of the Night, Fantastique Unfettered, ParABnormal Digest, The Absent Willow Review, Midnight Street, The Storm Is Coming* (Antho), *Behind Locked Doors* (Antho), *Black Ink Horror, Bete Noire,* and *Cover of Darkness.*

His collection, *Claw Marks and Other Disturbing Diversions,* was released in September of 2010 by Crossroad Press in all digital formats; it is also available at Amazon.

In December of 2011, his novella, *Infinity Twice Removed,* co-written with Michael McBride, was released in hardcover and all digital formats by Delirium Books; it, too, is also available at Amazon.

He is currently shopping around a novelette and a novella, as well as several other short tales of horror.

Them Ol' Negro Blues
by JG Faherty

Lester Bolls wiped crusted dirt and sweat from his forehead and opened the next tattered cardboard box, unaware he was about to discover a surprise ticket to fortune and fame. It was day three of moving his parents from the house they'd lived in for the last forty years to the new condo they'd bought in a retirement complex just south of Atlanta, and he was thinking about nothing except getting a cold beer. Or maybe ten.

It galled Lester to spend his time doing manual labor. Normally he'd have found an excuse not to help, but his record company had just dropped him, and helping his parents also meant a week of not spending money on food. Plus, they'd paid his airfare from LA to Atlanta. Of course, he'd drawn the line at actually moving the boxes down from the attic. Let his brothers sit up there in the hundred and something degree heat.

Instead, he'd volunteered to open the boxes and determine if the contents had any value or should be tossed in the dumpster out back.

Looking inside the latest box, he found a stack of old-fashioned vinyl records. Unfamiliar faces stared up at him, all African-American, most of them wearing the close-cropped hairdos popular among black musicians of the forties and fifties.

"Hey Ma, what are these?" He held one up. The cover read "Backyard Blues," by Willie Mo Gains.

Peggy Bolls put on her bifocals and looked at the album. "Oh, I remember these. Your grandfather worked at a recording studio for a while. Back when I was in high school. Sometimes he'd bring home free records. Mostly blues and jazz."

Lester flipped through the dusty album jackets. Some were torn; others mildew stained. "Gator Man Marshall. T-Bone Rex. Harmonica Joe. I never heard of any of these guys."

His mother laughed and handed the album back to him. "No, I don't 'spect you would have. The company was rather shady, from what I gathered. They took people's money for the studio time, made a few copies of the record, and then went on to the next poor soul."

"Were they any good?"

Peggy shrugged. "You're the musician. I haven't listened to them since the fifties. Probably no one has. But your granddad always used to say there was nothing better than them old Negro blues."

The idea of hearing music no one else had heard in decades intrigued Lester. He'd always enjoyed the blues—Clapton, BB King, Stevie Ray Vaughn, Muddy Waters. His strong point as a musician was lead guitar; all he had to do was hear a lead once and he could not only play it note for note, but improve on it. Unfortunately, he had almost no talent when it came to writing songs. Catchy melodies came his way about as often as million dollar lottery tickets. That, combined with a reputation for being hard to work with, had him well on the road to being a life time studio player.

"You mind if I keep these?"

"No, go ahead. I'm never going to listen to them." Peggy went back to folding towels and sheets into storage containers.

Lester slid the box of records to the side and called up to his brother to hand down the next box.

*****

The sounds of JD "Bullfrog" Castle's hauntingly melodic fingerpicking filled Lester's apartment. He looked at the album cover again. *Atlanta Blues.* He wanted to cry as the long-dead guitarist worked his way through a long solo based loosely on a minor scale in D.

I can't believe how fucking good these guys were.

So far, he'd listened to seven of the twenty-three records he'd salvaged from the box. The rest had been too scratched or warped to even consider playing. Each album had been better than the last, each guitarist a virtuoso in his own right.

And the songs—it was impossible to imagine that the people who'd written them had never made it in the music business. Compared to Bullfrog Castle or Johnson City James, blues icons like BB King, Robert Johnson, and Howlin' Wolf were nothing but rank amateurs.

Sure, the recordings were crude, and the playing slow by modern standards, but you could *feel* the greatness wrapping you in soulful notes, emotional chords, and crying leads. These unknowns didn't just play the blues, they produced them the way a generator produces electricity.

Lester still found it unimaginable that no one—not Clapton, not Vaughn, not Beck, not Setzer, not Page—had ever recorded their own versions of these songs.

It was as if no one but Lester Bolls knew of them.

Maybe that's because no one but me does know of them. I might have the only copies of these records in existence.

Dollar signs flashed in Lester's head as he thought about what a mark he could make in the music industry by re-releasing the old recordings.

But that would take a lot of work—digitally remastering them and cleaning up the hiss and pops, not to mention finding the relatives of all the songwriters and performers and getting permission to release the albums. And who knew how many ways the profits would have to be split?

The next song on the record started up as Bullfrog Castle launched into an up-tempo tune that had Lester tapping his feet from the first notes.

Christ, if I could write like that...

And that's when the idea hit him. If no one else knew about the songs, who would know if he released them under his own name? He could speed them up a bit, add his own twists onto the already superb leads, throw in a few horns and keyboards...

He could be the next Stevie Ray Vaughn or Clapton, start a brand new blues revolution.

There was enough material here for a whole career; after twelve or fifteen hit albums, he could live the good life just on royalties and the occasional live appearance.

But he had to make sure there was no official record of any of the musicians in the box. The last thing he needed was a scandal like the Led Zeppelin fiasco a few years back.

He turned on his laptop and started a Google search.

*****

"And the Grammy for Best Contemporary Blues Album, Instrumental or Vocal, goes to...Les Johnson!"

Lester Bolls stood up as the packed auditorium went wild. He handed his drink to his date, waved his arms to the crowd, and headed down the aisle toward the stage.

"Congratulations, man. Loved the album," whispered Steven Tyler, as he handed Lester the golden trophy. "Call me next week. I want you to guest guitar on the next Aerosmith album."

Lester stood behind the podium, stared out at the cheering faces, and felt a moment of awe.

The most famous people in the music industry, and they're cheering for me. Fuckin' Aerosmith wants me to play with them. And this is just the beginning.

He raised the trophy high in the air and shouted into the microphone. "Let this be a message to the world. Other music might come and go, but the blues will never die, people! Thank you, and I'll see you on the road!"

The noise level grew deafening as row after row of attendees stood up, clapped their hands, stomped their feet, and shouted.

Someone touched him on the arm. He turned and saw a pretty young thing in a sequined dress motioning to him. He couldn't hear a word she said, but he understood he was supposed to follow her offstage.

Behind the curtains and props, a line of people stood waiting to congratulate him. Among the faces he recognized were David Bowie, Bruce Springsteen, Eric Clapton, Sting, and Johnny Lang. The next fifteen minutes were a blur as celebrities patted him on the back and men in suits handed him glasses of champagne while tucking business cards—and drugs—in his pockets.

At one point, a twenty-something girl with innocent eyes and barely-concealed breasts latched onto his arm and whispered in his ear that she'd love to see his hotel room. He remembered seeing her on MTV—she was the newest teenybopper rocker—but he couldn't remember her name.

"I can't, sweetheart. I'm here with someone," he told her, looking around for the date he'd brought.

"That's okay," the Jessica Simpson clone said. "Three's always better than two." She took his hand and led him through the crowd towards an exit.

When she finally went home two days later, he still didn't know her name.

*****

"Les, phone for you. Your mother." Randy Levine held up the phone so Les could see it through the window of the sound booth.

"Shit." Aware the mics might still be live, Les controlled himself from saying anything else. The last thing he needed was a lecture on how little he appreciated his parents. Still, the idea of paying for unused studio time when his mother could just as easily left a message at his apartment was a tiny knife in his back. It didn't matter that he'd grossed two mil on the last album. He hated wasting his own money.

"What is it, Ma? I'm at the studio." He hoped she'd take the hint.

"It's your father, Lester." Peggy's voice trembled as she spoke. "He's...he died last night."

"Ah, shit. I'm sorry, Ma. I—"

"Don't bother with the platitudes, Lester. We both know you didn't give a damn about him. God knows you never came to see him in the hospital. But it might be nice if you could come and pay your last respects. The wake starts tomorrow, and the funeral is on Thursday." She hung up before he could respond.

Les clenched the phone in his hand. It was just like her to play the guilt card. So what if he hadn't been home in a while? That didn't mean he didn't care. It *was* his father, after all, even if the old man had never expressed any interest in Les's musical talents.

Shit, the life of a rock star wasn't as easy as it seemed. He'd been crazy busy the last couple of years, what with the touring, promotional parties, and recording sessions. He'd barely had time to relax at the mansion he'd purchased in LA, let alone...

Ah, who am I kidding? I haven't been home because that part of me is dead. I don't want to be Lester Bolls. Being Les Johnson is a helluva lot more fun.

"Problem, Les?" Randy asked. He'd been Les's manager since the first album, knew him better than anyone on the planet.

"What? No. I mean, yeah, but it's okay. My father passed away." Les set the phone down. "Don't worry. I'm not gonna blow off the record."

Randy shook his head. "I don't know, Les. It'd look awfully bad to your fans if you didn't go to the funeral. That kind of shit can turn into a scandal, get all the nosy reporters investigating your past. People have forgotten about Lester Bolls and his lousy music career. You don't want them remembering again."

"Fuck me hard." Les let himself fall into one of the chairs behind the sound console. "So now I gotta go back to Bugshit, Georgia and play the good son for the whole world to see?"

"That's the way the business works, Les. We make an announcement that you won't be making any appearances for the next two or three weeks. You're taking some time off to be with your family in their time of need. The press will eat it up. Good PR, my friend."

Les looked at his custom Gibson Flying-V waiting in the recording chamber. He wanted to just put it on and play, forget all the bullshit. The tracks they'd been laying down for the new album were killer. Who knew if he'd have the same magic a week from now?

Goddamn family.

"Fine. Make the arrangements."

*****

"You didn't have to stay, Lester," Peggy Bolls said as she put the last of the dishes in the dishwasher.

They'd had friends and family over after the funeral. A slew of faces he didn't recognize, packing the apartment tight. People had stayed until almost nine. Following his brothers' leads, Les had done his part, serving food and cleaning up after people. Chuck and Morris had left a few minutes earlier with their wives and kids, promising to check back in the morning.

"It's okay, Ma. I didn't mind." The truth of those words surprised him. It had taken a day for the family to warm up to him after his two-year absence, but then it was like he'd never left. Joking around with his brothers helped him get over the shock of seeing how much his mother had aged since the last time he'd been home.

Amazing how things can change in a short time. Five years ago I was standing in this same room, helping my parents put away their things and wondering how I was going to find enough money to pay the next rent notice. Now I could buy the whole damn building if I wanted.

Five years and five gold albums. Three Grammys and countless other awards. All thanks to a box of records I found in my mother's attic.

At first, he'd been afraid someone would come forward and announce him for the fraud he was. But by the time the third record came out, he'd given up on that particular worry. The critics hailed him as the best blues guitarist in the last twenty years, and praised him for his ability to produce hit after hit. "The Paul McCartney of the blues," they called him. Musicians from all musical genres requested the chance to work with him, and he'd fulfilled more than one lifelong dream by playing on albums by Aerosmith, Bon Jovi, and Walter Trout. He'd taken part in the all-star jam at last year's Rock and Roll Hall of Fame inductions, sharing the stage with Clapton, Mick Jagger, and Slash.

And I've still got enough music at home for seven, maybe eight more albums. By then he'd be forty-eight. Old enough to semi-retire, young enough to enjoy a long, rich life.

"I think I'm going to lie on the couch and watch TV for a while," Peggy said as she dried her hands. "You can sit with me if you want."

Les shook his head. "I'm too wound up to sit. I think I'm going to take a drive. I need to get some fresh air, maybe grab a beer. I'll be back later."

Peggy nodded. "Be careful." It was the same caution she'd been giving him since the day he'd gotten his license.

"Goodnight, Ma."

He was a mile down the highway before it struck him that her offer might have been a way of saying she wanted him to keep her company.

Too late now. I'll make sure to spend some time with her tomorrow.

He exited the highway and found himself on Rural Route 18. The road stretched out before him, dark and empty. Other than morning and afternoon commuter traffic to and from Atlanta, the town of Wilson was too far from anything of note to keep the roads filled at night.

Things sure have changed, Les thought, as he fiddled with the rental car's satellite radio. He put on the blues station, was rewarded with the sound of himself singing *Whiskey Bitch Blues. Used to be all sorts of bars and pool halls along this road.* He wasn't in the mood for a fancy club, just a place where he could sit at the bar and drink a cold beer without being recognized.

No sooner had he thought this than he saw neon lights up ahead. He slowed down as he approached the small parking lot.

"Well I'll be damned." The flashing sign announced the bar as The Blues Dimension. Below the words, a neon guitar blinked from pink to blue to green. A smaller sign said, 'Live Music Every Night.'

Les pulled in and parked next to a beat-up Ford pickup. Only a few other cars and trucks sat in the lot. When he stepped inside, he found a handful of patrons sitting at the dozen or so round tables arranged in front of the small stage. The bar itself was empty, the high-backed stools standing in single file like soldiers.

No one turned his way as he approached the bar, where a stout black man in a green apron polished glasses with a yellow-stained rag.

"What can I get ya?" the bartender asked.

"Bottle of Bud," Les said. He swiveled his stool around so he could see the stage. "Not much of a crowd. You do have a band tonight, don't you?"

"Every night, jus' like de sign say." The bartender placed a bottle in front of Les. Drops of condensation ran down the sides of the icy-cold brown glass.

"Who's playing tonight?"

The man smiled, his teeth bright white against his midnight skin. "You in luck. Tonight's open mic night. Never know who gonna show, but it's always hot."

Les glanced at the stage again. A three-piece drum set, a beat-up piano, and a couple of microphones were the only instruments visible. The equipment looked almost as old as the gray heads of the scattered audience. He turned to ask the bartender what time the show started, but the man was gone.

"Okay if I play something on the jukebox?" he called out. When no one answered, he muttered "Don't mind if I do," under his breath and headed for the old-fashioned jukebox at the far end of the bar.

It took Les a moment to figure out how to work it; it had been years since he'd seen a juke that actually played 45's. He smiled as he flipped through the listings; nothing but blues. Muddy Waters, Clarence

Gatemouth Brown, BB King. Fleetwood Mac, back when they were one of the top blues bands in the world.

A name caught his eye and he spun the selection wheel back. *Dancing Shoes Jackson? That sounds familiar. Where have I...? Shit. He's on one of the albums I've got at home, a record I haven't re-recorded yet.*

Other names leaped out at him as he continued turning the wheel: Gator Man Marshall, Bullfrog Castle, T-Bone Rex, Hightower Jones, The Tom Harper Trio, Harmonica Joe.

Les backed away from the jukebox. *If these songs are on 45's in a run-down roadside bar, where the hell else are they? And who knows about them?*

He bumped into a stool and turned around. Another bottle of Budweiser waited for him, a shot of whiskey next to it. He downed the whiskey and drank half the beer in one long swallow.

It was impossible. He'd spent days searching the internet, and when that didn't turn up anything, he'd had his manager dig deeper.

Was that it? Had Randy double-crossed him somehow? Found the families and made a deal with them?

No, that didn't make sense. There was no money in that for Randy, not compared to the megabucks he was making off Les. And the last thing he could imagine Randy having was an attack of conscience. Hell, the general consensus in the industry was Randy Levine would sell his own mother into white slavery for a gold record. It was why Les had chosen him.

"Another beer?" came the bartender's voice from behind him. "Show's about to start."

"Yeah. And another shot." He heard the clink of glass on wood, turned and grabbed the shot glass. The whiskey burned his throat, but it also calmed him.

If anyone had heard of these people before, someone would have threatened me with a lawsuit by now. Whoever owns this bar probably got hold of some old records the same way I did. Chances are he never even heard my versions. Hell, there was nothing on that jukebox recorded after the nineteen-sixties.

Les took a deep breath as the houselights dimmed and the stage lights came on. *Nothin' to worry about. I'll just sit here and enjoy the show, and in the morning I'll have Randy do another search.*

A tall, thin black man in a blue suit stepped came out from backstage and approached the microphone. "Ladies and gentlemen," he said, his amplified Southern drawl filling the room. "Welcome to the Blues Dimension. We got lots of music for you tonight; we gonna be jammin' all night long. So let's get things started."

A small chorus of cheers and clapping, accompanied by good-natured hooting, followed his words. Les couldn't tell for sure, but it sounded as if there were more people in the darkened room than before.

I haven't seen anyone come in. Then again, he'd been too focused on the juke to notice anything happening around him.

The emcee continued his patter. "We got us a special treat tonight, folks. Sittin' in the audience is one of the finest young blues musicians dis side of the Mississippi. Let's see if we can't git him to come up here and play a few songs."

A murmur went through the crowd, and Les found himself straining to see in the near dark. A spotlight came on, framing him in painful brightness. He dropped his beer and covered his eyes with his arms as the emcee's voice rang out.

"Folks, I present Les Johnson! C'mon up here, Les!"

The audience broke out in shouts and cheers. Still half-blind, Les allowed the bartender to guide him up to the stage. Someone handed him a vintage Fender Stratocaster and turned him around to face the audience. Through a fog of cigarette smoke drifting up under the lights, he saw dozens—no, *hundreds!*—of smiling faces looking at him.

Where'd all these people come from? And why do so many of them look familiar?

A deep bass note startled him, and he turned around. The emcee stood right there, grinning as if it was the happiest day in his life. Behind him, people were sitting down at the piano and drums, and a portly old man with a gray afro leaned lazily on a stand-up bass.

"This here the house band, Les. Don't you worry, you jus' play anything you want. They know *all* your songs." The man patted Les on the shoulder and left the stage.

Les's hand accidentally touched the strings of the guitar; crisp, clear notes burst into life from the sound system. He glanced at the mic stand, saw several guitar picks taped there, just like he always had them when he played.

The crowd clapped and stomped their feet, eager for the show to start.

Well, I can't disappoint them, can I? he asked himself, as the unreality of the situation gave way to the comfortable feeling he always got when he was onstage.

I'm more at home here than anywhere else, he realized.

He cleared his throat and tapped the mic. "Uh, hello. I'm Les Johnson. I didn't expect to be up here, but...well, here's a song off my first album." Trusting the band to really know his material, he launched into "Delta Life Misery," tapping the four-four beat with his foot as he strummed the opening A minor chord.

"Down in the delta, things just ain't right. Seems all that I do is get drunk and fight. I caught my woman cheatin' on me. Now my life is just

full, full of misery."

The band seamlessly glided into the first chorus as Les bent the strings in a blistering guitar solo.

House band? These guys are better than my regular backup band. I oughtta see if I can hire them.

From "Delta Life Misery" he moved right into "Alligator Blues," the band tagging along for the ride without missing a beat. The crowd roared and cheered, and Les opened up to full throttle, any traces of nervousness gone as he moved from song to song, automatically following the same order he'd used on his last tour.

It wasn't until he was starting the last song of the first set that he realized he'd stopped calling out song titles, and yet the band was still in time with his selections.

A man in a dark suit and a beat-up derby hat jumped on stage, a guitar in his hand. Before Les could say anything, the man let loose with a short but hot guitar solo.

That solo, I've heard it before...

The man stared at Les and smiled. Two gold teeth glittered in the spotlight.

Bullfrog Castle! I'd know that face anywhere. But how...?

He looked back at the bass player. Really looked at him this time. Another familiar face.

Bathtub Willy. And that's Terrance Brown at the piano.

As if he'd heard Les's thought, the piano player lifted one hand and waved, then went back to pounding the keys.

Les glanced into the audience. They were all there, the men and women from the record albums hidden in his studio at home. Only now they weren't smiling anymore.

One by one, they made their way to the stage. Les backed up, holding his guitar up like a shield. "Go away!" he shouted over the rhythm section's steady beat. "Leave me alone!"

A short man Les recognized as Willy Mo Gains shook his head. "Sorry, Mister Johnson. This heah the end of the line for you. You done the blues wrong. Now you gots to pay."

Les screamed as Willy Mo's face fell apart, exposing rotting flaps of skin hanging from raw muscle. Glimpses of shiny white bone peeked through the decayed flesh. The creature's eyes changed to a jaundiced yellow; its tongue drooped from the suddenly lipless mouth in dog-like fashion. Les swung the guitar at the walking corpse, batting away the reaching hands and knocking the dead bluesman backwards.

Before Les could bring the guitar back around, more revived musicians stepped forward, their decomposed faces unrecognizable but their intent obvious. Les fell to his knees as someone tore the guitar from his hands and the undead descended on him from all sides.

He continued to scream until yellowed teeth tore out his throat.

*****

ATLANTA, GA (AP) June 18
BODY OF FAMED BLUES GUITARIST FOUND

The body of Lester Bolls—known to millions of fans as Les Johnson—was found by police behind an abandoned building in Wilson, Georgia. Bolls had been missing for several weeks, following his father's funeral.

"Couple of hikers stumbled on the body," said Leroy Harris, Chief of the Wilson police force. "Forensic evidence showed that he'd been beaten up pretty bad, maybe even to the point of death, and then the body was dumped in the field, where the animals got to it."

Chief Harris offered the theory that Bolls may have stopped at the side of the road, possibly to aid another motorist. "Happens sometimes. Criminals pretend their car broke down, and when a good Samaritan stops, they jump him."

Bolls's car was found behind the building.

In related news, Bolls's production company has been implicated in charges of illegal copyright usage. The families of several musicians have come forward, indicating they have proof Bolls claimed songwriting credit for songs originally recorded by blues artists of the 1940s and 1950s. Bolls's manager, Randy Levine, stated…

*****

"Stop here," Kenny Holmdel said to his girlfriend, pointing at the dilapidated building on the side of the road.

"Is this where it happened?" Stacy asked, getting out of the car and looking around. She gave an involuntary shiver. The temperature had dropped several degrees as the sun prepared to finish its daily cycle. Dark pink and purple streaks spread across the dusk sky, highlighting the scattered clouds in pastel fire.

"They found him out in that field," Kenny said, pointing past the building. "But they think he was killed inside. C'mon, I want you take my picture before the light goes away." He trotted over to the front of the building, leaned against a crooked porch railing.

Stacy aimed the camera at him. "Smile." The flash went off, and she checked the view screen to make sure the picture came out. "All right, it looks good. Now can we get out of here? This place gives me the creeps."

"Sure. I…wait, do you hear that?" Kenny turned and stared at the half-collapsed structure.

"What?"

"It sounds like someone playing a guitar. Inside." He went up the steps and disappeared into the black interior.

"Kenny, wait!" Stacy ran forward and then stopped as the faint but distinct sound of a guitar solo reached her.

"Kenny?" She put one hand on the railing. Immediately, the sound grew louder. Now she could hear a whole band playing. At the same time, a cold chill ran up her back.

"Kenny?" She went up the stairs and peered into the black space. She recognized the song as one of Les Johnson's.

A deep voice spoke from within the black. "Come in, Miss Ross. The show's about to start."

Strong hands grabbed her and pulled her inside before she had time to scream. Hungry mouths descended on her.

On stage, Les Johnson cried and moaned as his bloody fingers played their unending song.

About JG Faherty

JG Faherty grew up in the haunted Hudson Valley region of NY, and still resides there. Living in an area filled with Revolutionary War battlegrounds, two-hundred year-old gravesites, ghosts, haunted roads, and tales of monsters in the woods has provided a rich background for his writing. A life-long fan of horror and dark fiction, he enjoys reading, watching movies, urban exploring, volunteering as an exotic animal caretaker, and playing the guitar. One of his favorite childhood playgrounds was an 18th Century cemetery.

JG is the author of *Carnival of Fear, Cemetery Club, The Cold Spot,* and *He Waits*. His YA paranormal adventure novel, *The Ghosts of Coronado Bay,* was a Stoker Award finalist in 2011. His other credits include more than two dozen short stories.

You can follow him at www.jgfaherty.com, www.twitter.com/jgfaherty, and www.facebook/jgfaherty.

HAPPY CTHULHU TO YOU
BY LANCE ZARIMBA

"Happy birthday. Kyle. I hope you get everything you want for your special day," Ben Hunter, Kyle's older brother said. "Have you chosen your present yet?"

Kyle's eyes were full of sleep and he was still in his PJ's when he arrived downstairs for breakfast. He ignored his brother as he walked over to the cabinet and took out a box of cereal and headed to get a bowl and milk.

But Ben refused to be ignored. "Mom left you a special breakfast."

Kyle could see his brother's eyes glowing with excitement. He knew that look. He always saw it before he was going to be scared or teased or something bad was about to happen.

Ben opened the refrigerator and pulled out a fancy tray with a silver dome over it. He carried it to Kyle. "Happy birthday to you...happy birthday to you." Ben started to lift the silver lid off the platter.

Kyle strained to see what was inside, hoping for eggs, French toast or waffles. But instead he saw something grey and gelatinous wiggling and jiggling on the platter.

Then he realized what he was seeing...tentacles, long slimy tentacles of a big octopus. The wet, fishy smell of dead seafood rose in his nose and made him want to throw up.

Ben crowed, "Happy birthday to you!"

In response, Kyle backed up to the kitchen table and set the cereal box down. He bumped the table and pushed it back a foot as the platter was thrust at him. Kyle screamed as the gooey, slimy mess slipped off the tray and landed with a sickening wet plop on the floor. The slime splashed over his bare feet.

In Kyle's mind it looked like the octopus was still alive—it seemed to crawl across the tiled floor, its tentacles reaching for his toes—but the he realized that the mush was simply spreading out across the floor, because the octopus was dead.

Kyle screamed again and ran from the kitchen. His father stepped out of the study and tried to catch him, but he ducked away. He grabbed the railing and pulled himself up the stairs to scramble to his room.

His dad raced up the stairs after him and found Kyle's bedroom door locked. He knocked. "Kyle, let me in."

"No."

His father spoke through the door. "Are you hurt?"

"No. Leave me alone." Tears coated his words.

"What did Ben do to you?"

"Forget it, it never helps. He'll only do something meaner next time if you punish him." Kyle punched his pillow and pulled his blanket over his head. He could hear his father walking away from the door.

If only I was tougher, Kyle thought. *Or, even better...if only I didn't have a brother. I wish I were an only child.*

*****

Ben cleaned up the mess, but there was still a wet spot on the floor.

"What did you do to him?" Their father stood, hands on hips, anger burning deep in his eyes. "It's his birthday; can't you leave him alone for one freaking day?"

Ben kicked at the floor and avoided his dad's eyes. He didn't think the joke would scare the little creep that much. It was supposed to be funny, not scary. "I'm sorry."

"Tell it to your brother. It's his birthday and you're ruining it." His dad walked over to the garbage can and opened it. A dead fishy smell rose out. Dad dismissed it. "I have work to do; I can't be running out here all day watching you. Why don't you go to your room?"

"But Dad, I was going to go fishing with—"

"You should have thought of that before you scared your brother. Enjoy your room." His dad turned and walked back to the study.

Ben went up the back stairs, flopped on the bed, and stared at the ceiling. Why did he have such a baby as a brother? Why couldn't he have had a fun one, instead of this crying little girl? Kyle always had to ruin everything.

Ben brought his fist down hard on the mattress, again and again. The impact hurt, but perversely felt good, too.

He thought, *If only I didn't have a brother. I wish I were an only child.*

Ben looked up and saw his sorry-assed brother run by. He lay back on the bed and wondered what he could do. Should he ask for forgiveness? Hell no. He had other ideas.

*****

Kyle opened his door slowly, and when he saw that the coast was clear, he ran as fast as he could past Ben's room to the bathroom. He carefully opened the lid on the toilet. Empty. No octopus.

He used it and then headed to the tub. He pulled the shower curtain back and peeked over the edge of the tub. Nothing lay inside. He let out the breath he had been holding and stepped out of his PJ bottoms. Just before he climbed into the shower, he locked the bathroom door so he wouldn't have any more surprises. The hot water washed over him, taking the slime and the smell off his feet and down the drain.

"I wish I didn't have a brother." He stepped under the spray and rinsed his hair. Maybe when he blew out the candles on his cake, that would be his birthday wish.

When he finished his shower, he quickly dried himself and wrapped a towel around his waist.

He peeked around the corner and then raced back to his bedroom. He got dressed and waited for a bit, then opened his drawer to get his birthday money. Finally he gathered enough courage to leave the house.

Kyle spent the morning at the bookstore in the French Quarter. He looked at all the sci-fi and horror books, making a list of what he hoped to get as birthday gifts because he really didn't want to spend his own money. At the top of his wish list was an H. P. Lovecraft book.

Once he had seen everything in the store, he spent the afternoon fishing off the Riverwalk, all alone. For a birthday, so far it was an awful one. His only friend said he would join him at the river, but never showed.

His skin burned in the New Orleans sun, but he refused to let it bother him. It was his special day, and he was determined to make the best of it and do anything he wanted, even if he had no friends to do it with. As the heat of the day increased, he decided to head home to see what his parents had planned for his party. He hoped that dinner would be shrimp po-boys and vanilla malts out in the summer house in the back yard.

But most of all, he hoped that the H. P. Lovecraft book would be his present; he wanted the leather-bound edition with the golden lettering. He couldn't wait to read it by flashlight under his sheets.

*****

Ben snuck outside and headed down to the dock. He had hidden the octopus in a fishing creel. If his brother wanted Lovecraft and Cthulhu and all that crap, he'd give it to him. When Kyle got ready to blow out the candles, Ben's plan was to pop up and scare him one last time through the summer house window.

The octopus floated in the water as he opened the wicker basket. The tentacles waved at him in the water. As the sunlight faded, he thought it looked alive, but as he touched it, he knew it was dead. He shook out as much water as he could and placed the slimy thing on his face. Then he walked over to the summer house.

A big splash sounded in the water, but he wasn't able to tell where it had come from with the tentacles dangling over his ears. He tilted his head to peek between the tentacles and saw a reflection of himself in the glass of the summer house window.

He almost let out a squeal of surprise, but then laughed to himself. If this scared *him*, what would it do to his brother? It would probably send him into orbit. He watched as his reflection grew bigger. How was that possible? He wasn't moving closer to the window and the glass didn't have any magnification powers, or did it?

He stepped forward and realized that somehow, the octopus was getting larger...

Then he realized that what he was seeing wasn't his own reflection; it was something behind him. He stood frozen in his steps, staring at the summer house window as the sight grew larger and larger, towering over him. The beast shrugged its shoulders and huge bat wings extended out from its torso.

He turned around to face the creature and was horrified. A low whale-sound resonated from its lungs as tentacles wiggled and reached for him, alive and hungry.

Ben tried to scream as a rubbery tentacle entered his mouth, blocking any sounds. The smell of dead fish and old sea water blew into his face. He tried to fall back, but the creature grabbed him and lifted him up by both arms. It opened its mouth and dove into the water, bringing Ben with it.

Cold water washed over him as the tentacles explored his face, his nostrils, his ears, his eyes and mouth. He felt the water swirl past as he was dragged into the murky depths and it was incredibly cold. The thought came to his mind that no one could see him through the muddy waters of the Mississippi, so no one would save him.

He struggled frantically but the air in his lungs escaped in a rush and then he tried to hold his breath. The pressure on his chest soon became an overwhelming pain and he tried to suck in air, despite knowing it would only bring more water. His last thoughts were to wonder what went wrong.

*****

"I can't find your brother," his father said. "Ben must have snuck out of his room. He'll be punished."

"He'll show up. Let's not wait," his mother said and then began to sing, "Happy Birthday to you, dear Kyle."

The song ended and his mother said, "Hurry up and make a wish before you blow out the candles."

"I already made my wish." He blew as hard as he could and watched the candles go out.

About Lance Zarimba

Lance Zarimba lives in a haunted house built by the man who invented Old Dutch Potato Chips. He is an occupational therapist living in Minneapolis. He is the author of the mystery *Vacation Therapy* and three children's books: *Oh No, Our Best Friend is a Zombie*, *Oh No, Our Best Friend is a Vampire*, and *Oh No, My Brother is Frankenstein's Monster*.

His short stories have been published in *Mayhem in the Midlands*, Pat Dennis' *Who Died in Here? 25 Mystery Stories of Crimes and Bathrooms*, Jay Hartman's *The Killer Wore Cranberry*, and Anne Frasier's *Deadly Treats*.

You can find Lance at www.lancezarimba.com or email him at LanceZarimba@yahoo.com

THE GREMLIN
BY DAVID W. LANDRUM

Willa and I were on Pumpkinvine Pike when the damned thing jumped up on the hood of my car. I thought for a moment it was a raccoon or a bobcat, but it was too big for that and it had green coloration. She screamed. I hit the brake. The car skidded and almost went over. The thing, whatever it was, hung on, hooking its claws into the space under the windshield where the wipers fit. We jolted as the counterforce from the skid pulled us back. The car came to a halt and then surged against its springs, the energy of the reaction throwing us against the dashboard and windshield.

I banged hard, hitting my shoulder on the steering wheel and my head on the windshield. I looked over at Willa. She had fallen to the floorboard. She looked up at me.

"You all right?" I asked.

"What the hell is going on?" she gasped.

I turned to get a better look at the thing looming on the other side of the glass and could only conclude it was some kind of monkey—maybe an orangutan, though it was green, not orange. Still, it had the same kind of long, shaggy hair as an orangutan. It did not have fingers but long claws like a sloth. It stared down from its perch on the hood—big, round eyes, nostril holes but no nose, and a wide mouth. I could see anger and malevolence in its gaze.

I was wondering if it would smash the windshield and try to get us, but it sprang back, gripped the hood, pulled it open, and bent it double. What was it doing to my car? It was like it was trying to kill the car. Would we be next?

I reacted without thinking. I hit the accelerator, heard a thump and felt the car jolt as the tires rolled over the thing that had attacked us. We got level again. I stopped and looked back.

The thing lay twenty feet back in the center of the road. I could see blood on its green fur. By now Willa was up. She peered over the seat.

"Call the cops," I said. "I'm going to see if we killed it."

"You can't go out there. What if it gets up again? It's better to take your chances inside the car. If it gets up, we can get away from it."

Not with the hood bent up, I thought. Like her, I worried about it coming after us again. The creature pushed itself up and got painfully to its feet. We had not killed it.

Down the road, I saw flashing lights, and the thing must have seen them too. It limped into the tree line beside the road, disappearing into the darkness of Foster's Grove.

The police arrived—a patrol car had seen us skid and responded before we even had a chance to call for help. First one cruiser came, then two. By the time we had told our story, five of them had clustered around us, lights blazing red and blue, flashing on the thick old trees of the grove. I was surprised that so many squad cars were interested in our accident with an animal.

Two female officers talked to Willa. A female EMT examined her. The cops gave me the usual interrogation. I told them what had happened.

"So, what did you say it was?" they asked.

"It looked like an orangutan but it wasn't orange—sort of grey or green."

Of course, they stared at me like I was psycho. One asked me, in police jargon, if had "consumed any alcohol."

Thankfully, I had not. We had been visiting one of Willia's aunts, who did not drink. After that we got pizza, but no beer with it. We were headed, in fact, to a bar when the thing sprang on our hood. They asked me if I would take a breathalyzer test. I said I would—or even a drug test if they wanted. Probably because of my willingness, they didn't do either one.

But the cops didn't like my story. "This is pretty unbelievable, Mr. Haynes," one of them said.

I shrugged. "I have no reason to make it up."

And they could not argue with the physical evidence. Something had pulled my hood back and bent it double, snapping the latch. The grill and headlights were intact, so they could not say I had damaged the hood by hitting a telephone pole or a tree. The thing had left indentations where its feet hit. Besides that, blood covered my tires—blood, flesh and hair (and, yes, it was green—I had not been seeing things). Ten feet back, a pool of blood covered the white line dividing the pike. Bloody footprints led into the Foster's grove.

Willa was my girlfriend, and her parents came to take her home. The police blocked off the road. I arranged for a tow. The police said they would give me a ride to my house.

By that time a news crew had arrived on the scene and begun shooting footage. The cops tried to shoo them off, but they said it was a public street and they were not interfering with the operation. They got a good shot of me as I climbed into the police cruiser. One journalist, I noticed, wrote down my license plate number. They would find out who I was and want to interview me. *Mysterious creature attacks car.* Just the kind of stuff they loved to put on the nightly news.

Though I had already made a statement, the cops took me down to the station, saying they wanted "a more detailed report." When I protested that I had given all the detail there was to give, they mumbled something about "concern for public safety" because a wild animal seemed to have gotten loose and they needed to gather as much information on it as they could.

The police took me to a room and got me coffee. Willa called to check on me. I told her the car got the worst of it.

"Has anyone figured out what that thing was?" she asked.

"Had to be some kind of orangutan. Maybe a rare species."

We talked. We were getting to the end of our conversation when the door opened. Two guys in suits came in. The velocity of the situation ramped up when I saw their name tags: Agent Reuther and Agent Argazzi, both from the Office of Homeland Security.

They were cordial. I could not figure out what an escaped zoo animal had to do with homeland security.

"We've read your statement, Mr. Haynes," Reuther said. "We would just like to hear it from you personally."

I repeated what I had told the cops. They listened closely.

"You think it was an orangutan?" Reuther asked.

"Well, I can't think of what else it might have been. I will admit, I only said it looked like an orangutan because it had the kind of shaggy hair they have. But it was a lot bigger and it was green, not orange."

They glanced at each other. Reuther nodded.

"The blood and tissue samples we retrieved from the accident site do not match any we have on file," Reuther said, "except some we have from a World War II aircraft."

I stared, incredulous. "Are you trying to tell me something from World War II went after my car?"

"We can't rule out the possibility. All the reports on their activities, of course, have been classified."

"Who do you mean by 'their'? You said *their* activities."

"We're not saying gremlins exist or do not exist. Let's say they do."

"Gremlins? Are you serious?"

"What do you know about gremlins, Mr. Haynes?"

When I was sure I had heard him correctly, I laughed.

"Gremlins? Well, it was a car produced by American Motors in the 1970s. Or a monster—one of them scared the hell out of William Shatner on an old *Twilight Zone* episode. Other than that, I'm not real up on them."

They smiled politely. Reuther said, "We're wondering why this one would emerge suddenly and attack you—or, more accurately, attack your vehicle. They have some sort of aversion to mechanical devices."

"What?"

"Well, they don't like machines. No one is sure why. Some who believe in the existence of gremlins say the noise and pollution from gasoline engines upsets them and destroys their nesting environments. All the reports on gremlin activity come from the Middle East, Malta, and India."

"So this gremlin thing might be working for Al Qaeda?"

My sarcasm seemed to go over their heads.

"We have no reports of Al Qaeda in Malta or India. But if operatives from any country have captured these creatures—assuming they do exist—and if they plan to release them to destroy our military outposts, then that would constitute a hostile action. We're concerned because we have no records of a gremlin in the United States."

Argazzi jumped in. "Is there any reason a hostile force might target you, Mr. Haynes? I notice your name here and there in this community."

"One of my ancestors got a lot of stuff here named after him. Elwood Haynes. He invented one of the first automobiles." My voice fell when I remembered and said, "He drove it on the road where I saw the creature. That was back in 1906. Could there be a connection?"

"We don't know. If you come up with one, give us a call."

And that was it. The cops dropped me off at home. Pre-dawn grey had lightened the sky by the time I finally got to bed.

It was hard to sleep. It's not every day that a green monster jumps on the hood of your car. I tried to get comfortable and finally did doze off.

I don't know how long I slept before a noise woke me. I sat up in bed and listened.

I heard the noise of metal grating on metal. Jumping out of bed, throwing on a pair of pants, I heard the noise increase. It seemed to be coming from the garage. I took up my cell phone, ready to call 911 when the window to my bedroom crashed as if an explosion had blown it in. The thing—the gremlin. It had found my house.

It stood amid the debris of broken glass and wood from the smashed window, leering at me. It reached for me with its claws. Frightened out of my mind, I thought my heart was going to burst in my chest. I flopped across the bed and rolled behind it.

I knew I was up against animal speed and instinct. It would be impossible to get out a window or out the door to the bedroom without the thing catching me.

I owned a gun, an old .22 my Dad bought for me when I was a kid. It was in a case in the living room and was not loaded, though I did have a box of hollow-point longs—probably not enough velocity to kill the thing but maybe enough to hurt it and drive it away.

How could I get from here to the living room without it shredding me?

I popped my head up to see over the bed. We faced each other. The gremlin stood about six feet tall. Like a gorilla, it hunched forward from its hips with its back parallel to the ceiling. Long green hair covered its body and hung in strands from its arms. Its narrow eyes—black, almost all iris—peered at me. I saw a row of sharp teeth, and claws that could rip me apart with one swipe. Its body heaved with labored breathing.

I had to act. I thought of throwing something at it and making a break for the door, but I knew it would be too fast for a move like that. As we faced off, one of those thoughts that come as a revelation at unexpected moments struck me. Argazzi—or was it Reuther?—had told me that gremlins only attacked mechanical devices, and not people. I glanced behind me. I had a room air conditioner in the north window, within reach. I flipped it on and dove under the bed.

The air conditioner began to hum. The gremlin roared in rage and leaped, the floor shaking when it came down on the other side of the bed. It went for the air conditioner. It roared as it ripped and pounded the unit with its huge, clawed fists. I wriggled out from the other side of the bed. When I was clear of it, I ran into the living room.

I vaguely thought that maybe I should run out of the house, but I knew how quick and strong the gremlin was. Would I be able to outrun it? I figured I'd better do something more effective.

As the gremlin demolished the air conditioner, I flung open the door on the glass case where I kept display items, got the .22 out, and loaded it. It had a barrel clip that held eighteen shots. Though my hands were shaking, I managed to load it full, close it, and pop a bullet into the firing chamber.

I heard the tearing of metal. The low pulse of the air conditioner stopped. Silence. It had destroyed the air conditioner. Now it would start looking for me again. I hurried back to the door of my bedroom.

In the dim light of pre-dawn, I saw the gremlin and how thoroughly it had torn apart the window unit. Twisted metal, carbon filters, and severed electrical wires showed the gremlin's destructive capacities. A pool of freon widened at its feet.

I raised the rifle. For just a second I hesitated, remembering that the thing had not harmed me in any way. Willa and I had been slightly hurt when it jumped on the car, and we might have been hurt more seriously had we rolled the car, but the assault had been on the vehicle, not on me or her.

It suddenly seemed wrong to shoot it. But I could not take the chance. I did not know the full range of its behavior. I had the rifle—a mechanical device—in my arms. The gremlin might try to destroy the rifle and end up destroying me in the process. I shouldered the weapon, took aim, and fired.

Twenty-two rifles are small-caliber and don't have a loud report. The gun popped as I let off two rounds. The gremlin jerked in surprise and pain. It turned on me. I gave it a burst of five shots, aiming at its midsection.

The shots did not knock it over, but it slumped and let out a cry. The sound was an unmistakable yowl of pain. The thing wavered on its feet. I wondered if I had, in fact, killed it, but it seemed to gather its strength and stood erect, then stumbled toward the window it had smashed through. I heard a series of high-pitched cries and gasps as it fled. The gremlin painfully climbed over the sill of the window and then fell outside. I realized it was crying.

I reached for my cell phone, intending to call for help. Then the air outside exploded with loud booms and the stutter of machinegun fire. I thought I heard a deep groan and the sound of a huge last breath being expelled, though I never have been certain if I did or if I only imagined it. Then came silence.

The silence lasted only moments. A loud bang scared me. I heard heavy footsteps. Three men in black military-style fatigues burst into my bedroom and leveled M16's at me.

"Throw down the weapon and lay on the floor!" one of them shouted.

I stared, too stunned to respond. He repeated the order in a more threatening tone. I tossed the .22 on the bed and lay on the floor as instructed. The officers of the local SWAT team (I could read their badges now) handcuffed me and hustled me outside.

The grey of pre-dawn had begun to yield to the light of morning. I saw at least eight police cruisers parked around my house. My neighbors had heard the shots and came out to investigate. The police were herding them back to their homes. I saw Luce Tenga, the only female member of our hometown SWAT team and someone I had dated in high school.

"Luce!" I called to her. "Why in the hell are you guys arresting me?"

She walked over, her expression apologetic.

"Sorry, Alex. I really am. It's standard procedure to handcuff and secure anyone we encounter who has a weapon."

"I was defending myself against a monster, that's all."

She started to say something but Reuther came up just then.

"Take the cuffs off," he said. He gave me a look that he probably meant as a smile, though it did not come off as such. "Mr. Haynes," he said, "I know it will be another intrusion in your schedule, but I'll have to ask you to come along with us."

Luce took off my cuffs.

"Am I under arrest?"

"No, sir. But this is a sensitive case relating to homeland security. We can't discuss it here in public and we need to find out exactly what happened. We'll head to the Federal Building."

The police were putting yellow POLICE ZONE KEEP OUT tape around my place. I noticed a van being unloaded and a group of men and women rushing toward the south side of my house where the gremlin had been shot. One of them carried what looked like a body bag. Reuther led me to a car. Argazzi was there.

"You hurt?" Argazzi asked.

"No. The thing seemed more interested in tearing up the air conditioner than tearing into me."

He and Reuther laughed.

Then I asked, "How did the SWAT team get here so fast? I didn't call the police."

"We thought it might be a good idea to stake your place out. We had it under surveillance. Sure enough, the thing stalked you and found you. We had all the units in place and ready to go. Sorry you were cuffed but we didn't expect you to be firing a gun."

Once we were at the Federal Building, we went to an office downstairs. I gave a statement about what happened. They listened carefully and wrote down all I said.

"You know, Mr. Haynes, this is a sensitive incident related to national security. We'll have to ask you to say nothing about it."

"How is it related to the national security?"

They looked at each other. Reuther nodded.

"If this was a gremlin, we need to study it. Unleashing such creatures on our military installations, especially in the Middle East, is something we must be concerned about. We want to learn as much about the creature as we can. And we don't want the existence of the creature to leak out so that we have an uncontrollable media event on our hands. We'll have to ask you to keep quiet about this—in fact, we'll have to insist on it."

"Okay, I get it."

"No need for trouble," Reuther said. "We don't like to restrict people, but security concerns make it necessary. We also want to continue the dialogue with you. We're curious as to why the creature targeted you. We don't suspect you of treachery in any way. Don't think that. But something made this thing go after you. Something enabled it to stalk you and find you. We want to discover why—and we will offer you generous compensation if you're willing to work with us."

Money, money, money—it's a rich man's world, I thought, remembering the old song by ABBA. If the government couldn't throw you in jail, it could always pay you off.

"I'll be glad to," I answered.

As I sat there I remembered the sound the gremlin made after I shot it. It did not understand machinery. It did not understand why I harmed it. Were there more of them? Had my ancestor, Elwood Haynes, first awakened the gremlin when he drove his automobile down Pumpkinvine Pike in 1906? He had only driven it once for a test run, and cars did not become common for another twenty years. Had the thing gone dormant...but now, with cars, flight paths, and human activity constantly throbbing, had it come out of its slumber once again?

It had sensed me—my smell and my blood. Perhaps it recognized that my blood and the blood of the man who first disturbed its sleep were the same. Would they start coming out of the woods and deserts to attack the technology that our society depended upon so much?

Argazzi brought me a cup of coffee. *How many gremlins*, I wondered, *would soon be waking up?*

About David W. Landrum

David W. Landrum's speculative fiction has appeared in numerous publications, most recently in *Love at First Bite, Deathly Encounters, Night, Hunters, Separate Worlds* and *Aofie's Kiss*. He teaches, lives, and writes in West Michigan.

FLAME OF FREEDOM
BY AARON J. FRENCH

The thing dragged itself toward the building of Holtz and Associates. When Pete Ackerwood's eyes first registered it, he lapsed for a moment and remembered the dream he'd had the night before.

In the dream, he was running from something unseen at his ankles, nipping at the flesh of his calves. He'd awoken with a dreadful cry. Tearing the covers back to look at his legs, he'd sent Jemma lunging furiously to her feet shouting, "Jesus Christ, what's the matter?"

Nothing had been the matter. It was only a nightmare. And his legs were fine, not a single scratch on them. So they had gone back to sleep. But in the morning the feeling, the *terror* of the dream remained with him all the way to his office building of Holtz and Associates.

So it happened like *that:* instantaneously, his mind vaulting back and forth between two states of consciousness—waking and dreaming—at the exact moment his eyes trained upon the crawling thing. He smelled burning chemicals and told himself he was imagining it. Dreams were funny in that they rattled in your head for a while, refusing to re-submerge into the unconscious.

But when the thing didn't disappear, he leaned forward with his face to the glass. What the hell?

He stood at the window of his office, looking outside and watching the thing. Several possibilities flipped through his mind: a homeless man, a drunk who might've been hit by a car; a wounded animal escaped from the zoo; someone's idea of a joke, a gag to frighten people and get captured on film, then later uploaded to YouTube; maybe someone actually *was* filming a movie in the gardens, and he had been too groggy this morning to notice the cordons.

The thing resembled all these possibilities…

…and it resembled none of them.

Fear entered his heart.

The thing reached the parking lot. Slinking, inching, clawing its way closer. The window to his office seemed to lie directly in its path. He was thinking that maybe he should leave, get out of the building…just in case.

His cell phone rang, startling him. With great effort, he turned his attention away from the window.

"Hello?"

"It's me." It was Jemma. "I just wanted you to know that I didn't get back to sleep until almost 4:30 in the morning after your little screaming fit—"

"You told me that already." They'd had a fight about it over breakfast.

"If you'd let me finish. Once I *did* fall back asleep, I had a dream—a nightmare—which I didn't tell you about."

"Oh?"

"Yeah, and I didn't think it was a big deal, but it keeps bothering me, so I thought that if I told you about it I could get it off my chest."

"So tell me."

There was a pause, then Jemma continued, "Okay, but I warn you to brace yourself."

"Oh come on, how bad could it be, especially after the nightmare I had? You know, my 'screaming fit' as you called it?"

"I was cheating on you."

She was right. It was bad.

"Still there, Pete?"

He swallowed—*gulp*—"Uh-huh."

"So there's a new guy here at work. Dan O'Banyon. Yeah, so he's cute, and yeah. so we've talked a little bit, but that's all."

"Uh-huh."

"Anyway, he's married too, as far as I know. He's got a ring. In the dream, he and I were having an affair, and then you caught us in some dirty hotel going at it like dogs."

Pete caught the image and felt sick to his stomach. His skin crawled.

"I was just about to orgasm—you know like how you do in a dream—when you barged in and stopped the show. You had a shotgun, and you were very angry."

He grimaced. "Damn right I'd be angry."

"You shot Dan right in the face and blew his brains all over the wood headboard. Then I hurled myself at you, wanting to claw your eyes out or something, when suddenly Dan's mutilated corpse slides off the

bed, crawls across the floor, curls right up to your feet, and—I dunno—
he starts making out with your feet or something, using his gristly,
broken-jawed bloody mouth, and then your feet begin to dissolve as if he
was pouring acid on them. God, it was awful."

He didn't know what to say. His stomach felt like the La Brea Tar
Pits, and he rummaged through his top desk drawer, searching for the
bottle of antacids.

He muttered something in agreement with how awful it was.
Suddenly she said, "Oh crap, gotta go, Mr. Leeds is coming and he's
been on our asses lately about making personal calls during work hours.
But you forgive me, right? For the dream? Talk to you soon."

The line went dead. He lit a cigarette, knowing that smoking was
not allowed in the workplace. Pete put his cell phone down, and tried to
arrange the pieces together. There was certainly a connection—his
dream, her dream, this ankle/feet thing—but hell if he knew what it was.
His mind was racing.

And then there was the thing outside—

Remembering it, he was about to turn back toward the window
when his office door burst open and there was John Holtz, his boss. A
tall man with a barrel chest, Holtz always wore expensive Valentino
suits, even on Casual Fridays. The boss had this Miami Vice air about
him that women seemed to love, but which drove Pete insane.

"Hey Pete, how's it going, my man?" Holtz plopped authoritatively
down in the chair across the desk.

Pete extinguished his cigarette, knowing how Holtz hated them. The
smoldering smell turned Pete's guts. The man glanced at it, as though he
wanted to say something, as if his own guts were turning, but he
remained quiet.

"What's up?" Pete said.

Holtz sighed. "Well, you know I hate having to do this…"

Suddenly Pete understood, and the knot in his stomach grew tighter.
He listened for about ten minutes or so to Holtz reprimanding him—in
Holtz's sneaky, passive-aggressive way—for a host of reasons,
principally his failure to complete the data entry forms on time, for the
fact that he hadn't gotten his entire list of "activities" completed these
last couple weeks, not to mention his being late that one time several
weeks ago, and well…Holtz hoped it wouldn't happen again because he
prided himself on running a tight ship…and one hole in the bulkhead led
to one more hole, and so on and so on, until the ship sank…

Pete listened patiently as he always did whenever Holtz came in his
office, which was two or three times a month. Usually Pete hadn't even
done any of the stuff Holtz would complain about, and that had driven
Pete crazy when he first started. It'd taken him a few months to realize it
was just something Holtz did in his role as president of the company, like

a captain monitoring the morale of his crew—though in the case of Holtz and Associates, the morale was supposed to be kept *low*, or at least in dire straits. It was sick, but Pete had gotten used to it.

He listened until Holtz finished. Then (and he knew this was a fuck you statement but he didn't care) he lit another cigarette and blew a smoke ring. "You got it, boss," he said.

Holtz acted as though he was going to have a fit about the cigarette, then abruptly his eyes flicked past Pete to the window, and he said, "What the hell is *that?*"

Pete's fear blossomed. He knew what Holtz was seeing. For a moment he had blissfully forgotten, but now it swam back into his mind: the thing scudding its way toward the building.

He wasn't sure if it was preferable that Holtz was seeing it too, if that made him less crazy, or if the fact that Holtz saw it too made it *more* crazy, made the whole *world* crazy. He steeled himself for total destruction and turned toward the window.

The thing was gone. What Holtz was referencing was a squat homeless woman dressed in rags, pushing a shopping cart filled with bags and junk, with a makeshift flag of some sort poking up through the jumble.

"Man, the losers they got in this town," Holtz commented, making a whistling sound.

Pete had the wild thought that he actually missed the thing, that he had expected it to be there, and wanted it even, and now that it wasn't there, the effect caused a trauma. Now he had no idea what was happening or even what was real.

"Yeah, quite the crop of losers," Pete muttered, chewing on the filter of his cigarette. And when he turned again, Holtz was heading out the door.

"Put out the cigarette, bud," the man said before disappearing. "Against the rules."

Pete found himself alone.

He toyed with the possibility of getting some work done but Holtz's sudden appearance pretty much ensured he wouldn't do a fucking thing the remainder of the day. It was, perhaps, a streak of rebellion, but he allowed himself this one character flaw. After all, he'd become one of the fastest working employees in the entire company since he started, with leading sales for three consecutive months at one point. The way he saw it, he had earned a little slack time.

He turned again to the window with a screen of smoke before his eyes. And through the glass he saw it. He squinted. Was it...? Yes, it was back. Goddamn it, there it was. Not only that, but it was closer.

Much closer.

Terror. Panic. Dread.

Run?

He was positive that less than sixty seconds ago it had not been there. Holtz would have seen it too, but neither of them had seen anything. Now there it was, humped upon itself in a pile of misshapen black clods, like a Rorschach image come to life. Creeping liquidly across the asphalt of the parking lot, slipping between the cars...

Coming for *him*.

Now there was a paranoid thought. What had he ever done to deserve the retribution of a black distortion of psychosis? Did it exist inside his head? If not, surely Holtz would've seen it.

Maybe he was losing his mind.

But what were the implications of that? Did it mean he was working too much? In need of more sleep? A problem with Jemma, with their relationship?

True: All of the above.

But none of his doubts changed anything. The thing was still out there and getting closer, it was heading toward his office window, coming for him.

He reminded himself to breathe.

It was on the lawn of the front courtyard now, weaving between the stone benches, the flowering dogwoods, and the cement planters with shrubs of various genera leaning out. The sunlight struck the earth in a bright vision of fire, glinting off its back, casting out rings of diamond-like shards in tiny bursts. Pete thought he saw faces in that dark: his mom, his dad, his older brother Andy, Jemma, a couple of old girlfriends, even himself.

He extinguished his smoke and turned away from the window. "Damn it!" he shouted, surprised by his own anger. He struck the top of his desk just for the sheer satisfaction of feeling his hand smart against the wood. He took a deep breath, tried to get himself under control, and hung his head. He was losing it. The fear was frying his nerves.

That's when a scratching sound drew his attention. His heart stopped, blood running cold. As rigid as a mannequin, he returned to the window. But the thing was gone. The quiet city scene of North Philly played itself out with becalmed regularity: cars whizzed past Thirty-Fourth Street and pedestrians in the gardens meandered about while the sounds of river boats honked in the distance.

He leaned closer to the windowsill, inching his way forward, until his nose nearly touched the glass. Where the hell was it? *Did* he imagine it—

A long wispy rope of black ichor flung itself up, slapping against the glass.

"Jesus!" he cried, leaping back and slamming into his chair.

Another rope joined the other, then more, until a bouquet of shadowy tentacles wove in front of the window, *pressing in on it*. The tentacles merged, growing globular, encouraging the black stuff to gather, pooling above the sill, until a grand portion had encompassed all the glass, eclipsing the outer world.

The office darkened. Pete became a Gothic statue standing next to his chair.

His cell phone rang.

He groped for it in the darkness, just as the faces began appearing in the black canvas, the images of smashed children, smashed relationships, smashed broken family, his beloved Jemma looking scornful.

Dear God, please save me from myself.

"Hello?"

"So I've been thinking," Jemma said. "I know I told you about my dream, but—"

"But what?" His free hand clasped around the lighter, gripping it like the hilt of a blade, when suddenly the glass split with a violent crack, and he jumped, nearly dumping the phone. A stream of black essence poured tarlike into the office, insinuating itself through the spaces in the glass.

"I think there's more I need to tell you."

"What is it?"

"Are you okay? You sound weird."

"I'm fine, now talk."

"Jeez, no need to be a jerk. This is difficult for me."

As she began explaining to him her situation—confessing it to him, he thought—that she and the new fellow at work had done a lot more than simply "talk a little bit" (hence her related dream), the black stain upon this world impressed itself fully into the office, blooming before him like a demonic flower. He watched it weave like a psychotic undersea plant of pure dementia, with the faces from his life looking back at him.

"Great pain...great misery..." he muttered into the receiver, before dropping it.

"What's that? I said it's over, Pete!" came the muffled reply.

"I'm sick and tired of my life."

The black appendages came at him like a clawed lion's paw. He held out the lighter, thumbing it to glittering life. The tentacles retracted, then came back with a roaring intensity.

"And I hate my job," he said. Now his heart was breaking. Something about the conversation he'd just had with Jemma...but he couldn't remember what. Why did it feel like his insides were melting?

The folds of the thing caught fire, turning into the flaming pyre of Lucifer, engulfing him in a watery web of dreamlike delirium. He flamed up with it, two balls of inferno, and down they went together into the caverns of the underworld.

He screamed, but the black shot down his throat, silencing him, suffocating him. It invaded his eyes, blinding him. He fell back, jerking into the arms of some savage primeval god, and it gathered up his calves and began to gnaw on them like a dog gnaws a bone, until they had been picked clean of flesh, and at the bottom of this well of pain he splashed into the waters of his own salvation, taking up his lighter to the rest, until the whole effigy of his polluted past had been torched into ashes…and he was free.

About Aaron J. French

Aaron J. French (a.k.a. A. J. French) is a member of the Horror Writers Association. He recently edited *Monk Punk*, an anthology of monk-themed speculative fiction with an introduction by D. Harlan Wilson, as well as *The Shadow of the Unknown*, an anthology of nü-Lovecraftian fiction with stories from Gary A. Braunbeck and Gene O'Neill.

Aaron's fiction has appeared in many publications: magazines include *Dark Discoveries*, D. Harlan Wilson's *The Dream People*, *Black Ink Horror*, *Something Wicked*, and *The Lovecraft eZine*; anthologies include *Potter's Field 4*, *M is for Monster*, *Chiral Mad*, *Zippered Flesh: Tales of Body Enhancements Gone Wrong*, and *Dark Tales of Lost Civilizations*.

Aaron's recent article on Thomas Ligotti appeared in issue #20 of *Dark Discoveries Magazine*, where he is also an associate editor.

THE EDITOR'S CORNER

RENANIMATED
BY JEANI RECTOR

Zombies had been a mainstay in popular fiction for years, even decades, before they became a reality.

And when the zombies actually appeared, it was discovered that all the books and films had gotten it wrong.

A college student raised his hand. "How did this happen?"

"That's for the scientists to figure out," the professor answered as he strolled back and forth in front of the class.

"Do you think it was something that the military did?" another student asked.

The professor stopped pacing and faced the class. "Look, this is not a science class and we are not a military school. This is a sociology class. That means we are having a discussion about how to fit these reanimated people back into society. There are millions of them."

The professor paused, then continued, "Let's look at the socio-economic impact. How will the governments around the world find jobs for these reanimated people? Jobs are hard to find even for those who have never died. Will the undead require financial assistance until they are situated? And who will pay for that? What about all the elderly, whose pensions stopped when their death certificates were filed?"

He waited for his words to sink in. Then he added, "Where will all these undead be housed, and are they technically refugees? And if they are refugees, from what? Not from dangerous dictators, but from death itself. For that, there is no precedent to give us information about the best way to proceed. But these are people nonetheless, and they have rights as citizens…of a sort."

A third student raised her hand. "Can't most be taken in by their families?"

The professor answered, "One would think so. But emotionally...well, a lot of taxpayer dollars will have to go towards psychologists. After all, the shock of a dead family member suddenly showing up on the doorstep can be a deeply traumatizing event for the living."

The first student raised his hand once again. "What if a zombie—"

"We don't call them zombies," the professor interrupted.

The student continued, "What if a reanimated person comes home to find her husband had remarried? Or what if another had been in a nursing home with Alzheimer's before death and that person's children thought they were finally getting out of debt from paying for it?"

"Ah," the professor said. "Now you are finally sounding like a sociology class."

*****

Janet was watching CNN when the story broke.

At first it didn't register; it was too incredible. Too impossible.

And then her thoughts rushed to Jeffrey, and her hand went to her heart. Could CNN be talking about Jeffrey? Was it indeed possible?

She rushed for her cell phone. But for the first time ever, a recorded message came on saying that "all circuits were busy."

So she sat back down on the couch, stunned and bewildered. What did this mean?

She thought of Jeffrey. They had been married less than a year when he suddenly became sick. Trips to the doctor and eventually to the emergency room left them without a diagnosis. How could doctors not know what killed him in this day and age of medical advancements?

The funeral had been a heartbreaking affair. Jeffrey's wealthy father wouldn't acknowledge her. His mother had a few choice words for her before she too turned her back. They hadn't wanted their promising son to marry a nobody.

She was indeed a nobody. Janet had come from the poverty of the Ozarks. But she was pretty, even beautiful, and she knew it. When she was old enough for boys to notice her, and notice her they did, she decided she would marry up to someone who looked like a prince and had money like one, too.

And that prince was Jeffrey Hall. Janet had been so happy when he proposed. It was a dream come true. Everything about the marriage was just as she had hoped.

Now she was a widow, a very young widow, and Jeffrey was gone.

Or was he?

She needed to find out. She reached for her cell phone again.

*****

The local high school gymnasium was temporarily converted into a Reanimated Center. Police were seemingly stationed everywhere to control the milling and anxious people in the crowd who were desperate to see their loved ones.

Janet attempted to push her way through the masses, but a policeman ordered her to go to the back of the line. Intimidated, she complied.

And there she found Jeffrey's parents.

"Janet," Mrs. Hall said, "how nice to see you."

Janet was dumbfounded. "Nice?" she echoed. "Since when did you think it was ever nice to see me?"

"Now listen," Mr. Hall came straight to the point. "You have legal precedent over us in this situation. As Jeffrey's wife, you have more say about what becomes of him than his mere parents, the ones who brought him into the world, and the ones who had him for twenty-four years compared to your one."

So that's it, Janet thought. *For once, they need me.*

"Look," Mr. Hall continued, "We can stop our legal proceedings against your taking Jeffrey's estate. All we ask is that you let us take him home instead of you. Do that and we'll leave you alone."

Janet realized she could finally stand up for herself against these two. "Estate? There is no estate for a person who is not deceased. I am Jeffrey's wife and everything is community property once again. And as his wife, I am taking him to my home. Because my home is Jeffrey's home."

"Let me see my son, please," the mother pleaded. Janet tried not to notice Mrs. Hall's tears, because it was disconcerting to see them in a woman so hard.

Janet told her, "I'm not completely heartless. But I don't know what to expect. If Jeffrey is still himself and seems okay, then let me get him settled first and then decide what to do."

They stepped aside, seeming to accept her decision, and Janet began to slowly inch her way in the line toward the gymnasium door. She left the Halls behind, moving steadily towards her husband.

When she finally entered the large gym, she found it just as crowded inside as outside. More police were sorting people and taking identification. When it was her turn, the police officer was young, dark skinned and dark haired. He took her ID, peered at it, then looked at her strangely.

"You're Janet Hall?" he asked. "You're not what I imagined."

She was used to that. After all, the death of a wealthy person usually made the news when it happened. Jeffrey's death had been displayed on television and in the newspapers. It made sense that the public would wonder what his wife was like.

"Is there a problem?" she asked.

"No," he said, still looking at her oddly. "Proceed to the left."

A social worker met her in front of a curtained section of the gym. "Did you receive the preparation package? You did? Good. Proceed inside."

The curtain was held open and Janet entered. The light was dimmer inside, but her eyes adjusted immediately and she saw Jeffrey.

He was seated in a metal folding chair. He looked pale and his hair seemed longer. He wasn't wearing his burial suit and tie but instead was dressed in casual clothes which had probably been provided by the social workers. It seemed so odd to see Jeffrey in jeans, because he never wore them.

She ran to his side, and crouched on the ground to be at eye level with him. "Jeffrey! How are you?"

She didn't know if it was proper to ask a dead person how he was, but then she told herself that he was not dead. He was reanimated.

"I want to go home," he said.

"That's fine, Jeffrey, we can do that."

*****

She held his hand as she led him up the steps to their very large home. At over four thousand square feet, it was luxurious and was surrounded by two acres of beautifully maintained gardens. The upkeep was quite costly, and Janet had been stressed over the legal battles for the inheritance.

But now that Jeffrey was back, everything would be all right once again. Now, life could be reset and rebooted.

She sat him down on the same couch where she had been sitting when she first heard the news on CNN. It was surreal; just a few days earlier all of this had seemed so impossible. Now that it was actually happening, she was amazed at how easily she accepted it all. One could get used to anything, she decided, even this, once the initial shock passed.

Except that Jeffrey seemed different; distracted. He wouldn't hold her gaze, but she felt confident that with enough attention and gentle care, she could bring him back to what he used to be.

"What do you remember?" she asked him.

He shifted on the couch, his hair falling into his eyes. He looked away, vacantly brushing the unruly hair from his face. "Most things, but not all," he finally answered.

"Not all about things in general, or not all about us? Do you know who I am?"

For the first time, he met her eyes. "I ought to know my wife."

She wasn't sure she understood his tone. "So you know I am your wife, and that we were married almost a year. We had an anniversary, but you were unable to celebrate it with me. Would you like to do that? Have a belated celebration?"

He looked away again. "Whatever you want."

"What about you? What do *you* want?"

"I want to be left alone until I figure things out."

Shocked, she stepped back. "Well," she said, "I see some things never change."

Janet was dismayed as she stepped into the bedroom, leaving Jeffrey alone as he wished. She felt hurt and worse, afraid. What did the future hold for him? For her? For them both?

But by dinnertime, she had gotten over it. After all, Jeffrey's behavior could be understood. He had been through unimaginable trauma. She wanted to ask him what death was like but felt afraid of the answer. Wasn't death the universal mystery? Perhaps now that millions experienced it and came back to tell about it, the mystery would finally be solved.

She was distracted by the ringing of her cell phone. She answered it to hear a strange voice. "This is Malcolm Harrison, attorney at law."

"I'm rather busy now, what can I do for you? Can you make it quick?"

"I'll try," Harrison said. "I wanted to notify you that Mr. and Mrs. Hall have filed a wrongful death lawsuit against you concerning Jeffrey Hall."

"He's not dead!" she cried.

"We are determining the legality of whether Jeffrey Halls is dead or not," he said. "You will receive court documents in the mail."

She hung up on him.

Jeffrey came up from behind and startled her. "Is everything all right?" he asked.

He reached for her and pulled her close. She rested her head on his chest and took in his scent. He still smelled clean like fresh wood shavings. She felt his warmth, just as he used to be. "I think things will be better now that you're back," she told him.

He took her chin in his hand and pointed her face upwards. She could see his golden brown eyes, his finely chiseled nose, and his masculine jawline. He looked like the prince he was when he rescued her from out of the Ozarks.

"Let's have our anniversary celebration," he whispered, and led her into the bedroom.

She didn't know what caused the change in him from earlier in the day. Perhaps he had come to grips with his situation and decided to begin living instead of dying. Perhaps he remembered the fire he had always felt towards her, the passion that clouded his judgment as to who made a proper wife, and who didn't.

Janet had always loved the power she had over his emotions. If that power transcended death, then she felt more powerful than anything else on earth.

He guided her towards the king-sized bed and shut the door behind him. "Take off those blue jeans," she told him as she lay on the bed.

Jeffrey complied, standing near the door, and the pants fell to the floor. She admired his strong, muscular legs. Then he unbuttoned his shirt and dropped it to the floor, where it landed in a heap on top of the jeans.

She gasped.

A huge, purple gash ran from his pubic area to above his nipples, where the single ripped and jagged laceration then branched out into two directions, each side tearing up to almost the shoulders where the y-incisions finally ended. Thick black stitches held the gaping wounds together, and when he moved to come towards her, the stitches stretched and the flesh seemed to pull apart, and Janet was afraid they wouldn't hold, and his insides would be disgorged onto the floor.

She screamed and tried to use her legs to propel herself backwards on the bed, but her dead husband kept coming.

He reached behind his head with a naked arm and yanked at his hair. With one move, he pulled his scalp forward until it flipped over onto his face, completely obscuring his features like an inside-out pelt. The skull gleamed brightly in the lamplight, glistening with wet red tint. She could see that the bone had been sawed and the top of the skull sat like a morbid hat, unattached but not falling from its perch.

"Stop it, please!" she cried in fright. "Whatever happened to you, please don't do this!"

He stopped walking. He took his scalp and gently placed it back on his head, covering his skull. His face was smeared with blood and it seemed pronounced against his unnaturally pale skin.

She thought the macabre performance was over. But then Jeffrey began pulling at the crude black stitches that covered his stomach and chest.

"The pathologist didn't put my organs in the same places that they were before the autopsy," he said. "He just sort of threw them back in afterwards and stitched me up. My heart and my pancreas are in my stomach."

Janet screamed, "Please! Why are you doing this?"

"Of course, the pathologist thought that was fine since I would just be going into the ground. How about your organs, Janet? Is your heart in the right place?"

"Please stop, please."

"Not yet. I gave you my heart in life. Now I will give it to you in death."

He tugged at the stitches and pulled them. They unthreaded in one long string, the cord like a ribbon, going into one hole and coming out another like a long black worm. The chasm that was his chest began to open, the skin rubbery and the yellow fat beneath becoming visible. Intestines began to tumble out of his stomach area, and from out of the mess a red, veined, globular heart fell to the floor, its ventricles cut and waving.

She vomited on the bed, and felt dizzy and faint.

"You asked me before how much I remembered."

Unable to look at him, she spoke into her hand that she held to her mouth. "How much?"

"You gave me Ricin. It's so rare, the doctors couldn't find out why I was sick. And the pathologist didn't find it in the autopsy. For a country girl from the Ozarks, you came a long way in life."

"Jeffrey, now I know it's better to have you alive. I had to learn the hard way. I want you back; it's too hard without you. Everyone hates me because they suspect me even though no one has proof."

"But now there's proof. The pathologist who did the sloppy autopsy didn't expect me to come back to tell about it. Neither did you."

She wiped the vomit from her mouth, and turned to face him. She gave him the look she had always given him. She unbuttoned her shirt to show him her charms. It had always worked before. She had power over his emotions. She was more powerful than anything on earth.

When he sat on the bed and reached for her, she knew her power worked. She still held him under her spell.

But suddenly he grabbed her neck and began to choke her. She clawed at his face, shredding ragged sheets of pale skin under her sharp fingernails. He squeezed his large hands tighter. She bucked like a bronco to try to knock him off, but he held on, pressing against her larynx until her hyoid bone broke.

He stood up, letting his wife's dead body tumble from the bed to the floor. He walked out of the bedroom and out of the house without looking back.

Three hours later, Janet reanimated.

THE FAMOUS FILM STAR
BY JEANI RECTOR

I freelanced, which meant that I sold my celebrity photos to the highest bidder. Call me paparazzi if you want, but I called it lucrative.

And why was it so lucrative? Because I got exposés. I caught the stars in compromising situations. And I did it by stalking them.

I was very successful in my chosen profession, not just because I was clever, but also because I am female. For some reason, stars expect the paparazzi to be male. They let their guard down when they see a woman, so I got the goods.

And then there was Jeremy Hayes, the famous film star and Hollywood heartthrob. It was in the news that once a month he would disappear for a few days. Lots of photographers wanted to know why, but no one could get the goods. Did I mention that I am better than most of the paparazzi? I knew I could find out what Jeremy was up to if anyone could.

So I began to stalk him. I tailed his Lexus. I followed him to restaurants and bars, to clothing stores, and even to the set of his latest film. But nothing he did stood out as mysterious.

I decided to stalk him day and night, to hold a stake-out of his premises in my car. I would eat and sleep in my car. The only time I would leave Jeremy's house would be to relieve myself or to shower. It was a lot of work and stress but I knew that this would be *the big one*.

I would park on the street outside his gate. Most Hollywood stars live behind tall fences, and Jeremy Hayes was no exception. His was an expensive home in Beverly Hills off of Highway 2, better known as Santa Monica Boulevard. Jeremy lived on North Rexford Drive, the same street where Boris Karloff had once resided. It was a neighborhood of stars and looked it.

A couple of times, I was rousted by the police as I was sitting in my car. But I was committing no crimes, none that they could see, anyway. I was simply parked on a public street. Besides, I had a press card, so overall I was left alone. No one knew that I had stuck a tracking device underneath the Lexus' car chassis one day when Jeremy had been inside a restaurant.

And then I got my break. It was a Thursday night at about 2AM. I was trying to stop from nodding off when I saw the gate open and the Lexus emerged, gleaming in the street lamps. Instantly I became alert and started my car, turning the GPS system on.

I followed the Lexus south to Wilshire Boulevard where we turned west. He got off Wilshire in Koreatown and stopped at a storage facility. When he drove the Lexus inside, I knew I couldn't follow him because first, I would be spotted and second, I didn't know the gate code.

I waited on the street, and was rewarded when a blue Toyota drove out. *So that's how he doesn't get followed,* I thought. *He changes cars. I guess the GPS is useless for me now.*

I tailed the Toyota and Jeremy returned to Wilshire Boulevard, this time turning east to backtrack. We entered a neighborhood and I followed Jeremy to South Curson Avenue, right across from Hancock Park in Los Angeles. The homes here were by no means cheap; but they couldn't begin to compare to Beverly Hills prices.

My adrenaline raced. Jeremy Hayes had never been connected romantically to anyone. Was I about to find out why? Was there a secret woman, or even a secret man in his life? At only thirty years old, there had to be a *someone.* If so, what about that someone could be so damaging to his career that Jeremy wouldn't want the world to know?

I aimed to find out.

I parked on the street, many cars away from the Toyota so as not to be seen. I exited my car with one of my cameras at my side. It was a Nikon Coolpix S9100, perfect for shooting photos in low light settings.

Covertly, I began taking pictures. I shot Jeremy as he exited the Toyota in front of a house and walked up to the door, which opened before he got there. As my camera clicked away, I realized that whoever lived in this house had been expecting Jeremy. Perhaps he had called ahead of his arrival.

The person who opened the front door was an older man who had graying hair and looked to be in his sixties. *So it's a man,* I thought. Romantic partner? Drug dealer?

The door closed with Jeremy inside, and I realized that would be enough for one night. I got back into my car and drove home.

But now I had an address to research. I intended to find out who the older man was, and why a famous film star would be visiting him in the middle of the night.

*****

As I expected, Jeremy Hayes had vanished again. And I was the only one who knew to where he had disappeared.

I researched the address, but for some reason, I was unable to locate the owner of the property, not through public inquiries and not through my private channels. That in itself was highly unusual.

So I decided to simply go to the house and knock on the front door. I was no stranger to a direct approach.

The morning was beautiful. April in Los Angeles is the perfect time of year; sunny but not yet seasonably hot, the air not exactly clean but not choked with smog either. The smog would envelope the city come July and August, trapped by the Santa Monica, San Jacinto, and San Gabriel mountain ranges.

The house was a modest one-storey, with a stucco arch above the front porch. It was painted an unusual color, a beige-pink, and looked like it was supposed to be a Spanish style, but just missed the mark. It sure didn't look like the kind of place a famous Hollywood star would use for a tryst, but then again, I reminded myself that looks are often deceiving. After all, most Hollywood stars did not drive Toyotas either, but this one did.

I parked my car on the street and went up the walkway. It was about ten in the morning, and I figured they'd be up by now.

Knocking on the front door, I listened for any sounds inside. I could hear someone walking on what was probably a hardwood floor.

The door opened and I was face-to-face with the older man. "Can I help you?" he asked politely.

In anticipation, I stuck my foot in the door as I said, "I'd like to talk to Jeremy."

Sure enough, the door began to close, but my foot prevented the man's success. I pushed at the door.

"I'll call the cops!" the man said.

"If you do," I threatened, "I'll plaster photos of this residence all over Hollywood. Now all I want to do is talk. If you let me in, I'll keep my mouth shut and my camera off."

I could feel the man's hesitation. "What do you want?"

"Just to talk. That's all. Here's my identification." I shoved my credentials at him.

I could hear the man sigh as he opened the door once again. "There is nothing here but I'll let you in anyway."

The living room was smaller than I expected, the walls painted cream. He gestured to an overstuffed chair and I sat down. He sat in an identical chair across from me.

"Listen," I said, "I know that Jeremy Hayes came here last night. I have proof. I just want to know why."

"Why can't you people leave him alone?"

"Jeremy Hayes is a public figure and his fans want to know all about him. I'm just the middle-man, or middle-woman, I should say." Then I got to the point. "What's going on between you two?"

The man sat against the chair, as if a wind had blown him backwards. "Going on? I'm his father."

I wasn't expecting that. No wonder I couldn't determine who owned this house. Sometimes money could buy anonymity.

"I'm Donna; what's your name?"

"George."

"Why does Jeremy come here every month and stay for three days?" I asked.

"Who says he does?"

"I say."

"You have a problem with a son visiting his father?"

I smiled grimly. "That depends. Is he here now?"

"Yes, in the back bedroom. He's sleeping and I am not going to disturb him."

No amount of probing made George open up any further. No amount of pushing or cajoling had any effect. Eventually I decided to leave. For now.

After he saw me to the door, I got back into my car and started the engine. I knew that George was watching me from inside the house through the window. I drove away.

Around the block.

Then I parked my car once again and snuck back, on foot.

As did most homes in California, this one had a six-foot tall redwood fence around the back yard. When I first arrived, I had noticed a tree stump next to it. I knew I could climb into the back yard using that stump. I also knew there was no dog, because the home was very quiet.

A perfect house to spy upon and snoop into.

The fence was easy to climb. It was well maintained so it bore my weight well and gave me no splinters. Once on top of the fence, I leaped to the ground inside the back yard.

I quietly approached one of the two bedroom windows. I was happy to see that they weren't covered by blinds, only curtains. In both rooms, the curtains were slightly parted, allowing me to peek inside.

The first bedroom was apparently used as an office, having a computer desk and file cabinet.

The second bedroom contained a bed, but it was empty.

George had lied. Jeremy wasn't asleep in a back bedroom. So then, where was he? I knew he was somewhere in that house. He had to be.

I would come back that night, after dark. I was an expert at breaking into people's homes, even when they were there at the time. The trick was to disable the alarm, go in silently, and not wake the inhabitants. This time I wouldn't even have to drug a dog. I could do it. I knew I could, because I have done it many, many times and never woken up a single homeowner.

Illegal? Yes. Immoral? Yes.

But even if my methods were not above board, I had no guilt. I was the paparazzi, and I always got the goods, no matter what. I agreed with the old saying that the end justifies the means. I also liked the saying that it takes a thief to catch a thief. I was a thief of secrets and since no one was as skillful at as I was, no one could catch me.

*****

Although the days in April were warm, the nights could get down to the low-60s. I wore a sweater over loose-fitting pants, everything black, of course. The pants were a cargo type with lots of pockets.

I parked my car three blocks away and walked to South Curson Avenue. The full moon enabled good visibility, so I had no trouble finding the stump at the redwood fence. Quietly I mounted the fence, held onto it on the other side, and let myself down gently. There would be no jumping over the fence tonight. Everything must be as silent as the grave.

Stealthily I crept through the backyard, staying close to the fence, using it as cover. I kept my mouth open so that I could hear well. I moved slowly, stopping every two steps to listen, and when I heard nothing, I continued on another two steps.

I had a tool for my profession in one of my pockets. Once I reached the sliding glass door on the back porch, I removed the tool from my pocket and slid it into the door frame. As anticipated, the door smoothly and silently opened a crack. Sliding glass doors were never a problem for me to open, even when they were locked. This one didn't have a bar placed in its bottom track, the best kind.

Again I hesitated; waiting, listening. I had already disabled the alarm. I knew I could continue inside. Still, I waited an extra minute or two just to be sure. Outside, I could still change my mind. Inside, I was committed.

It was now or never.

I slid the door open just enough to allow me to fit though. I pushed the drapery aside, entered the room, and stopped. I needed time for my eyes to adjust from the moonlight outside to the full darkness inside. And I needed to listen once again.

No sounds. So far, so good.

When my eyes adjusted, I could see that the room inside the door was a family room, complete with a brick fireplace. In the center of the room was an open doorway leading to the front of the house. To the left was the hallway leading to the bedrooms. To the right of the fireplace was an archway and I had no idea what was behind that arch.

Since I had already seen the front of the house, the logical place to start snooping would be the bedrooms. I crept down the hallway, hoping the doors were open. They were.

Silently peering into the first, I saw that the office was unoccupied. No one had placed a cot there for any guests. That left the second bedroom.

I could hear soft snoring from the second room, and slowly brought my face forward through the door to see the person asleep on the bed. I saw silver hair on the pillow that shined in the moonlight which peeked through the curtains. This was the father. I wasn't interested in George.

Only Jeremy.

Slowly I backtracked and made my way into the family room. What lay beyond the archway to the right of the fireplace? I needed to find out.

The archway was short, much shorter than the open space leading to the living room. I poked my head through, watching and listening. There was a closed wooden door inside the archway. Where did it lead? The basement?

Suddenly I heard something. I froze completely to wait. No quick moves now; I depended on my own silence.

I opened my mouth again in order to hear better. It sounded like a dog was sniffing at the other side of the door. *What?* I had been so sure there had been no family dog. I became angry at myself. This was a situation where mistakes would be incredibly costly.

I immediately calmed myself. Emotions were deadly, so I needed to keep my cool.

I slowly and silently reached inside one of my pockets for mace. I retrieved it, held it in my hand, and listened at the cellar door.

There was definitely something on the other side of the door. Something was moving against the door. Too tall to be a dog. Jeremy? Why would he be in the cellar? Perhaps it was a finished basement with another bedroom down there. But if that were the case, why would Jeremy be up at the door?

I realized that if Jeremy was at the cellar door, it was because he knew someone was on the other side of it. He knew someone was in the house. He was listening to me just like I was listening to him.

An impasse. No, that sort of thing was for quitters. I was no quitter. I would get the story no matter what.

I silently touched the doorknob, and tried to turn it. Locked.

But the key was right there up on the wall, hanging on a hook.

All I had to do was to quickly open the door, snap a photo, and run like hell back outside. The flash would blind Jeremy and I could make good my escape. By the time George got out of the bedroom, I would already be over the fence and running away at full tilt boogie. With my camera.

I carried a tiny camera meant for nefarious jobs. I put the mace back in my pocket and took the camera out of yet another pocket in the cargo pants. I aimed it as I grabbed the key off the wall.

Holding the camera in one hand and the key in the other, I unlocked the cellar door.

I was about to drop the key on the floor to free up my hand so I could turn the knob when suddenly the door burst outwards at me, throwing me backwards off my feet. I crashed to the floor and the wind was knocked out of me. The camera fell from my grasp and bounced away.

Gasping for breath, I saw a thing towering over me. It was huge and dark and smelled like musk. It was an animal, hairy and roaring with rage. I could see fangs and suddenly the creature swiped at me with razor-sharp claws, ripping the black sweater from my body in one fell swoop.

I grabbed the can of mace from my pocket and tried to raise it but it was knocked from my hand, clattering away on the hardwood floor. Why had I ever thought such a small thing as mace could protect me?

The thing attacked me again. I tried to shove my forearm sideways, because I knew that a sharp elbow could be an effective weapon. But the creature seemed to be everywhere. I began to feel disoriented and didn't know where to aim.

Desperate for survival, I tried another tactic. I tried to kick the creature; but again, the animal was quick, too quick, and it was a whirlwind of weight, razor teeth and slashing claws. I was aware of intense, searing pain coming from seemingly everywhere on my body, even on my face. It felt like the thing was attacking me for an eternity, although what was left of my rational thoughts was sure it had only been for a few seconds.

Suddenly I heard an ear-shattering BOOM and the creature fell away from me.

I didn't feel like a thief of secrets. I didn't feel like the paparazzi who always got the goods. I felt like a frightened, panicked little girl, and I screamed.

"Shut up, it's over now," I heard George say. He flipped on a light switch.

Still on the floor, blinking from the sudden light, I sat up. There was Jeremy, lying face-up next to me, naked, with a gaping hole in his chest that was dark with blood. The wet, maroon fluid dripped down his sides to pool upon the hardwood floor.

"What?" I couldn't say anything else. Somehow, that single word spoke volumes.

"We agreed that if he ever tried to kill someone, I'd shoot him," George said.

"What?" I repeated.

"If you're such a hot-shot reporter, why didn't you ever figure out that his disappearances coincided with the cycles of the full moon? Legends are always based on facts. The bullet was silver."

It dawned on me what he was saying. "That's not possible," I said, and managed to get to my feet.

"That's my son I just killed," George said. "But you are just as responsible for his death as I am. Why couldn't you just leave him alone? It was only for three days a month. I hid him and locked him up during those times. For chrissakes, he *volunteered* to have me hide him. He didn't want to hurt anyone."

Tears coursed down the old man's cheeks as he stomped violently upon my camera, smashing it. "He was a good boy, and he was a famous film star. Maybe he was a monster sometimes, but now he is human. You can't prove otherwise. You have no photographs."

Then he turned to look directly at me. "Where will *you* go for three days every month?"

About Jeani Rector (Editor)

While most people go to Disneyland while in Southern California, Jeani Rector went to the Fangoria Weekend of Horror there instead. She grew up watching the Bob Wilkins Creature Feature on television and lived in a house that had the walls covered with framed Universal Monsters posters. It is all in good fun and actually, most people who know Jeani personally are of the opinion that she is a very normal person. She just writes abnormal stories. Doesn't everybody?

Jeani Rector is the founder and editor of *The Horror Zine* and has had her stories featured in magazines such as *Aphelion, Midnight Street, Strange Weird and Wonderful, Dark River Press, Macabre Cadaver, Ax Wound, Horrormasters, Morbid Outlook, Horror in Words, Black Petals, 63Channels, Death Head Grin, Hackwriters, Bewildering Stories, Ultraverse,* and others.

Her historical fiction novel about the black plague titled *Pestilence: A Medieval Tale of Plague* was released in 2012 from *The Horror Zine Books*.

FOUNDLINGS
BY DEAN H. WILD

Officer John Macon drummed his fingers on the roof of the cruiser while Shelly, who worked the graveyard shift at the dispatch radio desk, ran the plates on the silver Toyota. He wanted her to hurry. He didn't like the deep haze that hung around his headlights tonight, he didn't like the tall roadside grass that towered over the car on this stretch of Quarry Road, and he sure as hell didn't like the way the Toyota's driver was slumped over the steering wheel. It was pure reaction that made him pull the guy over—on any other night he would have turned a blind eye to a traveler with a broken taillight. Now instinct was telling him to get this whole deal behind him.

Shelly came back on the radio, her voice sounding like a duck squawking into a tin can. The Toyota was registered to Sam and Gloria Kaplan from downstate. Clean records. A safe bet, she said and then told him to have a nice evening. He lingered near his cruiser once the radio fell silent, then took a deep breath and walked over.

The driver's side window of the Toyota was open and as Macon stepped up the man behind the wheel began to move laggardly. Macon felt his hand drop to the butt of his service revolver. He brought his other hand, which held a heavy-duty flashlight, to chest level and switched it on.

"License and Registration," he demanded sternly. It meant you were all business—a good ploy, especially when a stop got your hairs up like this one.

"Make it fast, please," the man said and turned his head slowly in the swooping red and blue glare of the cruiser's lights.

Macon aimed his light at the face and found a drab, middle-aged countenance tainted by hectic lines. Wet eyes were shot with blood from one corner to the other. The man's lips trembled like rubbery gills strung with mucus. *Crying*, Macon realized, as the man held out his license with pale fingers.

"Are you all right, sir?" Macon asked. Damned graveyard shift bullshit.

The man made a gurgling laugh. "I'm in a hurry, that's all."

"There isn't much to hurry toward, considering the direction you're headed. You're going to run out of road in about half a mile. There's a guardrail, then a thirty-foot drop-off into the local stone quarry. Did you know that?"

He shined his light at the license. He was in the presence of Sam Kaplan, rightful Toyota owner and licensed Wisconsin driver, he saw from the data in front of him. There was a smudge on the corner of the license, a filmy red smear, something Kaplan had left. Macon considered it while the unease that had swept toward him on the hazy roadsides now moved in to slip over him completely. He caught the heavy, coppery odor that hung inside the crying man's car. Blood, Macon thought, goddamn it, we've got blood.

"Step out of the car, Mr. Kaplan." He was always amazed at how calm he could sound even when his heart was jackhammering in his chest.

Kaplan's face crumpled and fresh tears spilled down his cheeks. "I can't, officer."

Macon pocketed the license so his hand could once again rest on his gun. He let the flashlight beam sweep down to the man's lap. A thick, checkered blanket was draped over Kaplan's legs, covering his feet. Near the floor, a red stain darkened the fabric. "Are you injured, Mr. Kaplan?"

An animal crashed through the ditch on the other side of the car. Kaplan twisted his head around, "You'd better go now, officer." he said. "Start walking toward town. You don't dare get back into your car."

Macon tightened his fingers over the butt of his gun, "This has gone far enough. Out of the vehicle. *Now*."

Kaplan sprang at him, wriggled out of the open car window like a bolting rabbit and snatched Macon's gun hand. Macon leapt back as Kaplan's grip fell on him and the man slid three-quarters of the way out of the car window to stay with him. Red and blue cruiser lights swooped silently in an odd countermotion. Kaplan's hot breath puffed at him.

The flashlight flipped away into the night as Macon clamped both hands over his gun. Kaplan's fingers grasped greedily, pulled Macon's hands up and pushed the gun barrel up to his own face. "Shoot me," he huffed, "shoot now."

Kaplan's thumb wriggled between Macon's fingers, seeking the safety and then the trigger buried inside. Macon managed to turn the barrel in a downward angle. The gun went off, sending a crackling echo that flared through the quarry half a mile to the north and whip-cracked against the face of the natural limestone ledges an equal distance to the south.

Macon's first impression was of the surprised look on Kaplan's face as he let go of the gun and found himself too far out of the car window to simply slide back inside. Kaplan raised his hands as if in beseechment and then he dropped onto the pavement, lap blanket and all.

In the same instant, hot pain bloomed just above Macon's kneecap. He looked down at the round economical bullet hole in his leg with something like disbelief. He took a step backward and his legs folded up. He sat down hard on the pavement. His gun bounced from his grip and skated into the roadside grass somewhere to his right. He clamped both hands over his wound and let a wave of black spots open in front of his eyes. They faded quickly and he vaulted to his feet once more with surprisingly little trouble. His next words roared out of him like something spilled and molten.

"*You* are under arrest for assaulting an officer, Mr. Kaplan. Face down. *Now*. Stay on the ground and keep your hands where I can see them."

"Fine, arrest me," Kaplan groaned and turned over obediently, hands above his head, "But I have to get to the quarry."

Macon gave the man a cursory pat-down with one hand and with the other he grasped the microphone, affixed to the shoulder of his uniform by Velcro tabs. "Shots fired, officer injured. Requesting backup. Shelly, do you copy?"

"We shouldn't have come." Kaplan submitted to the repositioning of his hands against the small of his back so Macon could cuff him. "I told her today was a bad day. I felt it in my bones. And I told her not to go into the cave. You never know what's sleeping in one of those ledge caves. That's what my dad used to say. But she didn't know, she didn't grow up around here. She's from Chicago. The only place she'd ever seen a badger or bear was in a cage with ten feet of zoo walkway between her and it. Badgers and bears, Jesus."

Sickening waves of pain began to radiate from Macon's injured thigh. He leaned against the side of Kaplan's car. "Who in the hell are you talking about?"

"My wife."

That would be Gloria Kaplan, co-owner of the Toyota. "And she is where, exactly. Still up on the ledge somewhere?"

"No. She's here," Kaplan rolled onto his side to address him with flat yet mournful eyes. "And she's dead, officer."

Macon thumbed the microphone again and put out another call but Shelly and her duck-in-a-can voice were not responding. He glared back at his cruiser with uneasy alarm. It waited, door open, roof lights spinning endlessly.

"I'm sorry about shooting you," Kaplan said and glanced down at the blanket still tangled around his legs. "But it won't matter much longer. It seems they've already moved into your car and got the radio. They're smart little bastards about some things."

"Who?"

"They know their human anatomy, too."

"Is there someone else in the vicinity I should know about, Mr. Kaplan?" Macon shuffled close and yanked at the other man's shoulder to get him to roll over and face skyward. Kaplan's response was a quivering chin and tightly squeezed eyelids. "I didn't think so. I'm taking you in."

Kaplan regarded the veiled stars, and then the blanket over his legs. "It really would be best if we stayed away from your cruiser."

As if taking a cue from the man, the cruiser's headlights squeezed down to fiery pinpoints and vanished. The siren let out a throaty unwinding sound and the engine died with a sputter and a gassy rattle. The red and blue globes spun down after that, once, twice and then faded into darkness.

"This is bullshit," Macon heard himself say.

He inched forward and his leg screamed with pain. The haze had moved in tighter and the only available light was coming from the Toyota's headlamps and single tail light on the ditch side of the road. He glanced to the south, reflected grimly that there might be no more traffic on Quarry Road tonight. No help, just him and Sam Kaplan and God knew what else.

"I'm not making anything up," Kaplan said. "Your flashlight is right here, under my car. Use it and see for yourself. My Gloria's right here in the back seat. I didn't cover her up."

"Is that so?" Macon crouched down and dragged his flashlight out and shone it in Kaplan's face. "Games are just going to get you deeper into trouble, you know."

"I won't run while you're looking," Kaplan assured him. "I can't."

Macon went to the back door of the vehicle, opened it, and aimed the flashlight inside. The first thing that struck him was another whiff of that thick copper smell. Next was the woman's body stretched out on the back seat, wearing only a bra and panties, her skin punched full of ragged, quarter-sized holes.

"Goddamn it."

He backed away. His gorge rose up and then faded quickly, so much like black blooms of pain. Something moved amid the grass in the ditch behind him and he froze, thought of Kaplan saying the words badger or bear as if those things were some kind of joke, and it brought gooseflesh to his arms.

"She did that to herself," Kaplan snuffled. Tears were streaming down his face again. "She was so afraid. So disgusted. She wanted them out of her."

"Wanted what out?" Macon leaned against the car once again. He needed to rest his leg. He thought he could feel the bullet gritting against bone in there.

"The things from the cave. We came out here to do some hiking on the ledges, maybe camp out overnight. She went off looking for arrowheads and dried out shrew husks and whatnot. There's a whole box full of that crap at home. Her foundlings, she calls them. She came across the cave about an hour after we parked."

Kaplan snuffled again, a harsh, sharp sound, before going on. "When she came out I knew something was wrong. She was gasping, choking, trying to talk. I thought I saw something shiny working inside her mouth. She picked up her shirt for me then. Something had chewed into her stomach, officer, something about the size of those minnows you can buy at the bait shop about six miles back, something silver and wriggling. It was buried in her like a goddamn tick, its pointy tail throbbing and pumping. I grabbed its tail and pulled it out of her. God, what a freaking ugly feeling that was. The thing was cold. It had no legs or fins or arms that I could see, just a slick silvery body. It twisted around and looked at me with these little black knobs for eyes and its mouth like a flap filled with needles, and then it shook loose from my hand and squirmed away into the grass. 'More,' Gloria said to me, still gagging. Blood was leaking from her mouth and I realized that more of the little bastards were inside of her. They were like freakish little cars traveling on the roadmap of her blood vessels. Crazy, but that's what I was thinking as I held onto her.

"The last thing my sweet wife said to me was 'They think they found *me*. Isn't that funny?' Then she grabbed the knife off my belt and walked away. I could see her arms pumping in and out as she stumbled toward the car. I didn't realize she was slicing into herself at first, not until I saw the blood, so much of it. Like rain. She fell over right behind the car. Her head hit the back bumper pretty hard. I guess it was her skull that crushed my taillight. I think I passed out for a minute after that, or maybe I was just in shock. All I know is it was getting dark when I finally put her in the car. They had gotten to me by then. Funny, but when they chew their way in, it doesn't really hurt that much."

"You've got something in you?" Macon checked the stretch of Quarry Road, shrouded in night, draped in haze. He'd heard a lot of stories in his day, lots of them bullshit, but he couldn't help but believe this one. Most of it, anyway. He shivered.

"In my legs," Kaplan said. "For now, anyway. They don't like us, but they're curious. And they have a godawful way of getting to know us. Chewing into us is no more remarkable for them than opening a car door is for you or me. Please, officer, let me get back in my car. I want to drive over the guardrail at the dead end and plunge myself and my wife, car and all, into the water, see how the little bastards felt about that. I don't think they're put together for swimming."

The grasses around them rustled again, on both sides of the road now. The smell of sweet timothy was heavy. The haze pressed in.

"We're going into town, to the station house," Macon offered, not demanded or insisted—the time for that was over. What seemed important, first and foremost, was that they get away from this desolate stretch of road.

Through the haze, in the weak light cast by the Toyota's headlights, he could see the grass twitch. Kaplan seemed to be waiting, resigned, his face aimed toward the sky.

"Take my car," he said to Macon. "Get out of here. It's too late for me."

"No," Macon said. "If what you say is true, you're safer in my custody."

Kaplan's eyes blazed, "I'm practically one of them, for Christ's sake. They're tinkering with my brain. I can't go anywhere with you. Not anymore."

The man pushed the blanket away from his legs. He was wearing hiking shorts, Macon saw, and something moved beneath the skin of his left calf, lurched between bone and muscle, sliding within millimeters of breaking through the membrane of flesh.

Kaplan began sobbing again, drawing deep breaths. "I'm sorry I stopped for you, officer. I kept them out of my head pretty good until then, but when I saw your lights I got distracted and they worked their way back in. They realized what I was up to and made me stop the car. Pain helps to keep your head clear, by the way," Kaplan pushed the blood stained blanket away completely, which left his feet uncovered. "You should probably know that."

Macon aimed his light downward. Kaplan's right foot was laced into a rather new-looking hiking boot. The left foot, however, was missing. The leg ended in a ragged stump, a garbled stew of plum and burgundy and red. The shredded, blood soaked cuff of a sock still clung around the anklebone.

"There was a hatchet in my camping stuff." Kaplan explained. "I figured if I hobbled myself I wouldn't be able to help them get around. And Gloria—well—you'd better leave us alone now."

Macon stole another glimpse of the thick humps that slithered beneath Kaplan's flesh. One of them surged up the thigh and disappeared beneath the barrier of his shorts. Grass rustled around them, and then something else from behind him: a delicate skittering like bits of tangled wire draggling across the pavement. He turned around. His injured leg screeched inside with the movement.

A trio of silvery blurs skated across the pavement like blots of mercury. He turned back to Kaplan. He meant to drag the man inside the Toyota with him but stopped when he saw the bulge expand at the side of Kaplan's throat. It swelled and then popped with a wet, dark explosion. One of Gloria Kaplan's foundlings waggled out and plopped onto the pavement, teeth munching on blood and tissue. Kaplan flopped over, eyes wide and glittering with tears. The foundling humped its way forward and began to nip greedily at the tip of the man's nose.

Macon slogged around the body and sat inside the Toyota, his breath coming in hectic gasps. Kaplan's key was in the ignition. As he fumbled over it with shaking hands, Gloria Kaplan sat up behind him, gangly and fitful like a funhouse dummy, her skin a roiling bladder of migrating humps, her mouth full of moving silver. Two wriggling shapes shot from a flaccid hole between her breasts. Macon's first instinct was to bolt from the car, but the icy tearing sensation at his shoulder told him it was too late for that.

*****

The car traveled the back roads for hours. Only a few people saw the Toyota as it weaved up and down the country by-ways surrounding Quarry Road, and only one of them got a good enough look to recognize the crying man behind the wheel as a Royal County police officer.

What none of them knew was that he had burrowed a finger deep into the ragged bullet hole near his kneecap; the pain helped to keep his head clear while he weighed his options. They could not see the riddled, bleeding carcass that had been Gloria Kaplan resting in the back of the car or how its limbs and nerves twitched occasionally. They could not see the streaks of blood on the back bumper where Sam Kaplan had been dumped into the trunk nor could they see the leeching silver mound that trolled around beneath the tissue and muscle in the officer's shoulders.

Finally, Officer Macon wiped his face on the sleeve of his uniform shirt and let his resolve push to the front. He turned the car one final time and tromped the accelerator to the floor.

Crazily, he thought that the graveyard shift just ended and he should be back at the station house punching out while listening to Shelly squawk her parting quips for the day. The Toyota engine built to a roar. The grass and the haze faded to a blur. He locked the car doors and lowered his head as the quarry guardrail loomed up in the weak dawn light. Then he closed his eyes and waited for the ride to be over.

About Dean H. Wild (Assistant Editor)

A Wisconsin native, Dean H. Wild lives in the town of Brownsville located in the east central part of the state with his wife Julie and their two cats, Siegfried (Ziggy) and Walter.

His work has appeared in the HWA anthology *Bell, Book & Beyond*, as well as *Vivisections, Extremes 5, Fantasy and Horror from the Ends of the Earth* and *Nine: A Journal of Imaginative Fiction,* among others. He also occupies the Assistant Editor seat for *The Horror Zine.*

When not writing, editing or proofreading for one project or another, he is busy working on a novel.

~ * ~

If you enjoyed this book, please consider writing a short review and posting it on Amazon, Goodreads and/or Barnes and Noble. Reviews are very helpful to other readers and are greatly appreciated by authors.

THE HORROR ZINE

The Horror Zine's mission is to provide a venue in which writers, poets, and artists can exhibit their work. *The Horror Zine* is an e-zine, spotlighting the works of talented people, and displaying their deliciously dark delights for the world to enjoy.

The Horror Zine is accepting submissions of fiction, poetry and art from morbidly creative people.

Visit *The Horror Zine* at: www.thehorrorzine.com

Staff:
Jeani Rector, Editor
Dean H. Wild, Assistant Editor
Christian A. Larsen, Media Director
Bruce Memblatt, Kindle Coordinator

Bat art created by Riaan Marais

IMAJIN BOOKS
Quality fiction beyond your wildest dreams

For your next eBook or paperback purchase, please visit:

www.imajinbooks.com

www.twitter.com/imajinbooks

www.facebook.com/imajinbooks

Made in the USA
Lexington, KY
26 May 2013